Pamela Hart is an award-winning author for both adults and children. She has a Doctorate of Creative Arts from the University of Technology, Sydney, where she has also lectured in creative writing. Under the name Pamela Freeman she wrote the historical novel *The Black Dress*, which won the NSW Premier's History Prize for 2006 and is now in its third edition. Pamela is also well known for her fantasy novels for adults, published by Orbit worldwide, the Castings Trilogy and her Aurealis Award-winning novel *Ember and Ash*. Pamela lives in Sydney with her husband and their son, and teaches at the Australian Writers' Centre. *The Soldier's Wife* is her twenty-eighth book.

To find out more about the true story behind the book and to sign up to Pamela's newsletter, visit:

www.pamela-hart.com
www.facebook.com/pamelahartbooks
@pamelahartbooks

THE SOLDIER'S WIFE

PAMELA HART

piatkus

PIATKUS

First published in Australia and New Zealand in 2015 by Hachette Australia
An imprint of Hachette Australia Pty Limited
First published in Great Britain in 2015 by Piatkus

1 3 5 7 9 10 8 6 4 2

A CIP catalogue record for this book
is available from the British Library.

Cover design by Christabella Designs
Cover photographs courtesy of Getty Images and Trove

ISBN 978-0-349-41018-0

Printed and bound in Great Britain by
Clays Ltd, St Ives plc

Papers used by Piatkus are from well-managed forests
and other responsible sources.

MIX
Paper from
responsible sources
FSC® C104740

Piatkus
An imprint of
Little, Brown Book Group
Carmelite House
50 Victoria Embankment
London EC4Y 0DZ

An Hachette UK Company
www.hachette.co.uk

www.piatkus.co.uk

PROLOGUE

The telegram read: *I HAVE LEAVE. MEET TODAY NINE A.M. CENTRAL DESTINATION BOARD. LOVE. JIMMY.*

Clutching the telegram tightly in her gloved hand wouldn't make Jimmy get there any faster, she knew, but Ruby gripped it like a talisman anyway.

Sydney Central Station Destination Board was so long – she didn't know which end to stand, and the space in the middle, by the clock, was so full of soldiers and women and children all waiting for their families that she had no hope of edging her way in.

The board didn't list arrivals, only departures, but the Liverpool train was due to depart from Platform 16, so she positioned herself at the eastern end, which was closer to that platform, and tried to be calm.

At least there was a lot to see while she waited. It was overwhelming to a country girl, even after a couple of weeks in the city. So many people! More in this one place than lived in the whole of Bourke, she reckoned. People of every class – beautifully dressed women in cashmere coats floating towards the country platforms, porters following behind with luggage carts; family groups off to the mountains for the day, complete with picnic baskets and blankets; men in hats clutching pink newspapers, queuing for the race train to Kembla Grange, some no worse than half flash and half foolish, others with the shifty glance of the tout; a few matronly looking women wearing Red Cross armbands, toting bags of wool back to their knitting groups. And soldiers, of course, soldiers and sailors everywhere. Clearly Jimmy wasn't the only one with leave.

The high domed roof echoed the sound back: laughter, winter coughs, shouts of 'Over here, Mavis!' and 'It's him, it's him!' Newspaper boys wandered through the crowds, yelling, 'German victory!' 'Troops fall back!' More bad news. And over all was the distinctive coal-and-wet-wool smell of a station in winter.

There was an old man with a white bushy beard playing the spoons in a corner, a sprightly rhythm she vaguely recognised. 'Click go the Shears', maybe. Some bush ballad. A pie cart smelling of gristle and fat, a fruit barrow, a news stand . . . everywhere she looked she saw someone being busy. It was galling to have to stand still, to wait and wait and —

There he was. In a group of soldiers, a head taller than the others, coming past the ticket collector in a rush. He looked around. For her. Even in that crowd of uniform khaki he stood out, handsome and strong and . . . and *keen*. More alive than anyone she'd ever met. He pulled off his hat and the light gleamed on burnished hair, slicked down ruthlessly to control those unruly curls.

Ruby felt her heart blossom – it felt just like that, as though inside her some enormous, tightly furled bud opened, exposing her heart, offering it irresistibly to him. Her whole chest was full of her expanding heart. The emotion travelled right through her, choking her throat, trembling her knees, blurring her sight with tears, lifting her up. She took a shaky breath. He turned and saw her. His expression changed – for a moment his face was stripped as bare as her heart, with the same emotion.

She was moving without thinking, walking then running, dodging through the crowd, and Jimmy was running towards her, too. They met in a confusion of handbag and hat and arms and then she was in his embrace.

He kissed her. She forgot all good conduct, closed her eyes and kissed him back, leaned on him, felt him real and warm and wonderful under her hands. His mouth tasted of tooth powder and tea, and he smelled so good, so much like himself, despite the cold wool of his uniform and the reek of boot polish.

For a moment she was held suspended in the physical truth that he was there, right there, whole and wholly himself, and then she registered the heat of his mouth and the strength of his hands and fire swept through her. She whispered his name and his grip tightened, his arms strong across her back. It was a desperate kiss, hard and needy and intoxicating. She had never wanted him so much. If they'd been in private she would have dragged him off to bed immediately.

But they weren't. Ruby pulled herself away reluctantly. It was the woman's job to put a limit on this kind of thing; which didn't seem fair, really.

'Jimmy,' she said, managing a tone of wifely reproach, but her eyes betrayed her, she feared, because he grinned as though he knew she was just pretending.

Tenderly, he tucked a strand of her hair back under her hat. His face had regained its usual lively expression, but his eyes showed how he really felt. It was going to break both their hearts to part again.

'Hello, old girl.'

Her eyes filled with tears at his tone.

'Hey, none of that!' he protested. 'Or I'll think you're not glad to see me.'

Valiantly, she brought out a smile and took his arm. 'Come and have a cup of tea.'

'No fear!' he said. 'We don't have time for that. I have to be back right here at nine o'clock tomorrow morning to march down to the ship. This is my first time in Sydney. What do you say to a spree?'

She blinked. She hadn't imagined that. She'd thought . . . well, she'd thought they'd go back to the house where she was boarding and spend time together. Maybe Mrs Hannan, her landlady, would go visit a friend or something and they could . . . she blushed. But sitting in a little room and talking, well, that wasn't much of a send-off for a soldier.

'Whatever you want,' she said, tucking her hand tighter under his arm. 'Whatever you want.'

•

They went to the zoo and fed the elephant. They went for a ride on a ferry and had afternoon tea at a tearoom on the Corso in Manly. On the ferry home they stood out on the forward deck, tasting the spray, Jimmy's arms around her, protecting her from the cold wind, his warm bulk reassuring and exciting at her back. As the ferry docked, she took her handkerchief out of her purse to wipe the sea salt from her cheeks, and found an envelope she was sure she hadn't put in there. Puzzled, she looked at the front. 'Certificate of Marriage', it read. She opened it – it wasn't her own lines, which were put away safely in the suitcase under her bed, but Maree and Theo Hannan's. Her landlady must have put it in without telling her. What a strange thing for her to do. Why would she —? Ruby's cheeks flamed in sudden understanding, and she closed the bag hurriedly, before Jimmy could see.

Then they were on the dock at Circular Quay in the middle of the afternoon, looking at each other with unbearable desire. Jimmy wet his lips, as though unsure of himself.

'There's a hotel, just down Bligh Street,' he said. 'I know we don't have any luggage, but maybe they'll let us stay if we show them your wedding ring.'

Ruby touched his cheek, her breath coming shorter, heat surging through her body. She must remember to buy her landlady a thank-you gift.

'Oh, I think they'll let us stay,' she said.

•

His body was a revision – a lesson she had to learn all over again, where flashes of memory overtook her. The hollow under his throat. The long line of muscle which linked thigh and hip. So male. Utterly male. His taste. Each flicker of familiarity making her think for a moment that she knew what she was doing, but the next moment leaving her tentative, unsure. She knew very little about being a wife. They had only had a week of honeymoon, after all, two months earlier.

But his hands she remembered. Under her hips, on her skin, cradling her face, alive and gentle and so tender that she cried, just to have him wipe the tears away, softly, and kiss her, murmuring her name, only her name, over and over and over again.

He came to her like a man who, starving, still forces himself to have manners, to behave politely, with restraint, but she didn't want restraint. If she was his meal she wanted him to devour her, to consume her completely.

So she touched him, encouraged him wordlessly until he lost that terrible self-control and buried himself in her as if she alone could keep him alive. She clutched him to her, wrapped legs and arms around him, wanting him closer, even closer, tighter, *nearer*. Dying inside while she loved him because he was going so soon, and she couldn't bear it; kissing him again and again until they fell back on the pillows and did it all once more.

The hotel room was small and badly furnished – a 'Family Hotel' patronised mostly by single men. It was painted a dark red below the dado and a deep cream above it, which reminded Ruby of fat around a piece of steak. She lay with Jimmy's sleeping head on her shoulder and stared at the dull red curtains as the room darkened. She didn't want to move, to wake him. Just to savour this moment, to memorise the feel of his body on hers, the rise and fall of his breath, all that curious mixture of strong and vulnerable which made him Jimmy. She tightened her hold on him and hung on.

Then it was morning, and time to bathe and dress and go to the station, grabbing a hasty breakfast on the way.

At Central, they found his company and he reported in. Collected his kitbag, his rifle, his canteen.

They kissed. Jimmy murmured, 'I love you' and she said the same, but none of it felt real. It was happening to someone else, surely. He pulled away from her, his face tight with misery, and none of it was real, until the last moment when his hand, the tips of his fingers, left the tips of hers and he was gone.

Turned into just another soldier.

PART
1

CHAPTER 1

16th July, 1915

'Mrs Hannan, do I look businesslike?'

Her landlady looked her up and down, amused eyes assessing Ruby's neat navy skirt and jacket, gloves, purse and well-shined shoes just peeping out from under her hem.

Mrs Hannan was trying to stir a pot on the range with her struggling two-year-old on one hip. Stooping, she set Eddie on his feet and gave him a gentle swat on his behind, pushing him towards the back door. 'Out to the garden for you, my lad.'

'Gerden!' Eddie shouted, and ran with arms wide.

Mrs Hannan pushed her hair back from her forehead with the back of one hand. She twirled a finger and Ruby obediently turned a circle. Mrs Hannan shrugged. 'I don't know what a businesslike woman looks like. You look respectable.' She smiled suddenly, with a touch of wryness. '*I'd* give you a job.'

Ruby wasn't sure what that smile meant. Her landlady wasn't easy to read; only a year or two older than Ruby, she was far more . . . sophisticated wasn't quite the right word. No one would look at her serviceable print dress and ample figure and think 'sophisticated', a word which called up images of social graces and sherry-drinking. Mrs Hannan drank shandies. But she did drink shandies, not lemonade. And putting those marriage lines in Ruby's handbag had been the action of an experienced woman – she was generous, but practical with it, and she'd accepted Ruby's thank-you gift of chocolates with a composed, enigmatic smile.

'Off you go,' she said, as if she were Ruby's mother instead of Eddie's.

•

Respectability wasn't much to offer an employer. As she walked down to Rozelle Bay, Ruby wondered what Jimmy would think of her going off to work in a strange business. It wasn't *strictly* necessary. Now he had embarked, she could go back to Bourke. Back to the family draper's shop, back to live with her mother.

It made her oddly shaky to think of doing so. The three weeks she had spent there after Jimmy left to enlist had been so odd; she had felt herself neither flesh nor fowl: not really a wife, because she had no home of her own; not a girl, either, thanks to that wonderful, astonishing honeymoon week. She grew warm at the insistent memory of Jimmy's lips, his hands, his loving voice. After that, after that total transformation of who she was, it had felt wrong to simply slip back into her old room, to sit at her old chair at the dining table, to serve the same picky and inquisitive customers in the store, to be dutiful and obedient as though she were still an unmarried girl.

But that was just it. There wasn't a word for what she was

now, and there wasn't a proper place for her in Bourke. She was better off here. It was silly, she knew, but she felt closer to Jimmy here. And if she never served in a shop again it would be too soon.

It was not as cold as she had thought, despite being midwinter, and Ruby hoped she wasn't going to walk into the office perspiring and looking frowsy. She slowed down a little so she would arrive fresh. The winter winds hadn't yet started to blow – her landlady had assured her they would come full force in August, but today Sydney Harbour shivered in bright sunshine.

Curry & Son's Timber Merchants were at the end of Johnston Street, facing The Crescent and backing onto Rozelle Bay. There were timber yards and docks all around Rozelle Bay, from one side of Glebe Island Bridge all the way round the foreshore to the other side, with a small break for Federal Park on the east. On the other side of the bridge was a quarry and commercial shipping wharves.

She had watched Curry's operations from Federal Park yesterday, judging if it were the kind of business which would warrant a full-time bookkeeper, or if the bookkeeper would be expected to do extra work, heavy work a woman couldn't do. They were a miller and wholesaler; the logs arrived on barges, were unloaded and then stacked in the yard.

She had watched as trimmed and shaped logs had been ferried across from Curry's to the new wharves being built on the western side of Rozelle Bay – a short trip, but tricky; the logs were huge, no doubt to make the pilings of the new docks. It had been an impressive operation.

Ruby swallowed a lump of pure nervousness and smoothed down her skirt before she crossed the street, avoiding an omnibus and a horse and cart without too much fear – a new skill she'd only just acquired.

It was a big yard, the size of a home paddock. A long paling fence ran along the street frontage to a cream weatherboard office with a green door and a couple of frosted-glass windows facing the street; further down was a pair of big green gates, which were open for business. She could glimpse the ends of stacked timber through the gate as she walked to the front door.

Should she knock, or just go in? She took a deep breath and opened the door to the office, a knot of hope and anxiety under her breastbone.

The office overlooked the yard from a storey's height, the far wall having three big sash windows. In the corner was a door which led down to the yard. She could see the sawmill to the left, a big open shed with machinery running down the centre, busy with men and lumber, the saws shrieking and buzzing as each log went through. To the right, stacks and stacks of timber were neatly aligned in open corrugated-iron sheds. Vaguely, she remembered that timber had to 'cure'. A bit like leather, she supposed, which got harder as it got older.

The building was one big room, with wooden filing cabinets along one wall and desks in the middle. An end was partitioned off for two equal-sized offices, glass above wooden partitions. In the corner a barrel stove gave off a surprising amount of warmth.

One of the small offices was empty. The other was occupied by a man talking on the telephone. Mr Curry, perhaps.

The wall to her left was faced with boards of many different kinds of timber, from bright gold to a dark red, the boards oiled rather than varnished. Although the wood had been put together without any concern for looks, it was curiously attractive, with the simple beauty of natural things. It took her a moment to realise that this was a sample wall, put there to show customers the different grades of timber available.

In the middle of the central two desks was a telephone, which was the only familiar thing she could see – it was the same model they used in the shop at home.

Two men were seated at the paired desks, checking over lists, and they looked like a pair, both older, both balding, in shirtsleeves with sleeve protectors on and looking up with identical expressions of surprise at seeing a woman. When they stood up, she realised they were not, after all, so alike – almost a foot in height separated them, and the shorter of the two was skinny as a snake, while the taller one's abdomen stuck out like a ball in front of him. Too much beer made a stomach like that, her mother had said and, sure enough, the blue eyes peering at her were a little bloodshot.

'Can we help you, miss?' the tall one said, politely.

'My name is Mrs Hawkins,' she said. 'I've come to enquire about the bookkeeper's position.'

They gawked at her.

The shorter one, whose bald head glistened with a light sweat, snorted and said, 'No jobs for the likes of you, young madam!'

His tone made it clear what kind of woman he thought she was.

'Now, Wesley,' the other man said. 'Lots of women are working these days.'

'God didn't intend it!' Wesley snarled. 'Get home to your children, woman!'

The door to the boss's office opened and a wide man came out. He was perhaps sixty, not so much corpulent as solid with muscle. It was his shortness which gave the impression of width. His hair was black but speckled with grey, and his eyes were Irish blue. Ruby realised that she'd seen him at Mass last week, and a flicker in his eyes suggested that he recognised her, too.

'What's going on?' His voice held an echo of Ireland. She was surprised that a man named Wesley – clearly a Methodist – should be working for an Irish Catholic. The shortage of men must be bad indeed.

When neither of the clerks spoke, the man turned his gaze on her, and she became aware of his authority. He was used to being obeyed. Clearing her throat, she said her prepared piece again. 'My name is Mrs Hawkins. I've come to enquire about the bookkeeping position.'

Before he could respond, the door from the yard opened and a big man in shirtsleeves burst through, bringing with him the smell of wood and woodsmoke, the sound of the big saw screeching, and the tang of the sea. He seemed to fill the office with movement and noise. Ruby registered his red hair and the width of his shoulders.

'Where the bloody hell is the carter? He's supposed to take that shipment up to Haberfield.'

'Tom,' the boss said, nodding at Ruby. She tried to look like she heard bad language every day, but it was hard not to stare coldly at the man. When he saw her he coloured red to the roots of his hair, and shuffled his feet.

'Sorry, missus, didn't see you there,' he mumbled. Then he regained his composure and looked at the tall man. 'But where's my carter, Wally?'

She almost laughed. Wally and Wesley.

'You'd better come in here,' the boss said to her. 'I'm William Curry.'

Mr Curry's office was more comfortable than she had expected. The visitors' chairs were upholstered in rich brown leather and there was a Turkish carpet on the floor. On the desk was a telephone handset and a bronze inkwell in the shape of a lion. It was all very masculine, and she wondered what she was thinking of, applying for a man's job.

Sitting down, she tried to look calm and professional, although her palms were moist inside her navy gloves. She resolved not to gush with nerves.

'So,' Mr Curry said. 'Bookkeeping. Done it before?'

'Yes. My father owned a draper's and haberdashery in Bourke. I kept his books for six years, ever since I left school.'

'Bourke. What are you doing in Sydney? Get married, did you?'

His manner was abrupt, but not unfriendly, though there was no trace of the blarney she had known in other Irishmen.

'My husband is in the Expeditionary Force,' she explained. 'I came to Sydney to see him off.'

'Hmph. Children?'

'No.'

He sat back in his chair and stared at her. It was an unsettling gaze and it brought out in her the defiance her mother had predicted would be her downfall, the same defiance that had led her to marry Jimmy despite the pronouncements of her acquaintance that 'marry in haste, repent at leisure'. She put her chin up and stared back, aware of the noise of the saws and the shouts of workers, the trundle of a cart and the clop of hooves down the street. Perhaps the carter had arrived. After a moment of standoff, Mr Curry chuckled.

'You won't want to use the privies here, I can tell you.'

Her heart lifted. Did that mean he was considering her for the job?

'I'm living only a few moments' walk away, in Wells Street. I would go home for lunch.'

'Might be best,' he nodded. 'The men won't want to mind their tongues around you at break-time. And I won't have them shamed into minding their tongues at other times, either. This is a man's business. If you come into it, you'll have to take us as you find us.'

'Certainly,' she said. 'It's not like I'm a child, Mr Curry, or an unmarried girl.'

'True, true. Wouldn't have a girl working here. Just lead to trouble. How old are you?'

That was rude – but what did she know about job interviews? Perhaps he asked all his applicants the same question.

'Twenty-two.'

'Old enough to know sense, then.'

He stared at her again, the light striking his face. She could see the line where he stopped shaving; above it a fine down of hair showed in the light. He had small flat ears, which lay back against his head. Neat ears, like a child's.

'My boy Laurence is with the Force,' he said. 'He's a lieu-tenant. I didn't want him to join up, but what can you do? His mother was English.'

She nodded to show she understood. Ireland was staying out of the war, hoping that Germany would weaken England enough to make Irish independence easier to achieve. Some said the Irish were active sympathisers, supplying the Germans with safe harbours and supplies, but Ruby didn't believe that. The British-led government ruling Ireland would never allow it.

'What battalion?' she asked.

'The 20th.'

Her heart lifted. 'That's the same as my Jimmy.'

Mr Curry pulled at his lip, his manner changing slightly, becoming less reserved. 'Well, then. We 20th Battalion families had better stick together. You can start Monday. Half-past seven. Start early, finish early. Half-past four. Half hour for lunch at twelve. Half day Saturday. One pound ten for the first month, while you're learning, two pounds after that if you're any good.'

That seemed low to Ruby, but what did she know? Only the value of men's wages.

'All right. Off you go. Be here bright and early.' He stood up and ushered her to the door.

'Thank you so much, Mr Curry,' she said, suddenly aware that she hadn't said anything appropriate. 'I'll work hard, I promise.'

'No trouble,' he said. 'No trouble with the men. That's the main thing.'

She nodded firmly. 'No trouble at all. I'm a married woman.'

He sniffed. 'Just you remember that when your husband is a long way away.'

They were at the street door before she could think of a response. As if she would *ever* – but she found herself out on the footpath before she could put her indignation into words.

As she began the climb back to Wells Street, she was filled with elation. *I have a position!* An actual, proper, paid position. She calculated. Two pounds a week. Jimmy got six shillings a day. The Army reserved one of those shillings for when he came back to Australia. Jimmy allotted her half of the rest, two shillings sixpence a day, so she received seventeen shillings sixpence a week and cabled the rest back to him. Once her month was up, she would have two pounds, seventeen shillings sixpence a week. Even paying her board, and even given the shocking price increases in things like stockings and tooth powder, she should still be able to put away a pound or so a week.

The thought filled her with an extraordinary sense of hope and excitement. Money of her own.

CHAPTER 2

Walking back to Wells Street, Ruby calculated. She would need more shirts. She really needed a clean shirt at least every two days, and she wouldn't be able to wash them until Saturday. Perhaps she could pay Mrs Hannan extra to do her washing.

Instead of turning left into Booth Street, she continued on to the draper's just past the corner. The bolts of fabric and the 'notions' in the window reminded her sharply of her father, who had always done the window display at home. She felt a twinge at the memory. He had been dead almost three years. Her sister Myrtle did the windows now.

'Hello, Mr Vincent!' she called. 'Mr' was an honorary title – Julius Vincent was only fifteen, and had left school to mind the shop when his father enlisted (primarily, Ruby thought, to get away from Mrs Vincent, who had a voice like a crow). She'd heard all about it from Mrs Vincent herself, the first time she'd come in – mainly out of curiosity about what a haberdashers in Sydney carried, compared to their own shop in Bourke.

'Mrs Hawkins. What can I do for you today?' He blushed, which just made the pimples on his face stand out more clearly.

'I need some shirting,' she said. 'Plain white, or a blue and white stripe.'

His face fell.

'Oh, I'm so sorry, Mrs Hawkins. I have some lawn, and some men's shirting, but no ladies', I'm afraid.'

She paused for a moment. She was a draper's daughter and knew that the only real difference between men's and women's shirting were the colours and the fact that the men's was a slightly heavier weight, so it didn't lose its shape under a suit jacket. 'Let me see the men's white,' she said. 'There's a war on, after all. We must adjust.'

He blinked in astonishment, but then he nodded. 'Quite right, quite right.'

She hid a smile. He was trying so hard to be grown up. He hefted down the bolt of men's shirting. It was perfectly acceptable. She doubted that anyone but herself would ever know.

'One and tuppence the yard.' It was interesting that men's shirting was always cheaper than women's, and yet men's suiting was always more expensive.

'I'll take four yards,' she said. She needed two blouses. From four yards, she wouldn't be able to create the intricate drapery that had been so fashionable before the war; fortunately, fashions were becoming more sensible.

She blessed her mother, who had insisted Ruby learn to sew. Buying quality ready-made was too expensive.

As a minor celebration, she bought a newspaper on her way home, from the newsboy on the corner. She was eager to read the war news, but she restrained herself from reading it as she walked.

Ruby let herself into the house. As with so many terrace houses in Sydney, there was a long hall with two bedrooms on the left. Past an archway, it gave onto a parlour. Behind the parlour was the kitchen and scullery, with the outhouse in the backyard.

Ruby had the smaller second bedroom, a simple room with a single bed and a narrow wardrobe with an oval mirror in the door. It had been Eddie's room, but Mrs Hannan had taken him into hers, to sleep on a small divan next to her bed. The walls were still a cheerful nursery yellow. Ruby laid her hat and gloves on the side table near the window and carefully hung her jacket over the back of the chair, then went to make herself a cup of tea.

Mrs Hannan was out. Perhaps she had taken Edward to the park. It gave Ruby a chance to read the paper in peace. As in every edition, war news dominated the summary on the first page.

The Minister for Defence announced yesterday that the number of recruits in Australia exceeds 100,000.

One hundred thousand. One hundred thousand sons and brothers and husbands. One hundred thousand families torn apart; sent to Turkey, sent to France and Belgium. God help us all, she thought. She paged through until she found the regular feature, *Heroes of the Dardanelles*.

Row upon row of photographs of young men in uniform,

and underneath each one: *Killed in action. Missing. Died of typhoid. Killed in action.*

The Dardanelles was where Jimmy was headed. No one would confirm it officially, but everyone knew it. After the shambles of the April landing at Anzac when so many men had been lost, it was common knowledge that the British had demanded reinforcements. There were articles, too, about the casualties in France.

Ruby started to shake, imagining her Jimmy, so tall and broad and forceful, writhing in pain, twitching in agony, pierced by bullets – she gasped and pushed back from the table. She mustn't read any more. It did Jimmy no good. She mustn't fill her head with these weak imaginings. She changed into an old cotton dress; it was chilly inside, away from the sun, so she wrapped a coat sweater around herself. Her sister Myrtle had made it for her before she left Bourke; it was a lovely cerulean blue but it was not a garment she would feel comfortable wearing to an office, so she might as well have the use of it here.

Mrs Hannan's voice, loud and cheerful, sounded from outside. Ruby took the *Herald* to tidy it away, noticing on the front page that Lasseter's had a sale on lisle stockings. She could write to them tonight and order several pairs. She would need at least one more pair, and hose were becoming scarcer. Better to stock up. She had put her one pair of silk stockings away until Jimmy's return. Most of her first week's wages were going to clothes, it seemed, but she had been saving ever since Jimmy joined the Army, and before that she had saved much of her pin money.

Edward toddled down the corridor and rushed at her. She

bent to cuddle him; he smelled of grass and wind. Over his head his mother looked a question.

'Yes!' Ruby said, overcome again by elation and a tinge of fear. 'I start on Monday.'

'How much?' Mrs Hannan asked, ever practical.

'One pound ten for the first month, two pounds after that.'

'That's half what he'd pay a man,' she said, shrugging, pulling Edward through to the kitchen to wash his hands. 'Come now, dumpling, time for tiffin.'

'Tiffin!' Edward cried, and rushed ahead of her, falling over the step down to the kitchen and beginning to cry.

'Oh, Lord.' She picked him up and dusted him off. 'Any blood? No? Well, then, show me what a brave sailor you are.'

Edward straightened immediately. 'Like Daddy,' he said.

'That's right, little one. Just like Daddy.' She went to get Edward his tea. Edward plucked something from her hand as she went past and brought it, eagerly, to Ruby.

'Look, missers awkins, Daddy!'

It was a photograph of a cricket match, with men in an assortment of cricket and work clothing assembled around a batsman at the crease, a medium-sized man with big arms who seemed, by the look on his face, determined to hit the bowling all over the ground.

Edward planted a plump, dirty finger on the face. 'Daddy,' he said.

'Theo sent it from Plymouth,' Mrs Hannan called from the kitchen.

Ruby turned it over. On the back, in pencil, Theo had scrawled: *The* Australia *crew against the Devonport shipwrights. We trounced them! That's me batting, 78 not out!*

'*Daddy*!' Eddie insisted.

'Yes, I can see! Daddy.' Satisfied, he took the photograph and sat on his chair, a low stool by the fireplace, his little finger stroking the image over and over. Ruby went to start a fire. The afternoon was drawing in with a nip in the air.

'Sounds like Theo's having a good time,' she said as she scrunched newspaper and laid kindling and some coals.

'All right for some,' Mrs Hannan answered, but she was smiling as she came back with milk and a scone for Eddie. He fell on them eagerly, the photo falling to the floor. Mrs Hannan picked it up. 'They're in port for repairs.' She pulled a letter from her pocket and showed Ruby black sections in the text. 'The censor's had a go at it, so who knows what else he wrote.'

Regardless of the censors, how wonderful, to know that your husband was safely ashore, playing cricket and working at his trade. The losses in the navy had been so low that Mrs Hannan didn't have to worry at all, really, despite the German submarines patrolling the Atlantic. They only targetted merchant vessels.

'Not too much coal. Price has gone up again.'

Ruby moved a lump of coal back to the shuttle, lit the paper and waited a moment to make sure the fire had caught.

'I'll just put the kettle on,' Mrs Hannan said.

Ruby went to her bedroom. There was just time before tea to add a P.S. to her latest letter to Jimmy. *I have a position as bookkeeper at Curry & Son's, a timber merchants – and just think, Mr Curry's son is in your battalion! So you see I am in good hands, in the 20th Battalion family. I start on Monday. The office is very nice and the men gentlemenly, so you must not worry about me. All my love, my darling.*

Ruby

She missed him so much. How she would love him to walk through the door, smiling as he always did when he first saw her, snatching her up and spinning her around, and then kissing her so passionately, so tenderly . . . She wiped her tears away with the back of her hand, sealed the envelope and put on a stamp. Letters for the front were sent to the Army, which forwarded them to the men, so who knew how long it would be before he read it. She bent her head over the envelope, saying a prayer for him.

It made her feel a little better. She would post the letter tomorrow morning.

Time to cut out the new blouses, she thought. She'd have precious little time to sew from now on.

•

17th July, 1915

My darling girl,

When we stopped at Aden, the officers got news of the front. From the looks on their faces, things are pretty bad over there. The good oil is that we'll only be in Cairo a couple of weeks before they ship us across the Straits. But I won't talk about that. Thinking about it just saps your strength. I think about you instead.

I know we probably won't live at Barkinji, but that's where I like to imagine us. Sitting on the verandah, watching the sun go down over the red hills, while the crested pigeons and the cockatoos are settling in for the night in those big gums around the homestead.

You in that yellow dress, with the buttons down the front. And all we can hear are the birds and the wind.

Funny, in training I thought the city coves in the company were on the back foot compared to us country blokes, but they cope with the noise better than us. One bloke's house was next to the railway tracks at Central. He can sleep through anything, he reckons. Lucky blighter.

As the sun went down you'd come and sit next to me on the old cane lounge, and turn your sweet face up to mine for a kiss.

You don't know how much I love you, Ruby. Not yet. I haven't had a real chance to show you. But I will. I swear. When I get home.

I can't let the censors go through this. I'll write you a nice normal letter instead. Something cheerful.

your Jimmy

CHAPTER 3

19th July, 1915

Heart beating fast, Ruby let herself in the office door at twenty-eight minutes past seven on Monday morning. Mr Curry was waiting for her, but Wesley and Wally were absent.

'They'll be in shortly,' Mr Curry said, noting her glance at their desks. 'You'll be over here, Mrs Hawkins.'

He led her to the small desk in the corner near his office. It was colder today, and a draught came through the big sash windows. Her desk was farthest from the stove. To be expected. A pile of ledgers awaited her – she recognised the brand, John Sands Ltd. Her father had used the same kind. The familiarity settled her nerves.

'Incomings,' Mr Curry said, indicating the blue ledger. 'Outgoings.' The red one. 'Correspondence.' Two brown ledgers, one for incoming letters, one for copies of letters sent. Just the same as home.

Next to the ledgers was a stack of papers. Invoices, no doubt, and receipts.

'Order forms,' he said, handing her a pad of forms with carbon paper behind the first page. 'Telephone rings, no one else here, you answer it and take down the order, give it to one of the boys. If they're not here, take it down to the yard.'

'Yes, sir,' she said, trying not to look apprehensive.

'Off you go, then,' Mr Curry said. 'Any questions, ask the boys.'

The 'boys' walked in a few moments later, shedding coats and scarves, staring at her the while, Wesley scowling. She would ask Wally if she had any questions. She wished she knew their full names. It put her at a disadvantage.

The easy ledgers first. Correspondence. She paged through them; letters carefully pasted in, along with message slips and telegrams. Mostly orders and replies to orders. Her heart beat a little faster when she saw the telegrams, which was silly. These were innocuous, from supplier to buyer, from interstate merchants waiting for shipments, even from overseas companies. They had nothing to do with the dreaded War Office telegrams.

Now the blue ledger. Incomings. A pile of Commonwealth Bank receipts to be entered against the last days' takings, a pile of cheques to be entered ready for banking. She traced the pattern of incomings: cheques coming in, most on the first of the month, of course, and then on the fifteenth. But also odd payments, small sums mostly, in cash. One-off sales from the yard rather than continuing clients.

There were pens on the desk, but they were scratchy and tended to blot. Ruby hesitated. She had her own fountain pen in her purse, but she didn't want to look as though the office pens weren't good enough for her, even though she suspected that the 'boys' – or at least Wesley – had stocked her desk with the worst pens available. She checked the desk drawers. There were spare nibs and nib wipers, so she changed the nib on one pen and went back to work. At least someone had had the decency to fill the inkwell for her.

It was soothing, working with numbers. So neat. So predictable. So controllable. After an hour or so Mr Curry looked over her shoulder and grunted, then left. She supposed that was a vote of approval.

The telephone rang a few times, but she never had to answer it. Wesley grabbed the handset like a snake striking. He didn't let Wal answer even once, so there was no fear he would expect her to. She relaxed a little more; talking on the telephone was so strange. She had had to do it in her father's shop, but it had always seemed slightly eerie to her, hearing a disembodied voice, as though she spoke to a ghost. Her mother had laughed at her for saying that, one of the few times she had ever given way to unbridled mirth. 'Thank the Lord you can't talk to the dead on the phone,' she'd said. 'God knows what they'd have to say to us!'

Most orders, it transpired, came through on the telephone and were confirmed by telegram or letter after Curry's had verbally agreed on a price and delivery date.

At nine, a whistle blew in the yard and Wesley got up to put the kettle on the stove. He glanced at her and smirked. She wasn't to be offered tea, then, but that didn't worry her. She had decided that she wouldn't drink anything while she was working, lest she had to relieve herself.

'Women's work, making tea,' Wesley said.

Of course it was. Ruby felt an immediate impulse to get up

and take the kettle from him, like a good girl. But something in his smile and a tension in Wally's shoulders made her hesitate.

'Did the last bookkeeper make the tea?' she asked.

From behind her, Mr Curry's deep chuckle startled them all. 'No, he did not,' Mr Curry said. 'That's the junior clerk's job.'

Wesley flushed with anger.

'I'm not serving a woman!' he snarled.

'I wouldn't ask you to, Mr – I'm sorry, we haven't been properly introduced.' It was a struggle to keep her poise in the face of Wesley's anger. For once she was glad of all those times Mother had made her 'act like a lady'. 'Remember,' Mother had said, over and over again, 'if a customer is rude, *they* are displaying a lack of breeding. There is no need for you to copy them.'

So she called on all the times a customer had treated her like a piece of dirt, and smiled at Wesley.

'Mr Wilson.'

'Mr Wilson,' she echoed. 'I won't be having tea, thank you.'

'Too good to eat with the likes of us, is that it?'

'Now, Wesley –' Wally said.

Ruby was mortified. It hadn't occurred to her that it might seem like that. 'No, Mr Wilson, not at all.' She paused, wondering what to say. She either had to have a cup or tell the truth. A lady would never mention needing to relieve herself. On the other hand, the truth would take the wind out of Wesley's sails.

'I shan't be drinking tea because I don't want to lose working time walking back home to use the . . . the convenience.'

It stopped them dead. Mr Curry roared with laughter, and after a moment, Wally did too. It wasn't unpleasant laughter, but it made Ruby go pink nonetheless. She could feel the heat of her face. Wesley looked her up and down; he clearly thought she'd spoken like a drab.

'Good thing, too,' Mr Curry said, after he'd calmed down. 'I'd have to dock your pay.'

As the men got their tea, Wally turned to her and said, 'I'm Wally Andrews. Sorry we didn't introduce ourselves properly the other day, Mrs Hawkins.'

'That's quite all right, Mr Andrews.'

'Come on, lass, I'll show you around the yard,' Mr Curry said, leading her out the door on the far wall.

The great thing about a timberyard was that it smelled sweet; a lovely tangy smell of sawdust and pine resin wafted on the breeze from the water. The worst was the noise; the whine and buzz and shriek of mechanical saws.

The door opened onto a steep wooden staircase, which Ruby looked at in dismay. Her narrow skirt would make the descent very difficult. She clutched the handrail and followed Mr Curry slowly, embarrassed by the knowledge that any of the men below could see her ankles – and perhaps more.

As she negotiated the last step Mr Curry looked her up and down. He opened his mouth but she pre-empted him.

'I'll make a new skirt. One with more, more – flexibility.'

He nodded but she saw the twinkle in his eye and smiled ruefully in response.

'New times, new times,' he said.

The sea lapped at the one long open edge of the yard. Fences went down to the water on either side; there was a dock built out onto the bay, taking up half of the width of the yard, together with a small beach, a mix of mud and sand, where logs lay waiting for the men to haul them up. The other half was taken up by the long stretch of open shed, stacked with different sizes and grades of timber.

The men, except for the ones operating the saw, stopped dead and stared at her, looking her up and down. She was suddenly aware that she had never before been a woman alone with a group of men. She felt – exposed. Vulnerable. Which was ridiculous! She took a deep breath and looked at the men as individuals, not a menacing group. As though her courage had been a signal, they returned to their tasks.

Around ten men, she thought. The tall, red-headed Tom was in the sawmill, directing three others in the business of sending a log through the huge whirring, grating saw. Ruby shivered. It looked so dangerous. It *felt* dangerous, even watching from a distance.

'You keep away from the mill,' Mr Curry ordered.

'Yes, sir.'

Another two men hauled the sawn timber from the mill on a kind of long trolley, and stacked it in the big open shed to their right.

To the side of the yard, a ramshackle old cart with only three wheels was being loaded with offcuts of timber by a couple of young boys, eleven or twelve years old.

'Firewood,' Mr Curry said. 'It's one of the perks of working here. What the men don't take home, we sell. If you've got a wheelbarrow, you can come down and collect some once a week.'

What a saving! Perhaps they could borrow a wheelbarrow. Ruby was struck by how appalled her mother would be to know that she'd wheeled free wood through the city streets.

'Or else you could pay one of the boys to take it for you,' he added kindly.

Ruby raised grateful eyes to his face, and realised again that she didn't have to look up – he was only her height. Coming from a family of tall men, with an even taller husband, it was an odd sensation to look a man straight in the eyes. 'Thank you, Mr Curry. I'll do that.'

He nodded and whistled through his teeth. All the men turned to the sound, but he beckoned one of the boys over. 'Tiddy,' he said, 'put a barrow load of firewood and tinder to the side for Mrs Hawkins. You can take it to her place after work, and who knows? You might get a farthing out of it.'

Tiddy was a dark scrawny boy, but she had watched as he had loaded the cart and he was stronger than he looked. He grinned up at her. 'I 'eard there was a donah workin' in the offis,' he said. 'I'll take yer wood every week, missus, no worries.'

'Thanks, Tiddy,' she said.

'And mind your language around ladies!' Mr Curry warned him. 'Or I'll give the job to Mick.'

'Ar, Mick don't know how to talk to ladies,' Tiddy said. 'He's a blooming idjit.' He hopped back to the cart with sprightly ease.

Ruby couldn't help but laugh.

'He's a scamp, all right,' Mr Curry said. 'Felt the back of my hand more than once, I can tell you. But he's a good worker. Tom!'

Tom came over, pushing a cap back on his head. He and the men had finished with the huge log – it had been reduced to timber astonishingly quickly. His shirt sleeves were rolled up, as were those on most of the men despite the cold; his arms were heavily muscled.

For a moment she remembered Jimmy's arms, similarly muscled, strong and warm around her. The feel of his skin, the hairs springing back under her fingertips. She swallowed and blinked, pushing down the sudden image. No time for memories.

'Mrs Hawkins, this is McBride, our foreman. Mrs Hawkins is the new bookkeeper, Tom. Show her around the yard. She needs to know the different sizes and grades.'

'Righto, sir.'

She braced herself for his disapproval, but all she saw on his face was friendly interest. Mr Curry went off to speak to a dark-haired man down at the dock, and Tom turned towards the long open shed. Ruby followed him, wishing she had a notebook and pencil.

Wood was strange to her. Cloth she knew: wool and worsted, cotton and linen, ribbon and thread and notions. She knew the difference between pine and oak, between mahogany and rosewood, but that was about all – and only if they'd been dressed and made into furniture. These logs were mysteries.

'Don't worry,' he said to her, flashing a sympathetic smile. 'It's not that hard to get the hang of.'

Did she look that worried? She straightened her back and nodded. 'I'm sure I'll get the – the hang of it soon enough.'

If he'd said, 'That's the spirit,' or something equally patronising she would have felt like slapping him, but he just grinned. He had an engaging grin, and she couldn't help but smile back.

'Three ways of organising: first, by size, second, by timber, third, by grade.'

'Really? I would have thought the type of wood would have come first.'

'Well,' Tom replied, 'builders need a certain size of bearer or joist, a certain size of board. If they can't get it in one timber or grade, they'll take another. Not much difference between Baltic pine and Hoop pine in the end, except price. It also means you can keep two or three different timbers on the same size frame. More efficient. Come and see.'

He took her down the line of wooden frames that held the cut wood. They towered over her, ten feet high, with three sections to each frame, each section, she now could see, filled with a different type of wood.

'Four be fours here: softwoods on one side, hardwoods on the other. Basically, most trees are hardwoods, except the pines. They're all softwood. But a lot of European trees are treated like softwoods in Australia, because our hardwoods are a lot harder than beech or elm. All the gums are hard. Different pines are different prices.'

She was overwhelmed by the smells: camphor and cedar, turpentine and eucalypt, the red paint which covered the cut ends, and over all the scent of pine.

'So, sizes: you've got four be fours, two be fours, two be twos. One be ones are a special order. So is routing, like for skirting boards or dados. Boards come in a lot of different widths, depending on the timber, but your basics are four inch, six inch and eight inch.'

Ruby nodded. Numbers. She could 'get the hang of' numbers easily enough. In her mind, the types and sizes of timber organised themselves into a matrix, clear and solid.

Tom looked at her, as if assessing her ability to absorb more. She smiled reassuringly at him and saw his gaze change, sharpen then warm, as though for the first time he were seeing her as a woman.

Ruby was abruptly aware that they were a long way away from the other men, out of sight of the office. Alone. She cleared her throat and looked down, feeling unaccountably warm, and fell back on that protection of all married women. 'My husband would find all this *so* interesting,' she said.

Tom smiled wryly. 'My fiancée thinks it's all a bit boring. She's in the VAD and all she can talk about is wound treatment!'

Ruby only realised how tense she had become as her muscles relaxed at his reassuring tone.

'Then there are the grades of timber,' Tom continued. 'We'd better go back to the office so I can show you on the board.'

'I don't want to take you away from your work,' she said quickly. 'I'm sure I'll figure it out.'

'Well,' he said, glancing at the mill. 'It's really just about how many knot holes the timber has, how strong it is, what it'll look like when it's finished off. So you've got structural timber, face timber, veneer —'

He stopped, seeing the confusion bloom on her face, and laughed, but not unkindly. 'I reckon you've had enough for one day. Come on, I'll walk you back.'

Ruby's legs were aware of how far they had walked – a city block up and another back, at least. This was a much bigger enterprise than she had realised, with a fortune tied up in stock, gradually maturing.

Mr Curry joined them at the foot of the stairs, with a shrewd eye at her.

Ruby nodded at him. 'Fascinating,' she said.

'Barge is due any minute now, Tom,' Mr Curry said.

'About time. We're low.'

Mr Curry turned to her and nodded toward the staircase. 'Off you go. Unloading's no place for a woman.'

She made her slow and awkward way up the steep risers and paused on the tiny landing at the top to watch as the barge laden with roughly trimmed logs came in, pushed by a hooting tugboat.

Tom stood by the water's edge, signalling to the tugboat captain as the other men stood around, ready to start unloading. She hadn't noticed the cast-iron crane hoist which the men swung out across the barge. Chains and ropes dangled from the arm of the crane and were secured around the huge logs. Some of them were ten feet across.

Reluctantly, she went inside to find both Wal and Wesley looking through the windows.

'Ironbark,' Wal said. 'From up Taree way. The Army wants it for barracks out at Liverpool.'

They watched for a moment, united in a grim understanding that they were part of the War, after all. She found her eyes tracking Tom's movement in the group of men, and turned away from the window. She had work to do.

•

At five to twelve, a bell rang in the yard and Ruby got up thankfully to go home for lunch.

'Half an hour,' Wesley said to her.

She hurried – she had to hurry because her bladder was full to bursting. Tomorrow she would have only half a cup of tea for breakfast. As she went, she heard, faintly, the noon bell for the Angelus ringing from St Brendan's. She gabbled the words: *Angelus Domini nuntiavit Mariæ* . . . But she couldn't concentrate.

Letting herself in, she rushed past Mrs Hannan in the front room, feeding Edward, and ran through the house to the dunny. The can was almost full; the nightsoil man came on Tuesday mornings, and this was Monday. She put down newspaper squares before she peed; she couldn't afford to be splashed with ordure.

The relief was enormous and finally she could concentrate enough to finish the prayer. Was it sacrilegious to pray on the dunny? she wondered, and started to giggle, not stopping even when she went inside to wash her hands.

'What's so funny?' Mrs Hannan asked.

'Me. Running back like my pants were on fire so I could use the outhouse.'

Her landlady laughed out loud. 'Just as well you're a fast walker, Mrs Hawkins.'

Impulsively, Ruby said, 'Call me Ruby.'

There was a small silence, long enough for Ruby to feel that she'd done the wrong thing, been too familiar. Her landlady's eyes were masked, but then she smiled wryly. 'I suppose if we're sharing the dunny it's a bit silly to keep calling each other missus. I'm Maree,' she said, and handed Ruby a plate with a sandwich on it.

'Ham!' Ruby said, disguising her sense of having been granted something greater than a first name.

'Celebration meal. It'll be corned beef next week.'

Ruby scoffed the sandwich, surprisingly hungry. Her appetite had been low since Jimmy left; this was the first time in weeks she could remember being properly hungry.

'I'll make you a cup of tea,' Maree said, but Ruby shook her head, laughing again.

'I don't dare!' she said, taking just a mouthful of water to wash away the saltiness of the ham. 'I have to get back.'

'Is it – is it all right?'

Excitement washed through Ruby, tinged with satisfaction and relief. 'I think it is,' she said. 'I'm going into the city this afternoon to buy some Amazonian cloth from Lasseter's. I'll need a new skirt.'

'Don't spend all your money before you earn it,' Maree said, which was something her mother would have said, but she was laughing, not scolding, so Ruby smiled and put her hat on.

As she walked back to work, she marvelled at the difference in feeling that just being able to *think* of Mrs Hannan as 'Maree' made. As though she might have a home here, instead of just a room.

CHAPTER 4

Tiddy walked her home, complete with a barrowload of wood and tinder.

Maree was struck dumb when she saw them, but she recovered fast enough and showed Tiddy where to stack the wood.

He held his cap hopefully between his hands and looked up at her, clearly trying to seem as young and innocent as he could.

'Come on, you young scallywag, I'll give you a ha'penny and I don't know but what I might find a piece of bread and dripping too.'

Ruby went to the privy, smiling. Maree was one of those women who needed to feed people.

As Ruby washed her hands in the scullery a few moments later, Maree came to stand in the doorway. She had an odd look on her face, and her hands were on her hips. 'If you want a reduction in your board because you've got free firewood,' she began.

'Oh! No!' Ruby hadn't even considered that. Although she was her father's daughter, and she loved to make a bargain. 'But I wouldn't mind some help with my washing instead.'

Maree regarded her with an assessing eye. 'I'll wash your shirts,' she said. 'But you have to iron them.'

'Of course,' Ruby managed. She covered up the awkwardness of the moment by straightening her hat and putting her gloves back on, then smiled formally at Maree and left, feeling rather as though she had survived some kind of ordeal.

It was odd, this negotiating of friendship. She'd never done it before – all the women she knew in Bourke she'd grown up with, and any negotiating had either been done in primary school, or was imposed by family connections. In a way, this was only her second adult relationship; Jimmy had been the first.

Ruby picked up the tram in Booth Street and rode it to George Street, the main shopping street of Sydney. She was still getting used to the hustle and noise of the city, but she loved to ride the tram. The ride down George Street took them past the brewery and Central Station, where the scaffolding for the new clock tower was rising higher and higher.

Lasseter's took up three city blocks, the biggest store in the Southern Hemisphere. She had been there before, once, to buy the silk stockings she had worn for Jimmy's leave. There were women clerks in every department of the store, even in menswear, behind the tie counter. She wasn't the only woman who had moved into a man's job because of the war.

The draper's section was some way into the enormous 'Cheapside' as it was known, and she felt dowdy as she made her way through the departments, noticing how the city women were wearing skirts that were actually showing their ankles – not straight skirts such as she wore, but a wide skirt gathered from a high waist. There was a lot more than five yards in those outfits. She would need at least six and a half if she wanted a jacket too. Which she did, looking at the smart silhouette and easy movement of the new fashion.

But would Mr Curry accept a skirt above the ankle in his workplace? When Ruby finally found the drapery and asked the clerk for the Amazonian cloth (a mixture of cotton and wool, one and eleven pence ha'penny the yard), she hesitated as the woman showed her the range.

Should she buy black? Or would that be too much like mourning? She didn't want to jinx Jimmy by dressing like a widow. 'Five and a half in the dark green,' she said firmly. Time to cut her cloth to fit her wallet. Her skirt would just have to be narrower and slightly longer than these elegant things around her. She had to make sure the men in the yard didn't get too good a look at her ankles as she came down the stairs.

'And some ribbon to edge the skirt?' the woman said, showing her some lovely grosgrain ribbon in a smart light green.

'No, thank you,' she said. If she were going to save, she had to start now, although she fingered the ribbon longingly. 'But I will have some lining.'

Perhaps she could embroider the lapels a little, just to lift the unrelieved colour. Some light green silk thread, then. And a couple of pairs of stockings.

There was a letter from Jimmy, postmarked Colombo, waiting for her when she got home. She opened it with hands that trembled, and with a tightness in her eyes which she knew was her body preparing for tears. But the first words allayed her fear.

Dear Ruby,

By Jove it was hard to leave you! And so good to see you waving goodbye at the pier. I'm missing you already.

I got your letter in Melbourne, which was a lovely surprise. We're settling into shipboard life, though it's given me a lot more respect for old Captain Cook, who braved these waters in a little tub of a boat. At least he was here in summer. The southerly wind has been fierce all night, howling and tugging at the portholes, straight off the Antarctic. Quite a few poor blighters have been hugging a bucket all night with seasickness. So far, cross fingers, it hasn't hit me.

I've chummed up with a mate, Arthur Freeman. He's a Bourke boy, though he's been mining down round Wollongong, Bulli, I think, in the last few years. One of his sisters is a Ruby, too – do you know her or Esther, the younger one?

So don't worry about me. Freemie and I will watch each other's back, and I'll be home safe and sound before you know it.

I've been assigned to a Lt Curry's company. He's not so bad for an officer – at least he knows how to give orders. The other subbie, Lt Gorton, is a ditherer. If it wasn't for Sgt Moss we'd never know what he wanted. But Curried Lamb is all right. You can tell he's been in charge of working men before now.

I never thought I'd be thankful for those freezing cold nights in the school dorm, but at least I know how to sleep in a crowded draughty bunkhouse, unlike some of the men. There's a chap here who'd never shared a room before he joined up. 'You should have been an officer,' Freemie said to him, 'you're too delicate for the likes of us.' He didn't take it well, so there was a bit of a stoush.

Well, I probably shouldn't be telling you about this kind of kerfuffle, but it was funny to see the two of them going at it hammer and tongs one minute, and the next Smithy yells, 'Corporal's coming!' and Freemie and Blakey sling their arms around each other's necks and Freemie starts singing 'Auld Lang Syne', as though they were the best of friends. He's quick, I'll give him that.

You don't want to be reading about that sort of nonsense, but there's not much to do but get our kit ready and stare out at the rain.

You'll be pleased to know that I've been avoiding the two-up games; there are three on our deck, most nights, and Blake has become cockatoo for one of them. He asked Freemie to join in, but Arthur's too spry for that.

'No fear,' he said. 'I don't want anyone owing me money who's going to be behind me on a battlefield with a loaded rifle.'

I say so too.

Oh, my darling, I miss you so much.

your loving husband

Jimmy

She laughed in the relief of hearing from him. Then she cried. Then she read it soberly, seeing how hard he was trying to write a 'nice' letter to her. Something cheerful, to stop her worrying.

Ruby Freeman? Yes, she had a vague memory of her; a few years older. It was meaningless, and yet somehow it was comforting that he was with someone from home.

She laughed over the references to Mr Curry's son, and then took the letter into the kitchen, where Maree was giving Edward his bath in a tin tub in front of the range.

'Jimmy says something here about Lieutenant Curry,' she said. 'Do you think I should show it to Mr Curry?'

'Oh, yes,' Maree said immediately. 'If he hasn't heard yet, it would be a kindness.'

Maree *was* kind, Ruby was realising, despite her matter-of-fact manner. She had thrown herself into Red Cross work. There was scarcely a moment when she wasn't knitting socks or scarves or rolling bandages. Maree was the salt of the earth.

•

The next day, hesitantly, Ruby knocked at Mr Curry's door, Jimmy's letter in her hand. He was immersed in a letter of his own, but it was a big and heavy legal document, not the thin paper the men sent from the Army.

'Mr Curry,' she said. 'I received a letter from my husband yesterday.'

He looked up and his whole body tensed, braced for bad news, every sinew taut. She smiled reassuringly and cleared her throat. 'From Colombo,' she continued. 'Just a hello letter, but . . .'

He stood up and motioned her in, then came around the desk and closed the door behind her.

'What is it, Mrs Hawkins?' he said.

The scent of his cologne was strong and reminded her of her father.

'He mentions your son,' she said. It was hard to give the letter to someone else, but instinct suggested that it was better for Mr Curry to read it himself. He took it carefully and sat back down in his chair, reading just as carefully. His mouth twitched with humour, and then a change came on his face. Pride, mixed with some other emotion; there was a glint of tears in his eyes.

'Fancy my Jimmy being in your son's Company!' she said brightly, to cover the moment over.

Mr Curry coughed and slid the letter across the desk to her. 'Yes, fancy.' Before he let it go, he pulled it back and read it again, as though memorising the words, then placed it into her hand. 'Thank you, Mrs Hawkins. It was good of you to show me.'

He was caught in his own thoughts and barely noticed when she stood up. She didn't know whether to leave or wait, so she hovered by the door, one hand on the brass knob.

'He's all I've got, you see.' He muttered the words as if to himself, but they were meant for her.

'Yes,' she said. It was all she could say, but it seemed to be enough.

He nodded at the desk, not meeting her eyes, and then pushed back from it with sudden energy. 'Right! Time to get that delivery organised.'

They went out into the office and he made his way to the yard door. As he opened it he looked back and chuckled. 'Curried Lamb! Your man's a cheeky bugger, Mrs Hawkins.'

She didn't answer, but she smiled. He clattered down the steps with more enthusiasm than she'd seen in him since she'd started, and the two clerks glanced at each other, and looked hopeful.

'What's got him so happy? Like his old self,' Wal said.

'Hasn't been like that since the boy left,' Wesley added.

How much should she say? The moment she had just shared with Mr Curry was private, surely, but these men had known him for much longer than she had, and they were genuinely concerned.

'I had word from my husband,' Ruby said. 'The Battalion is doing well on its journey.'

'Ah,' Wal said, nodding wisely. 'Good news. Well. We could do with some.'

'Amen to that,' Wesley intoned.

She'd never liked them more than at that moment, but then Wesley sniffed and looked her up and down.

'Some of us have work to do,' he said.

•

23rd July, 1915

My darling girl,

I got to the gold souk in Aden and managed to find a plain gold bracelet for you – the stuff they mostly sell here is a bit foreign-fancy for your taste, I think. I'll keep them in my kit. The post offices here are full of thieves, and it's not safe to send them back to you. But at Christmas you can imagine that I've sent them to you with all my love.

A lot of the fellows here are planning to go off on their leave to the fleshpots of Cairo, but Freemie and I have decided to head for the restaurants and feed ourselves up instead. Knowing you are waiting for me is the best possible thing to keep me on the straight and narrow, Ruby, and I want you to know that

I am as faithful to you as you are to me. I don't understand these married men who go off to visit the bordellos. Don't they know what they are risking? I don't just mean the diseases they could carry home to their wives, although those are bad enough. I mean the taint of it; how can they go home and kiss their children after – faugh! Forget it, I shouldn't have mentioned it. I only said anything because I know how people go on about 'soldiers on leave' and I didn't want you to worry about me.

I'm not saying I've been perfect before we met, but from now on – you can be sure of me. I've got a guiding light and she's shining strong and bright in my heart.

Well, I suppose I'm getting a bit sentimental because this will be our last leave before we head out.

Curried Lamb tries to keep the news from the front away from us, but you must know it's pretty grim. We see the hospital ships sometimes come in to dock, and they're always full, and we've been on burial duty a few times.

So before I leave here, I just wanted to say, my dearest, how glad I am that we had our week together before I left. Maybe that's selfish of me. I don't know. But the thought of you, the memory of us together, that's the thing that keeps me going. I know what I'm fighting for, and I know what I've got to come home to. You can believe I'll do everything I can to make it back to you.

That's enough of that.

I love you,

your Jimmy

CHAPTER 5

23rd July, 1915

Ruby paused at the point on the road just before it dipped sharply down the last ten yards to the bay. She could look out from here right across the harbour, clear to Glebe Island Bridge. It was a swing bridge – the middle section had moved sideways to let an elegant yacht go through. She wondered, idly, who could afford the time to go yachting during a war. Beyond the bridge she could see the intricate masts of some steam schooners tied up at a far wharf. The ferries were busy at this time of morning; one cut across Rozelle Bay headland as she watched, a small yellow and brown beetle scurrying over the water.

Such a constrast, this expanse of water, to the dusty, dry countryside around Bourke. She loved the red soil plains, and she was drawn to the water because only here did she get the sense of a vast open sky above her. City streets were so crowded, and Sydney had so many trees – she laughed. Trees were precious in Bourke; who would ever have thought she'd resent the way they blocked out the sky?

She walked briskly to the office door, enjoying the length of stride her new skirt gave her. It swished nicely against her petticoat as she walked; she could hear the quality of the fabric as it glided smoothly over her legs.

Was it wrong to enjoy these small pleasures when Jimmy was bound for such misery? She knew he would scoff at the idea, but she felt it deep within as a kind of betrayal. Without him, she was miserable much of the time, no matter how well she hid it, but she wasn't miserable *all* of the time, and she should be, surely, if she loved him as much as she thought? And she did love him. Oh, how she loved him.

The feel of it swept from her heart out in ripples through her body, a sweetness like nothing else. The essence of Jimmy. So much tenderness that tears came to her eyes. Ridiculous!, her mother would say. It was ridiculous, of course, not to be able to control her feelings. She took a breath, another, and waited for an omnibus to pass before she crossed the road.

This was how she'd first seen Jimmy, except that it had been a bullock dray she had been waiting for. He'd been on the other side of the street, his hat tipped back, his hands thrust into his jacket pockets, looking at ease with life and happy to be where he was, despite the dust and the heat and the smell of the dung the bullocks dropped as they passed.

Sometimes, Ruby thought that she'd fallen in love with him that very moment. He always swore that *he'd* fallen in love with her right then and there, and certainly when he'd seen her standing there he'd gone red, taken his hands out of his pockets, pulled his jacket down, and adjusted his hat. Then he'd smiled at her, a slow, lovely smile. She'd bitten a smile back. His clothes were well made and he clearly wasn't one of the drovers or abattoir hands who visited the town, but he was a stranger and no lady would flirt with a stranger on the street.

But two days later he'd come into the store and made a beeline for her, even though she was at the ladies' notions counter. Of course, the lingerie and the Ladies' Travelling Necessities (neatly done up in brown paper) were underneath the counter, but still! Ladies notions was not somewhere a man should be. The two women who were there looking at stockings left in a huff.

Looking back, she realised that he had had no idea what she had been selling. Most men didn't, of course, not understanding that women didn't always have enough cotton rags lying around the house for their monthly needs. There was a limit to how many times you could reuse them, no matter how carefully you washed them. And if you were travelling – well, Ladies' Travelling Necessities *were* a necessity. They would be a necessity to her, as well, now she was working.

Jimmy didn't have a sister, and his mother had died when he was young, so he hadn't lived with a woman until they were married. It had all come as a bit of a shock to him.

Ruby opened the office door to find Wesley there already, scowling at her. Her heart fell. She had hoped he would begin to adjust to her presence, but his resentment seemed to be growing.

Mr Curry called her in as soon as she had laid her hat in the desk drawer. He handed her a ledger before she had the chance to sit down. It was green, a colour her father had never used.

'Wages,' Mr Curry said. 'Calculate, draw it out and pay the men on Saturday. I've just given them all a rise, so you'll have to figure it out from scratch.'

He returned to his paperwork and she had no choice but to leave.

She sat and opened the green ledger, which had a list of men employed and rates of pay at the front, and weekly pays on subsequent pages. She was mortified to find that the only ones paid less than she was were the two young boys. But that was the way of the world. It would be bad business for Mr Curry to pay her the same as a man.

Which didn't make it fair.

Going to a bank. Asking to withdraw money. She knew that women had accounts, even married women, but her father had given her pin money before she was married, and Jimmy had done so for the scant week afterwards. Her allowance from the Army came through the Commonwealth Bank branch in the post office. She had never been inside a bank in her life. Banking was men's business.

But now it was hers. She'd *asked* for this job. She couldn't say to Mr Curry, 'Oh, I'd rather not, it's not ladylike.' How hard could it be?

Carefully, she calculated the amount she would need to pay the wages, and then, even more carefully, calculated what notes and coins she would need to ask the bank for. The wages were put into small envelopes and given out; the men signed the book. She had used the same system to pay her father's delivery boys and the man who kept the yard clean. But at the shop, she had simply gone to the till and taken what she needed. Here, she had to have exactly the right number of shillings and sixpences, or someone would go short.

Someone going short could mean someone not eating. It was a great responsibility.

When she had checked her figures twice she took the results in to Mr Curry.

'No offence, lass, but I'll check it myself this first time. Wages is serious business. Have you taken out the state income tax?'

Ruby felt heat rise in her face. How could she have forgotten? But her father's employees had never earned enough to warrant income tax. She must look completely incompetent.

Mr Curry grunted disapproval, but relented enough to say, 'Anyone earning over two hundred pounds per annum gets taxed at 2.5 per cent. Most of the men just scrape under that.' He looked up at her from under bushy eyebrows. 'Christmas bonuses don't count.'

She nodded, understanding. The bonus money would be given as a 'gift', keeping the men's income under the threshold and effectively paying them 2.5 per cent more a year. It was a way of keeping the men, of stopping them being lured into the Army.

'So it's only Mr Andrews, Mr Wilson and Mr McBride.'

'Aye. That's the lot. Two and a half from them. I draw what I need when I need it. We forward what we withhold to the government every quarter.'

'Yes, sir. I'll bring this back when I've calculated it, um, fully.'

As she left the office, Wesley scurried away from the door, a light in his eyes. He had heard. The feeling of mortification threatened to choke her, but she ignored him and settled back at her desk, recalculating.

When she was satisfied, she took it back to Mr Curry and he checked it over, nodding approval at last, and wrote a cheque out for the amount she had calculated.

'Pay them Saturday, just before quitting. Otherwise they'll slope off and have a beer.'

'Which bank do you use, Mr Curry?'

'Commonwealth, of course. Post office gets enough in for us.'

The post office. No need for a bank after all. The relief was overwhelming, even though she knew she was being silly. She felt light on her feet as she walked back to her desk, clutching the cheque, and smiled warmly at Wal as he looked over at her. She put the cheque safely into her drawer.

'The envelopes for the pay,' she asked him. 'Where are they?'

'Down the storage, under the stairs,' he said, jumping up. 'Come on, I'll show you.'

He led her down the stairs. Her new skirt swung free, allowing her to keep pace with him easily. She smiled with pleasure and Wal looked back over his shoulder and grinned back at her.

The storage area was tucked back behind the stairs, underneath the office. It was roughly floored and smelled a little of damp. There were long shelves against the wall, full of stationery and tools. Wal turned the light on and stood back against the wall to let her go in, then closed the door behind them. That was odd, she thought. She turned, but before she realised it he was beside her, hands on her arms.

'Hehe,' he said. 'Now we're alone.'

She could smell the egg he'd had for breakfast.

'Mr Andrews!' she said, astounded, moving backwards. That was a mistake. It brought her up against a set of shelves and allowed him to crowd against her. 'Mr Andrews, I'm a married woman!'

'Don't play coy, Ruby,' he said. 'I saw how you smiled at me. Couldn't mistake that look.'

'You *have* mistaken it,' she said, as forcefully as she could, although her voice came out in a squeak, about as forceful as a mouse. She pushed on his chest, but even skinny Wal was stronger than she was. She pushed again as he bent closer, his hand sliding down her arm to her waist, and even lower. 'I was just being friendly.'

'Hehe. Call it being friendly if you want,' he said. 'I know how lonely you women get with your men away.'

Tears came to her eyes. She felt so *weak,* so incapable. What did he intend? His body pressed against hers and she felt, unmistakably, what he intended. Fear flared up in her and she pushed harder, panic-stricken.

He fell back and moved away from her, astonished. 'What, now you're going to play the innocent? Don't give me that.'

'Leave me *alone*!' she shouted, tears rising.

'Keep your voice down, woman!' he said. 'Bloody hell. You *came* in here with me. What did you think was going to happen?'

She stared at him, astounded, tears on her face. She thought of her mother, who had warned her against ever going into a room on her own with a strange man, and drew herself up, trying to act as much like her as possible. Dignity, she thought.

'I *thought* that you were being gentlemanlike by directing me to what I needed.' Too late, she realised that the comment could be taken two ways.

His face changed and he grinned, but she froze him with a look, and he grimaced. 'Better get yourself presentable before you come up,' he said. He walked out, leaving the door wide open.

Outside, she could see the men craning to see her, and they called out as he went by. She couldn't hear the words, but the tone was unmistakable.

Wal was grinning as he turned onto the stairs, and he paused to throw a comment back over his shoulder. If she didn't act now, her reputation was gone. Completely. Not one man there would believe her innocent. She quailed. She couldn't do it. She *couldn't*. But then, she realised, Jimmy's reputation would be soiled, too, and she couldn't bear that.

She barrelled out the door and called loudly, 'And *keep* your hands to yourself in future, Mr Andrews. I'm a married woman!'

The men laughed and hooted. Wal's face went dark with anger and he glared at her. She had made an enemy. But what was the alternative?

She went back into the storage area and found the envelopes, taking her time, and then slowly, with dignity, walked to the stairs. The men eyed her curiously, and she stared back at them.

'Get back to work!' Tom's voice came. He walked across the yard and nodded to her. 'Nothing to see here.'

She went up the stairs knowing they were all sneaking glances at her.

•

Mr Curry had his door open when she came back in, but apart from a quick, fierce look at her, he didn't give any sign that he knew what had happened. Wesley sneered at her – no doubt he'd believe whatever Wal – *Mr Andrews* – had implied. Mr Andrews had his head down, ignoring her. Good.

The rest of the morning was torture. All the things she should have done taunted her in her imagination. She should have said, 'Thank you, Mr Andrews, but I'm sure I'll be able to find the envelopes,' and gone down alone. She should have waited until he'd opened the door and then left again before she'd gone in. She should have stopped him closing the door behind them. She should have slapped him across his grinning face and kneed him in the privates, just as Jimmy had showed her before he left.

Thank God she had an errand. Fishing the cheque from the drawer, she went to Mr Curry and said, 'What shall I carry the money in?' Wordlessly, he handed her a small brown satchel, then he coughed.

'Do you want me to send one of the men with you?'

Oh, yes, she did. She hated the thought of walking down the street with so much money. For a moment, she was poised on the brink of saying 'Yes'. But behind her Mr Wilson muttered something to Mr Andrews and he sniggered.

'No, thank you, Mr Curry,' she said, her heart speeding up. 'I'll be back soon.'

The room seemed oppressive; the heat from the stove, so welcome when she had come in that morning, was now smothering her. Opening the street door, feeling the men's eyes on her from behind, felt like an escape. As she walked up the street towards the post office, she found her legs wobbling and had to sit down on a low stone wall. The memory of Wal's heat and strength and her own helplessness overcame her and she shook.

Her mother had been right. The only thing that kept a woman safe was staying well away from all men except the ones in her family. How could she go back? How could she work with that man every day, when the sight of him would remind her constantly of how he had treated her? What he *thought* of her. Heat rushed into her face. How could he have thought *that* of her? What had she done to encourage him?

But her mother's words came to her rescue. 'There are men out there who believe that all women are sluts at heart,' she'd said once, after Myrtle had been kissed on the cheek by a boy at a church supper. The two of them, Myrtle and she, had gasped to hear their mother use such a word. 'They'll take whatever they can get, with encouragement or without. Don't expose yourself to insult, that's the main thing.'

Well, she had exposed herself to insult, but she didn't have to accept the insult. She didn't have to allow a dirty-minded man to force her out of the work she needed.

Ruby got up from the sun-warmed stone and dusted off her skirt. Her heart was still beating too fast and there was a knot of unshed tears in her chest, but she walked up to the post office with a determined stride.

What was it Jimmy said when someone irritated him?

Damn the blackguard to hell.

That was it.

CHAPTER 6

The post office was busy, full of conversations and queues. Ruby felt self-conscious standing in line at the Commonwealth Bank window, sure that the turmoil of the past hour would show on her face, but no one looked at her. Mrs Black, the Post Mistress, was tacking up a poster for the Red Cross on the wall: a meeting to be held in the Town Hall next Tuesday evening.

When Ruby reached the window, Mrs Mulligan was serving. The main assistant of the Post Mistress, Mrs Mulligan was lantern-jawed, with a massive bosom which almost rested on the countertop. Ruby knew her as a stalwart of St Brendan's, the Annandale Catholic Church. Ruby passed Mr Curry's cheque and the brown satchel over, along with her own request for the denominations of notes and coins to be given.

'Oh!' said Mrs Mulligan, '*you're* the new bookkeeper for Curry and Son's?'

The noise stopped. Everyone turned to look at her. Then the conversations buzzed up again, louder than before. One woman especially loud; a woman she'd never seen before, standing with some cronies in the queue for stamps.

'Shocking! Women in men's jobs. I'm astonished she can show her face, the hussy.'

Ruby could feel her face heating up.

'Some of us,' Mrs Mulligan said clearly, 'understand that when we take on a man's job, we free a man to go and do his duty by his King and country. The bookkeeper, he's in the 20th Battalion, I believe, Mrs —' she glanced down at Ruby's notes, which she had signed, 'Mrs Hawkins?'

'I believe so, Mrs Mulligan. The same as my husband. Mr Curry was unable to find a man to replace him.'

There. Let them chew on that. She knew it was true, otherwise she would never have got the position so easily. And the fact that she was a war wife gave her added respectability.

'Of course not,' Mrs Mulligan said, staring with scathing eyes at the loud woman. 'There's a war on.' She closed her jaw with a snap Ruby could almost hear.

Ruby bit back a smile. Thank you, Blessed Mother, for strong women who support each other, as Saint Elizabeth supported you in your time of need.

She took the satchel Mrs Mulligan handed to her.

'Thank you so much, Mrs Mulligan,' she said, with special emphasis, and Mrs Mulligan smiled dourly at her, and nodded.

Ruby went past the knot of women in the queue with her head held high. The sense of success lasted halfway down the block, and then the consciousness that she was carrying the wages of sixteen people on a public street with no protection hit her. Thanks to Mrs Mulligan, everyone knew who she was. Someone could have watched her take the money out. Someone could be following her right now.

She glanced nervously over her shoulder, but there was no one in the bright sunshine who looked at all suspicious.

Still, her heart beat faster all the way down the road until she was safely within the walls of the office – only to realise that there was a different kind of threat here. Wesley and Wal stared at her with identical scowls.

But she remembered Mrs Mulligan, and decided that the best way was to brazen it out. She was going to stay, no matter what they thought. *She* had nothing to be ashamed of. For King and country, she thought.

'Good afternoon, gentlemen,' she said brightly. 'It's a beautiful day out there!'

Taking the satchel to her desk, she walked past them briskly and unpacked it, neatly separating the notes and coins, organising the whole thing as she used to do while counting the till receipts at the end of the day in the shop. There was a satisfaction in it, both in the neatness and the way the men were nonplussed by her attitude.

She filled the envelopes and wrote each man's name on the outside. Filling her own envelope was a particular pleasure. Her very first pay packet. When she'd finished, it was almost lunchtime. She packed the envelopes into the satchel and went to Mr Curry's office. The door was open. She realised it had been open all morning, ever since . . .

Mr Curry was keeping an eye on things.

She was grateful and she smiled at him as she gave him the satchel. He grunted goodnaturedly at her and rose to open the safe in the corner. She looked away politely so she wouldn't see the combination.

'Right, then,' he said. She was dismissed, and yet she felt as though she had passed a test. Perhaps he hadn't expected her to stay after the incident with Wal; perhaps he hadn't expected her to handle going to get the wages. But there was a small crinkle at the corner of his eyes, as though he were pleased with her. 'Off to lunch,' he said, waving towards the door.

She went to lunch more sedately than she had earlier in the week, and with more dignity. Walking up the hill to Wells Street was exhausting. She felt as though she had run a race that morning, an enervating, unexpected race under fire. Baptism of fire. No, it was hubris to use the same words they used to describe the soldiers' ordeal. Baptism of insults, perhaps.

But she had survived.

•

That night, after Edward was in bed, while she was edging the raw seams of her skirt, she told Maree everything that had happened.

'Well,' Maree said philosophically, 'you had to expect someone to put the hard word on you.' She saw Ruby's surprise, and laughed. 'Men'll always try something, if you give them half a chance. I was a waitress in a tea room before I married Theo. You'd think that'd be respectable enough, but the number of times I had to slap someone's face!'

Somehow, that was funny, and they laughed together until they wiped away tears.

'There's never been enough women in this country,' Maree said, tucking a handkerchief into her bosom. 'So they grab the first chance they get, in case they never get another one.'

That set them off again. Eventually, Ruby sighed and got up to make a cup of tea. Maree followed her, and Ruby smiled. She'd never had someone she could talk frankly to. She and her sister Myrtle weren't close; Myrtle was several years older than she was and had been married since Ruby was thirteen. Her other friends were from church, and their conversations were modest and ladylike, full of giggling.

She had been married only a few weeks before she came to Sydney in the hope of seeing Jimmy again before he embarked. She and Jimmy had married in haste, the week before he left to enlist. They had intended waiting until they had a home of their own, but the war changed everything. Better to be together even for a week; she couldn't have borne it if he had died and she had never lain in his arms.

She had been astonished, in the three weeks between Jimmy leaving and her own departure, how even respectable married women had joked with her about her honeymoon being cut short. Even her mother had commented: 'Don't get too much of a taste for it, you'll be sleeping alone for a long time.'

The difference between being an unmarried girl and a married woman wasn't just in the wedding ring and the social status; she had been admitted to the inner circle, where discussions of birth and women's illnesses and the climacteric were the stuff of everyday. In retrospect, she remembered all those times she had come into a room where her mother and her mother's friends had been talking and they had abruptly fallen silent. So often, as a young girl, she had assumed they had been talking about her, and criticising her. Now she realised they had been talking about something 'inappropriate' for her tender years.

With Maree, she had no need to put a guard on her tongue. She paused with the kettle in her hand; Maree leant against the kitchen doorway.

'His breath smelled of eggs!' Ruby said and had to put the

kettle down and bend over, clutching her stomach, she was laughing so hard.

Maree stuffed her apron in her own mouth so she wouldn't wake up Edward. 'Got to have a hearty breakfast if you're going to romance a married woman!' Maree gasped. 'You might need the energy.'

'Well, he's a long thin streak of nothing,' Ruby said weakly. 'I daresay he did!'

•

The next morning, handing over Wal's pay, Ruby looked him straight in the eye, trying not to laugh at the memory. Her amusement disconcerted him, she could see, and she felt a flicker of satisfaction. Wesley and Wal were paid first, then they called the men.

The boys first, followed one by one by the men, each of them with clean fingernails and hair slicked back, hat in hand, ready for the weekend. Each of the men looked at her surreptitiously, and then glanced quickly at Wal. She kept her face still, smiled with friendly calm, and gave each of them their envelope and held the book for them to sign. One of them, an older man with no teeth but a wide smile, made an X instead, but she was ready for that, having looked at the earlier pages, and signed next to his mark as a witness.

'Thanks, missus!' each said, and disappeared down the stairs to the yard. She had no idea what conclusions, if any, they had come to.

The last two were Alfred Smith, the crane operator, and Tom McBride. Taller by half a head than any of the others, he seemed to fill the office and smelled, unmistakeably, of honest male sweat. It took her a moment to register that Alfred Smith was Aboriginal.

It was a like a breath of home. She hadn't realised until that moment how odd it had seemed to her that there were no black people on the streets of Annandale.

'Mr Smith,' she said warmly, and asked him where he was from. She could tell he wasn't from home; his face was quite a different shape to the Burundji or Ngemba men.

'Oh, I'm from down south, missus, round Jervis Bay,' he said. He was a stocky, greying man, about the same age as Mr Curry, with broad shoulders. He had the large calloused hands of a manual worker, but his signature was a beautiful copperplate.

Tom saw her admiring it and laughed. 'Don't you go taking him to do the office work, Mrs Hawkins. I need him on the dock!'

He hadn't yet washed up and had grease on his hands. 'Sorry,' Tom said, wiping it off on a kerchief the size of a small tablecloth. 'Table saw needed some work.' She smiled and handed him his envelope and he flashed a smile back, white teeth startling after the empty mouth of the toothless man. He too signed with a neat, educated hand and she wondered about him. He reminded her of Jimmy, who had been well taught as a boarder in a Christian Brothers' school in country Victoria.

She noticed a St Christopher medal around Tom McBride's neck, just like the one her mother had given Jimmy to wear. So he was a Catholic, too.

'Thanks, Mrs Hawkins,' he said, raising a hand in farewell as he headed down the stairs. The room seemed smaller without him, and the silence louder.

She tucked her own envelope into her purse and signed the book, then took the book and empty satchel to Mr Curry.

'Well,' he said. 'End of your first week, eh? All in all, not too bad.'

It was like he'd given her a blessing. Her face broke into a smile; she could feel how wide it was, and fought to bring it back to something more appropriate for the office, but failed.

'I'm glad you were satisfied,' she said.

'Early days,' he said, but she could tell it was just form; the sort of thing he ought to say to a new employee.

They all left together and Mr Curry locked up behind them. The two clerks headed off towards Glebe; Ruby and Mr Curry walked together up Johnston Street, up the western side instead of the east, where she normally went. She felt she couldn't just leave him without ceremony, even if it took her out of her way.

'Heard from your man?' Mr Curry asked.

'Not since the letter I showed you,' she said. 'Perhaps we'll get something from Cairo.'

'Mmm. Well, I'm here.'

He had stopped outside a gate in the tall sandstone wall. The gate to one of the witches' houses, she thought, so called because of their round towers, roofed with pointed cones like a witch's hat. Perched on top of the ridge with views across the harbour, they were some of the finest homes in Annandale. She revised her estimate of Mr Curry's wealth substantially.

'I'll see you on Monday, Mr Curry,' she said.

He lifted his hat. 'Mrs Hawkins.'

He seemed a little uncomfortable, and she understood why. It felt odd to her as well, to walk away from a man at his own door. She couldn't recall ever having done such a thing. A man – a gentleman – walked you to your door, not the other way around. But she was not a lady, she was an employee, and they had merely shared a little way of the walk home. Perhaps next Saturday she would walk the other way, up Trafalgar Street. It might be more seemly.

CHAPTER 7

Ruby, Maree and Edward always went to eight o'clock Mass at St Brendan's. Mr Curry was there, dressed as they all were in their Sunday best. He nodded to them and they nodded back, very polite, quite distant. Tom McBride was there too; he helped take up the collection.

After Mass Mr Curry stayed to chat with the parish priest, Father Ford. Ruby and Maree showed Edward the work that had been started on the extensions to the parish school, and then walked home.

'It'll be good for when he goes to school,' Maree said as she fed Edward an apple with a sprinkle of salt on it. 'It's just around the corner.'

The Sabbath was the day of rest, but Ruby had discovered that there was no such thing as rest in a house with a two-year-old. Maree looked tired.

'Let me take him for a walk,' Ruby said.

'Wark!' Eddie shouted. 'Wark, missus 'uby!'

'You'd better call me Aunty Ruby, sweetheart,' Ruby said, and then shot a look at Maree. Was that too much?

'You're a lucky boy,' Maree said. 'I must say, I wouldn't say no to five minutes to myself.'

They walked to the View Street park. Pushing Edward in the swing, Ruby yearned for the time when she would bring her own children somewhere like this. When Edward reached for her, she gathered him in and cuddled him.

'Auny Ruby,' he said, patting her cheek.

'That's right, lamb,' she said.

'Meat!' he said.

'Bread and butter,' she said.

He squinted his little eyes at her, as though he were gauging how far he could push her. 'Bread and burrer,' he agreed.

Laughing, they went home and cuddled up together on the couch, singing nursery rhymes and eating bread and butter, while Maree, smiling, knitted for the Red Cross.

•

Over the next weeks, Ruby settled into a routine. She finished making all the new clothes she needed; she worked out exactly how much tea she could have for breakfast and still make it safely back to the outhouse at lunchtime; she ignored Wal's glares and Wesley's blatant contempt.

Gradually, the men became people to her instead of names in a ledger.

Tom McBride was engaged to a girl who had decided to do VAD work, and he occasionally mentioned her – Helen – to Ruby. The Volunteer Aid Detachment was going to help the official medical establishment. Some of them were actually going to the front! But Helen was planning, after her training, to help at the Repatriation Hospital in Randwick. Some of the wounded from the Anzac landing were already there.

'There'll be more, sure enough, plenty to go around,' Tom said one day while Ruby was waiting for Tiddy to load her barrow of firewood. She winced, thinking of Jimmy.

'Gosh, sorry, Mrs Hawkins. I – er – I'm sure your chap will come through just fine.'

'I hope so, Mr McBride.'

'Helen and I are both praying for him,' Tom said.

'How kind of you both! Thank you!'

They smiled at each other in simple accord.

Tiddy trundled the barrow off and Ruby followed, wondering what kind of girl Tom McBride had become engaged to. Pretty, probably.

●

11th August, 1915

My darling girl,

Well, I'm a real soldier now. On the front line. Better not to describe what it's like here. I've been thinking about Barkinji. Our week together.

Last night, in the lulls, I closed my eyes and imagined I was back there with you.

In the old brass bed where your mother was born. Maybe our children will be born there too. We didn't have much chance to talk about kiddies, did we? But I know you'll want a big family. Six or so.

That bed . . . it creaked a bit, didn't it? Just as well your uncle's housekeeper was away.

But I'll bet that bed never saw love like ours before, sweetheart. You were so tender, so giving, so . . . well, so passionate.

It's not just that I remember, my darling. It's as though I can feel you against me, feel your skin, taste you, touch you. More than a memory. Those sweet days and night are with me. Part of me, forever.

Another letter I can't let the censor see. I'll have a pile of them by the time I get home to you.

all my love

J

•

There was a letter from Cairo two weeks later, on a Friday, which Ruby found in the letterbox when she got home; Maree was at a Red Cross meeting. The letter had a stamp in red ink on it that said 'PASSED'. All letters from the front were checked by the military censor, although not all were opened and read. This one hadn't been opened. Ruby thanked God for that – losing even one word from Jimmy to the censor's thick black pen would have been heartbreaking. It had a photograph included, of Jimmy and another man in a Cairo street. On the back Jimmy had scrawled 'Arthur and me' in pencil.

Jimmy looked well; astonishingly so, really, and happy. Smiling for the camera? Or feeling a genuine excitement to be out in a foreign city with a mate? It warmed her heart but she felt a slight flicker of annoyance, too. Couldn't he have looked a little dismayed to be so far away from her?

Dear Ruby,

Here we are in Cairo. Who would have imagined that I'd get to see the pyramids one day? Curried Lamb organised an afternoon trip for us and a guided tour. Supposed to improve our minds, I suspect, although I think he was on a sticky wicket with some of these blokes.

The guide tried to gyp us, but Curried Lamb wasn't having any of that, and bargained him down to almost nothing. It was an odd day, looking up at these shapes in the desert that you've heard about all your life. Like having a book come to life. I felt a bit like Alice in Wonderland. Mind you, they're pretty shabby. The Egyptians don't take very good care of them. Wouldn't do them any harm to slap a bit of mortar on the dodgy bits.

The hawkers came after us selling trinkets and jewellery. I was going to buy something for you, but Curried Lamb said we'd get better and cheaper in the Cairo markets, so we waited.

We should have some leave before we embark for wherever we're going.

The news from Europe isn't good, and this war looks like being a bit longer than we thought. I don't like leaving you alone for so long. I wish I could be there to look after you.

I think about the Family Hotel every night.
love
Jimmy

The Family Hotel. She had gone through a stage of thinking about the Family Hotel as well, and of Barkinji, her uncle's cattle station where she and Jimmy had spent their short honeymoon. The night he had left she had fallen into bed, expecting to be dragged down into sleep, but she stared wide-eyed up into the darkness, unable to stop thinking about him. To stop imagining what might lie ahead, the pain and death and destruction. She had distracted herself with memories of the hotel room, of his hot skin and tender hands, but that was a mistake. Her own body, tired as it was, awakened, yearned for his, *demanded* his, heat and need and an aching emptiness making sleep impossible. Her skin felt as though a layer had been stripped from it, like the skin under a blister.

She had pushed all those longings down, deep down, but that night, after reading his letter, she dreamt of him, wild, impossible dreams where she cast all restraint away and tempted him like a scarlet woman, where he took her and mastered her and loved her as only Jimmy could.

She woke chilled as the morning air hit her sweat-covered skin, half-ashamed and half-aroused. She wished that the house had a bathroom, as the family home in Bourke did, so she could have a cold bath. She wished she could ask Maree if she missed Theo the same way, but that was not a conversation she could imagine having.

•

At work, she was acutely conscious of the feel of her clothes against her skin. Tom McBride was waiting for her in the office, to give her details of a new man employed, a Chris Frieman (pronounced Freeman, which made her think of Jimmy's friend), an experienced sawyer who was a godsend at a time when too many men were leaving to enlist.

Frieman hovered uncertainly near the yard door, a young blond boy no more than twenty. Tom leaned his hip casually on her desk as he gave her Frieman's address and date of birth, and she could smell the soap he had used, and the male musk under that. It made her flush, remembering Jimmy's scent, remembering too much, losing track of what she was doing.

'Mrs Hawkins?' Tom said. Startled, she looked up into his eyes, hazel eyes with flecks of brown and deep green, and she saw them darken as they looked at her. His breathing seemed loud. For a moment she couldn't look away, and then Wesley moved and his chair scraped across the floor, breaking the silence.

'I'm sorry, Mr McBride, could you just give me the rate of pay again?' She sought for an excuse which would settle things, which would bring the feeling in the room back to normal. 'I had a letter from my husband yesterday, and I'm afraid I was thinking about it.'

'Can't keep their minds on their work,' Wesley muttered.

Tom's mouth quirked and he looked at her, brimful of amusement, inviting her to share it. She smiled back involuntarily.

'Four pounds a week,' Tom said. 'Rising to four pounds ten after a month.'

So she wasn't the only person who had been put on probation. That gave her some satisfaction and made her feel more like herself.

'He's working today?'

'Yes, but he understands he won't be paid until next week. Isn't that right, Frieman?'

'Yes, missus!' Frieman snatched the cap from his head and shuffled his feet nervously.

'That's fine, then.' She smiled at him, amused to find herself being treated like the boss. 'That's all I need.'

He disappeared out the door like a rabbit down a burrow and Tom laughed. 'At least he's not afraid of the big saw.' She shivered at the thought, and he noticed. 'It's not dangerous if you know what you're doing,' he reassured her.

He was a very nice man, she thought. His Helen was a lucky girl.

She gave Jimmy's letter to Mr Curry to read, and he told her that he'd had one of his own. He didn't give it to her, but he did read out a paragraph:

I've got some good men in my squad, Dad. There are a couple of crack shots from Bourke, Freeman and Hawkins, who'll be very useful in a scrap.

Mr Curry picked up Jimmy's letter again, and looked at the last few words.

'I'd better look after you,' he said, 'or I'll have that husband of yours coming after me with a rifle when he gets home.'

She looked down and smiled, feeling proud. 'I can look after myself,' she said.

'Can't blame a man for worrying,' Mr Curry said. 'Not when he's so far away.'

•

20th August, 1915

My darling girl,

Sometimes the only thing that keeps me going is knowing you'd mourn for me if I let Johnny Turk take me down. It'd be easier in some ways – but don't worry, I'm going to get through this and come back to you.

I don't think I ever told you what happened the day I first saw you. You remember, you were on the other side of the street and I was just mooching along with Tim Montrose, and there you were.

It was a cloudy day, remember? We were all hoping for rain before the winter sowing. But the clouds shifted and a ray of light came down right on you, as though God was saying, 'Pay attention, boy! Look at her!'

So I looked. Well, you know how I felt, right away. I told you. (Remember when I told you? Our first kiss.)

I didn't tell you, though, how — how low I felt afterwards. You were so beautiful. Such a lady. So genteel and innocent and lovely. I knew I didn't have a chance of deserving you. I mean, what was I? Nothing. Nobody's dog.

So I went and got drunk. Only my second time and I reckon it'll be my last. Woke up down by the creek with a head the size of a watermelon. I looked into the stream and I thought, What are you doing, wrecking yourself like this? If you don't deserve her, make something of yourself until you <u>do.</u>

That's when I made the plan to be a stock and station agent. I was happy enough as a jackeroo till then but a jackeroo's wife wasn't good enough for you. I wasn't good enough for you then. So I got that job at Stuart's, and came to see you. I couldn't believe it when you said you'd marry me.

But I will be good enough, Ruby. When I get home I'll get my old job back and we'll rent a home and set up together and I'll work all the hours God sends until I can give you what you deserve.

my darling girl,
all my love
Jimmy

CHAPTER 8

August—September, 1915

The August winds had come late, but gusty and cold. Ruby kept one hand on her hat as she walked down to work and wished she'd made an overcoat for herself. She had, in sheer self-preservation, started wearing the coat-sweater her sister Myrtle had knitted for her. The men, after all, were turning up in cardigans and sweaters and long Argyle knitted vests. August moved into September, but the winds continued, although the streets were ablaze with the vibrant gold of the wattles and every tiny front garden had daffodils bent half over in the wind.

In the first week in September, Ruby walked into the office with her hair a mess from the wind and found Mr Curry waiting for her. His face was grim. She cast a quick glance at the wall clock. Was she late? No, it still wanted a few minutes until half-past seven. She moved towards him uncertainly.

'They've been deployed,' he said. 'Laurie managed to get off a note at the last minute. Just a scrawl.' He proffered a single ragged sheet of paper, clearly torn from a notebook. She took it, her heart beating too fast. Laurence Curry had a strong hand, clear and decisive.

Father,
We're off. I'll write more when I can.
Look after yourself.
Laurie

That was all.

Mr Curry's hand shook as he held it out to receive the letter back. Wordlessly, she gave it to him, and they looked at each other in shared fear. His mouth was drawn back in a straight line, in an attempt not to show too much.

She put a hand on his arm. 'We'll pray,' she said, and was surprised to find her voice steady. 'We'll pray, the two of us, and they'll come back to us.'

'I haven't prayed for a good long day,' he said. He saw her surprise. 'Oh, a man has to go to church,' he shrugged. 'Have to do the done thing. But I haven't prayed to mean it since Jean died. Didn't see the point. Didn't do me any good when she was sick.'

'Do you think your wife is in Heaven?' she asked gently.

'If anyone is, she is. She was the closest thing to a saint I ever met.'

'Then let's pray to her to look after our boys; her boy.'

He bent his head. With her hand still on his arm, she whispered the Pater Noster. He joined in at the Amen.

The door opened as they moved apart, and Wesley and Wal came in. Wesley's sharp eyes narrowed – she just knew that there would be gossip doing the rounds by morning tea about the two of them.

'The boys have been deployed,' Mr Curry said. It cost him something to announce it, so she knew he had seen Wesley's look and was protecting her.

'I'd appreciate your prayers,' she said, looking Wesley straight in the eyes. She was surprised when he nodded gravely. Religion, at least, he treated with respect.

'I'll be pleased to put them on the roll at my church,' he said.

It was a sombre morning. Ruby tried to concentrate on her ledgers, but it was so hard. Every cart outside sounded like a gun barrage; every shout from the yard like a cry of pain. Mr Curry, for the first time since the incident months earlier with Wally, kept his door closed.

Ruby walked home at lunchtime slowly and was relieved when Maree wasn't there. A sandwich and an apple waited for her on the tiny kitchen table. She sat and ate mechanically. She didn't want to eat, but she remembered the last night in Bourke, before Jimmy had set off for Liverpool, to the recruiting office.

'Promise me you'll look after yourself,' he had said, stroking back the hair from her face, his eyes tender and gentle and sad.

She had promised, so she ate, without thinking of anything at all. She washed her plate; she dried it and put it away. Then she stood in the middle of the kitchen, quite still, eyes not seeing. Poised between moments. Blank inside and out. Blessedly unfeeling. For a long moment it seemed that she could stay there forever, never moving, encased in glass.

The front door burst open and Eddie came running through, shouting, 'Auny Ruby! Auny Ruby! Sickens! Sickens!'

Turning to meet him was like moving through molasses. Then his warm, hard little body hit her legs and his arms came around her. The glass surrounding her broke and she bent and snatched him up, burying her face in his shoulder. He wriggled to be free. 'Sickens!'

'Chickens,' Maree said, following him. She had a wicker lidded basket, and a soft protesting clucking came from inside it.

Hysterical giggles rose up in Ruby's chest. She fought to keep them down, but as she gasped for air to stop, the giggles turned into sobs, great, racking sobs with no tears, just gulping for air and blindness and pain in her chest.

Maree sprang forward and put Edward on the ground, wrapping strong arms around Ruby. 'Rube, what is it? Did you get a telegram? Oh, sweet Mother of God, is it Jimmy?'

Those were the questions she needed to hear. They reminded her of how much worse it could be. She caught her breath, and shook her head.

'No, no, it's not that.'

Maree let out a long breath. 'Oh, thank God. What then?'

'They've been deployed. Mr Curry got a note from his son. They're going into battle. They've already gone. That note would have been written weeks ago.'

'Who battle?' Eddie demanded.

'Uncle Jimmy,' Maree said automatically. 'Uncle Jimmy's going to fight the Turks.'

'Kill Turks!' Eddie shouted. 'Bang-bang-bang!'

'Oh my lord, where does he get it from?' Maree said. 'No, I know, it's playing with the older children at the Red Cross sewing circles. Yes, yes, that's right, Ed, Uncle Jimmy's going to kill the Turks.'

Ruby had had time enough now to find her composure. 'I'm all right. I'm just being silly. I'd better get back to work.'

'Are you sure you're all right?'

'Fine. Fine.' She looked at the wicker basket, abandoned by the corridor, and began to laugh. '*Chickens?*'

'The longer this war goes on, the more expensive things will be,' Maree said. 'We might be very glad of free eggs before it's all over. I'll set them up a roost in the laundry. They won't eat much. At least we don't have to worry about foxes in the city.'

Ruby walked back to work, through a wide, warming spring day, a day that was made for hope and lightheartedness, neither of which she could summon. Thankfulness, though, she could find that. God bless Maree. She was a rock in the wilderness, although she must be just as worried about Theo.

She prayed for them all as she walked: Jimmy, Theo, Curried Lamb, Arthur Freeman, the bookkeeper whose name she couldn't remember, all the boys she didn't know, even the Turks and the Germans. All mothers' sons, every one of them. *Bring them all home safe*, she prayed, and knew as she said the words that the answer to the prayer would be, 'No.'

•

4th September, 1915

My darling girl,

We've lost so many.
    So many. I used to be sure I'd come through this and get back to you, but now
        Forget that.

Sometimes the waves wash on the shingle and it sounds like the wind in the gums at Barkinji. Sometimes I fall asleep and you're there with me, holding me. Nothing racy. Just holding me.

I miss you more than I can explain.

your own Jimmy

CHAPTER 9
September, 1915

On the Monday, Maree ventured into the city to the Red Cross headquarters to collect a quantity of khaki wool for the Annandale ladies to make into socks and scarves. Ruby met her outside the front gate at lunchtime, coming home flushed and triumphant, her arms pushed out from her sides by the size of the bags of wool she was hauling.

'It was a scrum,' she said, 'but I got us enough for a month!'

'Where's Edward?'

'Carrie Skinner's looking after him.' Sure enough, the call of 'Mumeeeee, Mumeee!' came from next door and Eddie rushed out and wrapped his arms around Maree's legs.

They laughed, but Ruby felt a pang. When would she know that feeling, of little arms clinging to her?

Back at work that afternoon, she kept her head down, thankful that she had something – even something unpleasant, like the coming introduction of national income tax – to occupy her mind.

The rest of the time she fought a constant battle not to imagine Jimmy dead or dying. The daily newspaper was a litany of casualties. She had stopped buying the paper for a few days to try to banish the images from her mind, but it was better to know what was happening than to imagine the worst.

What was happening was bad enough.

There was anger everywhere at the British stupidity in putting the Australian men at such risk for such little gain.

The daily list of 'Heroes of the Dardanelles' grew longer and longer. Although the paper never listed which company the dead had been in, gossip said they were mostly 18th Battalion. They were fighting somewhere called Hill 60, and the 18th Battalion were suffering heavy casualties. Jimmy must be there by now, surely?

The telegram boy arrived and reminded her so much of Myrtle's cheeky little son, Matthew, that she couldn't help tipping him a ha'penny when he brought a telegram to her desk.

'He won't give 'em to us in the yard anymore, Mrs Hawkins,' Tom McBride told her as he walked over to her desk. 'He knows what side his bread's buttered on.' He sat in the small wooden chair reserved for visitors and said, 'I got me a white feather this morning.'

He fished it out of his pocket – a hen's feather, bedraggled and pitiful.

'You're not planning to join up?' she asked without thinking, then felt herself flush. She so wished she could stop blushing. It was a terribly revealing trait, and so embarrassing. 'I mean, the mill *is* part of the war effort.'

'That's what I told the old biddy who gave me this,' McBride said. 'But she didn't look too convinced.'

He brooded over it. It must be hard to be called a coward, for that was what the white feather meant. Women of the Order of the White Feather were committed to shaming men into enlisting. One of the carters, a militant Irishman who came to her for payment once a fortnight, was making a collection. He wore them proudly in his lapel and joked about collecting enough for a feather pillow.

'My girl laughs, but she's in the VAD. She's doing her bit.' McBride twirled the feather in his fingers and brooded over it. 'This is my fourth one.'

Not surprising, Ruby thought, since he was so tall and strong. No wonder the white-feather ladies believed he was shirking – no one would think that he was unfit for duty. For a moment, her gaze dwelt on the muscles of his arms, and then she recollected herself and looked away.

'The old man needs you,' Wal said. 'With the boy gone . . .'

As one, the four of them glanced to Mr Curry's office. He was immersed in some papers, so they relaxed.

'I know,' McBride said. He hoisted himself to his feet and went to the yard door. 'But I wish the government would give a badge or something to the men who are involved in the war effort behind the scenes.'

Wall and Wesley looked worried after he left, and Ruby wondered what would happen to the mill and the yard if they lost him.

She put the worry aside because, after all, what could she do? Look to the future, that was best. She was saving hard, almost a pound a week. Every month she cabled Jimmy his half of his pay; only one of them could operate his account, and they had decided it had better be her, but it meant she had to send him his part of the money regularly. Fortunately, neither the bank nor the post office charged for this service. He would be able to cash the orders when he got back to Cairo; she hoped that was a long, long time away, as the mostly likely reason for a return to Cairo was being wounded.

Jimmy would have seven shillings a week from the Army, too, the one shilling a day they reserved for after the war. That was more than eighteen pounds per annum, so over a year, if she could keep this up, they would save seventy pounds!

It was better to think of the future as a happy, smiling time, full of new houses and new babies.

•

Two more men left that afternoon to join the Army. Tom McBride scowled and wished them luck, and Mr Curry promised that their jobs would be there for them when they came back. 'If they came back' was what everyone thought, but no one said.

Interviewing men for the positions was McBride's job, although for form's sake Mr Curry inspected the new staff members and approved them.

'We didn't have much choice, really,' McBride said, drinking his tea while Mr Curry welcomed the two men – boys, really, too young to enlist and too young to even pretend to be old enough, as many boys were doing. 'The only others who applied were dropsical or senile. Still, we might keep these for more than a couple of months.'

The telegram boy stuck his head in the office door and brightened when he saw Ruby at her desk. He advanced on her, ignoring Wesley's outstetched hand, and took his check cap off politely, showing badly cut brown hair, as he handed her the yellow form.

'For Mr Curry, missus,' he said, waiting expectantly.

Tom McBride intervened. 'You get paid well enough, young feller-me-lad,' he said. 'No need for Mrs Hawkins to give you tips.'

Ruby smiled up at McBride. 'It's all right —'

'Go on, off you go!' He turned the boy around with a hand on his shoulder and gave him a goodnatured swat on the behind.

'Gi'us a job, Mr McBride?' the boy asked from the safety of the door. 'I'm sick of bringing bad news.'

'Just missed out,' McBride said. 'I'll let you know.'

'Ta.' He disappeared out the door and they heard the sound of his bicycle bell warning pedestrians, and some man swearing at him.

Ruby laughed. 'He's a character.'

'Don't be too soft on him. I've known him since he was a kid, and if you give him an inch he'll take a mile.' He grinned, showing white teeth. 'But he's a hard worker, I'll give him that.'

Smiling, she got up to take the telegram into Mr Curry, who was just showing the new boys out of his office.

'This is Mrs Hawkins. Come to her on Saturday for your wages,' he said, taking the telegram and nodding his thanks. He ripped it open and scanned it swiftly. His face went white, as though all the blood had simply disappeared from his body, and he grasped the back of Ruby's chair for support. His hand trembled.

They all knew. The men were struck still and dumb, not knowing what to do. Not knowing what to say. They looked to her instinctively, and instinctively she moved towards him, taking his weight, leading him back into his office, back to his chair. He was shaking like an old man with palsy; not saying anything, his breath coming in harsh gasps, his hand still clutching the bad news.

Tom helped steady him into the chair. Wal and Wesley came with them, impotent but wanting to help.

'Get some brandy!' Ruby snapped. Tom moved to obey, going to a cupboard on the right of Mr Curry's office and finding brandy and a glass. He poured some and handed it to her and she held it to Mr Curry's lips, which were almost blue.

He moved his head in rejection, but she pressed him. 'You need it,' she said. 'Come on, now.' She used the tone she took when Eddie didn't want to eat his dinner, and perhaps some long-buried memory of obedience to his mother prompted him, because he steadied the glass with the hand that still clutched the telegram, and sipped.

'Close the door,' Ruby ordered.

Tom closed it against the avid eyes of the new employees and came to stand on the other side of the chair. He said nothing, but his hand came down on Mr Curry's shoulder. Mr Curry's free hand sought Ruby's and she held it as comfortingly as she could.

Wal and Wesley stood in silence; Wesley was wringing his hands and she was ashamed of herself for wondering if he was more worried about Mr Curry or his own future if the boss died of heart seizure.

Finally, Mr Curry got his breathing under control. He held the paper out to her and she took it reluctantly.

*PLEASE INFORM MR WILLIAM CURRY THAT HIS
SON (NUMBER 1926) LT LAURENCE CURRY 20TH
BATTALION, 3RD CPY REPORTED KILLED IN ACTION
29TH AUGUST AND CONVEY DEEP REGRET AND
SYMPATHY OF THEIR MAJESTIES THE KING AND
QUEEN AND THE COMMONWEALTH GOVERNMENT
IN LOSS THAT HE AND ARMY HAVE SUSTAINED BY
DEATH SOLDIER REPLY PAID.*
COL WARD

She read it in silence and then nodded to the others. The worst. Tom sighed heavily and the other men shuffled their feet. Wesley folded his hands and bent his head, but he prayed in silence. Wal stood with tears on his cheeks. They had known Laurence, as she had not, and their grief was real.

They all stood quietly for a few moments. Ruby became aware that Mr Curry was gripping her hand still, but that his other hand reached out for the telegram. She put it back into his palm and his fingers closed over it tightly. What should she do?

She cleared her throat. 'Would you like to go home?' she asked, as gently as she could.

Mr Curry looked up at her with eyes as wide as a child's, and pupils which were almost all black. No tears. Shock had purged the tears from him. It was only a hundred yards or so to his house, but would he be able to walk? Could they call a cab for such a short distance? How long would they have to wait?

'Come on,' she said. 'Tom, help me take him home. Wesley, call his doctor, get him to meet us at the house.'

They leapt to it, glad to have something concrete to do. Softening her voice as much as she could, and ignoring the pain in her own heart (*Jimmy, Jimmy, Jimmy* was echoing in her mind, knowing they probably sent the officers' telegrams first, knowing he might be dead already and she not knowing), she said, 'Come now, Mr Curry, come with us and we'll take you home. You need to rest.'

He swallowed once, twice, again. Tom grabbed the brandy and gave him some to sip. 'Best to get busy,' he whispered hoarsely.

'Tomorrow,' Ruby said. 'Tomorrow is soon enough to be busy.'

After that, as though she had some authority over him, he allowed himself to be levered out of the chair and supported out the door. She didn't even pause to put on her hat. Tom handled most of the weight; she guided them.

It took them a while to shuffle up the street, and the people they passed looked affronted at first, thinking they were drunk, disapproving of their hatlessness, then surprised when they saw who it was, then shocked, dismayed, compassionate when they saw the telegram still clutched in his fist.

A woman helped by opening the gate to the house; an old man Ruby recognised as one of the wardens from church helped them get up the steep steps to the garden.

'I'll get Father Ford,' the man offered, and Ruby nodded. 'Yes, thank you.'

They made their slow way up the brick path, surrounded incongruously by beds of pansies and heart's ease. It wasn't one of the witches' houses after all, but the house next door, a solid Victorian with a bay front and verandah. Ruby eased Mr Curry's weight fully onto Tom and ran ahead to ring the bell.

Mr Curry looked up blankly as though he'd never seen the house before; then he blinked and fumbled in his pocket.

'Can you get his keys?' Ruby asked Tom, but before they could act the door opened slowly.

A woman – the housekeeper, almost certainly – looked at them in astonishment and some affront. Ruby had only time to see that she was around sixty, her hair in a scarf to keep it clean while she dusted, an apron across her print dress. Then she sprang forward, saying, 'Mr Curry! Here, let me help, come in, come in, oh God preserve us, a telegram, is it the boy, then?' all in a full Irish brogue.

'Yes,' Ruby said baldly.

The three of them conveyed Mr Curry through the high hall and into the drawing room on the right, a large room with big leather chesterfield couches on either side of the fireplace. They eased Mr Curry down on one of them. The housekeeper tried to push him down full-length, but he resisted silently, shrugging her off and sitting straight, still staring ahead and trembling slightly.

'We've called the doctor and someone's getting the priest,' Ruby said.

Tom seemed tongue-tied suddenly, or perhaps he was just catching his breath. Mr Curry was no light weight, despite his shortness.

The woman was looking her up and down. 'You'll be the bookkeeper?' Her Irish accent was less marked, now.

'Yes,' she said. 'I'm Mrs Hawkins.' She gestured to Tom. 'Mr McBride, the foreman. We brought him straight home when . . .'

They all looked at the telegram clutched in Mr Curry's white-knuckled fist.

'Aye, aye, best thing to do,' she agreed dourly. 'I'm Mrs Donahue, the housekeeper.'

'How d'you do?' Ruby said.

She thought how ridiculous it was, and yet how comforting, to fall back on the rituals of good manners.

'I'll make tea,' Mrs Donahue said. 'That's what he needs. Strong and sweet.'

'Shall I help?' Ruby asked.

'No. Sit you down, I'll be back in a moment. Best to let him be for a bit, now. Don't try to make him talk. That boy was the sun and moon to him.'

A spasm flickered over Mr Curry's face at the words, but he didn't move.

Ruby sat next to him, thinking that perhaps Mrs Donahue was right, it was best to wait until the doctor came.

She had nothing to do but look at the house. Fine, big rooms – lit by French doors onto the verandah, the drawing room was richly furnished, but all the furniture was twenty or thirty years old. It reminded her that Mr Curry had already weathered one deep grief – she suspected that nothing had been changed since Mrs Curry had died.

'I'll shut the front door,' Tom said, as though glad to have something to do.

Ruby laid a hand on Mr Curry's arm. It was rigid underneath the cloth, every muscle tensed. He was fighting some kind of battle, and she didn't know how to help him. Was he fighting to keep control of his feelings, or to let them out?

'I'm so sorry,' she said. Fear for Jimmy rushed in, making her gasp, tears in her eyes, her breastbone aching from a future wound she knew might come any day, any moment.

He turned his head, stiffly, like a marionette, and regarded her from bloodshot eyes. The huge pupils had contracted to pinpricks.

'Dead.' His voice scraped like a match on stone. From the corner of her eye she saw Tom, coming back from the hall, stop still in the doorway and hold a hand out flat to motion back Mrs Donahue.

'Yes,' she said, keeping her voice as steady as she could. 'Laurence is dead.'

His head began to nod, slowly, over and over again. 'Dead.'

'Killed in action.' Her voice trembled. 'I'm so sorry.' She couldn't stop saying it, but what else was there to say?

The fine trembling which had kept up ever since he opened the telegram got worse. He shook horribly, his face turning white just as it had before. She put her arms around him and he pitched forwards until his face was in her shoulder. He was dragging in deep, difficult breaths. As though he were Eddie, she rocked him back and forth, crooning deep in her throat. After a long moment, he began to sob, sobs just like Eddie's when he cried for his mother.

Tom moved out of the room altogether and Mrs Donahue didn't appear. Ruby understood why; later on it would be better if Mr Curry didn't know anyone else had seen him like this. But it left her feeling marooned in this plush room with its Victorian propriety, alone with his grief and her own fear.

She was rescued by the doorbell and, a few moments later, the doctor, a small bustling man with a limp who took one look and whipped a small metal case out of his bag. 'Water!' he barked.

Mrs Donahue scurried to get some. The doctor crushed a tablet into a vial and held out a hand impatiently, waiting motionless until Mrs Donahue placed a small jug in it. He poured a little water into the vial, holding it up to see a mark on the side, making sure the water just hit the mark. Then he corked the vial and shook it. Ruby silently urged him on. Mr Curry was so heavy, and he was still shaking, still sobbing those desperate, forlorn cries.

A moment later, the doctor plunged a needle into the vial and drew up the liquid. 'Get his coat off,' he ordered Tom.

Together, Tom and Ruby struggled to get Mr Curry's jacket off. He started to breathe instead of sob, beginning to pay attention to what was happening. The doctor pulled out Mr Curry's cufflink and rolled his shirt sleeve up.

'Benson?' Mr Curry muttered, bewildered. Then the needle went into his arm. Ruby looked away. It was too intimate a thing to see of a man she hardly knew. He grunted in pain.

A few moments later, his body sagged and his eyes closed. Tom eased him back onto the lounge, his head on a black-and-gold tasselled pillow.

'Lie him on his side,' the doctor ordered. 'In case he casts up his accounts.'

They made him as comfortable as they could. Mrs Donahue brought an afghan rug and covered him gently. Then they stood, uncomfortable and suddenly embarrassed, not looking at each other.

'I have to get on,' Dr Benson said. 'He'll sleep till morning, and he'll wake with a hell of a headache. Sorry, ladies.' They nodded forgiveness. 'It's just the shock. Probably be fine tomorrow.' He looked from Ruby to Tom to Mrs Donahue with keen eyes. 'I must go – in the middle of delivering a baby. First baby, won't have come yet. Call me if he's no better when he wakes.'

'Yes, Doctor,' Mrs Donahue said, showing him out. She came back, wiping her hands on her apron. 'Come out to the kitchen and we'll have tea.'

Ruby hesitated, glancing back to the couch, not liking to leave him.

'Well, if you're too good for the kitchen, I'll bring you a cup,' Mrs Donahue said with a sniff, and only after Tom followed her did Ruby realise that, like it or not, Tom had decided his place was in the kitchen and hers was in the parlour. Her mother would agree with him. She was too worried to be concerned about offending Mrs Donahue, but she hoped she hadn't offended Tom.

Mr Curry's coat was on the floor. She picked it up, folded it and placed it smoothly on the arm of the couch.

In the large mirror over the mantelpiece she saw the garden reflected through the lace, snowflakes with edges of green and blue and sand stirring in the wind from the open door. It was like their lives, all the harmony and smooth lines fractured and partial, colours split and scattered, nothing whole.

Knowing it was a liberty, she drew back the lace curtains until the outside was displayed, the fractures erased. For a moment she enjoyed the simplicity and clarity of the green garden. A currawong was warbling, there were sparrows on the garden bed, looking for worms. The continuity of the outside world comforted her. No matter what happened, there would be sparrows. And then she thought, Oh, no! the shades must be drawn. There'll be callers.

She let the lace down and unclipped the heavy drapes so that they fell back in a silent whoosh of air. The room was darkened immediately. Mrs Donahue paused in the doorway and fumbled for something. A click and there was light. Electric light in Tiffany shades. No gas mantles. At least one thing in this house was modern.

'I'll draw the blinds upstairs,' Mrs Donahue said. 'We have a black wreath up in the attic, from when the late Mrs Curry's father died last year. Should I put it up?'

'Yes,' Ruby nodded, ignoring the edge to Mrs Donahue's voice. If the woman didn't like the way things were, too bad for her. The fact was, she was a servant and Ruby was – what? An employee? A businesswoman? How ridiculous that sounded. She supposed, in the end, that they were both women who were paid by Mr Curry to do a day's work for a day's pay.

They stood for a moment, looking at Mr Curry, who was breathing stertorously but steadily, the tips of his neat ears red, one hand lolling over the edge of the couch.

'Might as well have shot him, too,' Mrs Donahue said, putting Ruby's cup down on a side table next to a red velvet armchair. 'What will he do now?' She walked out briskly.

Ruby had no answer. She sank into an armchair and took up the cup, a delicate English porcelain. She usually drank her tea black but she was glad of the sweet, milky taste. Mrs Donahue had given her a biscuit as well, a shortbread, but she couldn't eat it; her stomach was still in knots.

She sat, unsure of what to do after she had finished her tea; it seemed wrong to leave him, but she wasn't family or even a friend. She didn't know what she was waiting for, but she couldn't bring herself to stir. For a moment, a few moments, the world was in a lull, becalmed. When she moved the waves would come crashing in again, the wind would rise, and who knew if she would survive the storm? Fanciful nonsense, but still she sat unmoving, the cup on the table beside her, staring at the brilliant ruby-and-emerald glow of the Tiffany floor lamp beside the fireplace.

Father Ford arrived some time later; the sound of the doorbell roused Ruby from a daze. Mrs Donahue, no longer scarfed and aproned but in a respectable black dress, led him in. Ruby rose to greet him.

'Mrs Hawkins,' he said. They'd met, of course, at church. 'How is he?'

'As you see, Father. Sleeping.'

Mr Curry's breathing had calmed and now he was in a seemingly natural sleep.

'Good.' There was still a faint trace of Ireland in his voice, but he'd been gone from there longer than Mr Curry; Father Ford was in his seventies, small and round, with a ring of white hair around a bald head. She wouldn't have said he was a particularly kindly man. But with all that, he was an experienced priest, and he looked her over with shrewd eyes and said, 'You get along home now, and look after yourself. Mrs Donahue has things in hand here.'

'Yes, Father,' she said obediently, glad to be able to obey someone, glad someone had taken the responsibility from her shoulders. She had never felt so young.

'McBride went out the back way,' Mrs Donahue said. 'He sent up one of the boys with your hat.'

'Get away now before it gets dark,' Father Ford urged her. He reached out his hand and she stood still as he traced the cross on her forehead and murmured a blessing.

'Thank you, Father,' she said, grateful for both the touch and the gift of grace. She went into the hall as Father Ford sat in her armchair, contemplating Mr Curry. He was in good hands.

Mrs Donahue had her hat. Her earlier antagonism seemed to be submerged in the presence of the priest. 'You'll come back tomorrow, then?' she asked.

'If Mr Curry's not back at work, I'll stop by,' Ruby promised, wondering what would happen if he were not well. Not . . . capable. But by tomorrow he would have got over the first shock and be able to control his grief. Men did.

It was sunset, a mackerel sky reflecting rose and gold and dusky purple. Maree must be wondering where she was by now. Realising how hungry she was, she hurried down the steps and out onto Johnston Street. A wreath had been set up on the gate as well as the front door, and a small note attached to it said, 'Mr Curry is not at home to callers.'

How useful social niceties were in times of trouble. It was a comfort to know how to behave; to have forms and habits to follow; to have mutually agreed manners to tide one through the difficult moments. That was why this afternoon had been so hard. Mr Curry had forgotten how to act. Grief had scoured his mind clean of any knowledge of appropriate behaviour. Real grief did that.

But now the whole world was in mourning, and there was no stopping, no time for seclusion or the indulgence of continuing tears. They would give him, what, a day or two, and then the world would beat at his doors again, demanding that he be 'himself', demanding that he take up the burden of business and community.

She felt doubly sorry for him.

Striding home, she tried not to think about whether there would be a telegram waiting for her. Of course not. If one had come, Maree would have brought it to the office, and they would have redirected her to Mr Curry's house.

No. Not yet. Not today.

My darling Jimmy,
We've just received the news of Lt Curry's death and I am writing to you hoping and praying that you are well.
Beloved, my own dear, take care of yourself . . .

She wrote long into the night and posted it first thing the next morning, just in case. Just in case.

CHAPTER 10

The office door was locked when she arrived the next morning. It had never been locked before.

Wesley and Wal were walking up The Avenue from Forest Lodge. They looked worried to see her standing out on the street. As they passed the big gates to the yard, the left gate began to swing back, right on time, and then the right one. Two of the men looked out of the opening and saw them.

'Any news of the boss?' one asked.

She shook her head.

Wal took off his hat and scratched his head. 'McBride has the keys to the yard, but not the office,' he said. They both looked at her hopefully.

'You don't want to go up yourselves?' she asked.

They both took a half-step back and shook their heads. 'Better not,' Wal said. 'Boss doesn't like us going up to the house. Mr Lonsdale used to go sometimes.'

Mr Lonsdale was the old bookkeeper. The implication was clear. She was, however doubtfully in Wesley's opinion, a bookkeeper, one of the bosses, and therefore the boss wouldn't object to her visit.

'Women don't count,' Wesley added. He was actually trying to be helpful, she saw after a moment's annoyance. 'Not the same, you see. Not encroaching.'

'All right,' Ruby said, sighing. 'I'll go up and get the keys.'

She would have had to go and check on Mr Curry anyway, she thought, but the men's attitude worried her. If Mr Curry wasn't there, who would run things? She'd assumed Wal or Wesley would take over, but they seemed in no hurry to assume command.

She was probably worrying for nothing. Perhaps Mr Curry hadn't even woken up yet, or the headache the doctor had predicted was incapacitating him.

She let herself in the gate and went up the steep stairs to the garden. Like all mourning houses, the place had a look of closed eyes and abandonment. Today she had time to take in the Victorian solidity and spaciousness, the bow front on the left which went up to the top storey, the iron lace on the balcony over the porch, the fine slate roof. You could have fitted three of Maree's little house across the front of this one, and probably another three at the back.

Mrs Donahue answered the bell, in her black dress, and stared at Ruby with a mixture of annoyance and relief. 'Hm,' she said. 'Well, maybe you'll be useful at that. Come along in. He woke his normal time and went up to the room and now he won't get up and he won't let the doctor be ordered.'

'I'm just here for the office keys,' Ruby protested, but Mrs Donahue ignored her and led her up the stairs. She could have stood stock still in the hall, she supposed, but if Mrs Donahue was worried enough to welcome her help, she couldn't just walk away.

From the upstairs landing, richly carpeted, several closed doors indicated more bedrooms. The room at the front, with the bow window, was the master bedroom.

'I can't go in there!' Ruby protested. 'Not into the man's bedroom!'

Mrs Donahue hovered by the door, caught in a real dilemma. Convention versus need. 'He's just lying there alike to die!'

Ruby didn't know what to do. It was impossible to go into the bedroom of a man who wasn't family when he was in a state of undress. What should a lady do in these circumstances? What would her mother do?

She would do what had to be done, of course. An image of her mother dealing competently with whatever was presented to her flashed across Ruby's mind, and she took a breath. 'All right. I'll speak to him.'

She went in, hesitantly. The room was dark, of course, with the blinds pulled down. Mrs Donahue found the pull cord for the light and clicked it on, a sudden harsh brilliance.

'Turn it off!' Mr Curry muttered.

He was lying face down, head buried in his arms, across the bed. Ruby was relieved to see that he was fully dressed, and then realised he was in his clothes from the previous day.

'It's me, Mr Curry,' Ruby said. 'Mrs Hawkins.'

A sudden stillness in his body showed her that he had heard.

'Mr Curry, are you all right?' She realised how stupid the question was as soon as she said it. 'No, of course you're not. I'm sorry. Is there anything I can do?'

He raised a bleary head and stared at her, then let his head drop down again.

'No.'

'Have you had anything to eat or drink?'

He dragged himself upright, and the strong electric light showed the bags under his eyes and the lines sunk into his cheeks. He looked twenty years older.

'Eat?' he whispered. 'Drink? Why would I do that? Only the living eat and drink, and all that's best of me is dead. It's all my fault.'

She closed her eyes for a moment in sheer pain; understanding only too well what that might feel like.

'The boy'd want you to carry on,' Mrs Donahue said from the doorway.

Ruby made a motion to her to stop, knowing in her bones that this was the wrong tack to take, but it was too late.

'Carry *on*?' he roared, sitting up fully and glaring at her, at them both. 'Carry *on*? They've taken it all and there's no more to take and you want me to *carry on*? I tell you what happens. They tell you that if you work hard and make something of yourself you can be happy. You can be a man, a bloody gentleman. You can have a family and children and a home and be part of something bigger, part of *Empire*.' He almost spat the word. 'But the Empire charges a price, oh yes, and the price is *everything*. I did so well my son became an *officer*, but what good did it do him, eh? What good did it do his mother? All my work, all my wealth, and nothing, nothing could save either one of them. So tell me, *ladies*, what's there to *carry on* for?'

Ruby stared at him.

Mrs Donahue took a step closer to her and Mr Curry rounded, 'Get the hell out of my room!' She ran, with a squeak, back down the stairs. He turned furious eyes on Ruby. 'You too!' he roared. 'You think when they tell you your man is dead you'll feel any different?'

Part of her wanted to run away as fast as Mrs Donahue. Part of her wanted to hug him and say she understood. But there was another part of her, the part that knew how to get angry. It apparently had control of her tongue and wanted to slap him for bringing Jimmy into this. Temper had always been her besetting sin, and today it was rising fast.

'I want the keys to the office.'

'Office is closed!' he said. 'The business is closed!'

The anger flicked out like a lash. 'So you'll make every one of us wallow in your misery?' she snapped. 'I never even met Laurence and I'm supposed to have my life broken apart by his death, too?'

She was appalled, listening to herself. How could she talk like this? How could she *think* like this?

Mr Curry was taken aback but he didn't falter. 'It's my business and I can do what I like with it.'

'It's your business and you have a responsibility to every single one of your workers, not to mention your suppliers and customers.'

'Fine,' he said. 'You're so gung-ho about it, *you* run it.' He dug the keys out of his pocket and flung them at her feet. 'Now get out of here!'

She bent down, picked up the keys and slid them into her pocket. 'And for God's sake, have a wash!' she said as she left the room. 'You stink like a barnyard.'

•

She walked back slowly to give herself time to get over her own insensitivity. To get herself under control.

And to decide what to tell the men. They saw her coming and she forced herself to smile. No need to burden them with the situation. She had the keys. Life could go on. In a couple of days Mr Curry would come to his senses and things would be back to normal.

She waved the keys at them as she was waiting to cross The Avenue, and saw relief wash over their faces. McBride was standing at the gate, and he waved acknowledgement to her and went back into the yard.

By the time she reached the front door she had herself well in hand. 'We're to go on as usual,' she said. It wasn't exactly a lie. He had said she was to run things, so she would. Or at least, she would enable the men to.

But she couldn't do it alone. She braved the stairs and went to the yard to find Tom. He was standing, bare-headed, down by the dock with Alfred Smith, apparently counting the floating logs waiting to be harvested from the sea. The barge that had delivered them was being tugged slowly away, the tug boat's smoke a smudge against the blue sky. Ruby took a deep breath of sea air. The normality of the day was reassuring.

Tom turned to greet her, handing his notes over to Smith to continue, moving away from the dock edge to the base of the big crane. He bent his head to her and lowered his voice. She was aware of his height; taller even than Jimmy, she thought. 'How is he?'

She bit her lip, feeling the emotions well up again. 'Not good. He – he's in despair.'

Tom swore, and she welcomed it because it expressed her own feelings.

'If we can just keep things going here for a few days . . .' she said.

'Right,' he said. He steadied her elbow as they walked slowly over the rough ground. She could feel the heat of his hand through her jacket and felt, absurdly, that it was the first time she had been touched since Jimmy left. Which wasn't true. Not at all. 'We'll manage.'

Relief washed over Ruby at the 'we'. She didn't have to handle all this alone. She didn't dare look up at him; she didn't want him to see the panic still lurking in her eyes. Besides, she was aware of the men in the yard watching them, and the last thing she wanted to seem like was a fawning girl.

'Fine then,' she said, brushing off a clean skirt. 'I'll let you know if things change.'

'Good-o.' He raised his voice as Albert Smith came nearer, the count complete. 'I'll get onto that, Mrs Hawkins.' He raised his hand to tip his hat and realised it wasn't there – for a moment his eyes were alight with laughter at himself, and she smiled, and went away heartened and a little nervous. Tom was so *reliable*, and seemed to be the one man who believed she could look after herself. It was contrary of her to wish that he would take over altogether.

•

Mid-morning on Wednesday, the phone rang and Wesley answered it. Something in his voice made Ruby look up from her work.

'Oh. Yes. I suppose. You'd better talk to – hold on.' He gestured to her to pick up her handset. 'It's the *Sydney Morning Herald*. They want a photo and a paragraph.'

'They should call the house.'

'They did. He wouldn't talk to them.'

Ruby sat still, then slowly reached out her hand to the telephone. There should be a paragraph in the paper. Laurence Curry deserved to have his heroism respected. And there were no formal death notices for soldiers, only the articles on 'Heroes of the Dardanelles'. There was a photograph of him on Mr Curry's desk they could send to the newspaper. But she had never met Laurence Curry. What could she say?

Before she picked it up, she hissed at Wal, 'Where did he go to school?'

'Joey's,' he said.

'Born here?'

'In the house,' he confirmed.

'And the mother's name was Jean?'

Both Wal and Wesley nodded, like the twins she had once thought them to be. As she picked up the handset, the two of them came over to the desk and stood ready, waiting to support her if necessary.

'Hello?' she said, heart racing.

It wasn't so bad. The reporter was clearly used to doing this and simply asked questions. Most of them she could answer. A few stumped her.

'Sport?' she echoed, waving frantically at Wal.

'Cricket,' he said immediately. 'Leg spinner. Pretty good.'

'He was a fine cricketer,' she said, not losing a beat. 'A spin bowler.'

'*Leg* spinner,' Wal insisted.

'A leg spinner,' she said obediently.

'Excellent,' said the reporter. 'That's the kind of detail we like.'

'One more thing,' she said, feeling bold. 'My husband is in his company, 3rd Company. He was much liked by the men. Respected and admired.'

'Wonderful,' the reporter said. 'Thank you.'

When she hung up, Ruby felt as though she'd run a race. She slumped back in her chair, exhausted, her grandmother's order never to let her back touch a chair totally forgotten for a moment. Then she sat up straight.

'What if he doesn't like it?' Wal asked.

'Then he should have talked to the reporter himself,' Ruby snapped.

Wesley laughed. He went back to his seat and Wal followed him more slowly, casting a look equal parts admiration and doubt back at her.

'Get Tiddy up here,' she said, 'and we'll send him into the *Herald* with the photograph.'

The paragraph was in the paper the next day.

Lt Laurence Curry, 20th Btln, IEF, the only son of Mr William Curry and the late Mrs Jean Curry, was born in Annandale, NSW. He received his education at St Joseph's College, Hunter's Hill, and was working in the family firm, Curry & Son's Timber Merchants, at the time of his enlistment. He was a keen cricketer and a fine leg spin bowler and much admired by the men of his Company.

Knowing it was cowardice, she waited all day for a telephone call from Mr Curry blasting her for her impudence. She didn't know if it was good that he didn't call. Had he even read the paper?

Over those few days, Ruby learnt how much work Mr Curry actually did. How many decisions he made.

Some of them were easily handled by Wal and Wesley. Normally, when an order came in, they would take it down by phone, work out the costings and if the yard had sawn stock or raw lumber, then give it to Mr Curry, who would look at what work they had on, figure out a delivery date, choose a carter and get a price from him, and then give the clerks a final price for the customer. The clerks would phone that back to the customer, who would send a confirmation order by telegram or letter, depending on the urgency of the delivery. Then the order went down to the yard.

With the war, many of the orders came from the Department of Defence, and the prices for their materials had been set by contract. They also sent their own lorries to pick up the timber, so there was no carter involved. These orders were easy, and were given priority. A quick word with Tom McBride was all she needed to set a date for collection.

They met so often over the next two days that the men in the yard stopped watching them. Mostly, it was simply a matter of discussing the order and then moving on. Sometimes, though, Ruby found herself standing by the dock, staring at the slow-moving harbour currents, discussing other things with Tom: the uses of the different types of wood, the places the logs were shipped from and why Curry's used particular suppliers; Tom's own favourite timbers and their qualities. He was trying, she realised, to give her some of his own understanding of the business, and that made her feel panicky, because it hinted that he might leave.

But not, she hoped, until Mr Curry was back. Those moments on the dock were the only calm seconds in the day.

They needed Mr Curry back. The non-Army orders were causing everyone trouble. Neither Wal nor Wesley liked to ask her for advice. Frankly, she didn't want to give it. She knew far less about the business than either of them, and would have felt bumptious for offering an opinion. But she heard them debating the merits of one carter over another, and arguing about whether they could get enough timber from their suppliers to make the delivery date on a big order for tallowwood. Tempers were rising.

Tom had no problem asking for her advice, but when on the Thursday afternoon he pushed a delivery note across her desk and said, 'This bloke's put his prices up without telling us,' she looked instinctively at Wal and Wesley. They were listening, pens poised. I can either take this query, she thought, and have them think I'm too big for my boots, or I can pass it off to them and look weak and ineffectual.

'Do we have an agreement with him in writing?'

'Don't think so,' Tom said. 'Wal? Jenkins Carters and Conveyers. Have we got anything in writing with them?'

Both Wal and Wesley got up and came over to the desk.

'No,' Wal said. 'It's always verbal. But they agreed to a price, right and tight. They wouldn't try this if the boss was here.' He challenged Ruby. 'Your job to put them straight, Mrs Hawkins. That was always the bookkeeper's job.'

'Fair enough,' she said. She took the carter's invoice and reached for the phone, but they were still standing there, watching her. 'No need to keep you from your work, gentlemen,' she said sharply.

Tom grinned and went downstairs, while Wal and Wesley moved back to their desks slowly, glancing at each other and shrugging slightly.

She rang the number on the invoice. A woman answered. Ruby asked for Mr Jenkins.

'He's out,' the woman replied. 'Making a delivery. Do you have a job?'

'This is Mrs Hawkins, the bookkeeper for Curry & Son's.'

'Oh, Mrs Hawkins!' Suddenly the voice was full of sweetness and light. So they needed the work Curry's sent their way, or the woman wouldn't be fawning.

'And I am speaking to?'

'I'm Mrs Jenkins.'

'Excellent. Then I'm sure we can work out this little problem we have.'

'What problem?' Her voice was cautious.

'Your husband seems to have mistaken the charge for the delivery he did to Wollstonecraft for us last week. It's ten shillings higher than we agreed.'

A moment's silence.

'Well, we have had to put our prices up . . . with the war, and everything.'

'So you cleared this with Mr Curry? He didn't mention it to me this morning . . .'

Mrs Jenkins coughed. 'As to that, I couldn't say . . . Jenkins might well have done.' Trying to brazen it out, then.

'Or perhaps,' Ruby said gently, 'Mr Jenkins just made a mistake, and charged Curry's the price he's charging other companies – companies that don't give him as much work as we do?'

There was a longer silence.

'I expect that's it.'

'So we'll just pay our usual fee and amend your invoice, and we're all square, then?' Ruby made her voice as happy and pleasant as she could. The desire to shout at this harpy was surprisingly strong. They were trying to benefit from Mr Curry's absence. Vultures.

'Fine, thank you,' Mrs Jenkins said, with no gratitude at all.

As Ruby replaced her telephone handset, the two men looked at her, eyes full of admiration mixed with disdain.

'No need to play nice,' Wesley said. 'You're the boss, not her best friend.'

'Woman to woman is different,' Ruby said, shrugging. It was – you didn't have to explain things to women; they heard the threat under the words loud and clear.

She left Mr Curry alone. They muddled on, with a couple of decisions being put aside, 'Until the boss comes back' because neither Wal nor Wesley would take the responsibility, but neither would ask her. Thank God.

Although she had the keys, the men supervised her locking up at lunch and home times, checking the windows and the yard door before they left.

'If he doesn't come back tomorrow,' she said to Maree on Thursday over a delicious leek-and-potato soup, after Eddie was asleep, 'I don't know what we're going to do. He needs to sign the wages cheque.'

'You should go and visit him tomorrow,' Maree said. 'Do

what you always do with the wages and then take him the books and the chequebook. *Make* him sign it if you have to.'

Ruby laughed. 'Hold a gun to his head? He'd probably tell me to shoot.' The idea caught her in the throat and she choked, half crying, half laughing, until Maree stood and patted her on the back.

'It'll be all right,' she said. 'Go and see him. Remind him that the world goes on, whether he likes it or not.'

So Ruby let the men in the next morning, a brisk, surprisingly chilly day for late September, then did the wages as usual, gathered up the ledger, the chequebook and the satchel and put her hat on.

'I'm just going up to get Mr Curry to sign the wages cheque,' she said to the air, not looking at either man but aware of their hopes.

'Right you are,' Wesley said, the nicest tone he'd ever used to her.

She had to summon her courage to ring the doorbell. The blinds were still drawn. When should you raise them? she wondered. Normally it was the day after the funeral, but if the funeral had already taken place, far away on some foreign battlefield, what did protocol say about the length of time the signs of mourning should be kept?

She would tell Mrs Donahue to raise them after a week, she thought, and then she was shocked at her own presumption, ringing the bell before she could get cold feet.

Mrs Donahue answered. Her eyes were tired and she was, disturbingly, thankful to see Ruby. 'Mrs Hawkins. Come in.'

'Is he all right?' Ruby asked.

'No, not so's you'd notice,' Mrs Donahue said. 'I don't know what to do, and that's the Lord's truth.'

'Where is he?'

'In his room.'

'Still?'

'No, no, in the boy's room. He gets up every morning and washes and dresses, but then he goes in there and shuts the door and it's more than my life's worth to disturb him. But you should try.'

She led Ruby up to the second bedroom, at the back to the right of the house, over the dining room. The door to the front room, the one with the balcony, was open and Ruby glimpsed a spare, almost empty room with a grand piano.

'Mr Laurence's friends would come over and he'd play or they'd put gramophone records on and dance and sing. He was a lovely young man.' She sighed heavily. 'So gay, so merry.'

Ruby squared her shoulders and knocked on the bedroom door.

'Get away, woman,' Mr Curry's voice came, heavier and less angry than when she had last spoken to him.

'It's Mrs Hawkins,' she called.

'You too. Leave me be.'

Her heart ached for him, but she was also a little afraid. Was this what would happen to her? Surely she loved Jimmy as much as Mr Curry had loved his son. Would she descend into this darkness if he died? And if she did, who would rouse her? Part of her wanted not to love him, not to open herself to this agony.

Opening the door, Ruby walked into the room. She'd expected to find it dark, as his own bedroom had been, but here at the back the blinds didn't need to be drawn, and the room was alight with spring sunshine. Mr Curry was sitting in a small wooden armchair by a desk in the corner. He had swung the chair around so that he could stare at the room. He didn't bother looking at her as she entered.

It was a boy's room: cricket trophies on the shelves, books, tennis racquets in their wooden frames hanging on the wall, a single bed with a blue-and-brown coverlet, a portrait photograph of a young woman on the wall, showing the hairstyle of an earlier generation. His mother, the mother he had never known. She was torn with grief for this young man who had barely lived, who had barely loved, who had grown up strong and merry only to bleed that strength and happiness away on a dry and dusty shore.

She swallowed twice before she could speak. 'I've brought the wages cheque to be signed.' She had made it out. All he had to do was sign it. She put it on the desk next to him, brought her own fountain pen out of her purse, and held it out.

He didn't move. He hadn't shaved since she'd last seen him, but he was clean.

'Mr Curry, I need you to sign the cheque.'

'Why should I bother?' he grated.

'Because if you don't I won't have enough to eat this week,' she said baldly. It wasn't quite true, but it was true enough, and it was certainly true of some of the men. He still didn't move, his eyes on the portrait on the wall.

She wished the anger she'd felt before would rise up, but all she felt was a dreadful pity. 'Mr Curry, I will stand here and talk and talk and talk until you sign this cheque,' she said. 'I can talk about lots of things. Clothes, for example. I know a great deal about clothes. Are you aware that Amazonian cloth is not from the Amazon, for example? The term Amazonian was adopted —'

'For Christ's sake!' he exploded, grabbing the chequebook and signing it. 'Get the hell out of here and leave me in peace.'

She collected the chequebook and the pen and replaced them in her purse in silence. Pausing at the door, she looked back and whispered. 'God bless you, sir.' Tears came to his eyes, but his gaze was already fixed back on the room, roaming from portrait to trophies to a group of battered tin soldiers high on a shelf.

Mrs Donahue was waiting for her at the bottom of the stairs.

'Not out of the woods yet, Mrs Donahue,' Ruby said. 'But don't give up hope.'

'I'm not used to it,' Mrs Donahue said. 'He normally wants everything just so. Tells me what to get for dinner, what clothes he wants ironed, everything.'

'I know the feeling,' Ruby said. 'I think you'd better take up the blinds on Monday. But keep the note on the gate. How are you off for money?'

'Oh, naught so bad. He pays me monthly, first of the month, housekeeping and wages. I've got enough for a week or so.'

It was the twenty-first of September. The monthly accounts loomed up in front of her. Mr Curry had to pay all their suppliers on the first of the month. And she would need to bank all the receipts. She'd done it once, after he had made out the deposit slips; it was one of those things she hadn't quite had time to learn, because there were different accounts and she hadn't learnt which payment went into which account yet.

She had so much to learn.

•

22nd September, 1915

My darling girl,

Home seems further and further away each day. You're the only thing that seems close. Your warm eyes, your soft lips, the way you stroke back my hair, the way you feel underneath me – sorry. Enough of that.

There's another big do on tomorrow and if I get it in the neck they'll find this on my body and send it home to you. It may be my last chance to make you see.

All my life there's been a hole inside me. A longing for something, but I didn't know what. A reaching . . . you know when you look up at the stars on a clear night – at the spaces between them – and your eyes, your mind, your whole self gets lifted up, dragged into those spaces like a wave is sucked back from a rock pool. That's what I felt, always. Like there was something calling, dragging me, but I had no idea what.

Until you. It all stopped the first moment I took your hand. I was home. Lifted up to the stars.

Don't mourn for me. I couldn't bear to be the cause of a single one of your tears.

I love you, love you, love you

J

CHAPTER 11

At the post office, Mrs Mulligan asked the question everyone wanted to: 'How is Mr Curry bearing up?'

How much to say? Whatever Ruby said would be exaggerated and embellished.

'He had a shock, of course.'

'Of course,' the murmurs ran around her.

'But he's at his desk at home, and he's told us to run things as usual.'

There. The exact truth.

Mrs Mulligan nodded. 'Please convey to him our sympathy.'

'Of course,' she said. 'Thank you.'

When she got back to the office, she was more than a little triumphant as she showed the bulging satchel to Wal and Wesley and saw their relief.

She made up the envelopes and only thought of that first Friday morning, in the storage room, for a flicker of a moment.

That would never happen again. But when she had finished the envelopes, she came to a stop. She didn't know the combination for the safe.

'Do you know the combination?' she asked Wal and Wesley. They shook their heads. For a moment, she was stymied. And then she remembered something. In the wages ledger, on an earlier page, Laurence Curry was listed as an employee when he was a lad. Presumably he'd wanted a 'proper job' during the holidays. All the employees had their birth dates listed. Just like the others, Laurence Curry's birth date was there. 12th March, 1895. So he was only twenty – ah. That was why Mr Curry thought it was all his fault. Laurence would have required his father's consent to enlist, since he was under twenty-one.

She went into the office with the satchel and tried 1, 2, 3, 9, 5. The first time, when she turned the dial to the right first, it didn't work. But on the second, when she turned it left first, it clicked open. She should get him to change the combination. Anyone could have guessed that.

She put the satchel into the safe, trying not to stare at the papers inside. None of her business.

'Well,' she said when she came out. 'That's done.'

On Saturday, when the men came to be paid, she was surprised by how matter-of-fact they all were. Of course, Wal and Wesley would have tipped them the wink that the wages were there, but she'd still expected some glances towards Mr Curry's office, or some questions about when he'd be back.

She said as much to Tom McBride and he grinned. 'They think you're getting daily orders from the old man,' he said. 'That he's just away for form's sake, but he's really running things as usual.'

'And why would they think that?'

He winked at her and pocketed his pay with a flourish. 'Why wouldn't they, when you got the moolah *and* knew the combination of the safe?'

She realised that Wesley and Wal must have taken her question the day before to be about whether they could put the money in the safe for her, not a plea for information. They thought Mr Curry had given her the combination; that he trusted her.

Indeed, when Wesley came for his pay, he said snidely, 'Nice for some people, to get told all the secrets.'

She'd had enough of this. 'How long have you known him? Years, yes? If you'd been man enough to go up and see him instead of pushing it off onto me, maybe he'd have trusted you, too.'

His mouth clamped shut and he turned on his heel, but halfway across the room he stopped and came back. 'That was true, what you said. I have to admit it to the Lord. I didn't want the onerous task, and so the rewards are not mine. That's just.'

He crammed his hat on his head and walked out the front door, leaving both Ruby and Wal with mouths agape.

'Strewth!' Wal said, and Ruby had to agree. He came over to the desk hesitantly and took his pay, signing with less than his normal bravado. 'So, Mrs Hawkins, no hard feelings?'

It took her a moment to realise he was referring to the incident in the storage room. Oh, she wanted to say something nasty! Something to make him quake in his boots.

'No reason to have hard feelings that I can remember, Mr Andrews,' she said. A lady never dredges up the past, her mother had said. 'And I'm sure I'll have no reason to have hard feelings in the future, *will I?*' And a lady never forgets, either.

He cleared his throat, having turned a pleasing shade of pink. 'No. None at all.'

'Have a lovely weekend, Mr Andrews,' she said.

He nodded to her before putting on his hat and going out. She stood at her desk, looking down at her own pay packet, looking around the office, and realised that they had left her to lock up. That they had, effectively, treated her as though she were the boss.

It made her simultaneously nauseated and proud.

CHAPTER 12

The men thought she was getting her orders from Mr Curry. They had better go on believing it.

'It's not exactly a lie, is it?' she asked Maree that night, over a lamb stew.

'Stop worrying about what's a lie and what's not. You're too scrupulous. You have to concentrate on keeping the business going, for everybody's sake. Including ours.' She put a dollop of mashed potato on Ruby's plate, and then some peas. The stew smelled wonderful, rich and meaty, but Ruby's stomach was roiling.

'I can't run the business! I don't know anything about wood.'

Maree looked at her – not in concern, which was what she expected, but with an amused exasperation.

'Last week you explained to me how they costed everything, remember? That's all you need to know – how much things cost to buy, how much it costs to turn a log into planks and two-be-fours, how much profit you're supposed to make.'

'*You* should be running things,' Ruby said, more sourly than she'd intended.

'Not on your life. I had enough adding up when I had to work out my bills in the tea shop.'

The thought of running any business other than a draper's shop filled Ruby with terror. A ridiculous terror, composed of equal parts fear that she would fail, and fear that she would succeed and be saddled with a responsibility she had no taste for. All she wanted was a nice quiet little job where she could earn enough to pay her board and put some away for when Jimmy came home.

But there were sixteen people depending on that business. *Someone* had to take up the reins.

So on Monday morning she let the men into the office and said, 'I'm just going up to see Mr Curry about that Army contract.'

'Right you are,' Wal said. She marvelled that he could treat her with such casual friendliness now; as though all the past nastiness had been washed away with that, 'No hard feelings'. Men were very simple in some ways.

Mr Curry's house was bright and welcoming today, with the blinds all up and the wreath gone from the door. It looked homely, prosperous, shining cream in the flickering sunshine as the wind pushed scraps of cloud over the sun.

Mrs Donahue was looking out for her and had the door open before she knocked.

'He's worse today,' she said abruptly. 'Won't get out of bed. A letter came, from his boy's commanding officer. He went to bed Saturday morning and hasn't been up since.'

No no no. He was supposed to be getting *better*. Ruby almost ran up the stairs, barging straight into Mr Curry's bedroom without a second thought. He was still in his nightshirt, in bed, lying motionless, turned away from the door.

'Go away,' he mumbled. 'Leave me alone.'

Horrified, Ruby heard her mother's voice come out of her mouth. 'What do you think you're playing at?' She stood with her hands on her hips, for once letting that temper have full rein. 'There are people depending on you. I – *I'm* —' Her voice broke into tears. She couldn't get the words past the enormous rock in her throat.

He rolled over and stared groggily up at her.

'Mrs Hawkins?' The sheer inadequacy of the response unblocked her throat, but all she could find was anger.

'Don't you Mrs Hawkins me! You're supposed to get up and come to work. It's Monday.'

He passed a hand over his face. His hair was mussed and there were flakes of dandruff showing. The room was dim, despite the blinds being up. All the light was filtered out by thick curtains. Enough malingering. She strode to the windows and pulled the curtains back, hooking them over the ornate brass curtain holders which curled out from the wall in the shape of daisies. Morning light, harsh and invigorating, streamed in. Mr Curry put a hand up to shade his eyes.

'I need your help,' she said, somewhat more quietly. 'I'm doing my best to keep things going but there are too many things I don't know and the men are acting like I'm in charge.'

He snorted disbelief. Flopping back on the pillows, he put his arm across his face to block out the light. But at least he was listening.

'You don't have to come back – yet. But you have to help me. Please.'

Still he didn't speak. All the fury drained away from her, leaving her defenceless, like a snail without its shell. 'There's an Army contract for pine boards. Cypress pine. We've got two quotes in, exactly the same. Symonds and Lee. Which one should we take?'

'Take whichever one you like. It doesn't matter. Nothing matters.'

'Mr Curry, I can't make that decision.' She could hear the tears in her voice, and she cursed the weakness which let them show. 'I don't *know* enough.'

A long silence.

She sighed, and turned to go.

'Lee,' he muttered. 'More reliable.'

Another breath, this time of relief. It was like being thrown a life preserver when you fell overboard.

'Thank you, sir,' she said. 'Thank you very much.'

On the way back to the office, she was stopped on the street by a woman she recognised from church, a thin, fluttering woman whose clothes seemed to be composed mostly of scarves and shawls. Mind you, the scarves were all silk and the shawls were cashmere.

'Mrs Hawkins! How opportune,' the woman said. Ruby racked her brains for the name, but she couldn't bring it to mind. 'We were just wondering, you know I'm head of the Altar Guild . . .'

Patterson, that was it.

'Yes, Mrs Patterson?'

'Well, we wanted to make the church especially nice for the memorial service, but no one seems to know when it will be?' She ended all her sentences on an upward note.

Ruby had wondered about Laurence's memorial service herself, but what could she do? She had no authority at all in this area. On the other hand, she thought, perhaps that's what he needs. A public ending. A ritual of grief. Maybe he'd come out the other side of that better off.

'I'll be talking to Father Ford today.' Inspiration struck her, an explanation for why it had taken so long. 'We were hoping for the twenty-ninth. A month after he was shot, you know.'

Mrs Patterson nodded. 'Ah, so that's it. I'll tell the other ladies.'

'But Father Ford hasn't confirmed it yet,' Ruby said hastily. 'I'll get him to let you know.'

'Wonderful, wonderful. And we hear that you're doing a wonderful job keeping things going?'

'Oh, I'm just following Mr Curry's orders,' she said, thankful that she could speak this as the truth. 'He makes all the decisions.'

'A terrible thing, when a man has no one left. He should have married again, given the boy some brothers and sisters. Ah, well. He was head over ears in love, I remember, but you can take grief too far.'

She moved on with a wave and a nod.

The exchange had made Ruby feel ill on Mr Curry's behalf. To have everyone picking over your bones like that; to have all your actions interrogated and gossiped about. It was familiar; she had been used to it in Bourke, which was such a small place. But she had relished the anonymity of the city. To find out that it was an illusion was something of a let-down. Almost a threat.

'Mr Curry says to offer Lee the contract,' she told Wesley and Wal as she took her hat off.

'Good-o,' Wal said. Wesley nodded. There was a stack of letters on her desk. The first week the men had let them pile up, not liking to take over a task which had been reserved for Mr Curry. Now, apparently, it was her job.

Before she began opening them, she cleared her throat. 'Do we have anything important on for the twenty-ninth?'

Wesley looked up, immediately suspicious. 'No, nothing special.' His tone held a question.

'It'll be a month since Lieutenant Curry's death. An appropriate date for a memorial service.'

'I wish I could come,' Wesley said. 'I liked the lad.'

'I'm sure Mr Curry understands that, Mr Wilson.' As a Methodist, Wesley's religion forbade him to enter a Catholic church, just as a Catholic couldn't attend a non-Catholic church, a rule Ruby had never understood, given that they were all supposed to be Christian. But it was iron-clad.

She picked up the telephone. It felt somehow momentous. As though she were shouldering a burden, the way a soldier shrugged into his pack.

She dialled 0 and waited for the operator, then asked to be put through to St Brendan's Church. 'No, I'm sorry, I don't know the number.'

'I'll put you through,' the telephonist said.

She had a brief conversation with Father Ford, aware that both men were listening in.

'Does he know what you're planning?'

'No, Father,' she said. 'Not yet.'

'Best to present him with a fait accompli, eh? I won't say you're wrong, but you're playing a dangerous game, Mrs Hawkins.'

'What would you advise, Father?'

For a moment, all she could hear was the crackle on the line and the sound of her own breath.

'Eleven o'clock. I can do eleven o'clock on the twenty-ninth.'

She had jumped off a cliff and was falling, but at least she wasn't jumping alone. Father Ford had known Mr Curry for years. If he thought it was the right thing to do . . .

'Thank you, Father. And, er, could you tell Mrs Patterson? She wanted to do something special with the flowers.'

He let out a huff of laughter. 'Of course she did. God bless you.'

He hung up and she took a deep breath. 'Eleven o'clock on the twenty-ninth.' Wesley and Wal nodded and Wesley got up and headed for the yard door.

'I'll tell the men,' he said. 'We'll be closing, of course?'

'Naturally.'

She picked up the phone again and asked for the post office. Mrs Mulligan answered. 'Hello, Mrs Mulligan? This is Mrs Hawkins from Curry –' she almost said 'Curry & Son's' but it wasn't, anymore, was it? 'Curry's,' she recovered, just in time.

'Yes, Mrs Hawkins, what can I do for you?'

'I just wanted to let you know that Lieutenant Curry's memorial service will be at eleven on the twenty-ninth. I knew you would want to know.'

'Thank you very much for keeping me informed, Mrs Hawkins. Will there be refreshments afterwards?'

'In the church hall, I believe,' Ruby said, thinking, *Refreshments? I completely forgot.* 'People are so busy these days it's easier for everyone than going back to the house.'

'Let me know if there's anything I can do to help.'

'There is one way you could help me a great deal, Mrs Mulligan. As you know, I'm new to the area, and I'm not sure who should be informed about the service. I was hoping you would be able to spread the word to the appropriate people – or perhaps let me know who you think should be invited?'

Mrs Mulligan's voice warmed. This was power and pleasure, all at once, to have control over the information. 'No, no, Mrs Hawkins, you leave that to me. I'll make sure all the right people are told.'

Ruby thanked her warmly and rang off. Wesley was staring at her with stark disapproval.

'You're letting that brawling woman at the post office take charge of who is invited?'

Ruby smiled at him. 'Mrs Mulligan will invite the people *she* thinks should be there; and they will tell the people *they* think should be there. In the end, everyone will know and we won't have to do a thing.'

Wesley sighed and shook his head. 'Women. Devious as the snake which tempted them.'

Ruby sniffed. 'Practical, Mr Wilson. Unless you'd like to go up to the house and ask Mr Curry who should be invited?'

He glared at her, but Wal chuckled. Ruby would have liked to smile herself, but she had a task which was no joke at all.

She rang St Joseph's, as well, Laurence's old school, and the office assistant there, a woman, promised to put word out to all the ex-students.

'Of course, most of them are at the front, but some of their parents may wish to come. He was a lovely boy, Laurence.'

That seemed to be the consensus. What a waste.

Tom, at least, should approve of the plan. She found him at the back of the sheds, doing his regular check for white ants, the arch-enemy of the timber trade. He was at the back, crouching down to inspect the bottom layer of a stack of cedar boards, and didn't hear her come up behind him.

Ruby touched his broad back and he sprang to his feet, the movement bringing him right up against her. They both stumbled, and reached out to steady each other, ending up half embracing. The moment hung suspended; Ruby was aware of her own heart racing, of his strength, the warmth of his hand on her arm, the breeze of his breath on her neck. She twitched back instantly, removing herself from temptation, and started gabbling, 'Oh, I'm so sorry to have startled you, Mr McBride, I was just coming to tell you . . .' Out it all poured – Mrs Patterson, Father Ford, the lot, while Tom took a step back and a deep breath in and she tried not to notice that his trousers showed clearly that heat had surged through him, as well.

When she faltered into silence, he swallowed and said, 'That's a good idea, Mrs Hawkins. Let me know if there's anything I can do.'

She looked up, at last, into his eyes. They were steady, but there was something in them she couldn't read. A shadow, pain, regret, perhaps even shame.

'Thank you, Mr McBride.' Thank you, she thought, for not trying to kiss me. Because I don't know what I would have done if you had.

Damn this war. It raised too many emotions to the surface. She felt as though her skin had been scraped off so that everyone could see the blood and sinew underneath.

There was still the hardest thing to do. On her way home, she went to Mr Curry's. He was still in bed. Reluctantly, she stood in the doorway and cleared her throat. 'Mr Curry? I have something to tell you.'

'I don't care what contract you've got. Go away.'

'It's about the memorial service for Lieutenant Curry.'

The still body, turned away from her, went even stiller. She took a long breath and moved closer. How much responsibility to take? It wasn't that she was afraid for herself; she was afraid of saying the wrong thing and making matters worse.

'Father Ford has booked a time. Eleven o'clock on the twenty-ninth.'

'He had no right.' Mr Curry's voice was dark and deep and it made her heart race.

'People have been asking —'

He exploded up on the bed, sitting tall and shouting. 'Damn them all to hell! What is it to them? Vultures, carrion crows, the lot of them, yes, and you too, you bitch!'

She slapped him across the face. 'How dare you? How *dare* you speak to me like that?'

As he sat on the big old bed, his eyes were on a level with hers. They glared at each other for a long moment. His fists were clenched on the bedclothes; hers on the strap of her bag and her gloves. The tension of the moment couldn't last beyond a breath, two breaths, three.

He sighed out, finally. 'You deserve it,' he said, 'but I shouldn't have used that language.'

'*I* don't deserve anything but respect,' she said. '*I'm* trying to keep things running, with bugger all help from you!'

As soon as the words were out, she regretted them. She'd never used language like that in her life. And she'd thrown away any ability to reprimand him for his.

But he laughed in surprise. 'What's sauce for the goose, eh?'

'If that's the only way to get through to you.'

He bent his head, his hands loosening on the sheets, which he had rucked up as he moved.

'I just don't see the point,' he said, his tone flat, uninterested. It worried Ruby more than his shouting. It sounded so final.

There were half-a-dozen things she could say. Most of them were platitudes: Time will heal, you'll get over it, God will lend you strength. All of them might be true, but none of them would be helpful right then and there. She fell back on the truth her mother had spoken to her when she had been distraught by Jimmy's departure and hadn't wanted to go to work. 'I don't care about anything else!' she had cried, and her mother had said . . .

'Does that matter?' she asked Mr Curry. 'Does it matter whether you see the point? You have a duty to perform.'

He shook his head from side to side like a horse with the weaves. 'Why should I? I built that business for his mother and him. They're both gone. I have enough money to live on for the rest of my life. Why should I bother about anything?'

'That's called giving aid and comfort to the enemy,' she said bitterly.

He looked up at that, startled.

'Curry's is a part of the war effort,' she said. 'Just as much as the boys at the front. We have to do our part, or else we're letting them down.'

'I don't even believe in this war!' he snarled, his accent stronger.

Irish. She'd forgotten.

'I don't care what you believe!' she cried. 'My Jimmy's over there, and Maree's Theo, and thousands and thousands more of our boys. I don't care about the politics or the rights and wrongs. I just care about getting as many of them home safely as we can!'

He rocked back and forwards on the bed, his head in his hands. 'Not yet,' he pleaded. 'I can't do it yet.'

She stepped back from the bed. 'All right. The memorial service is in five days. You'll come, of course.'

'Maybe.'

'I'll collect you at ten-thirty,' she said. 'There'll be refreshments in the church hall afterwards —'

'No, no,' he said. 'Here. This was his home. Talk to Mrs Donahue.'

If daisies and daffodils had suddenly bloomed from the carpet, she couldn't have been more gladdened.

'I will,' she said. 'I will.'

He looked up at her, face anguished. 'I don't know if I can keep going, even one more day. Every night I lie awake, imagining his pain, and when morning comes I can't face it. It's not getting any better.'

'You're stronger than you think,' she said, knowing how inadequate the words were.

He turned aside, lying back down, his back to her, and she left, with tears in her eyes.

She arranged with Mrs Donahue for refreshments – Maree and the Red Cross ladies would help, she was sure.

Then, exhausted and not at all sure she'd done the right thing, she went home. But that night she dreamt that Jimmy and

Tom were both at the front, shooting into the enemy ranks, and the enemy looked remarkably like herself.

•

20th September, 1915

My darling girl

It's funny without Curried Lamb around. I wonder how his dad's holding up.

I've been thinking about my dad lately. He fought in the first Boer War. Never talked about it.

Now I understand why.

They're moving us around, shifting the positions. At least they've kept Freemie and me together.

Freemie says he might come back to Bourke for a while, after, to see his old mates. I said he could stay with us as long as he liked. I knew you wouldn't mind.

I can just see you now, welcoming them all in.

My darling girl

J

CHAPTER 13

29th September, 1915

Ruby went to Mr Curry's on Wednesday with Maree, who was going to help Mrs Donahue with the food. She had said ten-thirty, but they were there at ten.

Just in case.

She found him sitting in Laurence's room at his desk, as she had before. He'd shaved and put on his shirt and trousers. No socks, no shoes, no collar, no jacket. His collar was in his hand and the collar studs and tie were on the desk, as though he'd been just about to put it on when he'd run out of energy.

Swallowing down tears, she said briskly, 'Time to get ready, Mr Curry. We have to be there before everyone else.'

His head moved from side to side; not exactly a shake, not exactly a wobble.

Ruby hesitated. Mrs Donahue was behind her, peering in, shaking her own head dramatically, her hands bunched up in her apron. Should she speak to him as she had last time? Would a scolding or gentle encouragement work best?

'Get his shoes and socks,' she whispered to Mrs Donahue.

Carefully, as if they might break, she put her purse and gloves down on the hall table, a marble-and-gilt confection at odds with the rest of the furniture. Probably a wedding present, relegated to this upper hallway, out of the public rooms. Concentrate, she told herself.

Mr Curry hadn't moved when she went back to the bedroom. Ruby took the collar gently from his hand, then picked up a stud. She knew how to do it – she had helped Jimmy with his shirt studs, feeling like a proper wife as she did so.

'Come along, then,' she said. 'Let's just get your collar on.'

She fixed the back stud, finding it odd to touch another man, speaking quietly as one might to a nervous horse. 'That's it, now let's see . . .' He flinched when the back of her fingers brushed his neck, but he sat still, and raised his chin co-operatively as she brought the collar around to the front. It was the fiddly bit, putting the stud through two layers of collar and two of the shirt at once, but he stayed as still as a good child until she was done, his face blank.

Tying the tie was trickier, but she managed it. Perhaps the two ends weren't exactly at the right length, but the waistcoat would hide them. Mrs Donahue came back with the shoes and socks and garters.

'We'll need the waistcoat and jacket, too, Mrs Donahue, and the armband.'

She nodded, flicking a glance at his collar and tucking her mouth in at the corners. Ruby couldn't tell if she was affronted or approving, but she disappeared again towards Mr Curry's bedroom.

'Now, put your socks on,' Ruby said. She handed them to Mr Curry, and he automatically bent to pull them on his feet.

So far, so good. The garters were next – he slid up his trouser leg to put them on and she turned her eyes away. A blush began in her chest and climbed over her face. This was too intimate a situation for comfort, but she dared not leave him; without her prompting he might not finish.

He reached for the shoes himself, following a habit of years without thought. Slid them on, tied the laces, shifted in his seat to make them sit right on his feet; and then just sat, staring at one of the trophies on the shelf.

Mrs Donahue came back with the waistcoat and jacket, a full black mourning suit. Ruby took the waistcoat and considered. She couldn't get it onto him easily while he was sitting down. Getting him to stand up, however . . .

'Come on, Mr Curry,' she said, her voice high and singsong, cajoling, as to a child. 'Up you get.' She tugged on his arm and he looked at her blindly. 'Up you get now.'

He stumbled to his feet and she quickly slipped the waistcoat on and did the buttons up. She almost laughed – absurdly, helping Maree to dress Eddie had been good preparation for this situation. The jacket was next; it was as though he were sleepwalking.

Mrs Donahue handed her the black armband. It was black cotton, with two small pieces of elastic joining the ends.

Ruby held it out to Mr Curry, near his left arm. His eyes focused on it, slowly, and then sharpened. Stricken. He reached out for it with his left hand, but his hand trembled so badly that he couldn't take hold of it.

'I'll put it on,' Ruby said. She slid the cotton up over his wrist and took hold of his jacket cuff with her left hand while she pulled the armband up over his elbow with her right.

As it tightened into place he straightened, one hand going to his tie, which he adjusted unthinkingly. He stood more securely, his head no longer moving. He swallowed; looked around the room. Nodded once.

A faltering step towards the door. Outside, in the corridor, Mrs Donahue was whipping her apron off and putting on her hat. Hat. Ruby met Mrs Donahue's eyes and mouthed, 'Hat.' Mrs Donahue nodded and scurried away down the stairs.

Another step, and another, each step growing stronger. Ruby followed, thanking God and all his angels. She took her purse and worked her gloves onto her fingers, trailing Mr Curry down the stairs to where Mrs Donahue waited with his top hat. Maree was in the dining room, setting out cutlery and napkins. They nodded silently to each other.

Outside, at the bottom of the steps, there was a carriage waiting. Wesley had organised it; it was a mourner's carriage, the horses with their black plumes standing high, elaborate netting blankets ornamented with tassels hanging to their knees. Mr Curry stopped dead as he saw it and he half turned, as if to go back inside.

'The men organised it,' Ruby said. 'As a mark of respect.'

He stopped, breathed once heavily, and then moved toward the carriage. The driver held the door open for him. He motioned Ruby and Mrs Donahue in first. They exchanged glances. Traditionally, only the family rode in the first mourner's carriage. Then Mrs Donahue gave a little nod and Ruby knew she was right. He needed them, and that was more important than convention.

They climbed in and sat down, Mrs Donahue facing backwards, and waited with bated breath until Mr Curry followed them. The door closed and they started off.

It had been some time since Ruby had ridden in a closed carriage – her grandmother's funeral six years ago. Dark and uncomfortable, the old carriages were being replaced by modern motor vehicles, but it had been generous of Wesley to organise this and she knew that the form of things, the proprieties, mattered to him, so she paid attention to the black satin squabs and the silk-lined roof so she could report back to him that everything had been how it should have been.

Only a short drive to the church, thank God, and Mr Curry took it in silence, his hands clasped tightly together in his lap. When the carriage stopped, and he saw the crowd outside the doors, waiting, he gasped and said, 'I don't think I can.'

Ruby placed her hand over his and squeezed. 'They're here to express their support, not to gape. The men are all there. They knew Laurence too, and they want some way of expressing their sorrow. If you're not there, it won't be the same for them, or for his friends.'

A shaft of light caught his face as he leant forwards as though in pain. His eyes were bloodshot, scared, like a rabbit in a snare.

He *had* to get out of that carriage. If he didn't, everything would fall apart, she knew it would. He'd never leave the house again, he'd never recover. Forget the business, *he* would be destroyed. She and the men could find other jobs if they had to, but without the business he would spiral into dissolution and death. She could see it stretching out in front of him like the primrose path, so tempting, so easy to yearn for. She'd felt the temptation herself, in those early days after Jimmy had gone; it was easier to care about nothing than it was to face the fear and the pain. She couldn't let Mr Curry slide down that path without making every effort to help him.

'For Laurence,' she said. 'And for Jean. She can't be here. You have to do it for both of you.'

At Jean's name, he jerked and looked angrily at her. That was all right. Anger was good. Anything which cut through the fog of grief was good.

'Out you get,' she said. 'Take up your responsibilities like a man. Go and pay your son the respect he deserves.'

'I meant it,' he growled. 'You're a bitch.'

But he got out.

CHAPTER 14

The memorial service was everything Ruby had expected. Difficult, heart-breaking, hard to live through. At least the Catholic ritual was soothingly familiar. And the flowers *were* beautiful, great vases of daffodils, jonquils, freesias and white calla lilies. The mingled scents filled the church like the incense which would not be used because there was no coffin to purify.

She sat in the seat behind Mr Curry with Wal and Mrs Donahue and Tom McBride, who had come with his fiancée, a young high-coloured girl in a VAD uniform.

Moving through the crowd of his friends and well-wishers had tired him, she thought, but it had bolstered him too. Perhaps he had forgotten that he was more than Laurence's father, and they had reminded him he was a friend and respected community member as well.

Although not a funeral, there were still forms to be respected, so Ruby had organised for motor taxis to be available after the service for those who did not wish to walk to the Curry house.

Ruby sent Mrs Donahue, Wal, Tom McBride and his fiancée off in one of the taxis to help get ready for the guests. By rights, she should have been doing the same thing, but when she had whispered to Mr Curry, 'I'll just go back to the house,' he had shaken his head at her with something like panic, so she stayed where he could see her until it was time to leave.

Getting into the carriage with him was just plain wrong, but what could she do when he grabbed her arm with desperation and gave her a pleading look? His hand was shaking. The most she could do was play propriety and invite Father Ford to ride with them. His sharp, shrewd eyes flickered over them and he nodded, taking Mr Curry's other arm so it was clear to the watching, avid eyes that they were supporting him back to the carriage.

When they got into the carriage and had moved off, she said to Mr Curry, 'When they say something about me at the house, you have to say, "She's been just like a daughter to me."'

'Yes,' Father Ford said, 'that would be a good idea.'

'What?' Mr Curry was bemused, looking from one of them to the other as though he had no idea what they were talking about.

'The gossip's already started because I arrived with you,' Ruby explained. 'Now I've left with you, too, the knives will be out. They all know I've been visiting the house by myself. You have to make it clear that there's nothing going on.'

'That's a disgusting thought!' he said, truly shocked. It was the first time she'd seen him fully engaged with an idea other than grief and that gave her a spark of hope.

'Yes,' she said. 'But Mrs Patterson has that kind of mind, and so do most of her friends. If I'm to have any reputation left at all, you have to protect me.'

Father Ford was nodding.

Mr Curry blinked and settled back in his seat. 'Pack of old biddies,' he said. 'Don't you worry.'

He was as good as his word. At least half-a-dozen times she overhead him praising her as a daughter. 'You know, we're both part of the 20th Battalion family'; Wal didn't like it much, but too bad. It wasn't his reputation on the line, and he'd proven he didn't care about hers.

She heard him say it to Tom McBride's fiancée, Helen, and was surprised at the look the girl shot her. A measuring, assessing look, as if she were weighing up the truth of it. Ruby smiled at Helen and got a polite grimace in return. Perhaps Helen, like Mrs Patterson, suspected her motives.

Ruby didn't care. Having a task had been good for Mr Curry; it had allowed him to enter into the endless conversations of condolence with a purpose other than simple endurance.

She stayed back, discreetly, near the dining table, helping people with plates and napkins, arranging the platters as Mrs Donahue and Maree brought them out. Even little Brigid the tweeny came through, dressed in her best black and a blindingly white apron, to remove the empty platters and plates.

Normally, Ruby quite enjoyed funerals. Oh, the death itself was sad, but the wake wasn't, usually. People told stories about the dead person, and laughed and cried and knitted themselves back into the fabric of life while they did it.

Today was different from any wake she'd ever attended. For a start, every single one of the visitors, except for the Curry employees, had full black mourning on.

It wasn't in honour of Laurence Curry they'd bought it; almost everyone here had lost someone in the war already. Or else they had gone to so many memorial services that buying a set of blacks had seemed like good sense. Because it wasn't over yet, by a long way. The clench of her heart was almost comforting, it was so familiar. How long before Jimmy came home? She refused to think about any other possibility, although that refusal was a thin skin over stark terror.

The women, in their new full skirts and smaller hats, moved more easily than in the past; was it just her imagination that made them move with more purpose, too? No. As she went through the room, picking up empty plates and cups, she overheard their conversations. In the past they would have been talking about children and maids and spring garden parties. Now they were talking about the Red Cross and the VAD – Helen was spruiking the value of the Voluntary Aid Detachment and of the women who were helping out at the hospitals and aid stations, from Sydney to Cairo to France. Recruiting, and a couple of the young women looked interested. The others were talking about lines of supply, and organisation, and whether scarves or socks were most needed at the front.

Men and women always separated at these functions; the men were used to the women clustering in little groups, gossiping, as they thought. Ruby wondered how many of them realised their wives' and daughters' horizons had broadened.

The Curry employees were helping hand food and drinks

around, and Mr Curry clapped each of them on the back and thanked them for coming.

Wesley had come to the house as well. Mr Curry shook his hand. 'Thank you for the carriage, Wesley. It was a generous thought.'

'All the men chipped in for it, sir,' he said, but Ruby could see that the acknowledgement meant something to him.

'Mr Wilson has been wonderful,' she said. Astonished, his gaze fastened on her face, searching for sarcasm. She smiled at him. 'All the men have pulled together to make sure everything will be running smoothly when you come back.'

Wesley nodded at her, an odd look on his face. Was it annoyance at her presuming to comment on his behaviour, or something else? She couldn't tell.

Mr Curry looked exhausted, but it wasn't Ruby's place to wind things up.

She looked across at Father Ford with an unspoken appeal, and then at Tom McBride. Tom responded first.

'Come on, then, chaps, back to work,' he said, loudly enough that most of the room heard. The men grabbed some plates and cups and took them into the kitchen, then filed out again, leaving by the back door rather than making their way through the posh visitors. Ruby followed them, hoping that Mrs Patterson had noticed that she had left with the other employees, then stayed in the kitchen with Mrs Donahue, listening.

Father Ford followed up. 'Yes, it's time for me to go as well. Mrs Patterson, perhaps I can give you a lift?'

The motor cabs were waiting outside to ferry people home. Mrs Patterson flushed with pleasure and took his arm. That was the signal the others, women and men, had been waiting for. They dribbled out in ones and twos, shaking Mr Curry's hand as they left.

Ruby peeked out of the kitchen as the last one left. Mr Curry dropped into an armchair and she took him a cup of tea, placing it on the small table next to him, along with some cake and a small lemon tart.

He glared up at her from exhausted eyes. 'I will never do that again. I don't care what they say about you.'

'No, sir. Thank you, sir. I appreciate it.' She smiled hopefully. 'And my mother is in your eternal debt.'

'Hmphh.' He stared at his hands.

'I'll be back on Friday morning to take you to the office for the first of the month.'

'Go home, girl.'

'Yes, sir.'

But she went to the office, leaving by the back door just in case. The men were only just arriving. She suspected they'd nipped off to the pub for a quick drink before coming back, but she didn't say anything. They'd earned a beer or two.

'Mr Curry wanted me to thank you all very much for your help,' she said as she unlocked the door. He would have if he hadn't been so tired, she excused the lie to herself. The men took off their caps, nodded to her and mumbled things, the clearest of which was 'missus'.

She made a sudden decision, feeling giddy with relief that it was all over. It was presumptuous and it was outside her purview, but if Mr Curry was going to saddle her with all the responsibility, he could take the consequences.

'If you're all prepared to work a bit later tomorrow, you can have an hour and a half for lunch so you can go and see the *Brisbane* being launched.'

The HMAS *Brisbane* was the newest cruiser in the fleet, and it was being launched by the Prime Minister's wife, Mrs Fisher, at noon the next day, on Cockatoo Island. The whole city was going to turn out to see it.

'Thanks, missus,' the men said with real enthusiasm. 'That's nice of the old man,' Tom nodded to her. A good idea, then.

•

That night, as she wrote to Jimmy, she wondered how much to tell him. The facts, put down barely, made Mr Curry seem like a shirker, a coward, a malingerer. But that wasn't true. They were beginning to get reports of mental problems from men sent back from France. Mr Curry was like that, she thought, with the sense knocked out of him and no way to get it back to where it had been.

In the end, she decided it was beyond her ability to explain and concentrated on simply describing the memorial service, on the grounds that Lt Curry's men would want to know the details.

So you can tell the men that we did our best by your Curried Lamb, and that we hope and pray we won't have to do the same for any of you.

Oh, how I wish you were here in my arms, safely home again.
your beloved, always,
Ruby

She hoped it wasn't too dismal a letter, but perhaps it would remind them all that there was a home and loved ones to come back to, and renew their determination to stay alive.

•

30th September, 1915

My darling girl,

*The weather's broken, at last, and we can get some sleep at night
– when the shells aren't dropping.*

*I've been thinking about kiddies. They say this is the war to
end all wars, and I pray that it's true. It'd be a terrible thing to
bring up a boy and love him and raise him and then send him
to this. But we'll make a better world after this jaunt is all over.
You and me and our kiddies, we'll be part of that better world.*

*You just wait and see. Our boys will grow up safe and happy
and whole, with no fear and no cloud over them. All together,
the lot of us.*

love

Jimmy

CHAPTER 15

Thursday was a warm day, although overcast, and Ruby decided she just couldn't bear the crowds and the pushing and the shoving and the heat of trying to see the *Brisbane* hit the water, so she stayed quietly in the office, trying to sort out the paperwork ready for the first of the month.

One of her problems was the size of her desk – far too small to spread papers out on. Never mind. Better a small desk than looking across all day at Wal or Wesley.

It was oddly pleasant in the office without the shrill whine of the saw or the clatter of the carts in the yard. It was only when the noise stopped that she realised how much the clamour of the city put her nerves on edge; she missed the deep silence of the plains. She opened one of the big windows and sat down to do her work, enjoying the soft breeze coming off the water. The neatly controllable world of numbers surrounded her with spare, elegant comfort. For a time she could forget about Jimmy and Mr Curry and even Maree and Edward and simply be, a mind rather than a body and heart.

When the men came back, laughing, loud, excited, she smiled and nodded as they described the majesty and clamour of the launch.

'Never seen the harbour so full!' Wal exclaimed, hanging up his hat. 'Little boats everywhere, special ferries, the lot.'

'The *Brisbane*'ll give those Jerry submarines what for,' Wesley said with satisfaction.

Tiddy stuck his head in the yard door. 'Missus, you want me to take your wood up 's'arvo?'

'After work, thanks, Tiddy,' she agreed. The noise and the purposeful movement of the men swirled around her and for the first time she felt fully a part of it, an insider.

The afternoon seemed to speed by.

The next morning, at seven, she went to Mr Curry's house, nerves trembling in her chest like caged birds.

Mrs Donahue opened the door still in her slippers and bare legs, although she was otherwise dressed.

'Mrs Hawkins!' she said. 'What are you doing here?'

'It's first of the month, Mrs Donahue,' Ruby said. 'If you want to be paid, we have to get him up and to the office.'

Something flickered behind Mrs Donahue's eyes and her face changed. She straightened and looked Ruby up and down, as a madam might look over a new prospect for a house of ill repute. It was highly disconcerting.

'Think you're smart, don't you?' she said. 'Taking a man's job, taking over. Now the boy's dead, you think you can sweet talk your way in here? Become the daughter he never had, eh? I heard what he said at the wake.'

It was like being dunked in ice water. As though the ice had got into her veins, Ruby could feel a cold anger rising, an anger like she'd never felt before, vicious and uncontrollable. No. No. Not uncontrollable. She could control this. Ladies did not lose their tempers and shriek like fishwives. This woman wasn't worth her losing her temper. For a moment, she felt very young, but her anger overcame that; a sensation of total outrage buoyed her up.

She stared at Mrs Donahue. Silently, with as much distaste in her expression as she was feeling. 'Vulgar,' she said. That was all.

But Mrs Donahue flinched back as though she'd struck her.

Ruby walked past her and went up the stairs, shaking inside with the desire to turn back and throttle the old, the old, the old *bitch*. She climbed the stairs with her back straight and knocked at Mr Curry's door, which, for the first time, was closed fast. She prepared herself for a long argument and a lot of emotion.

After a moment, the door opened slowly. Mr Curry stood there, red-eyed but in trousers, shoes and collared shirt with braces.

Caught by surprise, Ruby gaped.

'Close your mouth, you'll catch a fly,' he said, turning and picking his waistcoat up from the bed. She closed her mouth tight. At last! The burden of being the boss had been far heavier than she'd been prepared for. At last she could give it back to where it rightly belonged.

Waistcoat, pocket watch, jacket (not frock coat), hat. Not the top hat, not today – it was a black homburg with a plain black band. He ran his hand back over his hair – longer than she had ever seen it but still respectable, just.

Without speaking, he led the way down the stairs and out the front door, leaving it to Ruby to close behind him. Mrs Donahue was nowhere in sight. Ruby was obscurely glad that the day was cloudy and dull; a bright day would somehow have seemed an insult to Mr Curry's courage.

He stopped just inside the gate to the street. Without looking back, he said, 'You there, girl?'

'Yes, sir,' she said.

He nodded brusquely and strode out onto the street. She walked next to him, not speaking, until they were waiting at The Crescent. The traffic – carts, omnibuses and motors – was thick, as it always was on Friday mornings. Loud and raucous, it was still reassuring, a sign of life. An Arnott's biscuit truck rumbled by, the bright parrot on its red side seeming to wink at her.

'Do you have the ledgers up to date?' She could barely hear him.

'Yes, sir.'

He nodded again and then, automatically, offered her his arm as they crossed. She took it, but dropped it as soon as they reached the other side. She didn't want the men to see her come in with the boss, arm in arm. Wal and Wesley were waiting, watching, with hope in their eyes.

Then she realised that she had the keys. She handed them over to Mr Curry, who nodded at her, then opened the door.

The three of them held back. Mr Curry looked at her, waiting for her to go in first, but she motioned him in.

'You first. You're the boss.'

'Hmpph.'

He walked through, not saying anything, not even looking, until he came to the offices. The empty offices, both of them. Staring at Laurence's old office, Mr Curry's back became rigid, his hands clenched. Then he shook his head sharply and went into his own room, closing the door behind him.

This wasn't working out as Ruby had hoped. The men followed Ruby in and they all three exchanged glances of mingled hope and fear. Ruby gathered up the ledgers and chequebook and went to his door. Knocked.

'Yes,' he said.

He hadn't sat at his desk. He was standing at the window, as though staring out, but the glass was frosted and he could not have seen anything.

'I have the ledgers, sir, and the list of cheques to be made out and the cheques to be deposited. If you would sign the cheques and tell me which accounts the deposits should go in —'

'Got me organised, haven't you?' he barked, not looking away from the window.

A measure of the same anger she had felt against Mrs Donahue rose up in her. This was all her fault, was it? 'I have the ledgers organised, sir, because that's my job.'

He laughed shortly, turning to look at her. His face was drawn and in his eyes she saw panic. 'You think I'll do this, do you? A job I don't give a fig for, a company that can go bust for all I care?'

'If you don't want the company, then sell it,' she said. 'But don't throw it away. That's not fair to the people who work here. They've built it up, just as much as you have.'

He rubbed his hands over his face and sat down heavily in his chair. The springs protested. 'Give them here,' he said. He sounded so tired. But she couldn't let pity rule her, not today. She handed him the ledgers, the chequebook and the deposit book.

'If you do the wages and Mrs Donahue's first, sir, I'll go up to the post office and collect the money.'

'No,' he said. 'Stay until I'm finished.'

So she sat in the visitor's chair and waited while he went through the ledgers and made out the cheques. There were three deposit books. He stuck the various cheques into each of them without doing out the deposit slips. It took more than an hour. Then he pulled a sheet of paper out of the drawer and wrote on it for a moment, then passed it over to her.

She read it. It authorised her to operate all his accounts.

'Sign there,' he said, pointing to a space he had left blank for her specimen signature.

'No!' she blurted out. 'If I sign this you'll never come near us again!'

'You want to be paid next week? Sign it.'

They stared at each other, and she was reminded of the moment in his bedroom when they had stared each other down. This was worse. This was his whole life, handed to her. She didn't want it. She said so.

'I just want a job until my husband gets home. I don't want any – any responsibility.'

'Then you should have left me alone. Sign it, or I'll never set foot in this building again.'

'You know what they'll say? What they're already saying? That I'm conniving to get Laurence's inheritance.' She shook the paper at him. 'They'll say I've succeeded if I take this to the post office. The whole of Annandale will know by tea time and the rest of Sydney by tomorrow.'

'What do I care?'

'*I* care,' she shouted at him. Outside the office, she could see Wal and Wesley stand up, hesitantly approaching them.

'Tell them that without Laurence, I need someone to be able to run the business if I get sick or something happens to me.'

'You should hire someone. A manager.' She cast a quick look at the other office, standing forlorn. He caught her glance and bristled. 'I did hire someone. You.'

Storming out of his chair, he brushed past her and opened the door.

'Wal! Move Mrs Hawkins' things into – into the other office.'

He slammed the door shut on Wal's startled, 'Yessir!' and faced her.

'I don't like that office standing empty,' he said, trying to bluster it out. 'Waste of space.'

'You need someone with more experience,' she said gently.

'You or no one.'

'Why?'

'Twentieth Battalion family's all the family I've got,' he said. It stopped her, as he had known it would. He picked up the letter to the bank.

'I'll put this in the safe. For emergency use.' He ran his hand over his face again and his voice trembled. 'Just in case.'

It was a peace offering. She looked at him with a mixture of exasperation and affection. Family. God help them all.

'All right. But you need to come to work. I don't know what I'm doing half the time.'

She took the letter and signed in the space then pushed the paper back to him. He took a spare set of keys from his desk drawer and handed them to her. She took them silently.

'I'll come when I can,' he said, slumping down to rest on the edge of the desk. 'You can always telephone me.' It was sheer exhaustion, she saw. He'd done what he came for, and now he was weary. She left him there and went out to the office, where Wal was ferrying her papers and pens to the other office.

'I'll do that, Wal,' she said. 'You help him home. He's done all he can today.'

It was cowardly of her, but she didn't want to face Mrs Donahue again.

Besides, she had to fill in the deposit slips and go and get the wages, as though nothing had happened.

CHAPTER 16

Over the next two months, Mr Curry slowly resumed control of the business.

At first, he came in only on Fridays to sign cheques. Ruby rang him on other days if there were decisions to be made which she couldn't handle; and sometimes, regarding decisions she could handle, just to make sure he was involved. She avoided the house; if she never saw Mrs Donahue again, it would be too soon.

Gradually, he began dropping in for an hour or so after lunch. The hour stretched to two, and then one Friday he came in for the morning, as usual, and stayed to sort out an issue between suppliers about delivery dates. He looked up at half-past four, surprised, as the others packed up to go home, and walked out with them with something like his old energy.

After that, they saw him more, although not full days, and not every day. But he was there enough that he could answer all the questions Ruby had dreaded, and take on all the tasks Ruby felt unqualified for: tendering for government contracts, pricing large orders, negotiating costs with suppliers. He insisted that she sit in on these conversations, either in person or on the telephone extension.

'I don't need to learn all this, sir,' she expostulated one hot summer day when they'd had to open the windows despite the noise from the yard. 'When Jimmy comes home, I'll be leaving.'

He braced his fists on his desk and glared at her, with a hint of pity at the back of his eyes.

'And if he doesn't come home?' he said bluntly.

She closed her mouth to stop the hot words escaping. He made her so angry, so often, but of course he was right. Perhaps that's why she was angry. The news from the Dardanelles wasn't good. People were talking about a retreat. A retreat! Defeat, they meant. It would make Lt Curry's death seem worthless, although the British government assured everyone that this was not so; that the Anzac and British troops had kept the Turks occupied long enough to mount a naval response to the German occupation of the Strait, that the Suez Canal had been safeguarded.

It was not a convincing argument.

Ruby had given up reading the news: there were too many 'Heroes of the Dardanelles'; too many wounded, too many dead. And there were no letters from Jimmy. Just before Christmas, she did get one of the postcards which were the only thing the British generals let the men send. It merely said, 'I am well, love Jimmy', but at least it had all the other horrible possibilities crossed off. No 'I am wounded', 'I am sick', 'I am very sick'. The men were supposed to black these out thickly, but Jimmy's pen had been scratchy and she could see the terrible words clearly enough.

She wondered if he had received any of her letters – she wrote twice a week, at least, but who knew what the mails were like over there? And the big Christmas parcels that Maree and Ruby had sent both Theo and Jimmy two months ago – there were terrible stories about those being stolen en route.

The postcard had come with the midday post on Saturday, and she had cried all night. She hadn't gone to church the next day – Maree had insisted that she stay in bed, and Ruby hadn't had the heart or the energy to disobey her. She burrowed down in the sheets despite the heat, burying her head, shutting out the summer light which carved its way through the curtains on the narrow window, and breathed in the scent of a bed in which only one person slept. A lonely smell. How she wished she had a child to cling to, to give her purpose. The only person she had to look after was Mr Curry, which was absurd.

•

After Mass, Maree served up a roast dinner, and gave Ruby a full plate, which she merely picked at.

'You're nothing but skin and bones!' Maree scolded. Her own response to fear was to eat, so she was getting bigger, and only their tight budget prevented her from growing out of all her clothes. That and the tireless work she did for the Red Cross.

Ruby had spent all one Saturday afternoon refitting Maree's best skirts and jacket. The result looked surprisingly good – when she had proper tailoring, Maree looked imposing rather than lumpy.

'It's very good of you,' Maree had said when Ruby suggested it. There was a faint air of – what, surprise? and Ruby had realised that perhaps she had overstepped a mark. But Maree smiled at her, with difficulty. 'It's been a long time since I had anyone to – to help.'

That simple sentence gave Ruby a pang of compassion. So the next weekend she made Maree one of the new overcoats; a bit late in the season, but it meant that they could get the wool gaberdine at half price. A nice navy, such as a sailor's wife should wear, with the military shoulders which were so much the fashion.

She finished it off after the roast dinner, over Maree's protests. It was intricate work, and it took several tries to get the shoulders to sit right, but it was very smart.

On Monday night, Maree wore it to her Red Cross meeting with a newfound air of confidence. 'I know I'm doing good work,' she confided to Ruby later, over cocoa and a biscuit after the meeting. 'I've never really done anything worthwhile before. Not like you.'

When, Ruby wondered, had she become someone who was 'worthwhile'?

CHAPTER 17

Mr Curry had a relapse in December. Not only was he dreading Christmas, but he received a letter from the other subaltern in Lt Curry's Company, who had been wounded in the same fight at the end of August and was only now fit to write.

He showed it to Ruby. It was a beautiful letter, praising Laurence highly, but it sent Mr Curry to bed for three days.

Ruby went back to managing things and realised, as she made her way down the stairs for the first time in several weeks, that she had missed her conferences with Tom McBride.

'Haven't seen you for a while,' he said, glancing sideways at her with a flickering smile. He was not exactly handsome, not like Jimmy, but he had a charm that lay in his openness of manner and his humour. She smiled back without meaning to.

'Silver lining,' she said, but didn't specify, even to herself, whether the silver lining was not seeing her, or seeing her now that things had gone wrong. Tom's mouth twisted with something that could have been pain.

'How's your husband?' he asked.

'I don't get many letters.' It was a short answer, but he seemed to understand that she couldn't talk about Jimmy to him; he nodded and passed her the clipboard with his summary of lumber in stock, keeping his hand well out of her way, so they didn't touch. The rest of the conversation was strictly business. But as she went back upstairs he smiled at her as if he couldn't help it.

She did notice that Wesley's nitpicking was a little easier to bear that afternoon.

On Friday morning, Ruby waited with the others by the office door. They looked at each other sideways, not wanting to be the first one to say anything.

Just after half-past seven, Ruby sighed and got her keys out, saying, 'I'd better go see him —' when they heard Mr Curry's heavy tread coming along the path from the bay. Walking towards them, he was drawn and pale. 'Just stretched my legs a little. Been indoors too much,' was all he said, but they all heard the apology in his voice.

It was just as well he wasn't there the next Monday, the Monday before Christmas. At a quarter to eight, when it was already swelteringly hot, Tiddy stuck his head through the yard door, as he often did, not wanting to muddy up the office floor.

'Missus!' he said in a loud whisper. 'Missus!'

Ruby went out of her office and over to him. 'What's the matter, Tid?'

'It's Mr McBride. You'd better come.'

Puzzled and not a little alarmed, Ruby went down the stairs to the yard. McBride was sitting on a log near the saw mill shed, singing. His hat was pushed back on his head and his waistcoat was unbuttoned, his shirt sleeves rolled up. God only knew where his jacket was.

The men stood around, half-smiling, some of them smirking, hands in pockets, waiting for her to catch on.

Drunk. Roaring drunk.

Ruby regarded him with a disappointed and disgruntled eye. This was the last thing she needed, and the last thing she had expected.

He had a surprisingly fine baritone.

'I put my arm around her waist
Mark well what I do say
I put my arm around her waist
She said, Young man you're in great haste.'

He hiccuped and laughed and the men standing around watching laughed too.

'I put my hand upon her thigh —'

The men elbowed each other and looked at her.

'Mr McBride,' she said, suppressing an amusement which startled her as much as it would have startled the men.

'Mark well – what?' He looked up and caught sight of her, then lurched to his feet, his arms outstretched. 'Misshus Hawkins! Lovely Misshus Hawkins, the saviour of ush all. *You'd* never leave a feller in the lurch, would ya?'

'Mister McBride,' she said, standing her ground, although that meant she got a big whiff of whiskey breath. She was reminded, inevitably, of her Uncle Stanley, a shearer who regularly went on benders when he got his pay.

'Misshus Hawkins,' he said, trying to stand up straight. He saluted, a wavering salute which only vaguely went near his head. 'Ready for duty, Marm!'

'Throw a bucket of water over him and put him to sleep in the shed,' she said to Alfred Smith, who was looking with fatherly amusement at Tom. 'He'll take no harm there.'

Halfway up the steps she turned back, remembering what had happened to Uncle Stanley's mate, Dan. 'And put him on his side so he doesn't choke on his own vomit!'

'Yes, missus,' Smith said, hauling McBride away.

As she closed the door she heard one of the men say to another, 'Ya gotta love a woman who knows what to do with a drunk.'

She laughed silently as she went back to her office.

Four hours later, just before lunch, an abashed McBride came to her desk, hat in hand. He'd spruced himself up a bit but was still missing a jacket; although, in this heat, most of the men went without. Ruby herself was perspiring in her cotton blouse and skirt. She had decided to ask Mr Curry for a fan for her office.

'Yes?' she asked McBride coolly.

'I was drunk,' he said.

'I could see that.' He looked over his shoulder at the outer office, and she said, 'Oh, come in and close the door!'

At least the office was half glass, she thought. It wasn't like going to the storage room and closing the door.

He sat down in the visitor's chair and stared at the hat in his hands, turning it around by the brim.

'My girl jilted me,' he said baldly. 'She's marrying a major she met in the Repat hospital. Says he's a *hero*.'

Ruby's heart sank. She knew what was coming next, sure as she sat there.

'Please don't desert us, Mr McBride,' she said. 'The war effort needs you here.'

He stared at her. She was abruptly aware of him as a man. The warmth coming off his skin, the muscles of his arms, the strong bones of his face. She would miss him far too much if he left. Perhaps it would be better if he did, before this friendship became tainted with something else. Yet, at the thought, her stomach twisted with an anticipated sorrow.

'I'll tell you the truth,' he said, 'because I might as well. She jilted me because she said I didn't really love her anymore, and her major did. Her major *needed* her, and I didn't. Go back to your Mrs Hawkins, she said, because you care more about her than you do about me.'

Hazel eyes, warm, guarded, desperate. A long mouth, mobile and expressive. Freckles across the bridge of his nose, highlighting the pale skin. The scent of a man, which she had almost forgotten. It was as though she had never seen him before.

She sat motionless, silent, because there was nothing to say.

'If you were Miss Hawkins, I'd stay,' he said. 'But better if I go, I reckon.'

She bit her lip and felt tears come to her eyes. This was too hard. Too hard. He'd been her one sure support here, the one person she could always rely on. But he was right. Better for them both. But —

'Better for us, maybe,' she said, acknowledging something she couldn't put into words, nor even into thought. 'But what about Mr Curry?'

He gave an involuntary glance at the empty office next door. 'He'll manage. I'll work out the week and leave on Friday.

That's a half day anyway, Christmas Eve. Go home to Dubbo for Christmas and enlist in the New Year.'

She nodded. 'Would you go up to the house and tell him yourself? He'd take it better from you.'

'Tomorrow,' he said, looking down at his stained clothes. 'When I'm more presentable.'

'No. Now. So you can tell the men today and they won't think I fired you for being drunk.'

He gave a short laugh and looked at her with admiration as he got up and went to the door. 'You think ahead, don't you, Ruby? Wish you could have seen this coming.' Then he walked out, straight through the office and out the street door.

She followed him more slowly and stood looking at Wal and Wesley, who had both got up and were poised, staring at her.

'He's enlisting,' she said. 'His girl jilted him for a major and he's joining up.'

'Damn,' Wal said. 'That's bad for us.'

'He's doing his duty,' Wesley said, but he was frowning. 'Will you have Johnson come back?'

'That's Mr Curry's decision,' she said, thankful that this was true. Part of her was thankful, also, that Tom was leaving. Best to avoid the occasion of sin, Father Ford would have said.

•

Ruby stayed up late that night and wrote Jimmy a passionate love letter recalling all the most intimate moments of their short time together. Then she burnt it, because the censors could read every word that went to the front, and no one on earth – including, possibly, Jimmy himself – should read that letter.

She had hoped that writing it would bring him back to her

memories alive and vivid and wonderful, and it had. But burning it . . . as the thin paper flared up white-gold and disappeared into black, he withdrew even further from her than he had been before.

•

20th December, 1915

My darling girl,

They're talking about pulling out, and the rumour is that we might get leave before they ship us off to France. How I wish I could come home for that leave.

We'd catch the train back to Bourke and see your family. Have a meal at the big table in your mother's house. Your sister and her husband and the kiddies, your uncle . . . all the family together like it ought to be.

Then we'd drive out to Barkinji just like we did on our wedding day, with you nestled up next to me and old Snowy finding his own way while I kissed you and kissed you and kissed you.

And then the homestead and sunset on the verandah and then bed.

Oh, my darling girl, what more could any man want?
your Jimmy
PS I've been thinking. How about Gilbert if the first one is a boy and Helen if it's a girl, after my mother?

CHAPTER 18

Mr Curry chose to make Alfred Smith the foreman and informed the three of them in the office first, at morning tea on Monday. Ruby wondered if it had been a difficult decision.

'Men won't like having a blackfella tell 'em what to do,' Wal warned, looking as if he didn't like it too much himself.

'He tells them now, on the dock with the crane,' Wesley said.

'Whose side are you on?'

'All men are equal in God's sight, Walter Andrews.'

Wal looked sour. 'They're not reliable,' he said. 'You can't trust them.'

Mr Curry looked him straight in the eye. 'That's what the English say about the Irish, Wal. They came to Ireland and took whatever they damn well pleased, and then told everyone we deserved it, and they did the same thing here. I won't be party to English oppression, I can tell you now.'

It was the first time Ruby had heard him make a political comment, and she was surprised at the depth of his anger. She didn't care who got to be foreman, but she was glad to see Mr Curry making a clear decision and sticking to his guns. It was like the old Mr Curry, before Laurence's death.

On the Tuesday, Mr Curry invited Ruby and Maree and Edward to his house for Christmas dinner. His eyes pleaded with her to say yes, and she knew why. There's nothing emptier than an empty house at Christmas time. Tom's resignation had left Mr Curry shaky again, and he'd gone home at lunchtime after he invited her.

She discussed it with Maree that night as they sat wrapping Edward's presents. Although Maree was a city girl, she had no more family in Sydney than Ruby did. Both her parents were dead, and her brother had moved to Cootamundra to start a sheep farm. It would be just the three of them for Christmas dinner.

'It'd be an act of charity,' Maree said thoughtfully. 'And I've got that big Christmas Eve concert for the Red Cross, where the soldiers' kids are coming to get presents. It'd mean I wouldn't have to prepare anything.'

So Ruby accepted the next day.

'There's just one thing, sir,' she said. 'Are you going to have a Christmas tree? Because there's no room for one at our house, and Edward would love it so.'

Pain flared up in his eyes. The memories of past Christmases, she thought, of decorating the tree with Laurence. He coughed, and turned aside politely to mask the moments he needed to regain composure. Ruby felt as though she were torturing him, but he had to get used to normal life again; and what better way than by doing something for another child?

'Bring the boy over on Christmas Eve before the concert and we'll decorate it,' he said, and then smiled. 'Mrs Donahue won't like it. She always complains about the pine needles on the floor, but bad cess to her.' He picked up his newspaper and shook it out, clearly dismissing her, and she returned to her own office with a smile.

'Mrs Hawkins!' he called a moment later, excitement making his voice sound like a stranger's.

She turned around and looked in on him.

'Wal! Wesley!' he shouted. 'They've pulled out!'

He brandished the newspaper at them. Wal and Wesley crowded her at the door, so she stepped inside the office and held onto the back of the visitor's chair. Pulled out?

'Evacuated?' she said in a whisper.

'Aye, lass, they're out of that hellhole! Here, it says right here: All troops at Suvla and Anzac have been transferred to another sphere of operations. The casualties attendant on the removal of men, guns and stores were *insignificant*!'

Jimmy was safe. He'd survived the Dardanelles. She felt so faint that she had to sit down in the chair. Wal and Wesley were slapping each other on the back while Mr Curry beamed.

'The bloody English should have pulled them out months ago!' Wal said, and for once didn't apologise for his language.

'Another sphere of operations,' she said. 'What does that mean?'

They quietened, sobered immediately.

'France,' Mr Curry said. The stories out of France were

terrible – wave after wave of casualties. Gas attacks, which left men with fragmentary lungs. Actual *aeroplanes* used as weapons!

But it would take some time for the men to get there. He would be safe for Christmas and New Year, at least. Possibly he might even miss the worst of the French winter.

'But he's safe for now,' she said, and the men looked relieved, as though they'd been dreading an episode of hysterics. She went back to her work with a lighter heart. It seemed like a good omen, that Jimmy had got out of Anzac Cove with a whole skin. He was a survivor, and he would survive France.

•

On Christmas Eve, the yard closed at midday, and the men came for their pay packets, excited, knowing there would be a bonus for each of them. Ruby had calculated the bonuses and knew they were more generous than in previous years.

'We've had a good year,' Mr Curry had said as he'd signed the wages cheque. His voice had been dry with irony. 'If you look at it from one direction only, it's been an excellent year for the business.'

It had almost broken her heart.

Saying goodbye to Tom McBride was difficult, not least because it was done with everyone watching.

Wal had organised a going-away present of a good khaki woollen jumper and Maree had sent three pairs of khaki socks and a scarf, courtesy of the Red Cross. Mr Curry had bought him a wristwatch, the kind the officers were wearing in Europe now, with a big leather cover over the face to keep out the mud. Ruby wanted to give him something herself, but felt it would be unwise. At the end, though, she had slipped a medal of Our Lady of the Way into one of the socks before she wrapped the parcel. He'd find it, somewhere over there, and know she had thought of him.

'I'm sorry to be leaving you,' he said. He looked down at the floor as he spoke, embarrassed, and the men looked there, too, in solidarity. 'But I guess I'm not sorry to be going.'

Smith had led a cheer as Tom walked out the door, and he'd looked back at her, just once, a long look which she couldn't read, before he closed the door behind him.

She was glad it was time to go home. Walking up Johnston Street with Mr Curry, as they did most evenings now, she realised she wasn't looking forward to the New Year.

Last year, people had said, 'Oh, it'll be over by Christmas.' And it wasn't. This year, no one was saying that. The war wasn't going to end anytime soon. The trenches of Europe were the new battlefield for Australian troops, and the conditions there were reported to be horrific. Even if Jimmy survived the Dardanelles, he would be shipped off to France.

The chance that she would see him again got smaller every day. And now Tom McBride was going, and she would never see him again.

As if he had heard her thoughts, Mr Curry said, 'We'll miss young Tom.'

'Yes,' she said.

He sighed and said nothing until they were at the steps to his house. The sandstone wall was in shadow now, but still gave off heat enough to make her perspire, just standing near it.

'Bring the boy over as soon as you can,' he said. 'The tree's here and I'll get the decorations down from the attic.'

'It's good of you, sir.'

'Not Christmas without a child,' he said, and went up the steps.

For the rest of the walk home, she forced herself into an unfelt cheeriness. She was fine, she had a good job, Jimmy hadn't been injured; neither had Theo. Maree and Edward and she were all well, and so were the folks back in Bourke. It was Christmas time! *And*, she had eight days off, the most she had had since starting with Curry's.

'Hello everyone!' she carolled as she came in the front door.

Edward was waiting for her, jumping up and down with excitement. 'Go go go!' he called.

'Just a minute, sweetheart, while I get some money. Maybe we'll buy an ice-cream on the way home.'

'Icekeem! Go!'

Ruby fished her pay packet out of her purse; she would take a few shillings and leave the rest here. She wondered, not for the first time, whether she would get a bonus too.

When she opened the envelope there was an extra twenty pounds in there. Ten weeks' salary!

It was too much. Much too much.

Wordlessly, she showed it to Maree, who was standing in the doorway to the corridor putting on her hat. She stopped dead, both hands above her, putting in the hatpin.

'Strewth,' she said inelegantly. 'That's – that's – that's a *lot* of money.'

Ruby looked at the four five-pound notes, with their pretty pink picture of the Hawkesbury River on the back. That was ten weeks' saving. One fortieth of their house, when Jimmy came back. Could she give it back? Should she? She felt completely helpless.

'What should I do?' she asked Maree.

'Well, I'd keep it!' Maree said, grinning. 'Tuck it into your stocking, dearie, for a rainy day.'

Carefully, as though they were made of crystal, Ruby put the notes away in her jewellery box and joined Maree and Edward in the walk to Mr Curry's.

'Can we stop at the post office on the way?' she asked Maree. 'I want to call Mum and Dad for Christmas, and I'll never get through tomorrow.'

•

'Mother?'

'Ruby? Myrtle, Myrtle, it's Ruby!'

The sound of her mother's voice took away all her strength. She began to weep quietly, slowly, feeling homesick and heartsick and very, very young.

After a few minutes of, 'How are you?' and 'How's business?' and 'Have you heard from Jimmy?', her sister got off the extension with a gruff, 'Look after yourself, Rube,' which she knew covered up deep emotion.

'Mum,' she said. 'I need to ask your advice.'

A blank silence on the other end told her how surprised her mother was. Ruby tried to remember the last time she had actually *asked* for her mother's advice. 'Miss Independence', her mother had called her as a child.

'Go on,' her mother said cautiously.

Ruby explained about the Christmas bonus and the twenty pounds. 'So should I keep it, or not? It just seems so *much* . . .'

'Is he forward with you?'

'Oh, no! Nothing like that.'

'Well, in that case, I think you should accept it.'

'Really?'

Her mother's voice took on that dry, amused tone Ruby had known and sometimes dreaded. Cecilia Carter had no time for fools, and that had included foolishness from her daughters. 'There are two reasons he might have given you the money. One is that he knows you're worth more than he's paying you, but he doesn't want to pay you any more than the men because it would cause trouble.'

'That's possible,' Ruby allowed.

'And the other reason is that, from what you've written, you've been a big support to him through his time of trouble and he wants to thank you.' Her voice took on a confidential tone, a lowering of pitch which made it clear that she and Ruby were in one of those female conspiracies men feared. 'Men like him aren't good at thanks, dear. Particularly to women. They don't know how to do it gracefully. So they use money. Your father was just the same. He'd much rather hand over cash than express his own gratitude.'

'So you think it's all right to take it?'

'As long as you do it graciously. Just say thank you as though he had given you a pound instead of twenty. You could use it to start your own bank account.'

The operator broke in to say, 'Three minutes. Do you wish another three?'

'No, thank you,' her mother said. 'Have a lovely Christmas, dear.'

'You too, Mother.'

●

Mr Curry opened the door himself. Mrs Donahue was still in the parlour, rearranging the furniture around the big pine tree which was backed up against the fireplace.

A tea chest with excelsior packing was nearby.

'Trrrreeeeee!' Edward shouted, wriggling down from Maree's arms and racing in. They followed, and helped decorate the tree with tinsel, candles and small porcelain angels, which they kept away from Edward.

Mrs Donahue was perfectly friendly, feeding them a huge afternoon tea of scones, egg sandwiches and biscuits. Edward was enthroned in Laurence's old highchair, beaming at everyone indiscriminately. Mr Curry sat silently and watched him with old eyes, the corners tightened against pain.

Then it was time for the star to go on the tree.

'Lights, lights!' Edward demanded.

Mr Curry laughed, finally, and lit the candles, and they all stood for a moment as the dusk drew in.

•

The concert in the Town Hall was a great success, with a whole slew of patriotic songs sung by the Red Cross choir – a hastily assembled collection of the local church choirs. War was doing more for ecumenicalism than all the theologians of the past centuries, Ruby thought. The choir sang their hearts out. *Belgium put the kybosh on the Kaiser* was the best received, and they had to sing it three times, the chorus getting louder each time as more and more children learnt the words.

> *For Belgium put the kybosh on the Kaiser;*
> *Europe took the stick and made him sore;*

On his throne it hurts to sit,
And when John Bull starts to hit,
He will never sit upon it any more.

The children found the idea of the Kaiser with a sore bottom hysterically funny, and in the end Maree had to intervene to get them to move on to the next song.

Soldiers' and sailors' and even airmen's children were there, some missing their father, some, like Edward, barely remembering that they had one. The children sat on the floor, the mothers clustered together at the back, a few of them still knitting socks. Then there was supper, and every child received a present of a sixpence and a little felt tree to hang on their own Christmas tree. Maree had been making those trees for weeks, and Ruby realised that the money for them had come out of Maree's own pocket.

They went home, exhausted, with a final chorus of 'O Little Town of Bethlehem' ringing in their ears, and Ruby, as she always did, thought that its description of a winter night sounded strange but beautiful here, in the hot antipodean summer.

Because of Edward, they didn't go to Midnight Mass; eight o'clock instead, where the big news was the retirement of Mrs Black and Mrs Mulligan from the post office. They were retiring to Bowral, where Mrs Black had grown up, and planned to grow roses. A Mr Studdert was taking over the post office.

'We'll be sorry to see you go,' Ruby said to Mrs Mulligan – and, indeed, she felt as though a prop had been withdrawn. She suspected the new male post master wouldn't look as kindly on her Friday wage visits.

'You keep your spirits up,' Mrs Mulligan said. 'It'll all come right in the end.'

They went home to open their presents – Ruby had bought Maree a beautiful lawn-and-lace dressing-gown and Edward a wooden train. It had given her a surprising amount of pleasure to choose the gifts, bought with her own money. She had sent small presents back to Bourke, as well, and it had been a heady experience, shopping without considering what her father, or mother, or husband would think of her extravagance. Not that she was extravagant. But she could have been.

Maree gave her some lovely blue floral print cotton to make up into a summer frock. 'I know you have to dress sensibly for the office,' she said, 'but you can have one gala dress, surely?'

Ruby hugged her. Her own sister had never judged her taste so well.

•

Lunch at Mr Curry's was a little awkward, with Mrs Donahue a disapproving presence behind the scenes. The adults didn't exchange presents, but Mr Curry gave Edward a little red tin truck, which he loved.

By the time he had said, 'Vroom!' for the thirtieth time, the ice was well and truly broken and everything was fine until Mrs Donahue brought the pudding in, with a jug.

She plonked them down on the table and strode back to the kitchen without a word.

Mr Curry stood up and stared at it. It sat on a round willow-pattern platter, its skin smooth and shiny, giving off an aroma of rum and almonds and raisins. Ruby could feel the heat of it from where she sat – Mrs Donahue must have just taken it out of the boiler. The small willow-pattern jug of brandy sent wavering fumes into the air.

'Laurence always lit it,' Mr Curry said quietly. 'It was a tradition.'

'New tradition,' Maree said, briskness overlying the kindness in her voice. 'I've got matches here somewhere.' She dug in her purse and produced a box of matches, then lit one. 'You pour, Ruby.'

So Ruby poured the brandy and Maree said, 'Watch this, Ed!' and lit it.

The whoosh! and Edward's excited 'Fire, Mummy, fire!' burnt away any awkwardness, but Ruby saw Mr Curry looking at Edward a few times with the ghost of Christmas past in his eyes, and she wasn't surprised when he went upstairs straight after lunch, after thanking them politely for a lovely day, like a well-mannered boy.

CHAPTER 19

3rd January, 1916

The Monday after New Year, when they all came back to work, was humid and cloudy, one of those Sydney days Ruby remembered from her childhood visits, when everyone yearned for the 'Southerly buster' to come through in the evening, bringing rain and cooler air.

One of the men was late – Chris Frieman, who had been one of their most reliable hands. Ruby sighed, assuming that he had headed off to enlist, following Tom McBride's example and all the encouragement in the newspapers to make up the 1000 riflemen Mr Carmichael, the parliamentarian, had pledged himself to recruit. Tom McBride would no doubt be among them.

But at ten o'clock Chris turned up, white-faced, sweating, tumbling through the yard door in a panic.

'They're after me, missus! Don't tell 'em where I live, missus, just give me time to get my gear together.'

She stood up and braced herself against the desk. 'Who is after you?'

'Military intelligence!' he gasped. 'They want to intern me 'cause my dad was born in Germany. But, missus, I'm not a traitor, straight up I'm not! Don't turn me in.'

For a moment she stayed stock still, weighing up her options. The government was interning any men who had been born in Germany or had parents who had been. Most of them, of course, were not German sympathisers, although she could understand the official mistrust. But they couldn't afford to lose Frieman. Now that Mr Smith had been promoted to foreman and Hopkins moved to the crane, Frieman was their leading hand on the big saw.

'Will you change your name to spell it with two "e"s?' she asked.

'You betcha.'

'All right,' she said. 'Get back to work. Don't come unless I call you. Here.'

She took the precious photo of Jimmy and Arthur Freeman out of her purse and gave it to him.

'That's your brother, Arthur, with my Jimmy. Now listen: you come from Bourke, like me. You've got two sisters, Ruby and Esther, and another brother, Bob. Do you understand?'

Fear lent him a quickness he'd never displayed before. 'Gotcha,' he said, pocketing the photo and heading for the yard door.

'And take care of that photo!' she called after him.

Grabbing the wages ledger, she turned to the page where the men's names were listed. Yes, she could change that 'i' to an 'e', but she needed a better pen than the office pens. She fished her own fountain pen out of her purse and began the job, only then becoming aware of Mr Curry standing at her right shoulder.

'Are you sure you want to do this?' Mr Curry asked.

'We can't afford to lose him,' she said. 'And he's been working on Army contracts for six months – if he was going to sabotage anything, he'd have done it by now.'

Mr Curry chuckled. 'Well, I'll give you your head, but you're on your own if they cotton on.'

'Fine!' she snapped.

He went back to his office, still chuckling.

The ink was barely dry when the door opened and two soldiers came in, dressed in the brown boots and flat caps of military policemen. They addressed themselves, naturally, to Wal and Wesley.

'Looking for a Christian Frieman,' the taller said. He pronounced it 'Fryman' with an exaggerated German accent.

Wal gestured silently to Ruby's office and they walked over, puzzled, to her doorway.

'I'm Mrs Hawkins,' Ruby said coolly, looking up at him but not rising. 'I manage the men. What can we do for you?'

The tall one blinked. He was younger than she'd expected, only twenty or so despite his corporal's stripe, but his companion, a private, was old and hard-bitten. He looked her up and down as though she were a tart.

'Oh. Um. Well, missus, we're looking for Christian Frieman,' the corporal said. 'To take him to be interned as an enemy alien.'

'Sorry, no one here called Fryman.'

'We've got him down as a hand here.'

'Spell the name for me?' she said, looking puzzled.

He did, consulting a list in his notebook.

'There might have been a mix-up,' she said. 'We have a Chris Freeman, but he's not German.'

Her heart was beating faster, and her conscience was roaring at her. But she wasn't lying. Oh, no. Not yet. She showed them the ledger. There, that was a kind of lie, but not a proper one. Chris spelt his name with two 'e's now, he'd said so. She'd just amended the ledger to match his preference.

They looked at each other, and the older one smirked a bit. 'Oh, they can often pass as Aussies, missus, but you can't trust 'em. Krauts is cunning, see? We've got orders to take 'em all in.'

'The Freemans are an old Bourke family,' she said. 'I know, I went to school with Ruby and Esther. Arthur Freeman is in the 20th Battalion with my husband.'

'We'd still like to see him, missus.'

She shrugged. 'Mr Andrews, will you call Freeman in, please?'

The corporal glanced at Mr Curry, who was on the telephone – or at least appeared to be so. 'Maybe it would be better if we spoke to the boss?'

'I'm in charge of the men,' Ruby said and realised that, God help her, it was true.

Wesley was listening to all of this with a frowning face, but he stared at the floor instead of at her, and she couldn't tell what he was thinking. Would his conscience get the better of him and make him betray her? Surely he would be glad of the chance to get rid of her? Mr Curry would have to sack her, at the very least. She might even end up in gaol. Her heart was beating wildly and her mouth was dry.

Wal reappeared with Chris, who had managed to throw some water on his face and cool down a bit. He held his cap in his hand and looked suitably overawed, but he looked at Ruby as if he were scared of her, not of the soldiers.

'Yes, missus?' he said.

'These men are looking for someone called Fryman,' she said, praying that his acting skills were good enough.

'Sorry, missus, don't know 'im.'

'Really, corporal,' she said, turning to him with a serious frown. 'What kind of proof do you need? Freeman, show the corporal your picture of Arthur.'

Freeman took his wallet out from his back pocket and carefully extracted the photograph Ruby had given him. He handed it to her and she looked at it for a moment, making the most of the emotion the image always called up in her. It made her ashamed, momentarily, to be using her feelings for Jimmy this way, but she'd be dashed if some silly law about enemy aliens was going to steal away the best saw-man she had.

Sighing, she passed the photograph over to the corporal.

'That's my husband on the left, corporal, and Arthur Freeman on the right. We grew up together in Bourke. They're sailing from the Dardanelles to France at this very moment. I hope you're satisfied?'

The soldiers looked at each other and shuffled their feet. The older one looked a bit abashed. 'I suppose —' the corporal said.

'Excellent,' Ruby said, taking the photograph back and passing it to Freeman. 'Then we'll bid you good day. Freeman, get back to work.' Explaining to the corporal, 'We've got a big Army contract on and Freeman's our leading hand in the mill. Why, he's personally sawn most of the timber for the new barracks out at Liverpool.'

'Right then,' the corporal said. 'Musta bin a mistake. Let's go, private.'

He even saluted before he left, and he closed the door carefully behind them.

The four of them listened carefully until the sound of their boots could no longer be heard among the traffic outside.

'Gorstrewth, missus, you can tell a whopper!' Wal said, with admiration.

'Nonsense,' Ruby said. 'I didn't tell a single lie. Weren't you listening?'

'That is so,' Wesley said. 'If she had lied I would have denounced her before God himself, but she told not a single falsehood. If they chose to misunderstand her, it must have been God's hand at work.'

Astonished, she stared at him and she would have sworn he winked his right eye at her, a mere flicker.

'God protects the righteous,' Wesley said. She didn't know if he meant her or Chris Freeman.

Ruby went down to the yard and found Freeman, who was working like a navvy. When the current log had been cut, he came down to see her, wiping his hands on a piece of rag. Silently, she held out her hand, and he put the photograph into it.

'If you betray this company or Australia, Freeman, I will personally shoot you,' she said. 'Don't forget, I'm a country girl, and I know how to shoot.'

'No fear, missus,' he said, fervently. 'I know when I'm well off.'

She nodded and went back up the stairs, aware that the eyes on her back were very different from the first time she'd walked up. She wasn't even sure she was the same person as she had been then. A year ago she would never have lied to government officials, never shielded an enemy alien, no matter how inoffensive. It would never have *occurred* to her to set up her own judgement in opposition to any kind of authority. She had changed, certainly.

She wasn't at all sure it was a good change.

CHAPTER 20

4th January, 1916

The next day, at seven minutes past eleven precisely – Ruby looked at the clock as the door opened – Maree walked in through the street door, hatless, rushed, ruffled, holding a telegram in her hand.

The windows were open against the heat and all morning Ruby had been cursing the noise of the saw, the traffic outside, the tug boats hooting on the harbour. But when she saw Maree a profound silence fell, so that all she could hear was the rush of blood in her ears, the slow, painful pounding of her heart, and a deep rustling which she realised, after a long moment, was the sound of her own breath.

She walked out of her office. Around her, work stopped. Mr Curry came to his door, a hand out to her, but she ignored him. Wal and Wesley stood as if in church, each holding the back of his chair, silent.

Maree put the telegram into her hand. It was damp from her sweat. Ruby pulled it open, as if it were any other message, as if her life wasn't about to crash around her like the *Titanic* hitting the iceberg.

REGRET REPORT HUSBAND PRIVATE JAMES HAWKINS REPORTED WOUNDED. WILL PROMPTLY ADVISE IF ANYTHING FURTHER RECEIVED.
BASE RECORDS 4/1/16

Wounded. Only wounded. Sound rushed back in a flash flood, overwhelming her. 'Wounded,' she said. There were black dots in front of her eyes and the room wavered, the floor swimming up to meet the windows. Wesley rushed to put a chair behind her and guide her back into it.

'Put your head between your knees,' Maree said, ever practical. 'And thank God.'

'Amen,' Wesley said, and the other two men murmured 'Amen' as well, softly, a little embarrassed.

Ruby handed the telegram to Maree and bent over at the waist – thanks be she didn't wear a corset anymore – and breathed as deeply as she could. The room settled into its accustomed place. 'How could he be wounded?' she asked, confused. 'They *left* Anzac! They pulled out! The paper said that there were no casualties. And he couldn't have got to France yet!'

'It didn't say "none",' Maree said. 'The official figure was three.' She put her hand on Ruby's back and rubbed up and down. 'But maybe he was wounded earlier. It can take time to get news out.'

Ruby read the telegram again, trying to make sense of it.

She had felt *safe*. What a cheat. What a terrible cheat, to tell people that their men had made it out safely and then this horrible, impossible news.

'Any details?' Mr Curry asked quietly.

'No,' Maree said. 'Just "reported wounded". Could be anything from a graze to —' She stopped short.

'All we can do is pray,' Ruby said. She was angry, yes, but she had to ignore her sense of outrage, which was not really logical, when you thought about it. She could feel calm descend on her, and was surprised at it. The lack of information was both maddening and comforting; surely if he'd been very badly wounded they would have said? Perhaps this unaccustomed calm was shock? Underneath the worry was a kind of relief – it had happened, at last, the thing she had been dreading, and it was not quite as bad as she had feared. She had been prepared for death; anything less was manageable.

'Let's get back to work,' she said. She tucked the telegram into her pocket and touched Maree lightly on the arm. 'Thanks,' she said. 'I'm all right. I'll be home at the normal time.'

Late that night, after saying the rosary with Maree, alone in her narrow bed her calm finally deserted her. She sat, rocking backwards and forwards, sobbing soundlessly, achingly, as images of Jimmy bleeding, pierced, limbs amputated, face blown away, paraded through and through and through her mind, like horses on a carousel, moving away only to return.

In the end, she turned up the gas mantle and brooded over the picture of Jimmy and Arthur Freeman – was it because she'd used this sacred image so lightly, so falsely that he had been wounded? She knew that was ridiculous, illogical, irrational . . . but part of her believed that she had tarnished her love for him by employing this most precious thing in a cause which was venal at best and traitorous at worst.

It was all her fault, wasn't it?

By dawn, she'd talked herself out of that idea, but a shred of guilt lingered and made her determined to get up and go to work. At least she could do her bit, help the war effort the only way she could.

Maree put the kybosh on that. 'Back to bed. You won't do anyone any favours by turning up looking like that. No one will be surprised when you don't come in.'

'They'll say I'm weak. They'll say it's because I'm a woman!'

'And what if they do? They'll probably be glad to know you *have* a weak side!'

She had to laugh at that, and returned to her bed. Maree brought her tea and toast and Edward sat across the foot of the bed, using her legs as highways for his red tin truck. The heat of his little body brought the summer in to her. 'Vroom vroom,' he said.

'Vroom,' Ruby said, more tears prickling her sore eyes. Thank God and his Blessed Mother that she had Maree and Edward.

'I have to ring Bourke,' she said. 'Jimmy's uncle will want to know. I'll get Mother to tell him. He's not on the 'phone.'

'We'll go up to the post office later. You know, I've been thinking it would be good to have the telephone on here. It would make my Red Cross work a lot easier.'

Ruby stared at her in astonishment. Although telephones had been around for decades, ordinary people didn't have them. They were for businesses and rich people.

'It costs four pounds a year and they're thinking about putting the call charges up to a penny a call,' Ruby cautioned.

Maree sniffed. 'I could save that on tram fares and shoe leather!'

'I'll go half. I'd like to be able to call home. Let's use some of Mr Curry's Christmas money for the first payment.'

'No, that's your special money. We'll just save up for it. It'll only take a few weeks. I think you pay the annual fee quarterly, so we'll only need a pound to start.'

'I've got that now,' Ruby said, indicating her purse. It felt odd, having this prosaic conversation while Jimmy might be dying in a Cairo hospital ward. Her brain had split in two. One half could think of nothing but pain and agony and dismemberment; the other could chat quite easily about where they would put the telephone.

'It would be expensive to talk to my brother, if I could find him,' Maree said wistfully. 'But it might be worth it to keep in touch. With Mum dead and the men away, we two seem to be all by ourselves. I'm not used to it.'

'How's your brother doing?'

'Oh, he's given up the sheep farming and gone droving up Castlereagh way. He'll never change.' It didn't seem to worry Maree.

Ruby thought wistfully of her own father, dead for three years, carried off by pneumonia in the midst of summer. They had been very close; it was understood in the family that it was Dad and Ruby, Mum and Myrtle. She had been distraught when he died.

The memory of that grief rose up in her as a taste of what was to come; she had cried so much for her father, and yet she had survived his absence. She had survived Jimmy's absence at the front, and she knew that she would survive his death, go on living and working and even laughing eventually. Did that mean she was hard of heart, in the centre of her, the true core?

What was it Maree had said, 'They'll probably be glad to know you have a weak side'? Perhaps she *was* hard.

She loved him so much, but she was not one of those women who jumped off bridges when their lovers died. She thought wistfully that it might be nice, to jump off a bridge and never have to worry again. It was a shame that suicide was a mortal sin.

'Ruby? Yoo-hoo, Ruby!' Maree waved a hand in front of her face to get her attention.

'Sorry. Wool-gathering.'

Taking her time, she got dressed and they walked up to the post office to call Ruby's mother. Mr Studdert, a tall man too old to enlist but too young to be happy about it, was very patriotic, and had hung the post office with recruiting posters and the Australian and British flags. He already knew about Jimmy, of course, having taken the telegram down the day before, but he kindly did no more than say, 'I'm sure he'll be back with us, hale and hearty, in no time.'

Her mother answered after only two rings. She always knew when something was wrong. A gift, her father had called it. 'What is it, Ruby? Is it Jimmy?'

'Yes,' she said.

'He's not dead, dear.'

That was a statement, not a question, and it soothed Ruby's fears. 'No, just wounded,' she said. 'That's all I know. Can you let Mr Hawkins know?'

'Yes, of course.' Her mother paused. Ruby could imagine her, gathering her courage for the next step, the one she always found difficult. Being comforting was not her mother's strong suit. 'Are you all right, Ruby?'

'Yes. Yes, I am. I'm all right.'

'Sufficient unto the day. Don't borrow trouble. It might be a blessing in disguise, if it brings him home in one piece.' When you're trying to be comforting, clichés were useful.

But although Ruby had the thought, she found she didn't mean it in a critical way. Her mother had lived through her father's death; and she had survived. 'Yes,' Ruby said. 'Pray for him.'

'Of course I will. I'll say a novena.'

'Thanks, Mum. I'll call if I get any more news.'

•

On Thursday, Ruby went back to work. She had slept a little better and she knew she needed activity to keep her mind off the worst.

Mr Curry came in early that day, and stayed all day, the first time he had done so since Christmas. Ruby realised, in a vague kind of way, he was making sure to be there in case the worst news came, and she was grateful for it, but it made little impression on her. It took all her concentration simply to add up her columns of figures. The calm safety of numbers had deserted her and only after an hour or two of solid work did she find it creeping back.

She had arranged with Mr Studdert that any further telegrams for her should go to Curry's during office hours. Every time the street door opened, she tensed. When it was Micky, the telegram boy, she could feel the blood drain away from her heart, but he was a good little soul and he always came in with, 'Just a business one, missus, don't worry.'

The days went past. Mr Curry came in every day, faithfully, and the office began to work as it had before Laurence's death. It was thin comfort. Every so often the fear would hit her, like a tram running on an odd schedule, and Ruby would be overwhelmed momentarily by a hideous imagining: Jimmy wild with pain, calling for her; Jimmy slipping away quietly on a sigh; Jimmy screaming. Every time, she had to freeze and fight for her breath, trying not to betray her weakness to the others. At night, she slept restlessly but did not dream at all, not even the flickering silly dreams she always had.

'I think I'm too scared to dream,' she said to Maree. 'Too much chance of nightmares.'

Every night, she looked at her wedding portrait. There she was, in her plain white silk with a machine-lace overdress, hastily cobbled together, so different from the elaborate wedding gown she'd always imagined, because Jimmy was leaving in a week to enlist, and there was no time for embroidery or beading or anything except the very plainest of dresses. She didn't even have a proper veil – she was wearing her old First Communion veil under a chaplet of boronia.

The strangest thing of all, she remembered, was that she hadn't cared. When she had arrived at the church, the vergers pulled the doors back and Ruby let her brother-in-law George lead her down the aisle, between the rows of mostly female guests. She spared one wistful thought for her father, and how he would have been so happy, and then she saw Jimmy.

She couldn't believe that six weeks ago she hadn't known him. Surely that tawny-brown hair, those warm blue eyes and firm mouth, had been part of her life always? He was standing in front of the altar-rail, waiting, staring at her as though she were a gift, a blessing from God.

The light from the window above the altar streamed through and surrounded him with glory. She advanced into that golden haze and knew that she had never been more sure of anything in her life: they were meant to be together forever. A perfect certainty, a joy which speared up through her whole body and brought tears to her eyes.

Jimmy smiled, slowly, as though the sight of her emotion had eased anxiety in him. He took her hand; she could feel the pulse of his blood even through her glove and her own leapt in response.

The priest advanced towards them and raised his hand to give them their first blessing together.

'*In nomine Patris, et Fillii . . .*'

She tried to pretend that it would be all right. That Jimmy would come home and she would see him and feel that glorious certainty, that golden joy, again.

•

More than a week after the first telegram, on the Wednesday, Micky came with two more. One he handed to Wal and the other, hand out as if he were serving a silver platter, he brought to her silently.

She looked at him pleadingly but he shook his head. 'Don't know, missus. Mr Studdert won't ever say.'

The men gathered as before. Perhaps Smith had seen Micky coming in, because he appeared at the yard door and stood waiting, silently.

Her hands were trembling as they opened the message. Make or break, she thought.

NOW REPORTED HUSBAND PRIVATE JAMES HAWKINS DANGEROUSLY ILL. WILL FURNISH PROGRESS REPORT WHEN RECEIVED.

'Dangerously ill,' she said through numb lips. 'What does that mean?' She looked wildly around.

'Probably got a fever,' Wal said, not unsympathetically. 'After a gunshot wound, you often get a fever.'

A fever had killed her father. Ruby began to shake. She had to pull herself together. She was at work. She was at the office. The ledgers were waiting for her.

'Take an early lunch, lass, and go tell Mrs Hannan,' Mr Curry said. 'It's your day for firewood, isn't it? Get Tiddy to walk her home, Smith.'

'Yessir.'

Tiddy trundled the barrow by her side with none of his usual cheeriness. 'D'ye think they'd believe I was eighteen, miss?' he burst out as they turned into Wells Street.

'What? No, no, they wouldn't, and don't you go enlisting. You're too young.'

The thought of little Tiddy exposing himself to the dangers of the front appalled her. Surely this war would be over before he was old enough? Oh, God, she thought, please don't let them kill him, too. It was then she realised that she was thinking of Jimmy as already dead.

CHAPTER 21

Ruby was drawn back, like picking at a scab, to reading the 'Heroes of the Dardanelles' in the newspaper. It seemed so arbitrary, who lived and who died. Or 'Missing in Action'. Everyone knew that meant dead, but the uncertainty must be the worst of all.

Dangerously ill. The words ran around in her head in a constant background litany. Whenever she was not fully concentrating on something else – anything else – she could hear them: *Dang*erously ill. Dangerously *ill*. Danger*ous*ly ill.

When they were children, Ruby and Myrtle had repeated words over and over until they lost their meaning, collapsing in giggles which were half-hysterical, because it wasn't quite right that something so well known, like the word 'milk', could empty of meaning like that. It was a kind of black magic. But she couldn't get the meaning to leave 'dangerously ill', no matter how many times she said it. It was crammed full of fear.

The telegrams kept coming, every six or seven days, every one striking her heart with a cold sword.

On the eighteenth of January:

NOW REPORTED HUSBAND PRIVATE JAMES HAWKINS STILL DANGEROUSLY ILL. WILL FURNISH FURTHER PROGRESS REPORT WHEN RECEIVED.

The words in her head changed: *Still* dangerously ill. Still dangerously *ill*.

Wesley said to her, diffidently, 'Though I walk through the shadow of the Valley of Death, I will fear no evil.'

She smiled at him, with difficulty. 'Jimmy is a man of faith,' she said, remembering early Mass with him the day he left to enlist, remembering the St Christopher medal she had hung around his neck, remembering kneeling at the altar with him as they were married.

He nodded, seemingly glad to know it.

Ruby prayed constantly, but perhaps she wasn't strong enough in her own faith, because she received little comfort from it. Wesley's faith, oddly, gave her more confidence than her own.

That Saturday, she answered a knock at the door, expecting it to be one of Maree's Red Cross ladies dropping off some knitting. It was Tom McBride, spick and span in his Army uniform. His red hair shone in the sunlight as brightly as the brass on his buckles.

Ruby just stared at him.

He held his hat in front of him with both hands, like a boy. 'I heard about your husband,' he said, uncertainly, 'from Jenkins the carter. I just . . . I just wanted to make sure you were all right.'

She was unprepared. A surge of emotions went through her, but she only recognised a few: surprise, pleasure and a strong sense of wrongness, that she shouldn't be standing here talking about her husband with Tom McBride.

Perhaps he read her face.

'I don't — I just —'

'I'm fine,' she lied. 'It was nice of you to be concerned. I'd invite you in, but Maree's expecting people.'

'Right. Yes, right.' He half turned away, and then turned back, his eyes too warm, too understanding for her own good. 'If you need anything . . . ever. Even if it's only someone to swear at.'

She couldn't help it; she smiled. 'I do need that some days,' she acknowledged. 'But I've learnt to swear at the mirror.'

He smiled too, a tightening of the muscles of his mouth which looked very much like pain. Staring down at his hat, he said, very quietly, 'Anything. Ever. Just write.'

Then he turned on his heel and walked away, towards The Crescent and the trams.

She watched him with her own pain welling in her; Jimmy seemed further away than ever, compared to Tom's health and strength and simple *presence*. This war would take both of them from her, and there was nothing she could do about it.

CHAPTER 22

27th–28th January, 1916

On the last Thursday in January:

> *AGAIN REPORTED HUSBAND PRIVATE JAMES HAWKINS STILL DANGEROUSLY ILL. WILL FURNISH FURTHER PROGRESS REPORT WHEN RECEIVED.*

Again still dangerously ill. Again *still* dangerously ill. Again still dangerously *ill*.

'He's a fighter,' Mr Curry said, patting her ham-fistedly on the shoulder. 'He's made it this far, he'll pull through.'

People kept talking in clichés, she thought wildly. There's nothing original to say. Men have been dying since the world began and there's nothing new to say.

That night she pushed Maree's mutton stew around on her plate. The smell filled her head until she felt as though she'd already eaten it; was full up to her gizzard, as her uncle used to say.

'Go to bed,' Maree said. 'You look like death warmed up.'

That was a good idea. There was a blanket between her and the world; perhaps it was tiredness that was making her feel so numb.

She got into her nightgown and sat limply on the side of the bed, but lying down felt too much like giving up. So helpless. Nothing she could do. She could feel the pain and the grief and the terror lurking just behind that numbness, threatening her. If it broke through, she would break too, into tiny sobbing pieces which might never come together again.

But the fear was coming, and the grief, and she couldn't stop it.

Like an old woman, she clambered down from the bed and onto her knees. Elbows on the smooth cold coverlet. Hands together, like the nuns had taught her. No, that wasn't right, her hands were empty. She reached to her bedside table and got her rosary beads. Better. Eyes closed.

In the name of the Father and the Son and the Holy Ghost. Amen.

The rosary was both comforting and demanding: comforting in its familiarity, demanding because she had to keep track of each decade. Only the Sorrowful Mysteries tonight. Keeping Mary company through the dark days. Each decade dedicated to remembering part of His journey. The Agony in the Garden. The Scourging. The Crown of Thorns. The Carrying of the Cross. The Crucifixion.

She prayed, and kept praying, even though the numbness wore away with each prayer, because each known word was a bulwark against the fear which seeped through, seeped up, from toe to knee to thigh to body, swamping her heart and lungs, catching her throat and closing it.

A great shadow loomed over her, pressing her down; she prayed as she had never prayed, her head buried in her hands, scalding tears sliding over her face and onto the blankets. She lost the words: all she could do was cling to the beads and say meaningless jumbles: God help him, Mary help, fruit of thy womb, as we do unto others, world without end, without end, bring him back, Lord Almighty, Blessed Virgin, help him, save him, help.

She lost the words, but she built his face in her mind and kept it clear. He was here, now, caught in her words and her prayers and her yearning, and she had to keep praying or he would be pulled away from her. Because behind all the words was the darkness and the looming shadow and the empty agony of a world without Jimmy in it.

•

She woke slumped against the bed, the thigh which rested on the floor dead with cold. Getting up was hard; every muscle shot pain through her. It was still dark outside; standing, getting her balance, she listened and heard the jingle of the milk cart in the distance. Not long until morning, then.

Last night she had been full of grief and pain and fear. This morning it was all washed away from her, leaving her as empty and resonant as a shell. A thin-walled shell, like the nautilus on Maree's mantelpiece.

She should try to eat; to fill up the shell with something real and solid. To plod through the days until the terrible news came and she had to face an empty world. Slowly, carefully, she dressed and went out to the kitchen to find herself a slice of bread.

Work was a refuge. A place where she just had to do her job. That was all. But when another telegram arrived, two days later, she couldn't bear to touch it. Micky held it out to her with an anxious look. 'Are you all right, missus?'

Mr Smith, in the office for a meeting about processing offcuts into paper for the War Office, advanced on Micky.

'Give it here, lad, and be off,' he said, holding out his hand for the telegram.

'No!' Micky said, dodging him and cannoning into Ruby. 'It's for Missus Hawkins!' He crammed it into her unwilling hand.

Wal raised his hand to the boy and she put her arm around him to protect him.

'It's all right, he's just trying to do his job.' They were all trying to help her in their own way, she knew. She had to do her part, so she opened the telegram.

NOW REPORTED HUSBAND PRIVATE JAMES HAWKINS PRONOUNCED OUT OF DANGER. WILL PROMPTLY ADVISE IF ANYTHING FURTHER RECEIVED.

Her legs gave out and she sank to the floor, Micky falling down with her. Tears ran on her face, unchecked, silent. She stared at the yellow paper in disbelief, hugging Micky.

'Oh, gawd,' Wal said.

Wesley started praying softly.

'Mrs Hawkins?' Mr Curry advanced and bent over her

solicitously. She looked up at him with wide eyes, unable to speak, and handed him the telegram.

'Out of danger!' he almost shouted. 'Pronounced out of danger!'

Wal clapped Smith on the back.

Micky shouted, 'Huzzah!'

Wesley cried out, 'Praise the Lord!'

Mr Curry sat in Ruby's chair and breathed deeply, reading the telegram over and over – and Ruby cried and cried and couldn't stop crying, feeling the tears fill up the emptiness, fill the spirals and curls inside her to brimming fullness.

•

1st February, 1916

My darling girl,

I know this is a scrawl – the first day I can hold a pen, and left-handed too, but they say the sooner I start the better. They talk about the Valley of the Shadow, and I swear that's what it feels like – a gigantic shadow looming over, pressing you down.

But I wasn't alone. I could feel you with me, my darling, all through that dark night.

I'm coming home to you, Ruby.

I'm coming home.

J

PART
2

CHAPTER 23

23rd March, 1916

Ruby was possessed by an insatiable impatience. The ward doors were closed and she waited with some other women. They had followed the ambulances from the troop ship in a convoy, but there were surprisingly few waiting, considering the number of men they had seen taken off the ship. No doubt the other men were from the country, or even interstate. How terrible to be here without visitors; Maree, more farsighted than she, had given Ruby chocolates for the ones far from home.

None of the women wanted to talk: they all stared at the doors, willing them to open. Ruby felt as though she stood on the edge of a cliff. Once the doors opened, Jimmy would be back. Really back, where she could touch him and talk to him. Hold on to him and never let him go again. She could feel all of the controls she had put on herself unravelling, all the careful packing away of need and desire and love coming undone. She trembled with nerves and anticipation.

At five minutes past two, a nurse, a pleasant-faced woman with high Irish colouring, pulled the door back and let them in.

A long room with tall windows, flooded with light. A row of iron bedsteads against each wall with crisp white linens; a small white locker next to each bed, a visitor's hard chair. The wooden floors glowed in the rectangles of light from the windows, dazzling her.

She scanned the beds anxiously. A series of unidentifiable bandaged forms, all alike in their weakness and their stillness. The nurse who had let them in whispered, 'Who are you looking for?'

'Jimmy Hawkins.'

'Private Hawkins is in bed seven.'

She pointed to the right-hand wall, and there he was. Jimmy. Quietly, half-afraid, she walked down to the bed. She had imagined this moment so many times: throwing herself into his arms, gripping him so tightly, kissing him over and over . . .

He was asleep, his head tipped back in a characteristic gesture. He was breathing shallowly, with a wheeze. She had known he would be thinner, but she wasn't prepared for this: he wasn't thin, he was emaciated. 'Skin and bones', such a common phrase, but this was what it really meant: skin stretched over a skeleton, cheeks sunken, the strong bones around the eyes protruding, the jaw jutting out. His thinness was painful, making her jaw ache in sympathy. She felt a kick of terror in her gut, and resolutely ignored it. He just needed feeding up, that was all, and then he would be her Jimmy again. His right arm and shoulder were covered with bandages, his left arm in a hospital gown. She must bring pyjamas. She fastened on to the comforting, domestic thought. Pyjamas, and some nourishing food.

Letting her bag drop to the floor, for a long, long ticking moment she simply stood there, looking at him, learning him all over again, learning the new angles of his face, the new lines of pain, the crow's-feet which hadn't been there, gained by staring into the hard desert glare, the broken fingernails. Jimmy had always taken care of his nails.

She was surprised that she didn't feel more; that she didn't feel that glorious spear of joy which she had imagined. But he was so fragile, he didn't even seem like her Jimmy.

Ruby took a step closer, wanting him to wake but not wanting to disturb him. She reached out, carefully, and slid her left hand into his left, and cradled it with her right.

His skin was rough and warm. Real, alive, human. She was content to just stand there, connected again even in so small a way. The moment stretched out in perfect equilibrium between past and future, between the marriage they had had and the one they must make, between who they had been and who they would become. Tears gathered and fell from her eyes onto the soft blue dress she had made especially for him. Her hands tightened, gently, wanting to feel him more firmly, and he stirred.

'Rube?' he muttered. Her heart flew up through the window in delight. He called for *her*.

'I'm here,' she said. She moved closer, stroked his hair back. 'I'm here.'

His long sandy lashes flickered open and those blue, blue eyes looked at her. His expression changed, in a way she couldn't read. Disbelief? Hope? Dismay? His hand clenched around hers, hurting her, but she didn't care.

'Ruby?'

'It's me, Jimmy. I'm here. Really. You're home, safe and sound.'

She bent to kiss him and he began to cry as her lips touched his forehead, his sobs so soft she could barely hear them. They cried together, and kissed gently, and she rested her head on the pillow next to him and felt as though everything inside of her was being shaken up and reorganised. His scent slid over her like a baptism.

Finally, she sat in the visitor's chair by the bed, still holding his hand.

She dragged a handkerchief out of her purse with her free hand and wiped his face, and then her own, and laughed shakily.

He was gazing at her hungrily, but there was still something . . . odd . . . in the way he stared.

'I didn't mean to drown you,' she said.

'I've wrecked my right arm, Ruby,' he said. She could see that he had to force the words out. That he was braced for her response, as though he'd been imagining her repulsion.

'I don't care what's happened to you as long as you're home alive,' she replied. 'Anything else we can work with.'

Tension went out of him and he looked suddenly tired. The strangeness in his gaze disappeared; she thought that it had been fear, and was swamped with pity for him. 'What do the doctors say?' she asked.

'Not much. More operations to get the shrapnel out. I'll be in here a while.'

Her whole face filled with a smile that stretched the skin across her cheeks. Happiness, finally, bubbling up and spilling over. 'If your arm isn't good, does that mean you won't be going back to the front?'

'Don't look so happy.'

'I can't help it,' she admitted. 'I'm so glad to have you home again.'

He smiled and said, 'By Jove! I almost forgot!' He scrabbled under his pillow and brought out a small calico bag, holding it out weakly to her.

Inside there were gold bangles, three of them. She had seen bangles brought back from Cairo before, thin cheap shiny things which were all soldiers could afford. But these were heavy in her hand: rose-gold, and beautifully chased. She slid them on immediately, and shook her hand so that they rang like bells. He must have spent all his pay for these. They weren't souvenirs, they were heirlooms.

'They're beautiful!' She leant forward to kiss his cheek as he sighed with relief. 'But they must have been expensive.'

He smiled, the same long slow smile he had given the first day she had seen him.

'Only the best for you. You're my girl.'

The man in the next bed coughed, a deep racking cough, and Jimmy turned to him.

'Freemie, this is Ruby.'

She wouldn't have recognised Arthur Freeman from the photograph Jimmy had sent her. He was too thin, too wasted. Oddly enough, though, his face in its vulnerability brought back a memory of him as a child, coming to school with his sisters, his dark straight eyebrows giving him a frowning look which belied his mischievous eyes. He'd been a scamp.

'I remember Arthur from Bourke,' she said, and moved across to shake his hand.

'G'day, Mrs Hawkins,' he said.

Arthur looked like a reflection of Jimmy – his left arm and shoulder was bandaged identically to Jimmy's right. He grinned at her, but she could see it took all his energy to do so. He noticed her looking.

'Pair of bookends, that's us. Shell came in between the two of us. Got me on the left and Jimbo there on the right.' He chuckled. 'Soon as we were wounded, they had to pull out. Couldn't go on without us.'

Jimmy laughed weakly, and Ruby tried to smile, but she shuddered at the thought of the shell, imagination filling in the horrible explosion, the pain, the dust and smoke and confusion.

To mask her horror, she dived into her bag, bringing out grapes and apples for Jimmy and the chocolates for Arthur.

'My oath,' Arthur said. 'I'm being spoiled.'

'Well, your sisters aren't here to do it, so I suppose I'll have to. The chocolates are from my landlady, Maree Hannan.'

'No chocs for me?' Jimmy said, aping disappointment. She fed him a grape, feeling his lips scrape her fingertips; his lips were rough, harsh with illness. But he kissed her fingers before she moved back, and a thrill went through her.

She turned to Freemie to disguise her response. 'We have the telephone on now. Would you like me to ring Esther and let her know you're home?'

'Oh, that'd be bonzer, Ruby – I mean, Mrs Hawkins.'

'We went to school together, Arthur. I think you can call me Ruby.'

She moved back to hold Jimmy's hand and he smiled at her, but she could see that he was exhausted. The nurse came over and checked his pulse.

'Time to let him sleep, Mrs Hawkins,' she said. 'He's not really up to any more today.'

'Not yet!' Jimmy protested, but the nurse was firm.

'Your wife can stay longer next time,' she said. 'But you need to rest now.'

Ruby got up and kissed him goodbye. His lips clung to hers; warm, tasting of tears and maleness, tasting of *Jimmy*. Desire flooded her and she was ashamed that she should want him so badly when he was still so weak. But when she lifted her head she saw that his eyes had darkened.

'I'll be out of here soon,' he whispered. 'Then you can really welcome me home.'

•

She made it back to work by four-thirty, floating in, dazzling them with smiles and the blue dress.

'Gosh!' Wal said. 'You look bonzer.'

There was a flicker of the old desire in his eyes, but she laughed it off. Nothing could cloud her joy today. 'Special homecoming dress,' she said. 'He's all right. His right arm is bad, but they're not planning to amputate, just get the shrapnel out.'

'Ring the boss,' Wesley suggested.

They all paused, considering that. Jimmy's return had upset Mr Curry – he was glad for her, but . . .

'Good idea,' she said. She rang Mr Curry's house and asked to speak to him. It was the first time she'd spoken to Mrs Donahue since Christmas.

'He's lying down.'

'Please ask him to speak to me, Mrs Donahue.'

'High and mighty,' she sniffed, but she clanged the receiver down on the hall table and went off. A few long minutes later Mr Curry answered.

'Something wrong, Mrs Hawkins?'

'No, no.' She told him about Jimmy.

'That could have waited until tomorrow,' he grunted.

'I wasn't sure I would see you tomorrow.'

Silence. A heartbeat, two, three.

'First thing in the morning,' he said, and hung up.

So it was a good day all around, and she bought Jimmy some nice new pyjamas from Mr Vincent on the way home.

CHAPTER 24

Ruby rang her mother that night, feeling strange about using their very own telephone instead of going up to the post office.

After she had given her mother the good news about Jimmy, she asked her to let Esther Freeman know about Arthur. No doubt the Army would have informed her that he was in Australia, but she would want to know *how* he was, as well.

'Do they have the telephone on, do you know?' she asked.

'Oh, I shouldn't think so,' her mother said. 'They're out on the edges of town.'

That was code for 'not very well off'.

'Would you let her know about Arthur, then?'

'Of course.'

'Give her my telephone number, Mum, and tell her she can ring me any time.'

'I will. I'm very glad it's all working out, Ruby.'

She had never felt so in charity with her mother. 'Thanks, Mum. I'll call again on Sunday.'

It was strange, she thought as she hung up the earpiece, how her move to the city had brought her mother and her closer.

The next day, there was a big sign on the front door of the hospital: Visiting Days: Monday, Wednesday, Sunday only.

It was Wednesday – yesterday had to have been a special exception because the ship had just arrived. They would have had a riot if they'd told the families they had to wait for two whole days.

Ruby was ashamed that she felt relief as she realised she'd only have to split her working day on two days a week. She should want to see Jimmy every day – she *did* want to see him every day. But if she couldn't, it was going to make things easier at the office. Mr Curry had agreed that she could take work home with her on the days she left early to visit.

At the door to Ward Four, she looked over at Jimmy's bed and waved gaily; her hand stopped midair. The bed was empty.

She felt the blood drain from her face. Her vision blurred and there was a ringing in her ears, like an unanswered telephone demanding attention. Sending her a message. He was dead. He was dead. Swaying, she put a hand out to the wall for support.

Terror washed over her. She was back at her bedside, on her knees, praying and entreating God and Mary and all the saints, racked by fear and grief and loss. Alone.

A nurse hurried to her and held her up by the elbow.

'Mrs Hawkins! Mrs Hawkins! Are you all right?'

'Jimmy —' Ruby managed.

'Private Hawkins has gone to X-Ray, Mrs Hawkins. He's fine. Come on, sit down and wait for him. He'll be back soon.'

Jimmy was fine. He was home. Everything was all right. This wasn't the Valley of the Shadow. It wasn't night-time but broad daylight, like the rest of their lives would be. No need for hysterics, or fear, or any kind of terror. She dragged in a breath.

She was led to Jimmy's bed and the visitor's chair and sat down thankfully. Arthur's bed was empty, too, and a couple of others. She was glad of the respite, grateful she didn't have to chat.

Part of her was afraid, still. How many times could she bear that terrible fear? It felt as though, each time, a section of her heart, her mind, her very self was scoured away. How many times could she survive that terror before all of her was gone? She had to get control of it. No doubt there'd be other times when Jimmy's condition would worsen; possibly even a time she would have to see him embark for France. The doctors hadn't given their final answer yet. If she let herself be overset every time something threatened him, she could – would – break down.

She *had* to get a hold of herself, and act like an adult. She had controlled her temper, she had controlled her desire, she could control this.

The sheet was wrinkled where Jimmy had got out of bed. She smoothed it down and fluffed up the pillow, glad of the small domestic duty.

'That looks very wifely,' Jimmy's voice said behind her.

She turned, laughing, to find him in a wheelchair, looking very pale but stronger than he had the day before. Ruby and the nurse helped him into bed and he sank back, exhausted by the simple movement.

He was too tired to talk. Ruby held his hand and chatted inconsequentially, telling him about Edward's latest trick of apologising to his food before he ate it, and Maree's work with the Red Cross, and a little about her own work at Curry's. She unpacked the pyjamas and put them away, keeping his hand in hers all the while.

Gradually, the white lines around his mouth and eyes disappeared and his cheeks lost their grey tone. But his blue eyes were still clouded. 'Sounds like you've got your hands full,' he said, wistfully.

'I've missed you so much,' she said, answering the tone and not the words. 'I'm so happy you're home.' She took his hand and held it carefully, then gave in to temptation and kissed his knuckles, uncaring of who could see them. The bangles he had given her slid against her skin with heavy coolness. She felt his hand on her hair, a gentle, caressing touch, and heard him sigh.

'So we're all right, then?' he asked.

'Yes,' she said, smiling mistily at him. 'We're all right.'

CHAPTER 25

Her life split into two: the brief, sweet, frustrating hours at the hospital, and the everyday world of two-by-fours, invoices and ledgers. The time on the tram was bizarrely precious, the only time of the week when there was nothing, absolutely nothing she had to do except sit.

It was only four weeks after Jimmy returned home that the first anniversary of the Anzac landing occurred. There was a big march in the city, but Jimmy was too ill to participate, although they took some of the other men, the walking wounded, in cars.

The next day's newspaper reported on all the speeches that had been made. It was odd, reading the praises sung of the Heroes of the Dardanelles, to realise that her own Jimmy was one of these exalted figures.

There was a gap between her knowledge of him and this publicly acclaimed hero, and the gap consisted of his memories of battle. The question was, did that gap have to be filled in, or could they simply bridge it and move on? None of the men at the hospital wanted to talk about Anzac; Ruby felt a deep reserve in all of them, and respected it. They had fought to protect their families, and they were still protecting them with their reticence.

As Maree served up the veal that night, Ruby was overwhelmed by affection for her. She had made life so easy, so pleasant, so *simple*. No wonder men wanted wives! Theo was lucky.

She didn't like to mention what must inevitably happen when Jimmy left the hospital; probably, the doctors said, in a couple of months, after at least three more operations. Ruby would have to find a house for them. Maree would be, in the words of the foreman, Smith, 'strapped for cash'. No doubt she would find another lodger. It was an odd thought; Ruby felt so at home here now that she resented the idea that she could be replaced.

'How about I make you that dress we've been planning?' she said. 'My treat. We'll go into town tomorrow afternoon and buy the fabric. Artificial silk, what do you think, a nice rich red to bring out your eyes.'

'Red? Really?' Maree said, flushing with pleasure. 'It wouldn't be fast?'

'Not scarlet – crimson. Perfectly respectable. Or emerald green. You'd look lovely in that. With a square neck and a drop waist, and an underskirt with stripes.'

'Sounds a bit fancy for me.'

'You need something nice for when you do speeches as the Red Cross representative.'

That was true. Maree was more and more in demand as a speaker at Red Cross fundraisers. She was surprisingly good at unclipping people's purses and eliciting donations. It was something to do with her sincerity and her straightforwardness; she spoke like a lady, but she spoke plainly.

'I suppose I do,' Maree said.

'In fact,' Ruby teased her, 'you owe it to the war effort to have a truly *beautiful* dress!'

The dress project was duly carried out. They found some lovely emerald art silk and a matching green-and-cream stripe for the underskirt and the wide elbow cuffs.

Ruby sewed it on the Saturday afternoon, feeling a little guilty that she wasn't, somehow, getting ready for Jimmy to come home. Perhaps even making herself a pretty dress to greet him in. But she had the blue frock, and Maree *needed* this dress.

It was a lovely time, just the two of them. (Carrie Skinner was looking after Edward to avoid the problems of swallowing pins.) They sewed and talked and laughed; Ruby wished she had been so close with her sister, Myrtle. She would miss Maree. The smell of the sizing on the cloth and the warm oil scent of the Singer machine as it whirred away were more than comforting – they seemed to create a small world in which everything was right, everything was *controllable*. If the facing on the neck didn't sit right, one simply did it again.

At the end, Maree tried it on for the last time and stood waiting for Ruby's judgement like a child in the headmaster's office. Ruby was surprised by how good she looked. She had lost weight, and the dress complemented her curves and her soft skin to perfection.

'You look *beautiful*!' Ruby exclaimed. 'It shows off your waist.'

'Never had one to show off before. Shame Theo can't see it.'

'Let's have a photograph taken!' Ruby said. 'You and Edward.

I'll make him a new sailor suit. Theo can't even know what he looks like, he's growing so fast.'

There were tears in Maree's eyes, and she hugged Ruby. 'You're a good friend, Ruby. I'll miss you.'

'We'll cross that bridge when we come to it.'

It wasn't until later that Ruby realised how strange it was, to refer to her husband coming home and taking her to their own house as a bridge to cross.

CHAPTER 26

11th May, 1916

'Missus,' Micky the telegram boy said, after handing over a yellow flimsy to Mr Curry.

'Hmm?' Ruby looked up from her ledger. 'What is it, Mick?'

'Um.' He leaned in to whisper to her. 'Not supposed to tell you, but I just took a cable up to your Mrs Hannan.'

Ruby felt the bottom drop out of her stomach. 'A bad one?'

'Can't say.' Micky was flushed and uncomfortable. 'Post office rules. But maybe you should go see her.'

Mr Curry had heard everything. 'Off you go,' he said. 'It's almost quitting time anyway. And don't come in tomorrow if she needs you.'

She walked back to Maree's house as quickly as she could, the clouds overhead making it seem later than it was. The front door was closed. She let herself in, calling softly for Maree.

The lights hadn't been turned up, despite the growing darkness outside.

'Maree?' she called, a little louder. She could just see the outline of the table and sofa, so she dumped her bag on the table and turned up the gas mantle.

Then she heard Edward crying in Maree's bedroom. She ran in. The room was quite dark, but she could hear Edward whimpering. Ruby turned up the light, fearing the worst.

Maree was sitting on the side of the bed, one foot back and one forward, as though she had stopped halfway in getting up. Edward was in her lap, his little hands patting her cheeks, saying, 'Mummymummymummmy,' but Maree paid no attention. She stared straight ahead, face blank.

There was a telegram on the floor next to her foot and, by it, a parcel wrapped in newspaper. It smelt of fish and chips.

Slowly, Ruby went across the room and sat on the bed next to Maree and put her arms all the way around her, rocking her back and forth as if she were a child. Edward scrambled across to her lap and burrowed in, frightened and demanding.

'Auny Ruby, Auny Ruby, *hungry*!' he said.

'Yes, sweetheart,' she said, not stopping her rocking. 'There's fish and chips. You have some.'

'Chips!' he crowed, and slid down immediately – but Ruby saw him cast a worried look at his mother.

'Mummy will be fine,' she said. 'She's just – she's just sad. You have dinner.'

Reassured, he sat at their feet and looked up at Ruby hopefully.

'Rip it open, Eddie,' she said.

He gave a happy little chirp and tore ineffectually at the paper, but eventually made a hole big enough for him to drag out a chip.

Maree had softened, her body leaning more heavily into Ruby's as she rocked. Ruby wanted to say something, one of those reassuring things one said to children: *Shh, shh*, it'll be all right, everything's fine. But all those things were lies in this situation. It was not all right. It would never be all right again for Maree or Edward.

The only thing that would help bring her to the next step was the truth.

'Theo's dead, isn't he?'

Maree's whole body shuddered, as though jolted with lightning. Her head went back and she gasped for air, and then it came forward and she nodded and kept nodding, over and over again. Ruby couldn't speak; her throat was hard and harsh with pain. But neither of them could find the release of tears.

'Chip, Mummy!' Edward said, offering Maree a precious half with a bite already taken. His big hazel eyes were clouded and his lip began to wobble.

'Edward needs you,' Ruby forced out, past the dense knot in her throat. 'He's scared. Take the chip.'

Maree stopped nodding. She blinked. Ruby could feel control seeping back into her body; her muscles were neither stiff nor flaccid, but moved as she breathed in and reached out for the chip.

'Good boy,' Ruby said.

'Chippy, Mummy,' he insisted. Maree had taken the chip from him but held it as though she didn't know what it was. 'Eat chippy, Mummy!'

'That's right,' Ruby echoed. 'Eat the chip, sweetheart. Show him you're all right.'

Maree cleared her throat and tried to smile; a horrible grimace, but a step forward.

'I'm all right, darling. Mummy's just not very hungry right now.'

He looked at her and seemed to be reassured. 'Eddie eat chippy,' he announced, and took it back from her, chomping it with relish.

Maree started to laugh; the note of hysteria was there, but it was buried. 'That's right, Eddie boy, you eat it. You grab onto life and hold tight!' Then she snatched him up and cuddled him and began to cry.

Ruby cried too, her arm still around Maree's shoulders, her face buried against her own arm, crying with real grief for a man she'd never met, with relief that it wasn't Jimmy, with fear for Maree and Edward, with shared pain for all the women and children who would be left husbandless and fatherless, thousands upon thousands, before this terrible war was over.

CHAPTER 27

Marriage and babies and dying, the pattern of everyone's life. And now they had to cope with the dying part.

She sank down on her bed, exhausted.

Maree had finally fallen asleep, curled around Edward, but she had barely spoken and had eaten nothing. The last thing she had said, drowsily, as if to herself, was, 'Who am I now?'

Ruby hadn't known what to say. 'Edward's mother' was the truest thing, but it was so trite. She had stroked Maree's forehead instead, until she fell asleep.

What would they do now? How would Maree manage for money? She would get a war widow's pension, but that was less than the allowance Theo had sent her. Even with a lodger, she wouldn't be able to make ends meet.

Don't borrow trouble, she heard her mother say. Good advice. There was always trouble enough in the present. Ruby hadn't realised that as a child, but it was clear to her now. There was always trouble enough. As if to confirm the thought, that night she dreamt of Theo, dripping, dragging other men from the sea. As they clambered onto the deck she saw that it was Jimmy and Tom, both of them with the clouded eyes of the dead and the blue–grey skin of the drowned. They turned to her with identical expressions of joy, and reached out swollen fingers towards her in a parody of desire. She jolted awake and lay panting, as though she had run from them in reality as she had in the dream.

•

The next day, Maree got up and washed and fed Edward without once mentioning Theo. She was pale, but perfectly composed. Ruby walked on eggshells around her, until Maree looked at her in puzzlement and said, 'Why aren't you dressed? It's past seven.'

'Mr Curry's given me the day off.'

The hand that was conveying a piece of toast to Edward stopped midair for a heartbeat, and then moved on. He took the toast and chomped away happily. After all, he didn't even remember his father. Theo had been in the Navy since 1911 and had been posted overseas as soon as the war broke out, when Edward was only a baby. Ruby found it especially sad that Edward would have no memory of his father to dwell on in the future.

'No need for that,' Maree said. Her voice was a little hoarse, but that was all. 'No need. I have a Red Cross meeting.'

'Do you think . . . ?'

'I have to keep *busy*,' Maree spat out, suddenly intense. 'I have to keep up my routine.'

'Yes. I understand. I'll get dressed and go to work.'

Maree nodded, sharply, as though Ruby had just escaped offending her deeply. 'I should think so.'

Ruby was reminded of the way Maree had acted when Ruby first moved in. She had to remember that she wasn't family, and had no say in Maree's life, even though it *felt* as though they were kin.

'Well. Have you thought about a memorial service?'

'I'm not sure I'll have one.'

Tread carefully, Ruby thought. One small movement at a time.

'That's up to you, of course,' she said, getting up and pushing her chair in. 'I'll get dressed and head off. If there's anything you want me to pick up on the way home, call the office.'

She closed the door behind her and stepped out into Wells Street into a grey, lowering day; yet as she checked that she had her umbrella, she had an odd feeling of relief, of having survived a dangerous situation. Who would have thought Maree could make her feel like that?

Mr Curry was surprised to see her when she appeared at his office door, but accepted her explanation that Maree just wanted everything to be as normal as possible for Edward.

'Poor little lad,' he said. 'It's hard for a boy to grow up without a father.' He walked over to the window and looked out, just as he had once before, not seeing the frosted glass in front of him. 'I lost my Pa when I was a lad. My mother remarried when I was twelve. Had a new family.' An old sorrow, an old anger, passed across his face. 'That's why I signed on to a merchant schooner when I was fourteen. They didn't need me.'

'That must have been difficult,' Ruby said. A not uncommon story; so often a woman married again only to have the new husband resent having to support her children.

He turned and looked at her, his eyes focusing on the present again, a little ashamed of his confidences.

'Do you hear from them?' she asked.

'No,' he said. 'They're all dead. I went back, ten years later, and the neighbours told me. The typhoid. Three years after I left.'

So much death – his family, his wife, his son. It was no wonder that sometimes he questioned if struggling on was worth it. She wondered if Edward might one day feel the same, and the thought brought tears to her eyes.

Mr Curry misinterpreted. 'No need to get upset about it,' he said brusquely, flapping his hand at her to get out.

She withdraw gratefully as Wesley brought her a question from a supplier about the grades of tallowwood required from the Tamworth area. Thank God for work! It was an escape from everything except itself. The thought made her wonder if men felt like this all the time; if their employments were a refuge rather than a burden. Ha! she thought. And we've been so grateful to them. Adding up figures in a ledger is so much easier than looking after a two-year-old!

Then a splatter of rain hit the windows and she looked out to where the men were dragging a huge log through the mud to the sawmill, and was ashamed of herself.

'Get in,' Smith yelled, loud enough to be heard upstairs. 'Lightning!'

With the metal crane there by the water, lightning was a danger to the men, although with today's rain they didn't have to worry about fire as a result. But Curry's was always careful about bringing the men away from the dock during a storm.

Ruby went to the yard door and looked down. Men ran for shelter as gusts of wind sent squalls across the bay, heavy rain pounded the street windows, thunder rattled the panes and Wal jumped up to stuff newspaper under the front door. Weather like this always came from the south-east in Sydney, straight up the coast. It was violent and wild; a drowning or a cleansing. She shivered at the thought of drowning, and sent a prayer for Theo's soul, shocked that this was the first one she'd said. How could she have neglected to pray for him? She had been so concentrated on Maree and Edward that she had had no thoughts to spare for poor Theo. She hoped he would forgive her for that.

At lunchtime she went home, pausing at the end of Trafalgar Street to look back over the bay. The skies had lightened and the rain reduced to a few stray drops, the clouds higher with the hint of light behind their grey; the proverbial silver lining. This rain was an aberration, she'd been told. April was normally the best month in Sydney, with beautiful blue skies and warm days but nights cool enough to sleep; at least, that was what Maree had said yesterday morning.

Only yesterday. It was a lesson she'd learnt so often lately that it had become meaningless: the world could change in a heartbeat. A flicker, a blink, and you were standing someplace you'd never been before; maybe somewhere you'd dreaded, or yearned for, but so often somewhere you'd never even imagined.

A stroke of lightning stabbed beyond the Glebe Island Bridge, in the distance, as the storm moved away. Over so soon. That was a Sydney storm – flashing lightning, deafening thunder, and then gone, striking like a bushranger only to vanish while others dealt with the consequences.

Maree was setting the table when Ruby let herself in. She looked a bit better; there was a little colour in her cheeks, at least. 'There you are,' she said, forestalling any enquiries as to her wellbeing. 'Lunch is ready.'

'I'll just wash.' Ruby went to the kitchen to wash her hands and stared out the back window, through rain-spotted glass to Maree's precious monstera in a pot outside.

Lunch was elaborate, with delicate sandwiches, a salad and a hot apple crumble for dessert. Edward ate happily, chattering about the storm, 'but I wasn't scerrid, Auny Ruby, no sirreee!'

'Of course not, Eddie, you're a big boy now.'

'Mummy was scared!' he said importantly.

Ruby put her hand over Maree's and squeezed gently. For a moment she stiffened, then her lips pulled in with a grimace of acknowledgement. 'I'm all right,' she said. 'The thunder startled me, that's all.'

Maree left her hand still for a moment, being polite, then pulled away.

All right, then, Ruby thought. She would offer nothing but practical help. 'I have some black wool gaberdine,' she said. There had been a sale at Mark Foy's just before Christmas and she had decided, with morose forethought, that at some point in the next while she might need full mourning, so she had bought seven yards and laid it away. When Jimmy had come home alive she had congratulated herself on not needing it after all.

Swallowing quickly, twice, as though to prevent herself from vomiting, Maree nodded. 'A suit would be most useful . . . later.' After her period of strict mourning was over, and she could dress up the suit with brighter coloured blouses. Yes. Ruby had a black jacket and skirt like that already – they weren't a full matching suit, such as she would need as a widow, but they were close enough for general use. She had worn them for Lt Curry's memorial service.

'I'll get started on it this afternoon. We should be able to get it done before Mass tomorrow.'

So they spent the afternoon sewing, as they had so often done before, but all contentment and fellowship was gone. Only grim intention was left: to do their best for Theo by mourning him appropriately.

Ruby made the skirt in the new style, with a high waist and wide at the hem, but she made it plain, without so much as an edging of black ribbon. The jacket was also in the new style, soft and relaxed, coming to the hips, with wide lapels.

It was horrible, Ruby thought as Maree tried on the suit, to set the hem, that she looked so wonderful in black.

CHAPTER 28

As soon as they walked in the door from Mass the next morning, Maree took her hat off and threw it on the couch, then started pacing up and down the small room.

'The old cats!' she said. 'Poking and prying. "How are you holding up, dear?"' she mimicked an old voice viciously. 'As if they care!'

'I think some of them care,' Ruby said.

'Ha! It's all gossip and finding fault. You don't hear them at the Red Cross meetings – pulling apart anyone who isn't there. I have to get them talking about the war or there wouldn't be a woman in the city with her reputation intact!'

'They like you, Maree. They respect you.'

She stopped raging around the room and looked at Ruby. Then she shuddered, and sat on one of the dining chairs. Edward climbed on her lap and began to go through her bag, looking for her keys, which fascinated him. She ignored him. 'I can't talk about him. I can't.' Her face had the same blankness it had shown when Ruby had come in and found her on Friday night.

'That's all right,' Ruby said, rubbing her shoulders. 'You don't have to. Go all Empire on them. "We have to Carry On, you know", "Stiff Upper Lip".' She put on an exaggeratedly British upper-class accent, and succeeded in making Maree smile briefly.

But then she put her head in her hands and sighed.

'Look on the bright side,' Ruby said dryly. 'Someone else will be dead by next week, and they'll forget about Theo.'

That made Maree laugh, at least. Ruby felt bad, however, when they opened the Sunday paper they had bought on the way home and read about the Irish Rebellion and the freedom fighters who had been so cruelly put down by the British. Of course, the paper didn't say that. It talked about 'rebels' and 'traitors'. But Maree, with an Irish father who had drilled her in Irish politics, could read between the lines. It seemed to give her a strange satisfaction to condemn the English so roundly. 'Ireland, the Dardanelles, it's all the same. Everyone is there to die for the Empire, as far as the English are concerned.'

It was hard to argue with Maree, and better not to try. At least it took her mind off Theo.

•

Maree's tense manner persisted all week. She even snapped at Edward once or twice. On the Sunday, Ruby convinced her to come to Randwick with her.

'Not to visit Jimmy,' she explained. 'They're only allowed one visitor, and no children. But if we get the Coogee tram, you can stay on and take Edward down to the aquarium. Give him a donkey ride.'

'I can't go pleasuring when my husband is, was —'

'You're not pleasuring. You're taking Edward out for some fresh sea air.'

That earned her a smile, and in the end Maree came, Edward hopping with excitement in his little sailor suit and matching cap. They never had got around to having that photograph taken. Perhaps they never would.

'I'll meet you by the donkeys at half-past four,' Ruby said just before she got off the tram at Randwick Junction.

Maree lifted a hand in acknowledgement. She already looked better. Freer.

As Ruby kissed Jimmy hello she was overtaken with thankfulness that he was still alive, and hugged him with vigour and with tears in her eyes.

'What's all this then?' he asked gently, stroking the drops from her cheeks.

Jimmy was saddened to hear of Theo's death, and sympathetic, but he hadn't known either Maree or Theo before he left, so it was a temporary melancholy. He was full of good news. 'Arthur's getting out next week!' he announced.

'That's wonderful, Arthur,' she said.

Arthur grinned at her, his black hair and eyebrows contrasting less with his face now the pale, pinched look was gone. They wheeled the patients out into the sun every day, without fail, and the boys were gradually regaining the tanned skin they'd had before they left. 'Too right,' he agreed. 'My sister Ruby wants me to come stay with her and Ted at Pendle Hill, so that's all right. I'll be able to get the train in for my sessions.'

'Sessions?'

'We have to come back for stretching and strengthening sessions after we're discharged,' Jimmy explained.

'Got to work the muscles so they'll come good,' Arthur added. He grinned. 'They've given up on me – so many little pieces of shrapnel stuck in so deep they can't get them.'

'They'll work their way out,' Jimmy said.

'Already are!' Arthur assured her. 'Look!' He showed her his forearm, where a small dark stripe showed under the skin. 'Couple more weeks, I'll be able to pick it out with tweezers.'

Horrified, Ruby shivered.

'Might need you to get the ones out of my back,' Jimmy added, and she felt sick at the thought. Yet it was such a small thing, compared to what they had gone through – were going through. It was up to her to bear up and make it easy for Jim.

'Yessir!' she said, mock-saluting.

The men laughed.

'Ya got a good one there, Jim,' Arthur said. 'Don't suppose you've got any chocs on you, Ruby?'

•

Coogee was one of Sydney's finest beaches, a perfect curve of sand bookended by high headlands of yellow sandstone. It had been tamed by a long paved promenade along the seafront, and was packed with pleasure-seekers enjoying the fine blue-and-gold afternoon. Ruby found Edward and Maree at the aquarium pleasure-ground, near the whirly-gig and the swings. Edward was in high excitement, his face sticky with toffee apple and the seat of his sailor suit marked by the saddle of the donkey.

'I on donkey, Auny Ruby! I on donkey on *beach*!' It had clearly been the best day of his life.

They walked back slowly along the promenade as Eddie rushed at seagulls and made them fly, squawking. The fresh sea air tugged at their hats and sand crunched under their heels on the pavement. Ruby loved the open sky of the beachfront. Living in the tiny house with Maree, she had almost forgotten the need for room to move. And today was Sunday, the one visiting day she didn't have to rush back to work. It felt as though this was the first chance she'd had to breathe deeply for months.

'Coming here was a good idea,' Maree said. She paused and looked out to sea towards Wedding Cake Island, a pile of rocks whose tiers were covered on each wave with white foam, like icing.

'I'm glad,' Ruby said.

They leant on the sandstone balustrade and watched a group of children playing chasings on the sand below.

'I should feel worse.' Guilt was heavy in Maree's voice. 'But he's been gone so long . . .'

Ruby stayed silent, allowing her the time to decide what she wanted to say. She put her hand over Maree's on the sun-warmed stone comfortingly. This time, Maree didn't move away.

'We weren't like you and Jimmy, you know.' She flicked a quick glance at Ruby, seeming somehow ashamed. 'We weren't desperately in love. I've seen how much you missed him, how much it hurt you when he was wounded. Theo and I weren't like that. But he was a good man, and I cared about him, and he was the father of my son.'

'Yes,' Ruby said. 'I understand.'

She did, but it was an effort. She felt as though her levels of understanding of human behaviour were being dug deeper with each day; as though the growing older and wiser which she had expected to do over a lifetime were being squeezed into these few months.

'I got used to being without him,' Maree said after a long pause. 'I suppose that's it.'

'Of course you did. He'd been gone a lot longer than Jimmy.'

Maree turned with a smile and a shake of her head. 'That's nice of you to say.' She sighed. 'I'll have to look for a job myself, I daresay. The widow's pension won't go far.'

'Not yet,' Ruby said. 'We can make do for now. I'll pay more board.'

Maree looked sideways at her. Would she refuse? She was so proud. Was their growing friendship enough to overcome that?

'I'll take on your ironing, then,' she said finally. 'But when Jimmy gets out of hospital . . .'

Yes. When Jimmy got out of hospital, Ruby thought, she would have to move out, and then Maree would need a job. And Edward, she supposed, would be looked after by Carrie Skinner.

'Whoosh!' Edward called. 'Whoosh, Mummy!'

'Whoosh!' Maree said, and smiled.

CHAPTER 29

'They're letting me out!' Jimmy called to her as soon as she appeared in the doorway of the ward on Wednesday. The other men cheered and clapped and whistled. One bloke yelled out, 'Watch out, missus, he'll come out of the gates raring to go!'

She laughed with delight and amusement, and kissed Jimmy right on the mouth. The whistles became louder. It was a lovely moment.

'When?' she asked, sitting down.

'A week from Saturday. They're taking the last bit of shrapnel out on Friday, and they'll give me a week after that to recover.'

Ruby bit her lip. Now was the time to decide where they would live. 'You could move in with me at Maree's, for the time being,' she said.

He blinked in surprise and struggled to sit up. She didn't try to help him – he didn't like being helped in front of people.

'We'll get a house of our own.' His voice was husky, almost as if he were in pain. 'Just the two of us together. At last.'

'Of course,' she said, wondering why she felt a pang of disappointment. She should want to be alone with him. She *did* want that. She smiled with deliberate gaiety.

He covered her hand with his left, the thumb stroking her skin, making the hairs rise on her arms and neck, making her shiver.

'All on our own,' he insisted. His eyes were brilliant with love and desire and a strange vulnerability, as though pleading with her not to hurt him. As if she ever would. She lifted his hand and kissed the rough knuckles and felt him relax.

'A little house all on our own!' she promised.

'Well,' he said, 'until baby makes three.' He smiled as though he were promising her a treat. She blinked. That was rushing things.

'Let's walk before we try to run,' she said. 'Time enough to think about a baby when you're better.'

He shrugged, mouth dissatisfied. 'I suppose so.'

'Besides,' she said, trying to cheer him up, 'I want you to myself for a while before I share you with a baby!'

That brought a smile to his face, and he kissed her hand.

•

On Thursday, Mr Curry didn't come in to work. Ruby normally ignored his absences, but there was a meeting with a new buyer from the Navy yards in the afternoon, and she was surprised that he would miss it, so she telephoned the house.

'May I speak to him, please, Mrs Donahue?'

'He's upstairs.' Her voice was flat with denial. Implacable. But that was just too bad.

'I need to speak to him.'

'He's upstairs and I'm not supposed to disturb him when he's upstairs.'

'It's important. I think you should.'

'And I'm sick of you giving me orders like you pay my wages!' she snarled. 'You're not the mistress here yet, Miss-high-mucky-muck, no matter how much you cozen him. Butter wouldn't melt in your mouth, you little tart —'

'What the hell is going on here?' she heard Mr Curry roar. 'Who are you talking to? Give me that!' His voice was suddenly loud. 'Hello?' Ruby knew a moment's craven desire to just hang up, but she mastered it.

'It's me, Mr Curry.'

'Bloody – sorry, sorry.'

'I just wanted to remind you about the meeting with the Navy officer.'

'I hadn't forgotten. I had an appointment with – well, never mind that. I'll be in before lunch.'

'Yes, sir.'

She put the earpiece down and looked up to see both Wal and Wesley staring at her. Did she look that shaken? The vitriol in Mrs Donahue's voice had been nastier than anything ever directed at her, and she was trembling. Then she realised they were waiting for news of Mr Curry. 'He'll be in before lunch,' she managed to say.

Not for the first time, she wished there was a ladies' convenience in the office to which she could retreat to regain her composure. She made do with burying her head in a ledger.

Mr Curry walked in before lunch with his face set hard, called her into his office and shut the door behind her.

'I've fired the auld bitch,' he said, his Irish accent strong. 'Why didn't you tell me?'

'What? That she was being rude to me? She didn't work for *me*.'

'You knew that I'd want to know —'

'I avoided her,' Ruby said. 'That was the best approach. What do you think she's saying about me now to everyone she knows?'

That stopped him in his tracks and he sank into his seat, thinking it over. 'Never mind the auld gossips. They'll see they're wrong.'

Easy for him to say. He wasn't the one they'd all whisper about.

'Once your husband's out of hospital it will die down,' he added.

'Yes. Eventually.'

'And in the meantime, I have to find another housekeeper!' He glared.

'Well, don't look at me as if it's *my* fault!' she snapped. '*I* didn't ask you to sack her!'

His mouth twitched, and then he laughed. 'Surely, surely.'

An idea occurred to her. Should she say anything, or ask first? But Mr Curry was a man of decision, once he got going. He might go and hire another housekeeper today.

'Um . . . would you need your housekeeper to live in?'

'You have someone in mind?' Then his head came up and he opened his mouth, closed it again as he considered, and then nodded. 'Mrs Hannan.'

Ruby shrugged and left it at that.

'That's a grand idea, Mrs Hawkins, but would she do it?'

'Frankly, sir, she might not have a choice about whether she works or not. And this way, she could keep Edward with her. Couldn't she?'

'Certainly, certainly, glad to have the boy around the place. Will you put it to her?'

•

Being a housekeeper was a step down, socially. It was a big decision.

'Beggars can't be choosers,' Maree said, practical as always. 'It's a good solution. I wasn't really happy about leaving Edward with Carrie for days on end.'

'The gossips will start on *you*, now.'

'Let them,' she shrugged. 'It's no skin off my nose.'

Ruby envied her phlegmatic attitude. On the walk home, she'd seen a couple of local shopkeepers, cronies of Mrs Donahue, stare at her disapprovingly. It shouldn't have mattered, but it was so *unfair*!

'Whoever said life was fair?' came the memory of her mother's voice, and she smiled at herself. That was when you grew up, she supposed, when you stopped expecting the world to be fair. She had a way to go yet.

Unexpectedly, her mother rang that evening.

'I'm planning to make a trip down to see you.'

'Oh. Oh, lovely!' Ruby said. 'But this might not be a good time . . .'

'No, I think it is. I think it might be the right time.'

Ruby knew that tone; Cecilia Carter only used it when she was referring to one of her 'feelings'.

'All right, Mum. I'm not sure if you'll be able to stay here . . .'

'I'll stay with Carrie Skinner,' her mother said briskly.

Her mother and Carrie had gone to boarding school in North Sydney together, at the Mercy sisters' convent. That was how Ruby had come to be boarding at Maree's in the first place.

Ruby's mother wouldn't travel on the Sabbath, so it was Tuesday before she arrived. Ruby came home from work to find her sitting in the parlour with Maree, and Edward taking a nap on the sofa. The remnants of Maree's best afternoon tea were on the table: scones, jam, the good china.

Seeing her mother again after the longest break they'd ever had, Ruby noticed the crow's-feet and the grey hairs, the upright posture and the French blue hobble skirt, modest in defiance of fashion. More than that, she saw the strength in her jaw and the determination in her eyes. They were qualities she'd never valued much in the past; she had wanted a sweet mother like her friend Annie had, a mother who would cuddle her and praise her and think she was wonderful.

Cecilia Carter didn't do any of those things. The most praise Ruby had ever received was 'Well done,' when she had made a hundred per cent on an arithmetic test when she was twelve. But her mother was here, now, and that brought an unexpected rush of relief and gladness.

Ruby kissed her on the cheek and put a hand on her shoulder. 'I'm glad to see you, Mum.'

'I've just been discussing with Maree that there's no reason she should have a memorial service for Theo if she doesn't want to.' Her mother's eyes warned her to agree, but that wasn't necessary. She *did* agree.

'Quite right,' she said, sitting down.

Maree gave her a grateful smile.

'If anyone asks, say that you don't feel right about having one if his parents can't be here.'

'Theo's parents are dead,' Maree protested.

'Exactly,' her mother said with a smile.

Jimmy's parents were dead too – Ruby had never thought it might be an advantage.

'At least you don't have to explain yourself to a mother-in-law,' she said.

It made them all laugh, and that woke Edward. Maree took him out to the kitchen to feed him his afternoon tea.

'I'm glad to have this opportunity to speak with you, Ruby,' her mother said, but instead of going on she fiddled with her teaspoon for a moment, and then sighed.

Ruby felt anxiety slice through her. Her mother never acted like this. 'Are you all right? Your health?'

'Oh, yes, of course,' her mother said, surprised. 'It's not me. It's your uncle.'

'Uncle Stanley?'

'He's dead.' Her mother made the declaration flatly, with the stiff back which said that she didn't want to be comforted.

Ruby blinked. 'When?'

A quick glance at her, and then away. 'It was just after you got the news about Jimmy. I didn't want to heap trouble on you.'

'That was very thoughtful of you,' Ruby said, breathing deeply to stop herself from crying. Uncle Stan had been away shearing most of her childhood, so she hadn't known him well, but he had been her mother's last relative – which meant . . . 'So, the station . . .'

'Yes,' her mother said, a light in her eyes Ruby had never seen. 'Barkinji's mine now.'

'What are you going to do?'

'George wants to take the store over.' George was Myrtle's husband, a man Ruby had never really liked but whom Myrtle adored. They had a son, Matthew, and two small daughters, Georgina and Ada. After their father had died, George had moved in to 'manage' the store – in reality, to take orders from her mother. He'd always resented that.

'You're not going to let him?'

Her mother sighed. The afternoon light came through the front window and lit up her hair, showing the black and white strands separately. How old was she? Ruby wondered. There were six years between Myrtle and her, and she knew her mother had to be at the least fifty, but she looked older. Her father had been fifty-nine when he'd died.

'I'm tired, Ruby. I turn sixty this year, and I'd like a little time to myself before I die.'

Sixty! Impossible.

'But you were married when you were twenty,' Ruby protested. 'How can you be sixty?'

'I had four miscarriages before Myrtle, that's how,' her mother said, an old pain resurfacing and darkening her eyes.

The first thing Ruby thought was, I must really be married if she's talking to me about miscarriages. It was one of those topics that wasn't mentioned to unmarried girls. The second was sympathy. 'I'm sorry, Mum.'

'Yes, well, it was a long time ago and no use worrying over it now. But the thing is, George and Myrtle are going to have the store sooner or later, so it might as well be sooner. I have the station now, so I'm going to make the store over to you girls and go back to live there.'

Ruby digested that. Did she want to go back to Bourke and run a drapery? Not with George in charge, she didn't.

'What I wanted to say to you, dear, is —' Her mother, for the first time Ruby could remember, looked embarrassed. 'I think you should ask George to buy you out.'

'Buy me out?'

'He's going to run it into the ground,' she said frankly. 'I've been trying to get him to understand that times have changed, that we have to adapt to new methods and new products, but he just won't listen. And Myrtle – well, she's a sweet girl, but she has the backbone of a jellyfish. Whatever George thinks is what's right. So you need to get your money out of the place before he loses it all for you.'

'Why give it to him, then?'

'I just can't be bothered with anything since your father died.'

Ruby had always known that her father had loved her mother devotedly, but she wouldn't have bet on her mother feeling the same. She felt abashed, as though she had been stupidly insensitive. Barkinji wasn't all that profitable, but it was family land and her mother had grown up there.

Ruby and Jimmy had spent the short, sweet week of their honeymoon there, in the old rambling homestead with its slab kitchen and wide verandahs. For a moment, the scent of eucalyptus and hot red earth enveloped her. The sky out there stretched forever. She understood why her mother wanted to live there.

'I've been thinking about going back home for a while,' her mother said. 'I like the peace and quiet. Now Stanley's gone . . .' Her face became almost dreamy as she spoke of it.

'You never really liked working in the shop, did you?'

Her mother looked at her sharply, and then away. 'I loved your father,' she said flatly, 'and that was his life, so I shared it. He came back to Bourke for me.'

A lifetime of mutual self-sacrifice. Ruby reached over the table and kissed her mother on the cheek softly.

'You're a good woman, Mum,' she said.

Her mother coloured and there was a suspicious brightness in her eyes. 'Oh, get away with you!' she said. 'Here, have a scone. You're skin and bones.'

They talked over the details and her mother said she would get a valuation done on the business so that each girl would get a fair share.

Ruby deliberately didn't let herself think about how much that might be. She had no real idea what a draper's shop in Bourke would be worth, and it was better not to set her expectations until after the deal was done.

'George will try to get you to keep your money in, but don't you let him sweet-talk you. Jimmy might need that money to set himself up in . . . something.'

'He's not that bad, Mum. The doctors are teaching him to write with his left hand. Once he can do that, and they've got all the shrapnel out, there's no reason he can't work.'

'Not too many stock and station agents in Sydney.'

'No. And he'll have to stay here for a while because of his rehabilitation. But there are other jobs he can do – lord knows, if they'll take women, employers will jump at a veteran!'

Her mother laughed, but held up a warning finger. 'It won't be as easy as you think, Ruby. It never is.'

She stayed only a few days, visiting Jimmy once, seeing old

friends, buying two new hats and, surprisingly, a quantity of artist's supplies.

'I always liked doing watercolours when I was a girl,' she said, shyly, when Maree asked her about it. 'I thought I might do some sketching again, now I'll have the time.'

She walked past Curry's and peered into the yard, but she refused to be introduced to Mr Curry.

'Do you think that one of the men would introduce their mother to him?' she scolded Ruby. 'You have to be more careful – it only takes one wrong step to start the gossip.'

A year ago, that caution would have made her roll her eyes, but now she knew her mother was right – even if it was unfair and unjust that it should be so.

On Friday night, Ruby took her mother to Central Station for the overnight train to Bourke and gave her a hard, heartfelt hug. 'It was so good to see you.'

Surprised but not displeased, her mother patted her on the arm. 'Yes, well, I thought we needed a chance to talk without anyone overhearing. You remember what I said.'

'Don't worry, Mum. Even if George could talk me round, he wouldn't have any luck with Jimmy!'

As the train pulled out with its characteristic puffs of smoke and steam, enveloping the waving bystanders in a wet white cloud which smelt of coal, Ruby felt a matching heat of tears in her eyes. When Jimmy was well enough, they would visit Barkinji, and see her.

CHAPTER 30

It wasn't just one operation, but three that Jimmy needed, and it wasn't until the end of June before he was released from hospital, finally back in his uniform. His legs were fully recovered, and Ruby exulted in the way he strode out of the lobby to the waiting cab.

She had found them a little weatherboard house in Taylor Street, a sweet cottage furnished simply but adequately with stout wooden pieces. It even had a telephone in the parlour. She had added a comfortable couch upholstered in midnight blue, using some of her Christmas bonus money. Jimmy would need a soft place to rest.

She led him in proudly, showing him the separate bathroom with an actual bath, just like they'd had back home in Bourke. She hadn't known how much she'd missed baths until her first night in the house, when she'd lain there for more than half an hour and only got out when the wood-chip heater ran out of chips. Even better, it had a WC; a lavatory with a pull-chain cistern. No more going out into the dark and the rain to relieve herself!

The kitchen was bright and modern, too, with a gas stove instead of a range and cupboards painted white and green. It was big enough for a kitchen table, a square one which would seat four.

The house was only a few blocks away from both Maree and Curry's, within easy walking distance.

She had told Jimmy about the house on her last visit, two days before he was discharged, but he hadn't been as happy about that as she'd expected. He plucked at the blanket that covered his knees and shifted restlessly in his bath chair. They were sitting in the hospital grounds under a gum tree; the shadows of the leaves moved over his face and made him look guarded and uncertain.

'It'll take me an hour at least to get to the hospital,' he'd said. 'Each way.'

She'd thought about it, of course she had. But his appointments at the hospital were only once a week, on a Friday. She'd already arranged to have Friday afternoons off so she could go with him. If they lived near the hospital, she would be travelling two or three hours a day, every day. She said so.

'But you'll be giving up your job now,' he said, as if it were the most obvious thing in the world.

She simply stared at him. Didn't he realise that wasn't possible?

He had been on full pay, but the minute he left the hospital his weekly stipend from the Army would be reduced to three pounds per fortnight. One pound ten shillings a week. A single man might be able to live on that, if he lived in a cheap boarding house.

'We need the money,' she said baldly. He flinched and looked at his right hand, lying limply on the coverlet, the fingers scarred and curled inwards. He still couldn't raise his arm to shoulder height, couldn't grip a pencil, couldn't turn a tap. They were teaching him to write with his left hand, but it would be a while before he would be able to do clerical work, even if they could find someone who would let him have Fridays off for his hospital visits.

'I've signed a six-month lease,' she said. 'Twelve shillings a week.'

He was startled by the cost. That alone was more than a third of his stipend.

'They're not building many new houses while the war's on,' she said. 'So rent has gone up.'

'Hold on. *You* signed?'

'Women are allowed to sign leases, Jimmy,' she said.

'Not when their husbands are alive.' Well. That was a mixed truth. Women with husbands were supposed to get them to co-sign any legal document, true. But during the war, that was clearly impossible, so for most day-to-day documents, like lease agreements, agents and solicitors were ignoring that requirement, and that had led to no one even asking women if they were married – the agents now just asked if they had a job and could show a pay slip or bank book. She suspected that Jimmy wouldn't like to be told that.

'There were three families who wanted that house. I had to sign on the spot,' she told him instead.

'Maybe we'd better go back to Bourke. I could work in the shop.'

Forcing herself to laugh, she disregarded the sinking of her heart. 'With George? There'd be murder in the first week!' She laughed some more, in genuine amusement, as she imagined Jimmy behind the counter. 'I can just see you selling ruffles and lace! "Oh, Moddom, this is the very latest style, I assure you!"'

He laughed too.

Best not to tell him that there might be money coming from the shop. Her mother hadn't referred to it again, in letters or in their weekly phone call, so perhaps it wasn't happening. Best not to get his hopes up. 'We'll just concentrate on getting you strong again,' she said.

'When you come to pick me up, wear that yellow dress.'

'I had to throw that out. It got machine oil on it in the yard.'

She was regretful herself – it had been a sweet dress, although a couple of years old – but she was surprised when Jimmy said, 'That's a pity,' with real feeling. 'You looked beautiful in that dress.'

She kissed his mouth tenderly. He returned the kiss with subdued passion, aware they were being watched by the other men and a few nurses, but she could feel the desire welling up in him. It gladdened her – not only for herself, but because it showed he was really getting better.

•

Now, finally together in their own home, she settled him on the comfortable couch and went to make a cup of tea. She thanked God that she didn't have to build up a fire from scratch. In this weatherboard house, she wouldn't have dared leave the fire banked while they were out, as they did in Wells Street. It gave her a pure thrill of pleasure to turn the tap on the stove and light the gas burner.

He came up behind her as she was about to put the kettle on the burner. He slid his right hand fumblingly around her waist and used his left to turn off the gas.

'Leave that,' he said, kissing her neck. Ruby's body flamed alight, and she turned in his arms eagerly, raising her mouth to his. At last she could loosen the reins on her own desire and return need for need, recover that part of herself she had packed away.

Hot, strong, passionate – he was her old Jimmy again at last, and they forgot everything as they rediscovered each other. His body was thinner than her hands remembered, but still so male, so hard and muscled and yearning for hers. They stumbled to the bedroom, still kissing, touching, wanting, and fell on the bed. Jimmy twisted them at the last moment so that he fell on his left side, and she pulled back.

'Are you all right?'

'Never better,' he said breathlessly. 'Come here.'

It was quick, an explosion of movement and need which was over before she knew it. A moment of disappointment was followed by joy as she saw his face, grinning with relief.

'Well, *that's* still working, at any rate!' he said happily, and she kissed him, not realising until then that he had been worried. It hadn't even occurred to her that some of the shrapnel fragments in his thighs might have done damage to something other than muscle.

They slid under the covers to escape the chill air. 'I love you so much,' he whispered. 'Arthur was right. I've got a good one!'

'I love you too,' she murmured, contentedly snuggling into him, carefully on his left side.

He fell asleep with the suddenness of exhaustion, and she was mortified that she'd let her own desires overwhelm her good sense. He wasn't strong enough, yet, for marital duties. Not time, apparently, to let her own yearnings free.

She lay for a while, wriggling to find a comfortable spot on the unfamiliar mattress, feeling odd at being in bed during the day, as though her whole life was topsy-turvy. She should be feeling that it had returned to normal; that everything was all right now.

After a while, when it was clear he wasn't going to wake up, she got up and washed her stockings for the next day. She was laying them over the towel rack when she heard a thrashing and yelling coming from the bedroom.

She ran. Jimmy was having a nightmare, a terrible nightmare. He tossed and turned and shouted out indecipherable words. Ruby went to him and shook his shoulder, racked with pity. He grabbed her hand, his eyes still closed, and flipped her onto the mattress with a swift movement. His arm was at her throat, pushing. She pushed back with both hands but he was so strong. He was trying to kill her, and he was still asleep. The only thing that was stopping him was that he had, instinctively, used his right arm, and it was too weak to finally finish her. It didn't seem real; she had to urge herself to struggle.

'Jimmy! Jimmy! *Jimmy!*' she choked out. His eyelids fluttered. The pressure on her throat eased. 'Jimmy, wake UP!' His eyes opened. For a moment which seemed to stretch forever there was no recognition in his eyes; no sign of Jimmy at all. Terror swept over her; a horrible wrongness. Then he blinked, and it was Jimmy again.

'Ruby?' He moved back, confused. 'What?'

She didn't move, just in case he was provoked again. She shook against the bed, trembling. 'You had a nightmare.'

From confusion and concern, his face shut down to a perfect blankness. He swallowed. 'Christ. What did I do?'

She sat up slowly, and touched her throat. Jimmy winced. 'I think you thought I was – um – a Turk.'

He turned away from her slightly. 'Don't wake me up if I'm dreaming,' he said harshly. 'It's too dangerous.'

Around her thighs, her skirts rucked uncomfortably as she slid to stand, and she had to pause to pull them down before she could get off the bed. Jimmy moved back as she stood up, and she backed away, a reflexive movement to put as much space as possible between them.

'You're awake now,' she said. Her throat was sore and her voice came out more harshly than she'd intended. She swallowed a couple of times and tried again. What could she say? What should she say? Her own shock and terror ebbed away, in fits and starts, at the sight of his guilt. 'It's all right now.'

Slowly, slowly, he took a step towards her. He reached his left hand towards her throat and she had to force herself not to flinch as his fingers, cold and shaking, touched her. Her breath came harshly.

'Don't wake me up if I'm dreaming,' he repeated. The blankness had left his face; his eyes were pleading for understanding.

A fleeting smile lit her face. 'No fear of that!' Getting her courage back, she stroked his cheek, feeling his body's warmth only a hair's breadth away. 'It will be all right.'

'Maybe I'd better sleep on the couch.' He mumbled it, ashamed, not looking her in the eyes.

'Nonsense!' she said briskly, as she might have said to Mr Curry in one of his moods. 'Now I know what to do, we'll be fine.'

She kissed him. His whole body was tense, and then he grabbed her and held her close. Fear rose up to swamp her, but she ignored it. Jimmy would never hurt *her*. She would just have to be careful.

'I get them a lot,' he confessed.

'*Shh, shhh, shhhh*.' She eased him back to bed and cuddled him as she would have Edward, and he held her and shook with shame and remembered fear.

•

Ruby missed eight o'clock Mass, because Jimmy was sleeping like a dead man and she couldn't bear to leave him. Vividly, she imagined returning to the house to find him still in bed, tossing and thrashing with another nightmare. The thought made her sweat and tremble with fear for both of them. She took a deep breath and forced herself to be calm. She had promised herself that she wouldn't react like this. Her fear was only a shadow of what he had gone through – was still going through. It was no wonder he had bad dreams, and she would support him through it.

He woke at nine, tired, but smiling weakly at her, still shamefaced. She made him breakfast briskly, not mentioning the night before, put the roast in the oven, and went to ten o'clock Mass, where almost everyone she passed asked after him. The news had clearly gone around.

'Got him home safely, then?' Mr Curry asked, looking past her to where the St Brendan's sign was shivering slightly in the wind.

'Yes, sir, thank you.'

He nodded once and walked away; she knew that tightness around his mouth, the low tilt of his shoulders. He was remembering Laurence, who would never come home. Part of him, surely, had to be wishing that it had been Jimmy instead of Laurence who had found a soldier's grave in the Dardanelles.

Maree and Edward came over for lunch. Instead of two half days, which domestic servants usually had, Maree had negotiated Sundays off. She had left Mr Curry a cold collation for his dinner which Brigid could serve and he was loud in his protestations that he could manage his own lunch. Maree made up for it with a lavish roast every Saturday night.

Their lunch was roast lamb with all the trimmings, and Ruby tried not to think about the eight shillings the leg had cost. It was worth it for Jimmy's recovery. He needed meat if he was going to gain strength.

He revived with the meal and entertained Edward by showing him how to aim his fingers as a gun and shoot at bushrangers, as he had as a boy.

'No need for him to worry about the war,' Jimmy said. 'With any luck, he'll never have to shoot at anyone.'

Afterwards, he was tired enough to accept that he needed a nap, and he slept right through to the next morning without any nightmares. It was odd, having a man in her bed again. She'd never really had time to get used to it, when they were married, in the single week they'd spent at Barkinji, far less in the night they'd spent awake in the Family Hotel. She breathed in his scent and relished the warmth at her back, but she woke every time he moved or made a sound, afraid of another nightmare, cold sweat breaking out on her skin.

He shifted and his hand touched her arm. Ruby came bolt upright, heart pounding in fear. She had to remove that fear or she'd reveal it to him and it would wound him as badly as the Turkish shell. Thank God he hadn't woken to see it.

Think of something else. Think of Barkinji, their honeymoon. Memories of Jimmy's hands and mouth, of his hot skin, of his body. Despite the winter chill, she pushed back the blankets on her side of the bed and used the cold air to calm her down. Time. All they needed was time, and they would recapture that honeyed frenzy. At least there was no room in her body for fear now.

She got up at six, as usual, ignoring Jimmy's sleepy attempts to pull her back down and her own tiredness. 'I have to go to work,' she said.

He sat up, his normally smooth hair tousled like a little boy's, and scowled at her. 'I don't like you going to work where there are so many men,' he said.

She bit back her first answer of 'Too late for that!' and smiled at him. 'Mr Curry looks after me like a daughter. I'll see you at lunchtime – half-past twelve.'

Thank God for the bathroom, where she could wash and dress in privacy; such luxury. Her hands were shaking a little; reaction, or tiredness, she couldn't tell. In the bright morning, last night's terror seemed unreal; but her body remembered.

She brought Jimmy scrambled eggs in bed, and hurriedly ate some toast herself while she braided her hair and pinned it up. Then she kissed him and left, walking the new route to the bay a little more quickly than she needed to. She'd heard enough honeymoon jokes when they got married. She knew what kind of ribbing she would get if she were late for work today. She got it anyway.

She came home to find Jimmy doggedly doing the exercises the doctors had prescribed for him. They looked so simple: raising his arms to shoulder height, first to the front and then to the side, but he was pale and sweating. The left arm came up easily, but the right came barely to waist height before it trembled and fell.

He grinned at her anyway and she blew him a kiss as she deposited the day's groceries on the kitchen table and returned to the parlour.

'Do you want a cup of tea?'

He had gone on to the next exercise, which consisted of putting his hands on his hips (not easy – he had to lift his right hand into place and curl it back so it would sit properly) and then twisting at the waist.

'Yes, please,' he gasped. As he twisted, his shoulder came into view. There was blood on his shirt.

'Jimmy! Stop! You're bleeding.' She leapt forward to examine him. He turned his head to peer over his shoulder.

'Popped a stitch,' he said ruefully. 'Darn.'

'Didn't you notice?' she asked, peeling the shirt from his back. There was a small tear in the scar on his shoulder and blood was seeping through it.

'You've torn your scar!' She rushed to the bathroom for bandages and bound it up, smoothing the sticking plaster over lint on the wound so that it held the edges shut together. 'Didn't it hurt?'

He shrugged, not meeting her eyes. 'No more than usual.'

She felt cold. If pain like that was 'no more than usual', what was usual like? Was it so bad?

He grinned at her. 'No sense, no feeling, that's what my father used to say about me.'

She let him reassure her, but it was still worrying. Hopefully the pain would improve as he got better. 'Don't push yourself so hard,' she said. 'There's no rush.'

He snorted. 'You wouldn't say that if you were me.'

Of course he wanted to push himself. Of course he wanted to be back to normal as soon as possible.

'Well, next time,' she said, 'take your shirt off before you start bleeding!'

Grinning more widely, he hugged her with his good arm. 'That's my girl.'

·

The next week was gentle, domestic and deeply frustrating. There were no more marital duties; Jimmy reached for her and kissed her every night, but didn't have the energy to continue to the end. It left Ruby restless and dissatisfied, yearning, but what could she do? It wasn't like he was withholding himself from her deliberately. She remembered their courting days, when merely kissing was astonishingly satisfying, and laughed to herself as she washed the breakfast dishes. At least there had been no more nightmares, although when he shifted in bed she saw the shadow of pain cross his face, and he avoided being touched on his right side.

Ruby went to work as normal, came home and made lunch, kissed Jimmy quickly and went back to Curry's, came home and made dinner, bathed and went to bed. The early finish at Curry's meant she could make it to the butcher and the greengrocer on her way home, and of course the baker and milkman delivered.

She hadn't realised how much a difference it had made to her, having Maree getting dinner ready each night, doing the washing, tidying up. Doing all that and working was more tiring than she had expected.

And yet, at night, there they were, curled up on the couch, reading and talking and simply *being* with each other, so that all the worries and duties and concerns of the day evaporated. Jimmy wouldn't talk about Anzac, which he called Gallipoli, unless it was to tell funny stories, about things like the biting lice they called chats.

'We all wore our uniforms inside out,' he said. 'They lived in the seams, so if you wore your clothes inside out they couldn't get to you as easily, the little buggers. Curried Lamb, he wore his shirt inside out all right, but he just couldn't bring himself to wear his trousers that way!'

He laughed. 'We looked like right Charlies! Freemie even wore his hat inside out, but they put a stop to that. Don't know why they'd care more about the hat than the trousers, but they did.'

His stories were full of the soldiers' 'they' – the officers, especially the colonels and generals; the powers-that-be which could determine, at a moment's notice, who would live and who would die. But mostly he didn't want to talk about the war; he reminisced instead about the voyage out, and the hospital in Cairo after he was wounded, and the strange customs of the locals there. Not once did either of them refer to the nightmare and what had happened afterward. Ruby wondered if they should discuss it, but she was more than reluctant to disturb Jimmy's equilibrium. Not because of fear, but because it was all he had.

On the Tuesday night, in return for his tales, Ruby told him about her life in Sydney and her work at Curry's, but like him, she realised, she was editing out the 'war stories'. No mention of the storage room. No mention of Mrs Donahue. And she touched only lightly on Mr Curry's response to his son's death; partly to protect him, and partly to skip over what must have been a difficult time for Jimmy and Freemie and their friends.

That night, Jimmy slept restlessly, waking often, sometimes with a grunt of pain as he turned awkwardly in bed, so she woke in the morning tired and a little irritable, although flooded with pity for him.

On the Wednesday afternoon, Tiddy accompanied her as usual with a barrowload of wood. Jimmy was waiting for her at the gate, enjoying the late spring sunshine in his shirtsleeves. He was getting his strength back.

'Hello, young feller-me-lad,' Jimmy said to him.

Tiddy was vibrating with the glory of being the first from Curry's to meet him, and he saluted briskly, dropping the barrow handles.

Jimmy used his left hand to salute gravely back.

'Good man,' he said. 'Take it around there.'

'Yessir, Mr Hawkins. I know where, sir.'

Jimmy shared a glance full of laughter with her, and she was plunged back to the early days of their courtship, when she had tumbled head over ears in love with him. She felt giddy with love and excitement. He was such a lovely man.

'I can see you've been well looked after,' he said, as they both followed Tiddy around the side of the house to the laundry.

'Yessir!' Tiddy said. 'We all looks after her. She's a bonzer sheila —' he caught sight of Ruby as he tipped the wood out, and froze, then scurried to pile it up neatly.

'Thank you, Tiddy,' she said, ignoring the comment as she'd learnt to do. 'Come in and I'll give you a bit of bread and dripping.'

'Oh,' Jimmy said. 'I ate it all. The dripping, I mean. There's bread.'

Tiddy's face fell.

'I'm sure we have some honey,' Ruby said, ushering him through the back door. 'But Jimmy – Wednesday is Tiddy's day for bread and dripping!' She meant it as a joke, and Jimmy laughed and said, 'Right you are.' But there was a shadow on his face.

After Tiddy left, replete, clutching his ha'penny in a sticky fist, Jimmy was restless, moving from kitchen to parlour to bedroom and back in a curious, formless back and forth.

'What's the matter?' she asked, finally taking off her hat and laying it on the mantelpiece.

'You've got a whole life,' he said. 'A whole life without me.'

'You had a whole life without me,' she said, fear slicing into her heart; surely without cause.

'That was different,' he said impatiently, still pacing. 'It wasn't *real*.'

She understood that. Of course Anzac hadn't been real. It had been a nightmare place, a strange interlude of blood and heat and fear and comradeship.

'My life here didn't feel real without you,' she said, and was glad, because he turned to her with a light in his eyes and held her as though he would never let her go. Guilt budded inside her heart; she had missed him, of course, desperately, hungrily, but life had been real enough without him.

CHAPTER 31

She had to do the laundry on Saturday afternoons, now that she didn't have Maree to do it. That Saturday Jimmy was well enough to feed the fire under the copper for her. Despite the hard work of stirring the clothes with the dolly stick, it was a happy time: the bright flames, the remnants of autumn leaves rustling at their feet, the steam rising from the copper.

Jimmy sat on a stool and joked with her just as he had in Bourke. This house came with a mangle – no more twisting the sheets by hand to get the water out. Jimmy turned the mangle for her as she fed the sheets through. They needed a wash, that was for certain; the past couple of days, the scent of lovemaking had wafted over her whenever she turned in bed, bringing both remembered pleasure and a kind of embarrassment.

Which made her worry about a baby. If she got with child now it would be, potentially, a disaster. They would have to go back to Bourke and live with her mother on Barkinji.

Jimmy wouldn't get the rehabilitation he needed – he might be permanently crippled. They would have to be careful.

But looking at him that day, with the breeze ruffling his hair and his eyes alight with laughter for the first time since he'd come home, she just couldn't bring herself to say anything. He had been through so much, how could she deny him the comfort of her body?

'Penny for your thoughts,' he said teasingly, and she blushed.

'Oh, just wool-gathering.' She fed the last of the sheet into the clothes basket and said, 'Can you let the line down for me, please?' She couldn't let him try to pick up the heavy basket, and equally she couldn't embarrass him by saying so.

He flicked her a quick glance and nodded, his mouth tucked in at the corners, but he went to the clothes line and took the prop out of the centre, bringing the line low enough for her to drape the sheets over it and peg them out.

That was women's work, after all.

Then Jimmy pushed the prop up under the heavy line, and she didn't try to help. He would suffer for it, she was certain, but the simple pain of a pulled scar might be easier to live with, in the end, than shame.

Perhaps it was because she had been around the house all the afternoon and they had done some of the household chores together, brushing past each other in the small kitchen, hands touching as they passed broom or rake to each other, but that night Jimmy reached for her with real energy, and made it all worthwhile.

He was almost like her old Jimmy. Warm and tender and loving; just weaker. His hands undressed her slowly, as if she were a precious gift, and reminded her of how much she wanted him. He had so many scars . . . she kissed each one, gently, slowly, and felt his breathing grow ragged. With his shoulder hurt, it was hard for him to prop himself over her for long; greatly daring, she moved on top of him.

'All right?' he asked her.

She kissed him in answer and surprised herself by finding that in this, as well, she didn't mind taking control. She smiled against his skin. Jimmy wasn't criticising her *this* time for assuming authority.

They slept in on Sunday morning and woke in a warm tumble of love and blankets, although they got up straightaway. Once a week was all he could manage, apparently. It would get better, she knew, and washed her face and wrists in cold water to cool her blood.

Jimmy insisted on coming to ten o'clock Mass with her, although she wasn't at all sure he should be walking so far. By the time they got to St Brendan's he was pale, though not unduly so, but by the end of Mass he was looking worse.

She wished he'd been able to eat something beforehand, just to tide him over. Ruby understood the theology which said that one shouldn't eat anything before taking Holy Communion, but what was just bearable at eight was more than difficult by ten – particularly when you'd used up quite a lot of energy the night before. She giggled quietly to herself at the thought, trying not to be impatient as every member of the congregation came up to congratulate Jimmy on being home safe and sound and to admire the bangles he had brought back for her.

Father Ford came over and held out his left hand to shake Jimmy's, doing it so easily that Ruby almost missed the small courtesy.

'Hello, Father,' Jimmy said. 'Thanks for looking after my Ruby.'

'A pleasure, a pleasure,' he said. Ruby tried not to get annoyed by this continuing male assumption that she needed looking after. 'Glad to have you home, my boy. Confessions are on Tuesday evening and Saturday afternoons – and don't tell me you don't need one, because I was an Army chaplain once!'

Jimmy laughed as if he meant it. 'I'll see you on Tuesday, Padre,' he said, saluting.

They walked home hand in hand, uncaring of who saw them, but Ruby's happiness was dulled when she realised that Jimmy was forcing one leg in front of the other. He was pale and sweating, despite the cool day. She got him to put his arm around her shoulders.

'I'm all right,' he said through gritted teeth, casting a glance at the other people walking down Nelson Street.

'We'll just look like we love each other,' she tried to tease him. It irked him that he needed her help, she understood, but she wasn't going to lose him back to that hospital because of misplaced pride.

Mrs Patterson chivvied her two daughters past them, saying, 'I have to get the chook in the oven,' in a driven tone.

Jimmy grinned and watched the elder girl, a slender blonde nineteen-year-old, with appreciation and some bemusement. She had a pair of short heeled boots on, and a skirt that was so short her ankles showed above the boots in flashes as she walked. The way she swayed her hips and flipped her skirt with her hand as she walked made it clear she knew how she looked.

'I'm amazed her mother lets her wear that skirt,' Ruby said. 'Although it is very fashionable.'

Jimmy sighed. 'Sometimes I feel like I've gone to sleep for a hundred years, like that fellow in the story. Like the hospital ship took a lifetime to get back. When I left, only a – a woman of the night would have dressed like that.'

His voice was not exactly critical, but it wasn't approving. She felt impelled to justify the changes. 'I was reading the other day that there are a lot fewer accidents now, with the new skirt length. Not so many trips and falls, and fewer women set on fire.'

'Set on *fire*?'

'If you have an open fire, it's very easy for an ember to set a skirt alight. Muslins and printed cottons go up like tinder.'

Jimmy grinned down at her, the tiredness showing in the white lines around his mouth. 'You learn something every day.'

She had thought that when he was home worry would be at an end, but she had merely exchanged one set of worries for another – instead of worrying about Turkish bullets or shrapnel wounds, she worried about pneumonia or gangrene or, almost as bad, melancholy. She would catch him sometimes, staring at the digger's hat on the mantelpiece, or rubbing at one particular scar on his forearm. He always rallied when she came in, but there were shadows on his face, eyes dark with memory.

His physical wounds were only barely healed. Every night she bathed them in rubbing alcohol and eucalyptus oil, but the scars were still red and proud, and she knew they were tender to the touch although Jimmy tried not to flinch. There was still shrapnel below the surface – the doctors had said it could be years before it was all out. He couldn't raise his right arm level with his shoulder; he couldn't straighten the fingers on that hand, nor curl them all the way in to hold something securely.

She had to cut his food up for him.

When Maree and Eddie had come for lunch, she'd done it discreetly, in the kitchen before she served the plates. When they were together, it was harder. He didn't like it – how could he? No doubt it made him feel like a child.

She began to make hotpots for dinner; dishes she could put on as soon as she got home, where the meat was cut up before it went into the pot. And mashed potato, which he could eat easily with a fork. Sandwiches for lunch. Jellies and custards and rice with jam for dessert. It was winter, it made sense to have casseroles, but she wondered what she would do when summer came.

Surely he'd be better by then.

He was certainly trying hard enough. Every day, he did the exercises the doctors had given him. She knew how much it cost him, because although Jimmy took off his shirt to do his exercises these days, the waist of his trousers became soaked with sweat. He did them even on Sunday, once he'd rested for a while after church. He stood and reached and twisted and flexed, grimly, for two hours at a time, his eyes as hard and determined as they must have been at Anzac.

CHAPTER 32

That night he was in a brown study again, staring at the fire after dinner without a word.

Ruby tried to start a conversation, but it petered out after a few words. She talked inanely about work. How hard it was to get good men. How many of the young ones were joining up.

'Fools,' he muttered.

In desperation, looking for something that would interest him, she told him about Chris Frieman and the military police. He looked up, his attention caught at last, and she felt a flutter of relief.

'So I said he was Arthur's brother, and they believed me,' she concluded, leaving out the way she had used his and Arthur's photograph as evidence. She still felt rather guilty about that. 'Just as well, we couldn't have managed the last few months without him!'

She made her voice lighthearted, a funny story to make him laugh.

But Jimmy wasn't laughing. 'You shouldn't have done that,' he said. 'He's an enemy alien.'

Too late, she realised how it must have sounded to him.

'Frieman's as Australian as you or I,' she said. 'He's a good man and a good worker. He was no threat to anyone.'

'That's not for you to decide.' There was a frown between his brows, a real frown, disapproving and definite. He sat up straight, staring down at her.

'We needed Frieman for the war effort.'

'You can't set your own opinion up over the Government, for God's sake!'

'I can when the Government is wrong,' she said, and wished she'd bitten back the words as soon as she'd said them.

'This is why women shouldn't be in charge of anything!' he flashed. 'You don't understand discipline. You don't know how to bow to a higher authority.'

He was right. God help her, he was right. She didn't know how to bow to authority. Look at the way she talked back to Mr Curry. And it was part of her insolence, impudence, whatever you wanted to call it, that she couldn't be sorry for it. But, in this case, there had been a higher authority endorsing her. More or less.

'Mr Curry knew all about it!' she said.

That stopped him. It was enough – just – to allow him to let it go.

'I suppose he knows his own men,' he grumbled, but he relaxed back into his chair with a wince of pain. She wanted – oh, how she wanted! – to say, '*I* manage the men,' but that would just make things worse. Resentment bloomed in her, surprisingly strong, that Jimmy wouldn't acknowledge she might have known what she was doing. Then she looked at the battered, stained digger's hat he'd put up on the mantle, and reminded herself that he'd done nothing but take orders for more than a year, and that he had to believe that following orders was a necessary thing. Or else how could he live with the consequences?

•

The next morning, Monday, Jimmy got up at the same time she did, and insisted on walking her to work. It was clearly meant to seem like a loving gesture, but it exasperated her. She had been walking herself to work for months now quite safely.

He nodded to the men in the yard, even had a word with Smith, the foreman, but he refused to come into the office.

By the time he left, he was pale, and she could see that the effort had taken a lot out of him. He could have stayed at home, she told herself, guiltily defensive; he should have stayed at home.

But the next morning, when he got up, she didn't suggest he keep indoors.

Mr Curry was standing on the doorstep of the office. He had his thumbs tucked into his braces, and he looked like he was just enjoying the crisp, bright morning, but Ruby knew he had been waiting for them. A fillip of panic made her heart hit hard against her ribs; she realised, feeling ashamed of it, that she hadn't wanted them to meet so soon. She didn't think this would go well, although she didn't know why.

'Well, then,' Mr Curry said, holding out his left hand to Jimmy, 'Nice to meet you, Mr Hawkins.'

Jimmy shook his hand and the two men assessed each other. Ruby was sharply aware of their different weaknesses. She didn't normally notice that Mr Curry was shorter than the men around him. His air of authority made it irrelevant. Jimmy was a head taller, leaner, younger – but he was physically weaker. Perhaps not in character, though. She couldn't imagine Jimmy giving in to grief the way Mr Curry had – and then she felt ashamed, again, of such an uncharitable thought. Who knew what Jimmy would be like if she died in childbirth and their only son was killed on foreign soil?

It was Jimmy's turn to say something; every instinct she had told her to keep her mouth shut.

'This is a big operation you've got going here,' Jimmy said, nodding to the yard and the double gates, where a heavy Army lorry was just turning in. They had to raise their voices to be heard over its motor.

'Yes. We're one of the main suppliers for the Army, now.'

They were sizing each other up, not so much like dogs before a fight as two bulls put into the same paddock. Mr Curry looked down, suddenly, and Jimmy swayed back in surprise – the older bull shouldn't have done that. But he was speaking, to the ground.

'I'd like – if you, er, just you, Mr Hawkins, could come over for a drink one afternoon after work. I've got some fine old Scotch . . .'

Jimmy was clearly puzzled; he hadn't expected the conversation to go this way.

Mr Curry, it was plain to Ruby, wanted to hear about his son, and just as clearly wanted the man's version of the truth, not one cleaned up for her ears.

'Oh, war stories!' she said, mock chidingly, squeezing Jimmy's arm to try to get the message across. 'I know, too shocking for my delicate ears!'

Jimmy stiffened, but was obedient to the squeeze. 'Certainly, sir, I'd be glad to come.'

'Today, then?' Mr Curry asked, trying to be casual. 'Might as well, eh? About five.'

'I'll be there.'

'Good, good, surely. Nice to meet you.' He went inside and closed the door firmly behind him.

'What the hell was that about?' Jimmy demanded.

She told him; he stood for a moment silently. 'I didn't think of that,' he admitted. 'Curried Lamb got it in the neck so long ago.'

So long ago. A few months – but she supposed it seemed longer, when so many had died in the meantime.

'Poor old coot,' Jimmy said, more comfortable now he could place Mr Curry as someone who needed his help. 'I'll go up and say the right things.'

•

Jimmy came back from the visit after dinner slightly drunk and a little maudlin, tolling over the names of the ones who wouldn't come back.

'And Jacko and Smithy and Horsencart . . . They were good blokes, good bloody mates. Maybe they're better off . . . better dead than a good-for-nothing cripple. You'd be better off, too, Rube, free, free as a bird. You could work all you wanted then . . .'

She ignored that, and the echo it set up in her own thoughts, although it made her feel sick to think that those thoughts perhaps accompanied him every day. Bundling him into bed, she resisted his attempts to pull her down with him.

'I'm going to eat my dinner,' she said. 'I'll come to bed later.'

She didn't mind the overcooked mutton; if this visit had cleared the air between the two men it was worth a lot more than a neglected dinner. But his comments worried her, and made her almost angry. Increasingly she was getting the feeling he didn't like her very much anymore. Didn't like the professional, competent woman she'd become. And if he didn't like her, could he love her still?

When she went to bed he was waiting for her: warm, male, but stinking of scotch. She wanted to pull away. With the memory of what he had gone through, the memory of lost comrades, still fresh in him, he needed her mercy, her kindness. That was what she told herself. But as he kissed her, she remembered that moment by the altar all over again, and the week that followed, the glorious week at Barkinji, and her own need bloomed up sudden and strong and cut through any reluctance.

'I love you, Ruby,' he said, propped on his left elbow, stroking her hair back with an unsteady, ungainly right hand.

She remembered their first night together, their wedding night. She had never been fully naked in the same room as someone else. It had been a silly thought, but it kept coming back to her, even when they were not merely in the same room but body to body, mouth to mouth, flesh to flesh.

And then there had been a flurry of skin and heat and touch. Mouths clinging, and a pause, his hand slowly tracing her limbs, slowly caressing her until she gasped and did the same to him, wanting to return favour for favour, and a part of her wanting to make him moan as he made her, to control him as he was controlling her.

'I love you so much,' he had said, poised over her. 'You don't know how much, Ruby. You can't know how much.'

'I love you, too,' she said. 'Just as much.'

He laughed, shakily, and held himself back so he could stroke a hair out of her eyes. 'God, I hope so,' he said. Carefully, he lowered himself on her. She tried to help him, shifting under him, tilting her hips. Time seemed to slow down, for just a moment, as he touched her, and then sped up until the glory of that light before the altar exploded in her mind and Jimmy clutched her close, shaking, and said, 'Together for good, Ruby. For good, you and me.'

'No matter what,' she had said, holding him hard, burying her face in his slick shoulder, smelling the *Jimmy* smell, feeling his strength and his maleness and his love, all mixed up in one astonishing bundle called her husband.

Together for good. No matter what. It had been so easy to say it. So simple. Then.

'I love you,' Jimmy repeated now, his voice tender.

'I know,' she sighed, almost despondent that it was true, and that she couldn't maintain anger against him, that her body betrayed her, that all she wanted in the world was him against her, in her, fused to her.

So she pulled him down for a kiss and was astonished at the fountain of need and pleasure which followed.

Afterwards, she lay and cradled him. He slept abandoned in her arms, and it was hard to remember why she was angry with him when her body still sang with pleasure.

CHAPTER 33

Jimmy now walked her to work every day.

They had to leave a little earlier, because he couldn't walk as fast as she could. She disguised it, to save his pride, but of course he noticed. His face paled with chagrin, but he made a joke of it.

'I'm just lulling you into a false sense of security,' he said. 'Then one day I'll race ahead of you!'

She wouldn't let him walk her on rainy days, just in case he had a recurrence of the fever, and he allowed her to persuade him.

Every couple of days, as she walked up Johnston Street to do some shopping on her way home, she found Jimmy and Edward in the park. The first time, it had caught at her heart to see Jimmy pushing Eddie on the swing, the two blond heads, looking like father and son.

'More!' Eddie screamed, and Jimmy pushed him higher, far higher than Maree or she would; that was what fathers did, she thought. Pushed higher, hugged harder, stood firm.

'And *up* we go!' Jimmy said, laughing. She came across the grass to them and he turned and saw her, his face lighting up, his whole attitude one of welcome and love. One day it would be their son in the swing . . . He would make a wonderful father.

'Time to go, old man,' he said to Eddie, slowing the swing down.

'No! More! More!'

'No,' Jimmy said, as Maree came across the park towards them, shopping bags in hand. 'Here's Mum.'

Astonishingly, Eddie accepted this and held up his arms to Jimmy to be lifted from the swing. Ruby would have hefted him onto one hip, but Jimmy swung him upside down, an arm around his waist, with Eddie giggling helplessly, joyously. Jimmy gasped a little and set him on his feet.

'Don't do too much,' Ruby said.

'Hello, bub,' Maree said. She reached for Eddie's hand but he tucked his own hand in Jimmy's.

'Two boys together,' he said smugly.

Jimmy laughed. 'That's right, mate. Us blokes have got to stick together.'

They walked back to Mr Curry's – just across the street – and delivered a flushed, happy Edward back into the garden while Maree took the groceries inside. On the way home, Jimmy was pale, but he brushed off her concern.

'He's a good little bloke,' he said. 'He needs a bit of time with a man.' But she made him sit down and put his feet up when they got home. He pulled her into his arms as he sat and she went willingly, laughing as they kissed.

She worried less as the weeks went past and he started gaining weight and strength. By the end of July, when she met him and Eddie at the park, he could swing Eddie upside down without trouble.

He insisted, now, that he could go to the hospital on his own, and Ruby didn't object, glad of the chance to catch up on some invoices.

'Time to think about getting a job soon,' he said that night over crispy fish and chips.

Thank God! She'd thought it would be too soon, but if the doctors had told him it was all right . . . 'What do the doctors say?'

He glanced at her and hesitated, briefly, barely noticeable.

'Oh, they're full of "you need more time" and "don't rush things",' he said irritably, pushing his fish away half-eaten. 'But a man can't sit around the house all day and do nothing!'

Not all right, then. 'If you go back to work too soon, though, you might never get fully better.'

He looked her straight in the eyes, mouth hard, and said, 'Do y'reckon I'm going to get "fully better", Ruby? Really?'

'Yes,' she said. She gathered her resources. She'd known this argument was going to come, and she'd prepared for it. 'Stand up.'

He blinked, surprised, but complied. Ruby stood in front of him and said, 'Put your right hand on my shoulder.'

With some difficulty, he lifted his arm and placed his hand heavily on her shoulder. There was no control to it – it flopped down. His face twisted with disgust at his own weakness.

'When you got out of hospital, you could only bring your hand up to just above my waist,' she said. 'That's a few weeks' work. Who knows what another couple of months will bring?'

He squeezed her shoulder as best he could, then turned away and mumbled toward the fire. 'We're living on your money.'

'No, we're not,' she said. 'Not only on my money.'

'One pound ten a week!' he said bitterly. 'It's a joke.'

'It keeps a roof over our head,' she said. 'And it's only ten shillings less than I get.'

'Oh, I know, I know all the arguments,' he said, waving his left hand at her in dismissal, 'but a man should be able to support his wife.'

'A soldier who's been wounded in defence of his country can take the time he needs to recover.'

'Hmmph.' He returned to the table and attacked the fish and chips as if it were a Turkish battalion. She sat and ate as well. The chips were all the more delicious because she hadn't had to cook them, and she noted that he ate them even more easily than the mashed potato.

When he'd emptied his plate she rose and started to clear, but he caught her by the wrist, still staring down at the tablecloth. 'I am grateful, you know,' he said. 'The way you've coped . . . but . . . you don't – you don't *want* to keep working, do you?'

'Don't be silly,' she said. She dropped a kiss on his head. 'Once you get demobbed, we'll be back to normal, and then we can decide what we want to do.'

He let her go with a nod, but he still didn't look at her.

In the kitchen, she began to wash up, staring out the darkened window. The wind was alive outside, whipping the branches of the camphor laurel in the next yard. She heard a clunk as some branch hit the side of the house. Her hands soaped and rinsed the plates reflexively, without thought, slowly. Did she want to keep working? Had she just lied to him?

She had only taken the job because she had needed the money. But if she left . . . she felt a surge of something close to panic. Maree's words after Theo died kept echoing in her head. 'Who am I now?' Ruby didn't know who she was anymore either. It was as though she had been fractured, like a mirror split into shards, each reflecting a different person: the sheltered girl from Bourke whom Jimmy had married, the bookkeeper revelling in the calm certainty of numbers, the woman who had hauled Mr Curry out of his slough of despond, Maree's friend, and someone else, the woman she would have to become to make a life for herself and Jimmy.

The problem was, she didn't know who that woman was, or how to find her.

CHAPTER 34

August, 1916

There was a piece of notepaper on her desk, folded over. Ruby read the scrawled words – an invitation to Saturday dinner at Mr Curry's. She looked up to find Mr Curry watching her through the glass. She nodded to him and he stuck his lips out in a satisfied grimace and nodded back.

So there they were, at seven o'clock that Saturday, shined and dressed and polished: Jimmy in his uniform and her in her black skirt and jacket with a peacock blue silk blouse, a blouse she would never have worn to work. She hoped it was a compromise between office formality and social smartness.

Brigid, the between maid, let them in, dressed in her best black and white, and ushered them into the drawing room, where Mr Curry was waiting with a tray of sherry and glasses.

It was a pleasant evening for the most part, although the two men talked about nothing but the progress of the war. She hadn't realised that Jimmy had been following the

French campaigns so closely, or the submarine chases of the North Atlantic. She concentrated on a delicious roasted spatchcock, so tender Jimmy could pull it off the bones with his fork, and was simply glad that Maree had already gone home and didn't have to serve the meal. That would have been too awkward.

After dinner, they moved back to the drawing room. Mr Curry went to stand in front of the fireplace, which was leaping with flames and gave off the sweet smell of cedar. Jimmy stood on the other side, pretending he wasn't tired; not showing weakness.

Ruby settled in an armchair and prepared for another discussion about troop movements.

'I've got a proposition for you, Mr Hawkins,' Mr Curry said.

Ruby's first reaction was dismay. No, no, don't let him offer Jimmy a job! I couldn't keep working there if Jimmy was there . . . then she was ashamed.

Jimmy had stiffened. 'Sir?'

'Mrs Hannan tells me that you were training to be a stock and station agent when you joined up.'

'Yes, sir.' Non-committal. Jimmy's face was carefully blank.

'A friend of mine's a selling agent at the new Homebush saleyards. Have you been out there?'

'No.'

'It's a big operation. Stock sales, auctions, deliveries for the meat-works from country suppliers . . .'

'Yes,' Jimmy said, still non-committal but with a faint trace of interest creeping into his voice.

Ruby sat forward on her seat. If Mr Curry was going where she thought, it could answer all their problems.

'My friend – Winchcombe, his name is, with Winchcombe and Carson – he'll take you on as a trainee stock auctioneer. You'll have to pay, of course. That's the norm. But you'd get your training and a lot of experience which would stand you in good stead later.'

'It's a grand idea, sir,' Jimmy admitted, 'and it's good of you to think of it, but I don't think we can afford —'

'Two hundred pounds upfront,' Mr Curry said. 'A year's course, eighteen months if necessary, and you'd be paid for any auctions you conducted as you learnt more.' Too much, she thought. She had fifty-two pounds saved, and Jimmy would have eleven or twelve from the Army when he was demobbed. But not two hundred. Not when they'd have to live on her salary while he was training.

Jimmy whistled. 'Gosh. No, we couldn't afford it. Shame, though. It sounds exactly the kind of thing I'd like to do.'

'Well, that's what I wanted to talk to you about.' As though embarrassed, Mr Curry stared into the fire and kicked an errant log back into the grate. 'I could stake you to it. Lend you the two hundred, pay you a stipend until you find your feet. You'd pay me back in your own time.'

Oh, he was so generous! So kind. He was doing this for her, she knew.

Straightening, Jimmy stared at him. Even with the harsh electric light on his face, Ruby couldn't read his expression, but she felt a chill run down her spine.

'And what do you get out of it?' Jimmy demanded.

Mr Curry turned his head to the side to look at him, so that he looked oddly like a bird twisting its neck to see something. Then he stood up and brushed off his trouser legs. 'I get to keep Mrs Hawkins as a worker,' he said. 'You don't take her back to Bourke.'

Jimmy nodded silently, a strange nod with a stiff neck.

Angry, Ruby realised. He's angry.

'Well, thanks, sir, but I reckon that'd make me feel just a bit too much like a pimp.'

She gasped with affront. Mr Curry took one step forward and slapped Jimmy right across the mouth. Jimmy's left fist balled up, but the older man pushed him in the chest and he lost his balance and had to step back.

'If you were my son I'd wash your mouth out with soap, you ill-mannered young cur. Your wife's a saint to put up with you. She's a saint all around, if the truth be told, and all I'm trying to do is make life a bit easier for her, because she's earned it. And the only way to make her happy is to make you happy, because God knows why she loves you, but she does!'

Jimmy recovered his balance and stared at him with contempt. 'Don't give me that,' he said bitterly. 'You want her to stay because she carries the business when you crawl into your hole. Think I haven't noticed?'

'Get out of my house,' Mr Curry said with tight anger.

'We're going!' Jimmy snapped. 'Come on, Ruby.' He grabbed his Army cap from the table and strode to the door, held it open for her.

Slowly, she stood up and went to Mr Curry. Touched him on the arm. 'Thank you, sir. It was a good thought. I'm sorry.'

'Don't you apologise for me!' Jimmy said, harsh and hard.

Mr Curry pushed his mouth out and blew a long breath through his nostrils.

'Off you go. I'll see you on Monday.'

'Yes, sir,' she said quietly. Mortified. But not angry. There was too much pain in this single room for her to be angry with either man.

As she and Jimmy walked down the steps to the street, he said, in an exculpatory tone, 'Ruby —'

'Best not to talk about it,' she said. 'Leave it be.'

Wisely, he did.

As they let themselves in and got ready for bed without speaking, she thought of this time last year. She had been learning the ropes at Curry's and writing letters to Jimmy about how nothing would change; how when he came home it would be just like it was before he left.

He was surprised when she kissed him passionately as they got into bed; he had assumed, she knew, that she was furious with him. But remembering that time, when she had been so worried about him, so simply worried about death, made her cherish him, made her grab this moment, this single precious moment, and hold it close. She felt, obscurely, that she *ought* to be angry with him; but life was too short for reproaches and arguments. Much too short.

Jimmy had nightmares that night, so she got up and sat in the dark in the parlour, listening to him struggle with remembered enemies, heart pounding with fear, helpless to do anything to protect him from the death stalking his dreams.

CHAPTER 35
29th August, 1916

'Rube,' Jimmy said, sticking his head into the bathroom where she was brushing her teeth, 'give my best to the old man today, eh?' His tone was conciliatory but there was a note of genuine feeling in it. He had avoided mentioning her work or Mr Curry for a week since the dinner.

Ruby rinsed and spat and enjoyed turning on the tap to wash the result down the drain. So much more sanitary than at Maree's, where they had to use the kitchen sink.

'Your best?'

'It's the anniversary. Twenty-ninth of August. Last day of Hill 60. When his boy got the chop.'

She had forgotten. How could she have forgotten? It was a Tuesday. Mr Curry had three meetings that morning: one with the Army and two with suppliers. She had made the appointments herself. 'I should have remembered,' she said, hairbrush in hand, but she couldn't move, couldn't make herself do the habitual things that would get her out the door.

God help her, she didn't want to face him today. If he came in at all. Perhaps that would be best; she could call the Army captain to cancel – he wasn't due until eleven. She could probably handle the two suppliers herself.

Guiltily, she wanted him to stay away. She was already looking after Jimmy – she didn't want to go back to looking after Mr Curry as well. She had a flash of annoyance at men in general. Why couldn't they look after themselves?

'I'll tell him,' she said. 'It's nice of you to think of it.'

'We lost a lot of men that day,' Jimmy said heavily. 'Freemie and me are getting together. He's living out Pendle Hill way with his sister Ruby and her husband, so we're going to have a drink in the city, us and a couple of other Gallipoli men.'

'Good idea,' Ruby said. It might do him good to consider that he could have been far less lucky. She hoped he came home more hopeful, less annoyed with his own limitations. 'I'll expect you when I see you, then,' she added.

Mr Curry wasn't at work.

Wal and Wesley looked to her for an explanation, and she gave it. They nodded fatalistically and got back to work while she rang the Army captain to cancel, but she couldn't contact him. 'Out,' was all his staff would say.

It was a difficult day. There were too many decisions to be made. The two suppliers didn't want to deal with a woman – one of them flat out refused to talk to her.

'You tell Curry I deal with him or no one!' he said to her, his face tight and closed. 'Tell him he's a fool to trust his business to a female!'

Wesley looked as though he agreed, but as the man slammed the door shut behind him, he said, 'The labourer is worthy of his hire,' to her.

She blinked. 'Thank you, Mr Wilson,' she said. 'Thank you very much.'

It was the only good note in the day. The second supplier, a thin, wiry old man from Taree with a brown, intelligent face, reluctantly agreed to sit down in her office – with the door open – and talk about schedules and log sizes and grades equably enough, but he would not talk money with her.

'Will can give me a call,' he said to her. It took her a moment to realise he meant Mr Curry. 'We've been doing business together for a mort o' years, and I trust him. No offence, missus, but I don't know you from a bar of soap.'

He got up and planted his battered old hat on his head and nodded to her, politely, then shook hands with both Wesley and Wal, and went on his way.

The men looked at her with identically dubious expressions.

'It's not my fault they won't talk to me,' she said, and knew as soon as she said it that it was a mistake. She bit back another excuse. No need to throw kerosene on the fire.

'If he's not back tomorrow I'll go up to the house,' she said. It felt like it had last year; the anxiety almost choked her. Then she remembered she had an ally, the only other person who knew the full story of what had happened to Mr Curry the year before, and she picked up the 'phone.

'Maree? How is he?'

'He's dressed, but he's sitting in the son's room,' she said. 'He's not good, but he's not as bad as you might expect.'

Relief flooded through her. 'You'll have had a hard day,' she said. 'Do you want to come over for dinner?'

'Lovely,' Maree said. 'A treat not to cook.'

Ruby clicked the earpiece down on its stand feeling vaguely comforted. At least she wasn't dealing with it all by herself this time. The outside office door opened. No doubt the Army captain, and he wouldn't be pleased, either, to be dealing with a woman.

But it was Jimmy. Jimmy looking thunderous, mutinous, more annoyed than she'd ever seen him, his right hand stuck in his pocket so hard she could see the tight curl of his fingers against the cloth.

He cast a look around the room, saw her and came to her office without so much as a nod to Wal or Wesley. They were staring and she blushed with mortification. What had got into him?

He slammed her door behind him with his left hand so that the glass panels shook, sending slivers of reflection trembling across her eyes.

'What's the matter?'

He scowled at her. 'I need money.'

Ruby blinked. 'Well, of course.' She opened her desk drawer for her purse. 'Why didn't you ask me this morning?'

'Because I thought I could go to the post office and get some, instead of crawling on hands and knees to my wife.'

Wallet in hand, she just stared at him. He went on, bitterly, 'But my signature doesn't match, does it? Because I can't use my right hand, can I? So I have to get the doctor to sign the form to say I can't sign the way I used to, before I can have my own bloody money, don't I?'

Oh, dear God in Heaven.

There was nothing she could say. She had begun using her father's old wallet for her notes back in Bourke, after he died. A small memory of him. Rather than dole out money to Jimmy, she handed him the wallet unopened. There was enough there to get him good and drunk and pay for a cab home afterwards. He took it from her ungraciously and then recognised it, remembered what it represented. It calmed him a little – he hadn't known her father, having come to Bourke well after his death, but she had spoken of him often.

She didn't smile at Jimmy; she didn't tell him everything would be all right. But she looked at him with all the compassion she felt; and she saw his face change, the hard lines softening, the hint of humour coming back to his mouth.

It would all have been all right if Wesley hadn't knocked at the door.

Jimmy took a short breath, surprised, and then his face hardened again as he turned to wrench the door open.

'Sorry to interrupt, Mrs Hawkins,' Wesley said, face carefully blank, 'but the Army chap is here.'

She hadn't even registered the outer door opening. The two men were blocking her view of the big room. Ruby rose and came around the desk and they moved ahead of her, out of her little office. There was a corporal standing, hat in hand, next to Wal and Wesley's double desk.

'Tom!' she said, not thinking, pleased to see him just a little beyond what was proper. Tom's eyes were fixed on her but his face was expressionless. Then Jimmy moved up behind her, warm at her shoulder, and she drew a breath in and turned to him. 'Jimmy, this is Tom McBride, you remember, I wrote to you that he was Curry's foreman and had joined up?'

'I never got that one,' Jimmy said shortly.

He nodded to McBride and Tom said, 'Glad you got back all right.' He grinned, 'You should thank Wesley here. He had his whole church praying for you, even though you're a heathen Catholic.'

Wal laughed and even Wesley smiled a thin, prim smile, but Jimmy didn't share the joke. There was an uncomfortable silence. The men seemed to be waiting for her to speak.

'I was expecting your captain,' she said, keeping it all light.

'They've put me to supervising the construction of the new barracks. That's why I'm here – they thought I'd know better what to order. And maybe get a better discount.' He made a disgusted face. 'Nanny duty for a wooden hut, that's what I've got.'

Jimmy moved forwards, brushing past Ruby and skirting the other side of the double desk to reach the door. He paused with his hand on the knob and looked at Tom, who had twisted to watch him go.

'Don't be in too much of a hurry to get over there,' he said. His eyes met Ruby's for just a moment, but there was no trace of softness in them, and he banged out the door the moment after without looking back.

Wordlessly, Ruby ushered Tom – Corporal McBride – into her office.

Ruby was reminded of the last time they had met; but both of them were strictly businesslike, concentrating on lumber and sawn timber and delivery dates and costs.

The Army was right; it was much easier to deal with Tom – with Corporal McBride – than with other clients. He knew exactly what they needed and was realistic about timelines.

He haggled on cost. He grinned at her when she was surprised.

'Got to do it, Mrs Hawkins,' he said. 'Have to be able to say I tried, at least.'

Yes, and he wouldn't lie. Tom McBride's honesty was like a horse's mettle – it showed in every movement and expression.

She gave him a discount; the kind of thing Mr Curry would probably have done anyway, since it was the Army.

'I'll have it drawn up for Mr Curry to sign,' she said.

'He's not in?' That wasn't the corporal speaking, it was the old Tom, his face concerned and compassionate.

'I should have remembered before I made the appointment,' she said. 'It's the anniversary of Laurence's . . .'

'Poor old bastard,' he said.

'Yes.' They looked at each other in a moment of perfect shared understanding. Ruby felt tears sharply hot at the back of her eyes. It wasn't Jimmy's fault that she couldn't lean on him; he'd been injured, he wasn't responsible for his weakness. But she had depended on Tom McBride, and she felt his absence every day.

'Is – is everything all right?' he asked, gently. 'Your husband seemed upset.'

The temptation to pour it all out to Tom was immense; almost overwhelming. But Jimmy was her husband. She had to be loyal to him, even though Tom's solicitude made her want to cry even more.

'He lost a lot of friends at Hill 60,' she said. Perhaps her eyes said something else, because his eyes darkened and his mouth tightened with concern.

'Ah. Yes. Of course.' He stood up, dusted off the seat of his trousers. 'Best be off, then.' He bent his head, fiddling with the stripe on his cap. 'Probably see you again soon, the way things are at Liverpool.' He glanced up, sharply, to gauge her reaction.

Ruby fought to put on her best 'visitor's voice', the way her mother had taught her. 'Yes. That will be nice.'

He nodded, his mouth clamped, then wiped his hand across his face as though ridding himself of whatever sentiment it had exposed, and left after a few moments with Wal and Wesley.

He went out by the yard door, to say hello to Smith and the men, and the sound as the door closed, cutting off the whine of saws and the hammers from the packing crate factory next door, was like a full stop at the end of a long, complicated sentence. Done with. Over, that's what that noise said. Ruby shifted her shoulders to resettle herself and handed the sheaf of orders to Wesley.

'That's what we've agreed on, Mr Wilson. Would you draw it up ready for Mr Curry to sign, please?'

A moment later they were all back at work as though nothing out of the ordinary had happened.

CHAPTER 36

Ruby went by the butcher's on the corner of Nelson Street and got some chuck steak and kidneys and some suet. She would make a steak and kidney pie and chips – one of Jimmy's favourites, and they hadn't had it since he came home.

Maree and Edward arrived at seven, after Maree had served Mr Curry's dinner.

'Not that he'll eat it,' she said gloomily, making a slice of bread and butter for Edward. 'Where's Jim?'

They sat at the kitchen table, which was ready laid. Ruby had even had time to pick some flowers from the garden.

'I don't know,' Ruby said. 'Out with Arthur Freeman. Drinking.'

'Ah, well,' Maree said. 'We might as well eat. They could be out all night. You know they've changed the closing time in pubs to six o'clock? Only some temperance idiot would have thought of that one. They'll just come home and drink and get in their wives' way.'

Ruby wished that Jimmy would come home and drink. He was strong enough now to go around the city by himself, but he wasn't fully recovered, and she couldn't believe that a day and an evening drinking would do him any good.

She served up the pie, which looked so good it seemed a shame to cut into the gleaming crust. Edward was jumping in his seat; he loved pie too.

'Careful, it's hot,' Ruby warned him, then the front door slammed back and Jimmy lurched through the hallway into the kitchen.

'What are you doing here?' he demanded of Maree.

She stared him down. Ruby was reminded that she had been a waitress before her marriage – no doubt she had seen her fair share of drunk men.

'Having dinner,' she said. 'Here, Eddie, have a chip.'

'Steak and kidney pie!' Ruby said brightly, for Eddie's sake. 'Your favourite.'

He sniffed the air, swaying a little, then said, 'Oh, Christ!' and ran for the bathroom.

They could hear him being sick. The unpleasant noise echoed around the little house.

'Let's hope he made it to the basin,' Maree said.

Ruby grimaced, then they caught each other's eye and collapsed into laughter, the helpless, resigned laughter of women who knew they'd have to do the cleaning up.

Jimmy came back, wiping his face with his handkerchief, glaring at them.

'So I'm funny, am I? Go ahead, laugh.' His speech was still slurred.

Ruby and Maree sobered but neither of them got up to help him.

'Chips, Unca Jimmy?' Eddie offered, doing his best to help.

Jimmy glared at Ruby and avoided looking at Eddie. At least he has the grace to be ashamed of himself, Ruby thought.

He stared with loathing at the pie, which was oozing gravy and smelled delicious, and not-quite-staggered to the bedroom. He shut the door behind him with a sharp clack.

'He'll have a head on him in the morning,' Maree said.

Eddie frowned and told her, very seriously, 'He already has a head, Mummy.'

They laughed again, but quietly. After they'd eaten and Maree had helped her wash up, Ruby saw them out to the street and watched as they walked away home, Eddie snuggled in Maree's arms, his head on her shoulders.

The familiar pang of envy went through her. Every time she saw a baby lately, she wanted one of her own. It was an ache in her belly, her nipples, under her breasts, a tightness in her throat, a prickling behind the corners of her eyes.

They couldn't afford a baby. They should be careful. She'd had a scare last month, when her monthly flow came late, and light. There were ways . . . the Church forbade them, however, and she knew she could never resort to such unnaturalness. Which left abstinence. There were so many different theories about *when* to abstain; she could never get it all straight. Even the doctors didn't agree.

Which left them with only one choice: total abstinence. In her heart, she knew that it would never happen. She wouldn't even bother to discuss it with Jimmy. Marital relations were the only real moments of joy in his life, and she couldn't take them away from him and remain his wife.

It was a fine evening with high cloud reflecting the city lights. The wattle was everywhere and the scent of freesias from the neighbour's garden went to her head. She was reluctant to go back into the stuffy house. To Jimmy. The Lord knew he had every right to get drunk with his mates, on today of all days, but she hoped he was already asleep.

The lights in the bedroom were out, so she tiptoed in. Jimmy was standing at the window in his undershirt and trousers, looking out into the dark, at the clouds massing over the hills to the south. She stood in the doorway and watched him, aware as she always was of his lean good looks, the carriage of his head, the perfect line of his spine. Despite herself, she felt warmth creep into her blood.

'That McBride,' he said. 'He's in love with you.'

'What?' She was unprepared.

'I read your letters in the hospital in Cairo. You talked a lot about this bloke McBride, but I didn't think anything of it. Thought he was an old bloke, like most foremen. But today –' He rubbed the back of his neck, and his hand shook – 'I saw him look at you. *And* he's a bloody corporal!' As if that were an insult.

She hadn't thought about it. But of course he was. Jimmy had joined the Army as a worker, used to taking orders from his employers. Tom had joined up used to giving them. Of course the Army had realised that and made use of it. It took the best and the worst in men and used all of it. The heroism, the courage, the young boy's idealism – and the desire to bully and kill and maim; authority and despotism, bravery and deceit. All of it.

'He's in love with you,' he said again. If there had been suspicion in his voice, or anger, she would have known how to react, but there was nothing except pain. She felt a stupid, juvenile impulse to protect Tom, but this was her marriage and she could offer Jimmy nothing but the truth.

'Yes, I think he is.'

He flinched as if she'd struck him, and then took a deep, steadying breath.

'He seemed like a good bloke.'

Memories flickered over her. That time in the back of the storage shed when she had been glad Tom hadn't tried to kiss her; staring into his eyes as she wrote down Frieman's details; day after day of being glad to see him, of being happy he was there. The day he had left.

'Yes. He's a good man. That's why he joined up,' she said, going to him and sliding an arm around his waist, laying her head against his bare, warm shoulder. The good shoulder, so she wouldn't hurt him.

'He knew nothing could ever happen,' she said, just to make sure he understood.

'It's hard, looking at someone like him – someone . . . whole.' He was fighting to find the right words, and his left hand gripped the curtain as if for stability. 'Hard not to think you'd be better off with him.'

A shudder ran through her, quick and instinctive. 'No!' she said sharply, perhaps more sharply because she had had flickers of wondering what it would be like, to be with Tom. 'I belong with you.'

He turned eagerly to her, reaching out his good hand.

'Then come back with me to Bourke!' he said. 'I'll pick up a job there, we'll get a house. It'll be just like we planned.'

The thought of it made her feel sick to her stomach; she was surprised by how strong her revulsion was. To go back, to turn back into that naïve, dependent country girl, that was what he wanted of her; that was what Bourke meant to him. A Ruby who no longer existed. A life she couldn't bear to live. Could she say that to him? No. No. She couldn't hurt him like that, not now, when he'd think it had something to do with Tom McBride. Later they could talk more sensibly. Time. They needed time. And there was another good reason not to go back.

'You still have rehabilitation to do,' she reminded him, but she took his hands, the fingers of the right curled hard against hers, reinforcing her purpose. 'We can't go until the doctors say it's all right. For that matter, we can't go until you've been demobbed.'

Jimmy was officially still part of the Army, on medical leave. Probably they wouldn't care if he went back to Bourke, but he couldn't take another job without being discharged first.

His shoulders slumped and he let her hands drop.

'And you have to work,' he said, 'because we need the money.'

'Yes,' she whispered. It hurt her badly to deny him, but she had to stay clear-headed.

'And you'll see that McBride all the time, I suppose?' His voice was despondent.

She jerked back in surprise and hurt. 'You think that would matter?'

'Couldn't blame you for wanting more than I can give you.'

'If you think that, you don't know me at all.'

He simply stared at her, leaving the words ringing in the silence. Ruby could feel a part of her heart break off, leaving a sharp edge behind. It hurt. Blindly, she picked up her nightdress and went to the bathroom to change and brush her teeth, because there was nothing she could say in reply to the dumb misery in Jimmy's eyes.

•

Mr Curry wasn't there again in the morning, but she didn't care. She just got on with her work. If he wasn't there the next day, then she would go up to the house. For now, she sought refuge in the calm certainty of numbers. At lunchtime, with a full bladder and reluctant to see Jimmy, she changed her mind.

'I'm going up to the house,' she announced at noon.

Wal and Wesley just nodded, and she realised how normal this all was now. How they all took it for granted, that she would deal with the emotional crisis and give the orders until Mr Curry came back.

She wondered what might happen to Mr Curry – to all of them – if she went back to Bourke with Jimmy. The thought gave her a curl of unease in her belly, and the sense of a burden settling on her shoulders.

As soon as Maree answered the door Ruby dashed to the downstairs WC, the servants' lavatory. When she came back through the kitchen, Maree was waiting with a sandwich and a glass of milk. Ruby gulped them down.

'He's up in the boy's room,' Maree said as Ruby ate.

Eddie came running in from the garden, smelling of new grass and, faintly, of manure.

'Auny Ruby!' he cried and flung himself at her in rapture, knocking over the thankfully empty glass.

'He misses you,' Maree said dryly, setting it upright as Ruby cuddled Eddie.

'I miss *him*,' she said.

They looked at each other and Maree's face changed, becoming concerned.

'I'll tell you later,' Ruby said. 'Come on, Eddie, let's go and say hello to Mr Curry.'

'Do you think —?'

'It'll do him good,' Ruby said firmly.

Eddie climbed the stairs laboriously, holding her hand, chattering about the sparrows and the willy wagtail in the garden, 'And I foun' a *worm*, Auny Ruby! It was *wiggerally!*'

'Goodness me,' Ruby admired. She knocked briefly on the door to Laurence's room and then opened it. 'Look who I've brought to see you!'

As she'd feared, Mr Curry was only half dressed, back in his old spot on the chair by the desk. He glared at her with bloodshot eyes but the expression faltered as he saw Eddie.

'No place for him,' he said, his voice grating with disuse. He cleared his throat and said, 'Off you go, Eddie.'

But Eddie had found an old cricket ball on one of the shelves. 'Ball!' he said with delight.

Mr Curry reached out as though to snatch it from him, and then slumped back. 'Well, why not? It might as well get some use.'

'Go to the garden, Ed, and try it out,' Ruby suggested. She went the door with him, checking that Maree was waiting outside. They nodded to each other as she shut the door.

'Will you be coming in tomorrow, sir?' she asked Mr Curry.

'I suppose,' he said, sounding thoroughly put upon. She had to shake him out of it, and she had only one weapon.

'Tom McBride came in yesterday to negotiate the new rates and orders. You missed him.' It was petty of her to add that, but she wanted to spur him to movement. She didn't think she could bear a long, lingering renewal of mourning. Not now.

To her astonishment, he turned and stared at her with concern. 'That why you couldn't sleep last night? For seeing him?'

'Don't be ridiculous!'

'Fight with your husband, then?'

She didn't answer, but perhaps that was answer enough. He hoisted himself to his feet and went to stare out the window. She was reminded of Jimmy, the night before. Was this something all men did when they were thinking of unpleasant things?

'When's Tom coming back?'

'Next week,' she said. 'Tuesday.'

'Better be there, then. Better if I handle those meetings.'

'You don't think —'

'I know Tom. And I had a pretty good guess as to why he joined up. I'll handle the rest of the Army negotiations.' He paused, looking down at the garden, avoiding her eyes. 'For his sake.'

She swallowed against a lump in her throat. 'Thank you,' she said. 'For his sake.'

She left without another word and went down the stairs and out the front door without saying goodbye to Maree or Eddie, and back to work, to reassure the men that the boss would be back the next week, to finish the end-of-month accounts, to begin to write out the cheques which Mr Curry would sign on Friday, to work and work and work so she wouldn't have to think about anything, anything at all.

CHAPTER 37

September, 1916

'Well, it's not as bad as it might be,' Maree said as they found seats on the tram back to Annandale.

'You have the house,' Ruby said. 'And you'll have *something* behind you.'

They had been to see Theo's solicitor for the final settlement of his affairs. The Army had released his pay at last. There would be some money; but not enough for Maree to stay where she was without working.

'Mr Curry'll be pleased,' Ruby joked, and Maree smiled.

'Things could be a lot worse,' she agreed.

They spent the rest of the trip talking Red Cross and the war. Ruby wondered, not for the first time in the past few days, whether she should ask Maree for advice. She was three weeks late. But how late did you have to be before you went to the doctor?

The idea of a baby simultaneously excited, uplifted, terrified and dismayed her.

They would have to move, to go back to Bourke as soon as the doctors released Jimmy, to move in with her mother.

Well. That might not be so bad, if her mother was living at Barkinji. For a moment her mind filled with images of the station: the wide skies, the space, the silence. A lorry next to the tram had shrieking brakes, and she winced. In Barkinji, the only sounds were the wind and the birds and the cattle. She could bear to live at Barkinji – living with her mother might be another thing altogether. How embarrassing to ask her for free board and lodging. It would be a long time before Jimmy could make himself useful on the station, if he ever could. They would be dependants, hangers-on.

Maybe she was mistaken. Maybe she was just late, or had skipped a month. That had happened to Myrtle once.

'Are you all right?' Maree asked.

Should she tell her? No. Better talk to Jimmy first.

'Fine,' she lied.

Maree's eyes searched her face and then, disconcertingly, dropped to her belly. Instinctively, Ruby put her hand protectively over her abdomen.

Maree nodded once, and settled back in her seat.

Ruby was filled with a strange satisfaction. Being understood without words, having her privacy respected; that was a friend indeed.

•

All through dinner she hesitated over whether to tell Jimmy. The knowledge of his inevitable delight and excitement delayed her – she wasn't sure she'd be able to match it, and she didn't think he would understand her divided heart.

She stacked the dishes in the sink and filled the kettle still undecided. She felt so odd. Even thinking about a baby was making her light-headed.

The full kettle was heavy. She swung it across to the stove and, as she set it down, felt a pain, sharp and scraping, across her stomach.

A short pain, and then another, which doubled her over, as though a cramp had been magnified a thousandfold.

She cried out.

Jimmy pushed back from the table and caught her by the elbow, his weak hand unable to steady her so that she stumbled and would have fallen against the hot stove but that he pushed himself in front of it and she fell against him.

The pain came again and again and with a sick inevitability she felt her thighs grow wet.

'Ruby! You're bleeding!'

'Bathroom,' she breathed through set teeth. He half-dragged her through the door and she managed to get her drawers down and sit on the toilet, leaning forward, grabbing her stomach with one arm and the side of the basin with the other.

There was a trail of blood on the floor behind them. A mixture of old, dark clots and bright red. Grief rushed through her. Any doubts she'd had about the wisdom of having a baby were washed away; she sat and mourned, rocking herself as shaft after shaft of pain went through her.

'I'll call the doctor!'

He was gone only a few minutes, but it seemed so long to

be alone. She was crying, she realised. When he came back he crouched beside her and rubbed her back.

'Women's troubles?' he asked diffidently.

'A slip,' she gasped. His face showed that he didn't understand the term. 'Baby. Losing the baby.'

His face went absolutely still and he stood up, taking his hand away, but she couldn't attend to him. Surely it shouldn't hurt so much when she was still so early? Three weeks was nothing. Thinking back, her last monthly had been very light, hardly more than spotting. She had put it down to stress.

She bit back a scream as another pain hit.

The doctor came soon after, but there was little he could do but reassure her that these things happened. After the pains stopped, he gave her an injection of something, she didn't know what, and packed bandages between her legs; she was past embarrassment at that point, but she vaguely knew that she would feel embarrassed about it later.

She heard the doctor say to Jimmy, 'Oh, two months, maybe three. She'll vomit when she wakes up, probably, with what I've given her.'

It speared her heart; she didn't know why it was worse to lose a two-month-old rather than a three-week-old baby, but it was.

She curled on one side and let the tears flow as she drifted off.

•

She didn't wake until afternoon, and lay there, drained and feeling curiously light, floating, as though the baby had tied her down to the world and now there was nothing to tether her.

The house felt empty, filled with the yellow light of an early spring day. She wondered where Jimmy was; it seemed odd of him not to be there. Shopping, maybe. They didn't have much in the house.

A door banged – the back door. Jimmy came through to the bedroom, bringing the scent of grass with him. It made her feel as though she wanted to vomit. There was a bucket by the bed.

He stood looking at her, his face blank. She waited for the questions: Are you all right? Can I get you anything?

'Why didn't you tell me?' he asked, voice clipped.

Oh, God. Not now. She didn't have the strength for this conversation. But it had been his baby, too.

'I wasn't sure.' Her voice was whispery, faint. She cleared her throat.

'Two months, the doctor said. Maybe three.'

She shook her head. 'Not that long. Two, maybe, but I didn't suspect anything until the last week or two.'

He stared at her. She was reminded of that first night home, when he had come up out of sleep looking at her as though she were an enemy.

'Why didn't you tell me?'

'I was waiting until I was sure.' It sounded weak, even to her.

His face broke from its mask, his mouth working, his eyes tormented. 'Did you get rid of it? Is that why you went to the city? To get rid of it before I found out? So you could keep your precious job?'

She had trouble understanding him. Surely he didn't mean . . . he *couldn't* mean . . .

She vomited into the bucket next to her, twisting over it although her whole midsection protested, muscles and organs sore and tender. Jimmy waited until she had finished. Until she was wiping her face.

'Did you?' he asked, implacable.

'I'd as soon shoot you,' she said viciously, and let him take that as he might. 'Get away from me.'

His face worked again, as if he were going to cry, but she had no sympathy for him, staring back at him with a hardness she hadn't known she possessed. He turned on his heel and went out, slamming the door behind him, and the front door after that.

Ruby vomited again. When she felt better, she realised, she would feel anguished about this, but now she seemed to have been reduced to blood and vomit and tears, with no room for thought at all.

•

Some time later, she made it to the telephone to call Maree, who came with chicken broth and fresh bread and removed the vomit and cleaned the bathroom floor and washed the bloodstained clothes, and helped her, eventually, to sit up in a chair in the lounge room while she changed the bed.

Ruby rested her head back against the chair and thanked God for her friend.

Maree heated the soup and gave her a mug of it, just warm enough. She hadn't asked any questions about where Jimmy was, but she deserved an answer.

'Jimmy thinks we went to the city to get – to get rid of the baby.'

'Bloody moron.' Ruby had never heard Maree swear before. She smiled with gratitude.

As though called, Jimmy came through the front door. He stopped and looked at the two of them as though he'd caught them red-handed in a bank robbery.

'You,' Maree said, 'are the stupidest man I've ever met. No matter how big an apology you give her, it won't be big enough.' She put her hat on and kissed Ruby on the cheek. 'I'll be back tomorrow.'

Jimmy moved aside for her as she left, but she didn't look at him, nor he at her. He was staring at Ruby. She wondered what she looked like. She *felt* white; as though drained of everything that made living possible. She hadn't even come back to life enough to feel grief. Everything was very far away and unimportant. Jimmy was still suspicious, but she didn't care.

It was a woman's job to keep peace in the home; no doubt she should explain, and placate, and soothe. Bugger him. Let him stew in his own bile.

She became aware she was still holding the mug of soup, and put it down, shakily, on the side table.

Jimmy stood for a moment and then went through to the kitchen. She heard him light the gas. Making tea? He came back – had she drifted off to sleep? It had seemed only a second, but he had a tea tray. He put it on the other side table and poured tea, but she shook her head when he offered her the cup. He put it down and contemplated it, tension in his shoulders and down his arms, his face dark with anger or shame.

'All right. Maybe I was wrong. But you should have told me.'

So he was going to force her to talk about it.

'If you ever accuse me of anything like that ever again,' she said, quietly, politely, like a lady, 'I will ask you to leave this house.'

His hand shook as he poured himself a cup of tea, sprinkling the table with spots of brown, which reminded her of the bathroom floor.

'Fair enough,' he said, but she realised that the shaking was suppressed rage. Or humiliation, perhaps. 'Your name's on the lease. I guess you're the boss.'

She wouldn't rise to that. Part of her, a distant, uncaring part, realised that he didn't love her. No one who loved her could accuse her of that. No one who loved her would believe it. No one who loved her would sit there and not see that her heart had been torn out. But she didn't have the strength to feel anything about that, not right now.

'Sorry,' he muttered.

'All right then,' she answered, just wanting it over with.

He relaxed, immediately, as though it were all over. As though she would forget.

As if she could.

•

'If he goes back to Bourke, I could divorce him for abandonment and move to Melbourne,' Ruby said. There was a pleasure in saying the terrible words out loud. The scandal, the gossip, the social disgrace. Who cared? Her baby was gone and her husband didn't love her. Social disgrace would just mean that she didn't have to talk to anyone. She felt, right now, that she could cope with that easily. Maree would still talk to her. Ruby cast off another three stitches at the beginning of the row. Finally, under Maree's tutelage, she was getting the hang of turning the heel of a sock.

'Yes, you could,' Maree said, knitting industriously, the light coming over her shoulder from her lounge-room window. On the street outside, some children played late afternoon games. The sound of young voices made Ruby cold. 'You think I'm joking!'

'I think that you need to fully recover before you make any decisions.'

'The doctor says I'm fine.'

'The doctor only cares about your body. Have you cried yet?'

A shiver ran through Ruby. Even the word 'body' brought back memories of the blood and the pain. How could her mother have gone through that four times and come out sane?

She was her mother's daughter, after all; she just wanted to pretend it had never happened. No, she hadn't cried. 'He doesn't love me,' she said.

Eddie ran in from the garden, going full pelt as he always did, and threw himself into Ruby's arms. She had to put her hands in the air so he didn't spike himself on the knitting needles. He buried his head against her waist, and she felt a shadow of pain, like an old bruise being pressed.

'Auny Ruby, there's flaars! Yerrow and red and blue.'

'There's no red,' Maree said, laughing. 'Just hyacinths and daffodils.'

'Yerrow and *white* and blue!' Eddie amended. He hugged her and she wrapped her arms around his strong, little-boy body. He smelled of child. She tried to breathe; a long inhale turned into a hiccuping sob, and then she was crying, finally, helplessly.

Maree sent Eddie back out into the garden and sat next to Ruby on the daybed, patting her back. 'That's it,' she said. 'Get it out. Better out than in.'

Gasping, Ruby said, 'Like shit.'

A thread of humour in her tone, Maree nodded, patting a little harder. 'Yes. Just exactly like shit.'

A while later, Ruby rang her mother. She had been putting it off; part of her was surprised her mother hadn't called her, hadn't known that something was wrong.

'I didn't want to call,' her mother said after the first greetings. 'I know how it is – you don't want to talk to anyone.'

So she *had* known. Ruby was filled with gratitude for her understanding. 'Thank you.'

'The grief stays with you the rest of your life,' Cecilia said baldly, 'but it moves to the back of your mind.'

Honesty. She could depend on her mother for honesty.

'Thanks, Mum. I'll be all right.'

'Of course you will. But take care of yourself.'

•

Much later, on the walk home, she considered divorce again. Unless Jimmy left her, it was unobtainable to her. But she could simply leave. If she left Jimmy, she would never marry again. She couldn't, in the eyes of the Church. She had sworn a sacred vow to be faithful to him, and she would keep it.

Which meant she would *never* have children. An echo of pain swept through her. Was it worth living with someone who didn't love her in order to have children?

Perhaps it was.

Because, unfortunately, she still loved him.

CHAPTER 38

6th October, 1916

The calendar said it was still spring, but summer was blowing in on the back of a westerly wind; red dust from the inland made the sunset glorious.

Ruby paused at the top of Taylor Street to look at the vermilion and gold clouds, glad of a moment's respite from carrying the heavy grocery bag. She wished she could shift shopping to Monday; it would be lovely to have a quiet Friday afternoon in an empty house. Friday was the only day Jimmy wasn't waiting for her, and things were still tense between them. Perhaps he wouldn't be back from the hospital yet, and she could have a cup of tea in peace without the sense of pressure surrounding her, without the feeling that he was silently asking her for something she couldn't identify.

As she set down her bag to put her key in the lock, the door opened.

'What's the matter?' she asked. Jimmy looked terrible. White. It was a look she knew – the face of grief. 'Is it Arthur?'

'No,' he said. He picked up her bag of groceries with his left hand and took it through to the kitchen, Ruby following. The bag thumped down on the table, the jars of jam and honey rattling.

'What's happened?'

'I'm being demobbed. Next Friday.'

'That – that's good, isn't it?'

'There's nothing more the doctors can do for me.' His voice was flat.

He turned to fill the kettle and put it on the stovetop, doing every action with an unthinking avoidance of his right arm; left hand only. So it was grief. She felt it herself, a terrible grief welling up for the death of hope, the end of progress, the failure of the future.

'What did they say?' She made her voice serene. He was fighting so hard to keep it under control, she had to help him by being as calm as possible.

'I can keep doing my exercises, and they want you to come and learn how to do the massage on my shoulder, but apart from that there's nothing they can do. The pieces of shrapnel are in too deep. If they operate they might take out a big blood vessel and kill me. So I'm on my own.'

'Not on your own!' Her protest was quick and instinctive, and it brought a swift, unreadable glance from him. 'If you keep doing the exercises –' she ventured – 'surely you'll improve slowly over time.'

'Not enough to be useful to the Army,' he said. 'Not even

as a paper-pusher.' His voice was full of the scorn of an active man for a clerk.

He said nothing else until the kettle boiled. She filled in the silence by putting the groceries away. There was a bag of jammy biscuits; she laid them out on a plate and at the sweet scent, her tummy rumbled. It felt like a betrayal, that she could still be hungry despite him being so upset.

When the kettle whistled she moved to make the tea, but he shook his head and made it himself; perhaps he had to show that he could be useful still. They sat at the table and went through the ritual of pouring, sugaring and milking. Throughout, Jimmy avoided looking at her.

He fiddled with the sugar spoon and turned his cup in its saucer, round and round. Ruby sipped the tea thankfully. Its sweet warmth was a comfort, but even more comforting was the ritual, having something to hide behind. She bit into a biscuit and ate it quickly.

'I think we should go back to Bourke,' Jimmy said. Quietly. Not with any authority, as he might have said it a week ago, or two. A statement. This is what I think.

She'd known it was coming. Of course she had. But she still didn't know what to say. All the reasons for going tumbled in her head: it was cheaper to live there, they could survive on his stipend and what she could earn at the store. He might get a job . . .

'I'll be writing to Stephen and Co, to ask for my old job back.'

There was an odd look on his face; a shuttered, closed look. 'But —'

'I've been practising. My left-hand writing'll never be as good as my right was, but you can read it. I can keep records. And I'm getting stronger all the time. Long as I have a dog, I can move stock around all right, open and close the gates in the yards.'

If he got that job back – and he might, with so many men away, even in his present condition – did she have the right to say no? Did she have the right to put Mr Curry and the other employees at the yard before her husband's happiness?

'We can get a house of our own. Just like we planned.' His voice was low, but not hopeful, as though he expected her to object. 'Remember?'

She remembered. The plans, the excitement of looking forward to a life together. For a moment she lost herself in a lovely, false vision of the two of them playing house, the kind of vision she'd had as a girl when she thought about being married, full of light and laughter and love. But she wondered who would get Mr Curry out of his son's room if she wasn't there. Maree? She wouldn't know what questions to ask him, what decisions needed to be made, and none of the men would go to the house. The business would go to rack and ruin, and a dozen good men would be out of work. And there was something wrong about letting a thriving concern go under when you could save it. She supposed she had her father's instinct for trading; it went against the grain to walk away and let the company sink. Her father would never have done it.

And if she did? The pretty vision of playing house shifted uncomfortably. She had an image of herself stuck in a little old-fashioned house, perhaps with a baby, perhaps without, cleaning and cooking and never having to make any choices apart from lamb or beef for dinner.

'You could work in the shop, if you like,' Jimmy said, as though he were giving her a present, a great concession.

Back behind the counter at the shop, being painfully polite to the jumped-up wives of shearers, to the hoity-toity dames from the houses along the river, smiling and smiling and never making a decision. Leaving all the decisions to the customers, because that's what a shopkeeper does. Taking orders from George, who was a fool and a bully and didn't know half of what she did about business. But he was a man, so would expect to manage things. She imagined having to 'handle' him so he wouldn't take the wrong fabrics, wouldn't ignore the new fashions. She wouldn't be able to talk back to him the way she did to Mr Curry – he'd never forgive her.

She imagined it too clearly; horror overcame her. It showed in her face, because Jimmy pushed back from the table and stood up, his expression darkening, his hands on the back of his chair.

'Can't give up your precious job, eh? So much for better or worse.'

She resented his tone, but she reminded herself of the hurt he was suffering, the hurt of mind and spirit as well as body. This was the moment of decision. Now or never – did she want to be married to this man or not? The sight of his maimed hand made her heart cry out with pain, and that decided her.

'If you can wait until I've trained someone to take over for me —' she said, seeing a way out, a way to safeguard Wesley and Wal and Smith and Tiddy and all the rest. If she could find another woman to do the job, and explain it all. She could explain it to a woman, and then she could leave Mr Curry safely.

'You're a bloody bookkeeper!' Jimmy shouted. 'What's to train? They replaced the old one with you, the job can't be that hard to learn.'

Ruby felt anger spiral up from her gut to her heart to her throat and spew out. She tried to call the words back but it was too late, the dam had burst and the anger had won. Her vision darkened and her hands shook. 'I'd like to see *you* do it!' she hissed. 'Mr High and Mighty I'll Take Care of You, You'll Be All Right With Me. Well, the only reason I'm all right is because I looked after myself. I don't need you, Jimmy Hawkins, half as much as you need me! And I'll stay here until I'm good and ready to move, and maybe that'll be never, because if I had the choice I'd never set foot in Bourke again! If you'd taken Mr Curry's offer we wouldn't have to make a choice, but you were too good for that, weren't you? Too good to take help from a fine man —'

'A fine man? He's a bloody emotional cripple!'

'Better than being a real one!'

He moved back as though she had hit him, and his face went white. He swallowed hard, and took another step away. She was appalled by her own words but at the same time there was a satisfaction in saying the unsayable. She should say she was sorry; she couldn't. The words choked in her throat, strangled her, her anger still alive and vicious.

'If that's what you think of me, you're better off without me.'

Blindly, he picked up his coat and hat and walked out the front door.

The fury drained away as quickly as it had risen, and shame replaced it.

'I'm sorry —' she called after him.

He kept walking.

She wasn't even sure he had heard her. Should she run after him? She went to the gate, hurrying so she got there as he shut it, and put her hand over his on the wood. He snatched his hand away.

'It's my temper, Jimmy,' she said. 'I say things I don't mean.'

He gave a short, terrible laugh. 'Temper? You don't have a temper worth talking about, Ruby. That was the truth.'

He turned away with finality and walked off, the slight halt in his step more noticeable from behind.

Ruby was shaking inside, a churning mix of guilt and residual anger and resentment that he wouldn't listen. He'd never seen her angry before; she was struck anew by how little they knew of each other.

Her right palm was sore where he had pulled his hand away, scraping hers against the gate. She cradled it with her left hand, and wondered how angry and sorry and humiliated she would feel if it never got better, if it ached and cramped and refused to obey her commands.

And yet. And yet. She couldn't quite forgive him for saying those things. For implying that she was worthless, that the work she had done was worthless. That the enterprise she had given heart and soul to over the past year was a job anyone could do. It just proved that he didn't love her. All he wanted was a version of the girl she had been in Bourke; and that girl was long gone.

CHAPTER 39

Jimmy didn't come home that night, at all.

Ruby told herself not to worry. He was a soldier, who had survived Gallipoli and the streets of Cairo and Alexandria. What could go wrong in Sydney?

Too much.

She lay awake, listening for the clack of the gate latch, imagining the worst, feeling guilty and angry by turn, hoping he would come home and wanting to hit him when he did. She had got used to sleeping with him, and now she couldn't sleep alone.

The night was full of noises. She started at every footfall on the street outside, at every distant shout. Friday night, and despite the new six o'clock pub closing laws, she could hear drunken shouts from Booth Street. Jimmy had left just before six. He wouldn't have had much time to get drunk before closing time. But there were so many other places to get hold of drink. The bottle-o was still open and the men bought beer then congregated in the parks and on the steps of public buildings until they were moved on by the police. Was Jimmy one of them? His uniform and his wound should protect him, surely, from any harassment. Every drunken cry made her start. Her fear was real, but so was her anger.

If he insisted on going back to Bourke, would she go with him?

The lure of freedom, of having to look after only herself, was so strong. She could train a replacement at Curry's, leave Jimmy (she flinched at the thought of the scandal, the sin of it), and move to Melbourne where no one would know she'd ever been married. Mr Curry would give her a reference and she would get a fine, interesting job.

Maybe Jimmy would divorce *her*, for abandonment.

The thought brought her up sharp. She edged herself back until she was sitting against the headboard, hugged her knees and watched the curtains at the window stir in the night breeze. She had got used to that, too, the windows open all night. And to the smell of sheets a man had slept in, and to coming home to find all the bread eaten, and to the feeling of his hand on her in the night. To the pleasure and the tenderness and the intimacy of spirit and heart. It would cause her heartache to cut that out of her life – but was it Jimmy she would miss, or simply marriage?

Jimmy,

Please call me at work if you come home.

I'm sorry about what I said. You think I don't have a temper, but that's because I fight against it as best I can.

I love you,

Ruby

She looked at the note, propped against the teapot. It was too abject. Too much like a spaniel begging for a bone. She scrunched it up and threw it in the fireplace, then left for work. If he came home, they could talk. If he didn't – well, if he didn't, she'd make a new life and be damned to him.

As she closed the gate behind her, she became aware that she was blinking furiously to stop herself crying, the tears scalding her already reddened eyes.

When she got home, on a windy afternoon with the branches of the camphor laurel tree next door whipping the roof with stiff twigs so that the whole house echoed with it, the first thing she saw was a man's dark head on the arm of the couch. Too dark for Jimmy. It gave her a jolt, and then she saw that it was Arthur Freeman. He woke as she stood there, sensing her somehow, and came to his feet in a rolling spring, the response of a soldier startled by the enemy. The fact that he was in uniform, no doubt for his Friday check-up with the doctors, as Jimmy had been yesterday, just emphasised his battle readiness. The uniform looked surprisingly smart, considering it had been slept in. Good quality wool, the draper's daughter in her noted.

'Oh, it's you, Rube,' he said, yawning. 'Scared the life out of me.'

'*I* scared *you*?' she retorted. She tucked the wind-blown hair away from her face and put her hat on the small table by the door, pushing aside two Army caps. Two. A wave of thankfulness slid through her core.

'Yeah, sorry about that. Jimbo's asleep in there.' He gave a sideways tilt of the head towards the bedroom and again she saw the soldier, who didn't nod forward because his tin hat might slide off, leaving him unprotected. He looked her up and down, and she knew that he had noted the rings under her eyes, her pallor. Her exhaustion. Now she was listening for it, she could hear snoring coming from the bedroom. Lucky Jimmy. She pushed down the instinct to go and check on him. The loudness of the snores was a guarantee of his good health.

'I'll put the kettle on, shall I?' Arthur said. She realised, as he went with confidence to the kitchen and began to make tea, that he had been in this house many times, that he'd come here to have a cuppa with Jimmy while she was at work.

It was a curiously comforting image, the two men sitting down at this little square table with their cups and biscuits. No wonder there was never any food in the house. But why hadn't Jimmy mentioned it?

As she washed in the bathroom and relieved herself, she was suddenly aware that she rarely asked Jimmy how his day had gone, assuming he'd done nothing but do his exercises or walk Edward to the park, because there was no evidence in the house that he'd done anything else, such as shopping or washing or cleaning. Perhaps he hadn't told her simply because she hadn't asked. What else didn't she know?

Arthur set the pot down on the table as she came out. She sat facing the window and turned the pot around to make the leaves settle. There was a small piece of sky framed in the window, where clouds with a leading edge of dark grey raced towards the north. They would have rain soon. The air smelled of it; and of tea.

'You can be mother,' he said, so she poured for both of them. 'You know, Jimbo tied a real one on last night.'

The cup trembled in her hand and clattered against the saucer. It was one of the cups belonging to the house, white porcelain with daisies on it. The flowers seemed to shiver in an unseen wind.

'Yes,' she said. 'We had a fight. I said some things . . .'

Arthur's hazel eyes assessed her with an unexpected intelligence. The Freemans were poor – their father had died when the children were only small, she remembered, and Arthur had gone to work in the meatworks as an eleven-year-old. She had been misled into thinking poor meant stupid.

'His shoulder was hurting something fierce, too.'

'Hurt? But the doctors said it was all right now.'

He laughed, unamused. 'Nah. They just can't get the last few pieces out. Mine're closer to the surface, so I've got another two or three ops to go, they reckon. Jimmy's are buried near his heart – they can't operate there. Have to wait until they work their way up, then do the op. Might be years. But he's in pain, all right.' He moved his left arm, wincing as the elbow came level with his shoulder. His fingers were curled in like Jimmy's, but not as badly. 'I can tell you, it hurts. Nothing you can do about it, either. Except have a drink.'

He sipped his tea and let it sink in.

Another thing Jimmy hadn't shared with her. She knew why; he hadn't wanted to seem weak in front of her. Not in front of the professional bookkeeper who kept a roof over his head. That would have been just too much humiliation. But wasn't that what a wife was for? Someone a man could tell the absolute truth to, all the things he couldn't admit to anyone else?

So she'd been a failure there, well and truly. 'He wants to go back to Bourke,' she said.

'Yeah, well,' Arthur fiddled with his cup and then took a swig, draining it in one gulp. He set it down in the saucer with exaggerated care. 'Bourke . . . he used to talk about Bourke. At Anzac. While we were waiting.' He flicked a glance at her; his eyes were hooded. 'There's a lot of waiting, in the field. More than you'd think. It's not all guts and glory.'

She nodded encouragingly.

'He used to talk about Bourke, Jimbo. 'Cause I grew up there, so I knew it. It's one of the ways we got to be friends. In the night, when we were waiting for the shells to come over, he'd talk about Bourke. About going home to you, getting a house together, getting his old job back, having a family.'

A candle against the dark, Ruby thought, tears pricking her eyes again. She was wrenched with pity for them, for all the boys over there, talking of home to ward off fear. For Jimmy, her Jimmy, her beloved, crouched in a bunker made of foreign soil, tin hat on his head, lice in his clothes, his rifle ready to hand, talking of her. Of her.

She took a long breath and let it out again. 'Yes,' she said.

Arthur nodded and sat back, then forward again to pour himself a second cup of tea. 'Just thought I'd say.' He swallowed the tea down and put his cup back on the saucer. 'Best be going.'

She saw him to the door and, to his evident surprise, kissed him on the cheek. 'Thank you, Arthur,' she said.

He paused, as though struggling with a decision. 'He used to write letters, in his notebook,' he said. 'Never posted 'em, though. Blokes did that, wrote things they didn't want the censor to see.'

He smiled at her, a difficult smile, and lifted a hand in farewell, then strode off into the darkening afternoon, settling his cap back on his head.

For a moment, she paused at the door. The storm was coming. The wind had dropped, as it did in Sydney before the full fury hit. The fruit bats flew over in a silent flurry of air and a single high call, heading for the Moreton Bay fig trees down at Federal Park; she would have to net the peach tree in the backyard for summer, she thought automatically, or they would have the lot.

Then the first drops fell, heavy and fat, and the wind came behind them, swirling up dust and leaves and the smell of automobile exhaust. Ruby was overcome with homesickness. She wanted to smell red earth and the crushed termite mounds they used for gravel in the backyard of the store; saltbush and spinifex, the dry prickling on the inside of her nostrils which said 'desert wind'.

She missed the soaring of wedgetail eagles, the harsh cawing of crows, the small flickerings of zebra finches in the shrubs by the garden gate at home. She missed the sky, the great, arching, flaming blue sky of the outback; and the stars at night, not the friendly twinkle-twinkle stars they taught city children about but the blazing, unforgiving, uplifting stars of the plains.

She let the dirty Sydney wind push her inside and leaned back against the door, fighting tears.

The town of Bourke she missed not at all, nor the people, always excepting her family, but the earth and air and water of Bourke, the colours and textures and shape of the land, she missed that with a deep solitary ache.

But was she prepared to give up everything she had here for a big blue sky and some red bulldust?

•

Jimmy slept through until dinnertime. He came out barefoot, still in his khaki shirt and trousers, his braces off his shoulders, his goldy-brown hair rumpled, stubble gilding his face. She had made a chicken stew out of an old boiler cooked slowly for four hours. Silently, she served him a plate at the already laid table.

He sniffed the aroma like a dog scents the air, half-asleep, and went into the bathroom, coming out a few minutes later with his hair slicked down. He sat down as silently as she and took up a fork with his left hand, eating with the stolid concentration of a hungry man who had to face something unpleasant after the meal.

'I've never thought of you as a cripple,' she said conversationally, trying to still the quiver in her tummy. Only the truth would save them; save that perfect love she had glimpsed at the altar. If they couldn't face the truth together, they were doomed. Sentiment, declarations of love, wouldn't help right now. 'But I don't know what else to call you.'

He hadn't expected *that*. He looked up in shock, fork poised half-up.

'What do you think?' Her palms were sweaty. 'What shall we call you? Impaired? Handicapped? Lefty?'

'Bitch.'

'It's the truth, and we have to deal with it.'

'No, *you* don't bloody have to deal with it. *I* do.'

He pushed back from the table and stood up, towering over her, left fist clenched and right curled.

Jimmy would never hurt her. She knew that, deep down. But at that moment, her heart fluttered with fear and the hair on the back of her neck stood up.

She felt her lip quiver like a child's. 'I don't know what else to do,' she said.

Slowly, he sat back down. 'Ball's in your court,' he said.

'Jimmy —' The words were hard to force out past the block in her throat. 'I – I don't want to go back to Bourke. I don't belong there anymore.' He pushed back from the table a little and she put a hand out to stop him leaving. 'There are jobs here, we could have our life here —'

'Not the life we planned.'

The chicken stew had congealed on her plate, a thin rim of fat turning white as it cooled. She licked dry lips, and tried again. 'When we got married, we didn't really bank on the war changing things. But it has. It's changed me. It's changed you. If we're going to be together, we both have to be prepared to change.'

'Seems to me I'm the only one around here who's being asked to change. You want everything to go your way. Fine. But you'll have to go that way on your own. I'm going back to Bourke.' He stood up and went to the bathroom door, then looked back at her. His expression was a mixture of determination and something else, fear or anger or perhaps even longing. 'You think about it, Ruby. You decide. Bourke or Sydney. Married or divorced. Your choice.'

He closed the door gently behind him, and she wished he had slammed it, so she could be angry with him. Her hands were shaking; a deep desolation opening up inside her, threatening to consume her.

Why did it have to be so hard? She couldn't find the words to explain to Jimmy. He didn't understand about Mr Curry – he didn't understand about *her* – about what it was like to finally be someone other than her father's daughter or Jimmy's wife.

She didn't have any words to explain it. All the words the suffragists used were wrong. She wasn't interested in women's rights or women's issues. This was between him and her. She didn't want the world to change. She just wanted to do a job she liked and that she was good at.

She thought, with a mixture of despair and astonishment, that the only one who might understand was her mother, because ever since the miscarriage it was as though she had turned into some other woman, a woman who couldn't make a decision, a woman who shifted from certain to uncertain between one breath and another. Part of her still felt disconnected to the real world; even to Jimmy.

He came out of the bathroom fully dressed and headed for the door.

'Expect me when you see me,' he said.

•

Arthur wouldn't have told her about the notebook unless it was important. Feeling like a cheat and a spy, she went into their room and looked through Jimmy's duffel bag, the one he'd thrown into a corner and never opened since he'd unpacked.

The detritus of war. A canteen, the stub of a pencil, old bootlaces, a pair of frayed braces. And a notebook tucked into an inside pocket.

Small and dirty, with rubbed edges.

She opened it, heart thudding, and read the first words:

My darling girl,

Things are pretty bad here, but I won't talk about that.

I know we won't live at Barkinji, but that's where I like to imagine us . . .

She moved to the bed, and sat, reading with a mounting emotion, some mix of shame and joy and deep compassion.

Words leapt out at her.

If you don't deserve her, make something of yourself until you do . . .

. . . *a hole inside me* . . .

. . . *Lifted up to the stars* . . .

. . . *what more could any man want?*

. . . *Gilbert if it's a boy* . . .

The ache in her heart, in her womb, bloomed sharply. She had grieved for her baby without ever realising that Jimmy would be grieving just as much. Not realising a man could long for children just as strongly as a woman.

. . . *Helen if it's a girl* . . .

And then, astonishingly, in a barely readable scrawl, *I could feel you with me, all through that dark night* . . .

She was back, suddenly, on her knees in Maree's second bedroom, praying and sobbing and begging God for help, for Jimmy's life. She was bending under the terrible shadow looming over her, frantically trying to do anything, say anything, which might reach out to him and keep him safe.

It overwhelmed her like a wave, and then was gone again, and she was in the bedroom, holding Jimmy's notebook with shaking hands, remembering how afraid she had been.

What she felt, mostly, was shame. For so many reasons. That she had held herself back from him, when he had given himself so completely to her – and done it out of fear, fear of grief, fear of loss, fear of not being strong enough to survive his death if she allowed herself to admit how much she loved him.

That she'd never really *talked* to him since he'd come back. Never told him how much she'd missed him, never told him how scared she'd been after he'd been wounded, never talked about that night she had wept and prayed and hoped. She had treated him like she'd treated Mr Curry, as though he wasn't strong enough to cope with anyone else's pain – but that wasn't marriage, that was being a nanny. She should have respected him enough to burden him with her grief and fear.

A deeper shame. They had been given the thing everyone wanted. The kind of love that poets wrote about and singers sang about. The kind that lived forever, that could cross continents and unite them in the Valley. And she – they, they were both responsible, she with her fear and pride and Jimmy with his anger and suspicion – they had almost killed it.

Mr Curry was not her family. She could sustain him only so far, and then he had to walk by himself. She could not put Jimmy's happiness at risk for a business, or for the welfare of a friend. If she had to go to Bourke and serve in the shop every day of the rest of her life to keep him happy, she would, just as her mother had done for her father.

Tenderly, she put the notebook back in the bag, tears standing in her eyes. One day, when everything was healed between them, she would ask Jimmy about it. But now, it was time to write a letter of her own.

Dear Mother,

I hope you are well and in good spirits.

Jimmy has been told that there is nothing more the doctors can do for him. He must continue with the exercises and massage, but there will be no more operations. While this is, in one sense, good news, in another sense it is the worst possible, as Jimmy has taken it to mean that he will not improve any further, which I do not think is the truth.

Ruby felt disloyal writing those words, but it was important that her mother understood how thing were.

He has suggested moving back to Bourke and trying to get his old job back at Stephens & Co. For various reasons, I don't think that is a good idea.

No need to go into the reasons. Her mother knew them.

I was wondering if you had given any more thought to the plan we talked over while you were here? If you have decided not to go ahead with it, I understand completely. But if you were going to go ahead, it might be a godsend for us.

Was that too strong? Putting too much pressure on her mother? Ruby thought of Jimmy's white face, and what it would mean to him to be able to retrain as an auctioneer, or something similar, and let the words stand. It was the truth, after all.

Please give my love to Myrtle and the children.

your loving daughter,

Ruby

Ruby blotted the letter and sealed it in an envelope, her hands trembling. She would post it now, right now. She'd had to do something, and this was the only thing she could think of which might help.

It was better to think about the possible future than to consider she might have ended her own marriage with a few unforgiveable words, with months of insensitivity. She wrenched her thoughts away from the memories of his stricken face, from his accusing face, from that last, unreadable expression. She felt, even though she was ashamed of it, a flicker of anger at his accusation, a flicker of her belief he no longer loved her.

Those letters had been written before he came home. Before he met the new Ruby.

Just telling him she loved him, just trying to have the conversations they should have had weeks ago, wasn't going to be enough. She had to be able to offer him something other than the same old dreary choices. Because without her mother's money, they needed her job. It was the first time that Curry's had seemed like a prison sentence.

Better not to tell Jimmy about the money, even now. If he got his hopes up only to be dashed down again . . . that would be too hard for him, she thought. She realised that she was thinking again about him the way she thought about Mr Curry, as someone delicate and fragile, easily broken, easily hurt. Well, that was the Jimmy in those letters; someone she could hurt as easily as she could crush a butterfly. It just increased her sense of responsibility. One day they would share everything, as equals; she still had some fences to mend before she could ask anything of him.

Jimmy came home well after midnight, but he didn't come into the bedroom. Ruby lay in the darkness and listened to him settle on the sofa. But she was too much of a coward to go out to him.

CHAPTER 40
8th October, 1916

Ruby thought she had prayed hard on that night of the shadow but at Mass the next morning she realised that those prayers had been just babbling fear. She hadn't wanted guidance or help, she'd just wanted everything to be all right. A fairytale ending.

Today, she put her head against her hands – her wrists rich with Jimmy's bangles – and prayed with an understanding that there would be no happy ending – at least, no ending where everyone got everything they wanted. There would be adjustments on both sides if they were to have an ending together at all.

Dear Lord, she said, kneeling after Communion with Jimmy's warmth bathing her side as he prayed too, *lead me to the right path. Help me to see what you want me to do.*

Deep down, she knew she was hoping Stephens & Co would take their own good time replying to Jimmy's letter. Time enough for her mother to answer her own letter. Still hoping for a happy ending, despite everything.

Jimmy spent Sunday brooding, just sitting by the fire in the parlour, staring at the flames. Once she caught him glaring at his hand with loathing. If Stephens & Co didn't want him, and her mother didn't have the money, what would they do? This dark mood was foreign to him, but it showed no signs of lifting.

She vacillated all day – one moment thinking she should just throw herself into his arms, the next afraid he would reject her if she did.

Perhaps they should go back to Bourke even if he didn't get the job; but she suspected that if they did, the reality wouldn't satisfy Jimmy. She thought of those wonderful, heartbreaking letters. He wanted what he'd described: the perfect life, the job he loved in Bourke, the domestic wife, the children, the bush. She understood that he'd clung to it so hard it was difficult to let it go, but he had to let it go, no matter what happened. Even if she gave in, that life was gone, vanished with the war and his wounds, and it wasn't coming back. She didn't think he realised how much things had changed in the bush, as well as in the city. She couldn't say so. Things were bad enough without that.

She got up her courage as dinnertime approached. Jimmy was still sitting by the fire. She moved across the room as gracefully as she could, and dropped to beside his chair. He looked at her with surprise. Protestations of love would seem pretty thin, she guessed. She needed something more substantial. At another time, she would have led him to the bedroom, but the doctor had advised against it, for now. Perhaps that was the way.

'The doctor says that it will only be a few more weeks before we can try again.'

He blinked, as if bringing her into focus.

'What's the point?' he asked. 'If you don't really want it.'

'You never asked me if I wanted it,' she said, realising that this had been a mistake, that her still aching grief made talking about children too hard, too easy to get angry about. 'You never asked me if I —'

She choked on the words, and pushed away from his chair, got up and went to the kitchen. Only someone you loved could make you so angry, so hurt. That was something to cling to.

Jimmy came in and started setting the table. A kind of apology. 'Do you?' he asked, face averted.

'I think we should call the first boy Arthur,' she said, dishing up the chops and peas, trying for brightness, not feeling strong enough to discuss it.

Jimmy smiled slowly. 'He'd like that,' he said.

They ate and talked about small things; Maree's Red Cross work, war news, the new wharf being built along Rozelle Bay and whether it would be used for troop ships. It felt like a victory for normalcy; for marriage. But in bed they lay separately, with no part of them touching.

•

At lunchtime the next day she came home to find that Jimmy wasn't there, which was odd, and then she remembered he'd said he was meeting Arthur and some mates in the city. Something about forming a Gallipoli League. There was a letter in the letterbox, from Stephens & Co.

Ruby itched to open it, but of course she couldn't. She

picked it up and put it on the hall table where Jimmy would see it when he came home.

The phone rang. She answered it with her heart in her mouth, hoping it wasn't bad news.

'Hello?'

'Hello, dear.' Her mother. Her heartbeat jumped and settled. 'I thought it was best to ring. I've sold the shop to George and Myrtle and I'll be sending you a cheque as soon as it's settled.'

'Oh.' She felt so stupid; she couldn't think it through. What was happening to her brain lately?

'This way he can't pressure you into investing. Myrtle will have the house for her lifetime and then it will go to the children; so George can't sell it out from under her if things go bad. You get a bigger slice of the sale price in compensation. I thought you'd prefer that.'

'My letter —'

'Oh, I'd already put it in hand before I got that, dear. But I thought I'd better call. Best if you know where you stand.' She named a figure which made Ruby blink. 'That should be enough to let Jimmy train in something new, yes?'

'Yes. Yes. Thank you.' There were tears choking her throat.

'No need to thank me. To tell you the truth, I feel as free as a bird. Like a weight's been lifted.' Her voice sharpened. 'You need to tell Jimmy about this as soon as you can, Ruby.'

'I will. I will. Thanks, Mum. Thank you so much.'

As she placed the receiver on its cradle, fear washed over her. She didn't understand why, at first, and then realised that she was afraid that it wouldn't be enough, that even this money wouldn't free them from the mistrust that had slowly built between them.

She forced herself to look on the bright side. She had an alternative to Stephens & Co to offer, an alternative to Bourke, where everyone would pigeonhole her and treat her like a silly girl, a shop assistant with the brains of a galah. The person she had been when she left, she admitted wryly.

No doubt she could change their minds in time, but the thought of the effort that would require made her quail. She just didn't have the energy.

She waited until the very last minute to go back to work, but Jimmy didn't come.

That afternoon was the time for Tom McBride's next appointment.

Mr Curry was waiting for him and called Tom into his office without giving him a chance to say anything to anyone. A tad overprotective, she thought with a smile. She gave Tom a small nod through the glass, and he grinned at her, happy to see Mr Curry back in the saddle.

When she left for the afternoon he was still there, but Mr Curry had pulled out the brandy, so she assumed the meeting was over. She nodded goodbye to them both and went home, not sure what she would do if Jimmy waved an offer of employment happily in her face and demanded that she go back to Bourke.

He wasn't there. The house had a quiet, waiting feel to it and for a moment she was relieved that she had time to settle and ready herself for the conversation to come.

Then she saw the envelope from the Stephens & Co letter on the floor, opened. She picked it up automatically. So Jimmy was home. In the bathroom, maybe?

She went through to the kitchen – the bathroom door was

open and the room was empty. He wasn't in the backyard, either. Had he gone out to celebrate with Arthur?

Coming back to the kitchen to make herself a cup of tea, she saw the letter from Stephens on the kitchen table. Her heart fluttered with anxiety.

Slowly, she picked up the letter and read:

Dear Mr Hawkins,

Thank you for your letter requesting employment with Stephens & Co. Unfortunately, Mr Bernard Stephens, to whom you addressed your letter, left the company to enlist not long after you, and we are sorry to have to tell you that he perished in the first day of the battle of the Somme in July of this year.

Since his enlistment, and due to the current downturn in agriculture due to the War, Stephens & Co. have reduced our staff to a minimum.

We must therefore, with regret, decline your offer of assistance. After the present conflict is over we would be glad to hear from you, and wish you all the best in the future.

yours sincerely

Wm Connors

Relief swept over her, and grief. Bernard Stephens had been a fine man, in his early thirties, with a wife and four children. They had danced at her wedding and given Jimmy and her a lovely plated fish slice.

Where was Jimmy?

She put the letter back on the table. Beneath it, she saw, was a note in Jimmy's handwriting. Shaky, left-handed writing. Foreboding swept over her.

My dearest girl,

Stephens & Co is a wash-out. At the meeting today I saw what had happened to the Gallipoli crowd who've been demobbed for a while. All of them out of work, most of them drinking themselves to death, half of them separated from their wives or jilted by their girls. I took a good long look at them, and promised myself I wouldn't turn into one of them.

Then I got home and found the Stephens letter, and I realised it wasn't my choice.

You're better off without me, Ruby. You can look after yourself, you told me that and you were right.

If a man can't look after his wife, he's better off – he had scratched a word out there, but she could imagine what it was, and her body turned cold, ice sending slivers outwards from her heart and inwards from her skin.

No.

I love you, Ruby. Always did. Loved you the first time I saw you. Loved you more than I could ever say. I guess that's why I've been a bit of a bastard. Afraid you'd leave me and I'd never hear the sound of your voice again.

You've got a beautiful voice.

I don't blame you for not wanting to go back to Bourke as the wife of a cripple. You'll be better off with McBride.

Take care of yourself,

Jimmy

Where would Jimmy go if he wanted to – wanted to —? She couldn't think the words. She ran through to the lounge and rang Maree. As she waited for the other line to ring, she realised that Jimmy's digger's hat was gone from the mantelpiece. He hadn't worn it since he came home from hospital – he always, *always* wore his cap.

'Did Jimmy take Eddie out this afternoon?' she said as soon as Maree answered.

There was a brief silence.

'No,' Maree said. 'What can I do to help?'

'I'll call you later.' Ruby hung up, hand shaking. Arthur. She needed to contact Arthur. But she didn't know how.

She needed help.

She rang the office, praying that someone would still be there. Mr Curry answered and she couldn't speak, couldn't get the words out.

'Mr Curry —'

'Ruby? What is it, lass?'

'Jimmy . . .' She couldn't articulate it. Couldn't say the words.

'Calm down, lass. What's happened?'

'He's not here. And. And. He's left a . . . letter.'

There was a silence, full of comprehension. 'Tom,' Mr Curry called. 'Who's left in the yard?'

Tom's voice came, distantly. 'No one now, sir.'

'Blast. We'll have to look ourselves, then. Come down to the office, lass.'

'Yes,' she said. She hung up and picked up her hat and bag, as if she were going to work on an ordinary day. If he'd known about the money coming from the shop, he would have had hope, still, even after the letter from Stevens & Co. If she hadn't treated him like a child, too weak to take disappointment, he would have been strong enough to bear it.

She hurried down the streets to the office and found Mr Curry waiting for her in the main room.

'I've sent Tom out to check the ferry.'

'Should we call the police?' It was odd, she thought, that Mr Curry wasn't doing anything. He was a man of decision followed by quick action, but he wasn't moving.

'Lass . . .' His Irish brogue sounded suddenly stronger, as it did in moments of strong emotion. 'Are you sure you should try to find him?'

'What?' For a moment she didn't understand. She stared at him blankly.

'He's never going to be whole. That's what you told me. The doctors have given up on him. He's in pain all the time. It's a hard life for a man, living like that. Are you sure he's not doing the best thing for himself?'

A deep shudder went through her. A revulsion at the very thought. But Mr Curry had seen a lot of death and hurt and pain. She should consider it; consider the possibility that he was right.

'No!' she said, not considering it at all, unable to even begin to think about it. Her whole body rejected the idea; it made her feel sick, made her tremble with a kind of terror. She knew what he meant. Should she condemn Jimmy to the pain, the sleepless nights, the sense of being less a man than he had been?

Maybe she was being selfish. Maybe she was. But she couldn't let him go.

'No. It can't be the best for him.'

'All right, then,' he said heavily. He picked up the telephone.

Tom banged back into the office, shaking his head. 'He didn't leave by ferry,' he said. He went to the filing cabinet and pulled out a map of the area, spreading it on the big desk.

'Yes, returned soldier,' Mr Curry was saying. 'Not sure, but we fear the worst. Six one, sandy brown hair, a private, injured right arm. Yes. Yes. Call my house if you have any news, my housekeeper will take the message. Good. Yes.'

We fear the worst. Ruby started to shake. That was the police he was speaking to. Because of the worst. The worst was too hard to think about, but she had to. The police would understand. Everyone knew that the returned soldiers were prone to – to the worst.

Mr Curry put down the telephone and turned to her. 'Did you bring the letter?'

'It doesn't say – it doesn't give any clues,' she said. She had to fight to keep her voice from squeaking, but she couldn't stop it trembling.

Mr Curry nodded sharply, then called his own house and explained the situation to Maree.

'So I'd appreciate it if you would man the 'phone there,' he said. He listened, and nodded. 'Yes. I'll try.'

He hung up. 'She wants you to go up to the house and wait with her.'

'No,' Ruby said. 'I have to help look.'

'How long has he been gone?'

'I don't know. He came back some time after lunch.' She forced herself to think. 'He doesn't have a gun. They keep those at the barracks. And there was no medicine he could take . . .' She trailed off, unable to say the words. As though saying them would make them true.

'What about his razor?' Tom asked.

Her stomach lurched at the image the question conjured up. She swallowed and made herself remember the bathroom. She had looked in there, thinking Jimmy was there. His comb, his shaving things had been on the side of the washstand.

'Yes,' she said, with relief. 'His razor was in the bathroom.'

'How would you go about it, Tom?' Mr Curry asked.

'Can he swim?'

'I don't know. He never said. The river was down in Bourke when we were living there . . . he had no occasion to.' She knew so little about him, after all. Even now, even now, she didn't know him. Not really. She didn't even know how he'd choose to die.

'The bridge, then, maybe,' Tom said. 'Or off the docks.'

'I'll check the Glebe side of the bay,' Mr Curry said. 'Fewer docks there, and a longer walk to the bridge. You take the western shore.'

'Yessir,' Tom said.

'I'm coming with you.'

Tom assessed her as he might have assessed a new recruit, a young private. She tried not to look hysterical, no matter how terrified she was.

'Come on, then.'

•

On a normal day, it took fifteen or twenty minutes to walk to Glebe Island Bridge. But what little light there was now was filtered through grey clouds, so thick they didn't even hold a spray of rose or gold from the setting sun. The electric lights that kept the main streets of Annandale so bright at night were few down on the docks, and that slowed them down.

The air smelled of tar and wood. The first timber yard, MacKenzie's, was locked tight.

'Hullo the yard!' Tom called at the gates, but there was no one there. The timber merchants together, including Curry's, paid for a night watchman to make the rounds, but he wouldn't start work until the sun was fully gone. Four pounds, Ruby thought, her thoughts flying, catching on anything, that's what their contribution was every month.

Tom rattled the wooden gates. 'He's not going to get through these,' he said. 'Nor the fence.'

Like all the timber yards, there was a tall paling fence surrounding MacKenzie's. Too tall for Jimmy, with his bad arm, to scale.

After MacKenzie's the road swung up to skirt around the work being done on the new wharves.

Ruby set off down Commercial Road, the street that ran at the back of the new work, where trucks came to dump the stone which was being used to form the foreshore, or bring the heavy logs that formed the pilings. We supplied those, she thought wildly. Her feet felt heavy, but she could hear her footsteps and they ran lightly, swiftly. The road was rough gravel, but it was level, a heavily used thoroughfare kept up to standard by the construction crews.

Tom followed her, past gate after gate. The boys, like Tiddy, would sometimes make their way around the front of the fence at low tide to fish from the rocks after work, but the tide was high now. She could hear the small harbour waves slapping on the thick tarred pilings of the new docks, even so far back. Did that mean the wind was rising?

At least it was a southerly. It pushed at her back as she ran, lending her strength.

Gate after gate and then a narrow pathway between two dock areas. A right of way for fishermen – no, a path to a small public dock where water taxis could bring their fares in. She swerved down the dark gap and ran a little faster, but Tom, behind her, pulled her back. She jostled against him; the strength of his chest, the tight hold he had on her arm, were like a threat. She had to get to Jimmy.

'Slow down or you'll have a fall,' he said. 'I've brought a torch from Curry's.'

He shone the torch down the wood-lined path and it was only then that Ruby realised how dark it had grown. They continued, too slow for Ruby. She could feel recklessness rising in her; she cared about nothing, including her own safety, except finding Jimmy.

The pier was narrow, too, and jutted only a short way over the water. There was a figure on the edge of the dock.

'Jimmy!' she called urgently, and sprang forward, but the figure turned and it was an old man, whiskers grey under a tightly pulled down old hat. He started as she moved towards him and Tom put a hand on her shoulder.

'Sorry,' he said. 'We're looking for a friend. A private. Seen him?'

The old man fumbled with his fishing line and shook his head. 'Gor, you gave a man a fright, missus! No, sorry, haven't seen 'ide nor 'air of 'im.' Curiosity brightened his eyes. ''E in trouble?'

'No,' Tom said definitely. 'Thanks.'

Ruby had no time for good manners. She turned and ran back down the pathway without a word, cursing Tom's torch which had taken away her night vision. She stumbled and kept going, breathing harder now, perspiring down the centre of her back and under her arms.

The southerly chilled that dampness as soon as she turned the corner and started for the bridge again, but she welcomed even that strike of cold as long as it pushed her closer to Jimmy.

Another dock, silent, and then the night watchman was at the gate, looking at them with suspicion. She dredged up his name from the monthly accounts.

'Mr Postlethwaite!' she called. 'Have you seen a man go past? A private?'

He shook his head. 'Just arrived myself, missus.' He came forward as she neared. 'Is that you, Mrs Hawkins? Want a hand?'

'Oh, yes, thank you, Mr Postlethwaite. It – it's my husband. We're a bit worried about him.'

For the first time in her life, she welcomed euphemisms. She thanked God she didn't have to put her fears into words. Postlethwaite understood immediately. He was a veteran himself, short half an arm courtesy of the Boer War, Mr Curry had told her.

'That's the one back from Anzac, eh? I'll take a look down all the docks. You go for the bridge.'

'Thank you so much,' she gasped, and kept running. Tom took the lead as her wind gave out and she had to pause, hands on knees, to get her breath back. He stopped to wait for her, but she waved him on, unable to speak, but urging him to forget her and find Jimmy. He nodded and ran, panting himself now.

She tried to breathe deeply. She was in front of where the old abattoirs used to be; the taint of tallow and the tannery still lingered and made it hard to catch her breath.

Commercial Road came up from the docks and curved around to meet Victoria Road and then climb the bridge, but they had to cross the road – thank God, light of traffic at this time of night – to get to the pedestrian walkway on the northern side.

Following Tom, Ruby dodged a dray and a private car and ran down the footpath on the side of Victoria Road, towards the bridge, where Jimmy, if he were going to do something rash, would head. The bridge rumbled and Ruby stopped for a second, shocked to see it was opening, the middle of the span slowly creaking around to create two channels, one on either side of the central pier, which held its midsection.

Why would they open the bridge at this time of night? It chilled her more than the wind. Normally, Jimmy would have had to climb the railings to jump. Now he could simply duck under the boom gate at the end of the bridge section and just walk off.

She ran faster. The bridge seemed too far away – why did they make the approach so long?

A line of cars, lorries and carts was waiting by the boom gate, and the walkway was crowded with a group of people, dark shapes under the streetlamp.

'Jim! Jimmy! Sweetheart!' Her voice was breaking, almost sobbing. Would that make him more or less likely to reveal himself if he was in that group? She tried again, forcing herself to be calmer. Hysteria wouldn't help Jimmy.

She couldn't see Tom anymore; he had got too far ahead. She turned her back on the slope to the sea and kept going, picking up her pace now she had her second wind.

The wrought-iron railing was cold under her hand, and gritty with dust from the quarry on Glebe Island. The iron grids that formed the walkway rang under her feet, a hollow sound, full of foreboding. No, that was just nerves. She had to get hold of herself.

It was a long way; she saw the tail of Tom's coat disappear between two men. She'd been wrong to wave him onwards. It would be bad if Tom found him first. Her lungs actually hurt now, a deep ache, but she made herself go faster, her knees and thighs burning, a blister on one heel, her whole body simultaneously drenched in sweat and freezing cold as the wind cut through her sweater-coat as if it were butter muslin.

On the bridge at last. The evening traffic was light, but piling up, trucks and omnibuses and trams and drays, horses standing patiently in front of carts. One lifted a tail and plopped a pat of steaming manure onto the road.

Tom had heard her behind him and stopped, came back.

'I think he's there,' he said, pointing ahead at the cluster of people by the boom gate; the ones who'd been caught by the bridge opening. All were men. Two were in uniform. One was Jimmy's height and colouring, his sandy hair burnished by the lights of the bridge.

'Yes,' she said, breathing out a long, long sigh of relief, followed by a sharp intake of fear as the man – as Jimmy – edged forward. 'Careful, now. I'll go.'

She walked up to the group, trying not to breathe hard, trying to control the desire to pant for air, to drag in great gulps of it. She had to be calm. She *had* to be.

'Jimmy?'

He turned and saw her. Then, lifting his eyes, he saw Tom behind her. She hadn't known what to expect when he saw her – anger, shame, alarm, horror, hope – but she hadn't been ready for a face that was totally exposed. He had nothing left.

No resources to put on a public face. Nothing to stop himself showing how the sight of them together – even though they were searching for him – was destroying him. Nothing left to fight the pain with, the pain of his injury and handicap, the pain of misunderstanding, the pain of fearing that he had lost her. She hadn't realised, until that moment, how much he needed her.

He was crumbling in front of her, and she couldn't get to him. There were too many people between them. The few men seemed like a hundred. She shouldn't have said anything until she was in touching distance, until she could grab him and hold him tight.

She slid between the men and reached out for Jimmy, but that was a mistake, too, because he backed away from her until he was against the boom, which blocked off the edge of the bridge. She hesitated, and that was another mistake, because it gave him time to duck under the boom.

'Get out of my way!' she screamed, as the men around her exclaimed and called him back. She wrenched them apart and got to the boom, reached for him, but it was too late, she was too late, and he looked at her and said, 'I love you, Ruby,' and took a step back and was gone, falling like a doll to the dark water below.

No. No. No. She knew this silence. It was the same one that had overtaken her when she got the first telegram; it was the silence of death. Nononononono . . . her arms were outstretched uselessly but she couldn't bring them down. Caught in a long, long single moment, a heartbeat of time when everything that had happened to them took itself and shook itself up like a snow globe, rearranging everything, because she didn't care about anything, anyone, *anything,* if she didn't have Jimmy.

She saw, as the past shifted to show its true colours, that she had held herself back from Jimmy after he got home because she'd been afraid of exactly this: this terrible, impossible pain, the destroying loss of his death. She had protected herself from the fear of it with anger and work and discontentment, but it had been there all the time, all the time, and if she had only shown it to Jimmy, if he had only known how much she needed him, this would never have happened.

Tom pushed his jacket and boots and cap into her hand and launched himself off the bridge, dropping feet first.

'Tom! No!' Now she could find her voice, now that it wasn't Jimmy disappearing into the dark.

She turned and ran back to the end of the bridge, where she could cross and get down the side of the embankment. The tide was still coming in; they were almost at ebb, but the current would still be taking them towards the timber yards.

As she rounded the end of the bridge railing, her heel caught in the fretwork and she almost fell; for a moment she swung by her one free hand, gripping the railing, and then she was back on her feet and crossing the road, scrambling down the steep bank instead of going the long way around by road.

Rocks rolled under her feet and she staggered, but kept running. The descent was a rush of night air and cold and terror, the lights behind her hiding her footing in her own shadow, so that she had to trust God, luck, at every step. She ran and fell and shuffled down the last, steeper section on her bottom, slashing her hand on the rough rocks.

She held still for a moment, trying to control her breathing so she could hear. Was that splashing? Yes, and curses. Someone was alive. She couldn't tell who.

She ran down the broken, rocky ground which sloped to the water. The shadow from the bridge was black. She could see nothing, nothing at all.

There – there, was that a hand flung up? Splashing, voices – two voices, oh thank you God, thank you God, thank you.

'Jimmy! Tom!' They were moving. The splashing was further away. She tried to keep pace and at last they moved out from under the bridge. Tom was struggling with Jimmy in the water, dragging him to shore. Jimmy was trying to fend him off. She dropped Tom's bundle of clothes and boots and cupped her hands around her mouth to shout to him.

'Jimmy, no! Oh, God, darling, no! *Please!* Please come back!'

Was he looking at her? All she could see in the darkness was a confusion, a blur. But the splashing stopped, no, just lessened, and now they were coming closer. She ran to the shoreline, bent over, hands out to avoid the small boulders that tried to trip her, tried to cripple her before she could get to him. She couldn't fall now, so she felt her way down as slowly as they were moving towards land.

'Here, here!' she called, and Tom brought them around. Their heads were close, but Jimmy's lolled back on Tom's shoulder, his eyes closed.

New fear. New and agonising. They'd been so *close* to saving him.

The drop-off at the shoreline was steep. She couldn't even wade in to help. Tom brought Jimmy close and she knelt on the sharp rocks and pulled on his uniform jacket, dragging him half out, beached on the shore.

Tom scrambled up beside him, shaking with exhaustion, and helped her drag Jimmy completely out of the water. Jimmy was in full uniform, boots and all, a terrible heavy load to have borne in that cold water, but she couldn't spare thanks for Tom. She put her face to Jimmy's and felt a blessed, faint breath touch her face with cold. Shaking him, she yelled his name, over and over.

He opened his eyes and coughed. Relief warred with rage in her, and rage won out, even over the guilt she felt at having brought him to this. It was an anger so deep it had to find outlet.

She began to shake him and hit his shoulder with the side of her fists.

'Don't you dare leave me! Don't you *dare* leave me! Don't you *dare*.'

Tears were on both their faces. His hand came up shakily to touch her face; his eyes were full of wonder. As she had seen his true face on the bridge, she thought, he was seeing hers now. Seeing her need of him.

'*Promise*,' she said fiercely. '*Promise* you won't leave me like that.'

He gulped, trying to find his voice. 'Promise,' he whispered, and she clung to him, and he to her, and they kissed, cold lips turning warm, salty with tears and the sea, the brine from his clothes seeping right into her until she was as wet as he was.

Finally, she pulled her mouth from his and turned to thank Tom, but he was moving away, finding his clothes, pulling on his jacket and boots. She made a move to call him back, but Jimmy stopped her.

'Let him go, love. Just let him go, for his sake.'

Before he left, Tom took one look back at them and half lifted a hand. Ruby did the same; exactly the same, the small half-wave one used to say goodbye to a friend without words.

It was a wave which meant that goodbye was nothing much, a temporary thing, soon over, but she knew she would never see him again.

'He's a good man,' Jimmy said. 'He could have let me go, and had you.'

But she knew with sudden certainty that she could not have married again, and certainly not Tom, if she had lost Jimmy like that. She shook her head, not able to explain it, aware of her exhaustion and cold and cuts and wrenches as an echo of what Jimmy must be feeling.

'Come on,' she said, 'let's get you home and into a hot bath.'

Jimmy touched her face again and made her pause. He cleared his throat. 'I guess I can stay in the city,' he said, rubbing his thumb over her cheek, 'if you don't want to go back to Bourke.'

She thought of the wide plains and red earth of the bush, and the two of them together under that vivid blue sky.

'There are other country towns,' she said, feeling, at last, the singing in her heart she had expected to feel when Jimmy came back. The same joy she had felt at the altar, when they had sworn to each other without doubt or hesitation. As though they had both, finally, come home to where they belonged. 'You can learn auctioneering first, while I train up my replacement. There are things I have to tell you. We have money.'

'What?' he asked, bemused.

They clambered to their feet using each other as crutches, and began to walk towards home as she told him all the things she should have told him before. All the things she'd never told him, all the things he needed to hear.

351

EPILOGUE

April, 1932

The Essex grumbled as Ruby changed down to negotiate the cattle grid into Barkinji's home paddock. The engine was happiest at full speed on the open road. She grinned and patted its dash. Buying this car had been the best use of money she'd ever made. Her trips into Bourke to pick up fabric and post off completed orders were so easy now.

The sun was westering and the road ahead of her, leading up to the homestead, was a dark red, the vaulting sky beyond blue with a brilliant band of orange around the horizon. The best kind of autumn day.

Her mother and Jimmy were on the verandah, having afternoon tea. She wondered where the children were – Arthur and Helen rarely missed an opportunity to eat; they burned up so much energy running around the property that they were always hungry.

Ruby waved and her mother waved back; Jimmy blew a kiss. She took the car around to the shed and signalled to Elsie, her foreman, to unload the bolts of lightweight gaberdine and silk jersey and take them back to the workshop. They had lots of orders in, from women all across the outback. The new long line, cut on the cross style, needed more fabric than the straight dresses of the twenties, but they were so much more flattering. Women had taken to the new style gleefully, despite the Depression, and Ruby and her seamstresses were happy to supply the demand.

She went in through the kitchen, washed her hands and face in the hall bathroom and joined her mother and Jimmy. His face lit up as it always did when he saw her, and she was flooded with that never-failing gratitude at the sight of him. They kissed, lightly, and their hands found and clung for just a moment.

'Where are the kids?' she asked, helping herself to a plate of pikelets while her mother poured her tea.

'Out boundary riding with Martins,' Jimmy answered, buttering a scone for her. His right hand was still crooked, but unremitting exercise had brought back a far wider range of motion than the doctors had expected. 'They wanted to come mustering next week and I said they had to show they could take a full day in the saddle.'

'They'll be stiff tomorrow,' her mother said.

'Epsom salts in the bath tonight!' Ruby laughed.

She loved the fact that Jimmy made no difference between Helen and Arthur – mustering, fencing, yarding, they both did it all. She thought, in the end, it would be Helen who took over from Jimmy; she would bet on Arthur heading for university to study mathematics in a few years.

Ruby took a bite of pikelet and fished in her handbag. 'Letters,' she said indistinctly, passing them to her mother. She swallowed. What was it about motoring in the open air that gave you such an appetite? 'One from Maree. Edward has finished his bookkeeping course and joined the business.'

'Good,' her mother said. 'He'll be William's heir, then?'

It was strange, still, to hear her mother refer to Mr Curry as 'William', but he had visited Barkinji several times with Maree and Edward over the past decade, since Jimmy had given up auctioneering to manage the station, and Ruby had set up her mail-order dressmaking business.

Ruby nodded, still eating.

'Odd to think of little Eddie having your old job,' Jimmy said comfortably. 'What about Mrs Bennett?'

Edna Bennett was the woman Ruby had trained to take over from her at Curry's. A tall, plain, religious woman, she had got on better with Wesley than Ruby ever had.

'Going to be a missionary in India, would you believe?'

Her mother laughed and pushed herself up out of the chair, waving aside Jimmy's move to help.

'Time for a bath before the children come home and use up all the hot water,' she said. 'Don't you two sit out here holding hands too long.'

Jimmy smiled and held out his hand. Ruby took it, sliding her fingers around his. They sat together in contented silence, watching the sun go down over the red hills, while the crested pigeons and the cockatoos settled in for the night in the big gums around the homestead, until the blazing, uplifting stars of the plains began to shine.

ACKNOWLEDGEMENTS

My thanks go to many people for help in the writing of *The Soldier's Wife*.

Firstly, my father, for telling me about his father, Private Arthur Freeman, who died before I was born; and to my brother Paul, who unearthed the copies of the telegrams sent to Freemie's family when he was wounded, which were the original inspiration for this book.

In terms of research, I'd like to thank the National Library of Australia for their magnificent Trove database; the weather in this book is the real weather for 1915–16 because I could read all the daily newspapers on trove.nla.gov.au, and I was saved from many errors of fact by being able to so easily check contemporary accounts of the fighting in the Dardanelles.

Cameron Atkinson at the Australian War Memorial was terrifically helpful, as was Glenn Howroyd at the Commonwealth Bank Archives Centre, who not only explained how army wives drew their pay in World War I, but sent me copies of all the forms they had to fill out. Dr Nigel Stapledon from the School of Economics at the University of New South Wales helped me figure out the rent for Ruby and Jimmy's house.

I had several beta readers for this manuscript, and I would like to thank them all – particularly my husband, who is my first reader and greatest help.

Finally, my thanks go to the inspiring Bernadette Foley, my publisher, Fiona Hazard, and editor Karen Ward, who encouraged me through the process and made *The Soldier's Wife* a much better book.